STUMBLING BLOCKS
AND OTHER UNFINISHED WORK

Stumbling Blocks

AND OTHER UNFINISHED WORK

DELORES PHILLIPS

Edited and with an introduction by Delia Steverson

The University of Georgia Press • Athens

Published by the University of Georgia Press
Athens, Georgia 30602
www.ugapress.org
© 2023 by the Delores Phillips Estate
Foreword, Introduction, Parts I, II, and III, and
Afterword © 2023 by The University of Georgia Press
All rights reserved
Designed by Melissa Buchanan
Set in Minion Pro
Printed and bound by Sheridan Books

The paper in this book meets the guidelines for
permanence and durability of the Committee on
Production Guidelines for Book Longevity of the
Council on Library Resources.

Most University of Georgia Press titles are
available from popular e-book vendors.

Printed in the United States of America

27 26 25 24 23 P 5 4 3 2 1

Library of Congress Cataloging-in-Publication Data
Names: Phillips, Delores, 1950–2014, author. | Steverson, Delia, editor,
writer of introduction.
Title: Stumbling blocks : and other unfinished work / Delores Phillips ;
edited and with an introduction by Delia Steverson.
Other titles: Stumbling blocks (Compilation)
Description: Athens : The University of Georgia Press, [2023] | Includes
bibliographical references. |
Identifiers: LCCN 2023018069 (print) | LCCN 2023018070 (ebook) |
ISBN 9780820364964 (hardback) | ISBN 9780820364933 (paperback) |
ISBN 9780820364957 (pdf) | ISBN 9780820364940 (epub)
Subjects: LCGFT: poetry. | short stories. | novels.
Classification: LCC PS3616.H455 S78 2023 (print) | LCC PS3616.H455 (ebook) |
DDC 818/.609—dc23/eng/20230614
LC record available at https://lccn.loc.gov/2023018069
LC ebook record available at https://lccn.loc.gov/2023018070

For Delores, Linda, and Shalana

And for Kemeshia Randle Swanson,
who first placed *The Darkest Child* in my hands

CONTENTS

Linda Miller

We are, all of us, akin to books that have been done well. We have a beginning and an end, and the best parts are where, when, why, and how we do what happens between the pages.

Delores Faye Phillips seemed to know the importance of those best parts.

She loved words, the rhythm and the sound of our mother's voice reading fairy tales or poetry at the end of the day. Delores stated that was where it began for her. Words became lifelong friends when she used them while reciting poems before our church congregations and listening to their heartfelt calls of "Yes, Lord" or "Amen." She could feel the appreciation that further ignited little sparks of the joy of words that grew into flames and continue to burn within her throughout her life.

As for many shy people with artistic talent, her silences, intolerance for stupid acts and meanness, and inability to engage in small talk were not always understood. And neither was the bottomless well of love she had for her family and close friends. It was simply Delores Faye being Delores Faye.

For as long as I can recall, she could and did write. And it did not matter to her if the writing was poetry, short stories, editorials, personal or business letters. It was detailed and right to the point.

She enjoyed reading her work aloud and was open to comments from listeners, though not always happy with the responses. However, after taking time to think about critiques, she often learned from and utilized them.

Delores's writing was a gift I had the privilege of reading and listening to. However, I was not influenced by it. Awed? Yes. Influenced? No.

Yes, we loved to read and to write, but I saw quite early (forty years ago) that there was absolutely no comparison to how she structured her writing, scheduled her time, determined inside her head where and when she wanted to take her characters between those pages, and how she planned to get there. She was able to sight obstacles, then figure out how to overcome them. So very similar to what we do in real life.

Unfortunately, as much and as often as Delores encouraged me, cajoled me, fussed at me, I had to admit to my sister that I preferred to read.

Still, she gave me her time and patience to read whatever unfinished drivel I managed to write. She gently critiques the writing, tried to find a complimentary word or two, and always reminded me of the importance of character. She'd say, "Di, you can't just write descriptions. A story is about characters. You have to have them." And I'd reply, "Uh huh, thanks." And I would very soon begin writing my drivel again.

She never gave up on me, and after we reached our forties, we began to put our heads together to write short stories. I was okay with that. Delores excelled at it.

Creating art alongside Delores was an unimaginable delight because I had the joy of seeing her mind at work. My little sister shared who she truly was and the special blessing that added such meaning and happiness to her life.

Between the pages of Delores's life, she encountered rough roads, sharp curves, hills, valleys, and detours. Because she was determined to be taken seriously as a writer, she returned to university at the same time that her daughter, Shalana, was attending Kent State University. She was one of the oldest students in her classes. A small bump in the road. Five years before the Quinn family's story was written, Delores was diagnosed with multiple sclerosis. It slowed her down, but it never stopped her.

Two years before completing *The Darkest Child*, while mowing her lawn, Delores had a heart attack. As a nurse, she knew what was happening, went into her house, washed freshly mown grass off her feet, and drove herself to a hospital. One of those unexpected curves. But she continued to write, to fill the pages in her own personal book.

During most of her writing of *The Darkest Child*, and the beginning of *Stumbling Blocks*, Delores was living in Cleveland, Ohio, while I resided in Silver Spring, Maryland. Every day, sometimes two or three times a day, she would call me. "Di, you got time to listen to this chapter?" "Sure, just let me nuke my coffee first," I'd answer. Then she would read the pages to me. And after hearing them, often, I was silent, but at other times, I'd be laughing, or even crying, just trying to take in something that was so huge and mesmerizing coming from my sister.

But most often I was held spellbound by the blessing she had been given to be able to bring Rozelle Quinn, Tangy Mae, Martha Jean, and their story to life.

I was honored to accompany Delores on her book tour and many speaking engagements. To witness how much work is involved in traveling, greeting interested fans and signing copies of her book for hours so as not to disappoint people who had waited patiently to say a few words to her.

I observed that as shy as she was, Delores was always friendly and gracious, and she managed to talk easily with her fans.

There were evenings when we returned to our lodgings, too tired to do anything more than eat a late meal, look into each other's eyes, and incapable of talking, just laugh out the happiness we were experiencing.

One of the questions Delores was asked most frequently was, "Is your book auto-biographical?" The answer is no! But yes! Our mother, Annie Ruth Miller, was warm, loving, and attentive. She also wrote and read constantly. Her children were 5, 12, 16, and 17 when she died at age 39. So we raised each other. But yes!

Delores was born in the Jim Crow South, so much of the topography, speech, behaviors, work, and day-to-day 1950s life she wrote about are a reflection of the Georgia she heard and observed and lived.

She continued to write and to accept invitations from colleges and book clubs for ten years after the publication of *The Darkest Child*. She also was a volunteer reading teacher in the Cleveland Public School system.

In February of 2014, Delores encountered a roadblock she was unable to surmount—pancreatic cancer. That soon put a stop to her weekly senior line dance classes.

Did she stop writing and just give in? No, she did not. Delores accepted her closing chapters by writing on her good days and trying to prepare her family for the days after her last chapter was completed.

She wrote brief letters to each of us. She held us while we cried for her. She prayed with and for us.

And thank goodness Delores had the presence of mind to hold on to so much of her earlier poetry, short stories, and unfinished novels—these fascinating glimmers into the mind of one extraordinary woman, writer, sister, and friend.

ACKNOWLEDGMENTS

. . . .

I could not have completed this work without the love, labor, and support of five incredible Black women who helped anchor this project. First, thank you to Linda Miller and Shalana Harris for trusting me without question to care for and preserve your family's legacy. I am truly honored. My research assistant, the newly minted Dr. Ashley Clemons, meticulously captioned videos, listened to and transcribed numerous interviews, and provided invaluable feedback on my writing. My mother and best friend, Carolyn Steverson, assisted me in conducting several interviews with Phillips's family and was pivotal in organizing the thousands of documents, photos, and artifacts that would become the Phillips archives. Thank you for believing in me, being my rock, sharing my triumphs, and comforting me through failures. There has perhaps been no other person who has made a greater impact on my growth and trajectory as a scholar than Dr. Trudier Harris. Even as a graduate student, I knew I just had to convince you to be a part of my first book project, and I'm so delighted that now you are! Thank you for pushing me to think deeper, strive for excellence, and not accept mediocrity.

I'm so thankful that this project has a home at the University of Georgia Press, as I believe Delores would find it fitting that it is published in her home state. I'm particularly grateful to Nate Holly, who believed in the project from its inception and who has consistently been kind, responsive, a great listening ear, and a detailed and incredibly sharp editor. Thank you for making this process manageable and enjoyable!

I am also blessed to have an exceptional support system at the University of Florida that has sustained me in vital ways throughout this journey. Stephanie Birch was instrumental in helping me find and access Phillips's published poems and newspaper articles, while Cera Keene patiently guided me through using the microfilm machines. Flo Turcotte taught me useful practices on how best to preserve Phillips's archives. Barbara Mennel and Sophia Acord at the Center for the Humanities and the Public Sphere read several drafts of my research proposal that led to funding. I'm so grateful for my senior colleagues, especially Leah Rosenberg, Steve Noll, Pamela Gilbert, Debra King, Marsha Bryant, Kenneth Kidd, Malini Schueller, and Jodi Schorb, who have all mentored me in distinct ways and have really made me feel like family over the years. Uwem Akpan, Laura Gonzales, Victor Del Hierro, Rae Yan, Paige Glotzer, Rachel Gordan, Ivana Parker, and Margaret Galvan have been inspiring writing partners. Having consistent writing dates (even when I didn't want to) ensured I remained accountable for the work, and I am so appreciative of that. LaToya O'Neal, Della Mosley, Dillon Vrana, Tanya Saunders, Jillian Hernandez, Chris Busey, Rebecca Hanson, and Vincent Adejumo—your kinship has consistently nourished me since the first day I moved to Gainesville. Thank you for sharing your extraordinary scholarship, creativity, and friendship with me. My heart is so full.

Several people in the Cleveland area were crucial in helping me piece together various biographical aspects of Phillips's life. Leonard Trawick, Neal Chandler, David Weizman, and Jeff Karem were instrumental in filling in the gaps of her college years at Cleveland State University. La'Tia Adams, Vanessa Bradfield, and the Cuyahoga County Clerk of Courts located several records of Phillips's life. Donna Marchetti graciously scoured her notes from decades ago to locate her interview with Phillips. Delores's youngest brother, Gregory Green, openly shared his memories of his sister with me. Outside Ohio, many others gave me a platform to share widely about Phillips's life and works. Caroline Lieffers hosted me on the *Disability History Association Podcast* for a rich discussion on *The Darkest Child*. Thank you to Chris Krentz and the *Journal of Literary and Cultural Disability Studies* for housing my first article on Phillips. My graduate students in my fall 2019 Gender and Sexualities in African American Literature course offered fresh perspectives on Phillips's work.

Finding Phillips's published poems was a tedious process, and I am incredibly grateful to the University of Michigan, Auburn Avenue Research Library in Atlanta, and Bowling Green State University for access to the *Black Times*. I must thank my close friend Chantal Revere for taking time out of her workday to help me read through several hours of microfilm. Laurie Rossi and Andrew Majcher at Brown University helped me gain access to *Jean's Journal*. Paul Oliver and Amara Hoshijo at Soho Press—which published Phillips's *The Darkest Child*—were instrumental in providing me with every review of Phillips's novel that they had archived over the years.

This project was funded by the Rothman Faculty Summer Fellowship at the University of Florida, which allowed me to travel to Cleveland for research. Additionally, the Career Enhancement Fellowship through the Institute for Citizens & Scholars granted me a much-needed one-year sabbatical to finish the project. Special thanks to fellow recipients Jamall Calloway and Erica Richardson for writing with me during this time.

My dad, Dennis Steverson, continues to give me spiritual guidance that strengthens me and gives me the will to persevere. My brother, DJ, always makes me laugh and never hesitates to be there when I need him, even if it's just to take a mental break to play some video games. My friends Charmaine Morrow and Jeremy Donald are always on my side.

I must give a special thank you to my dear friend and colleague Kemeshia Randle Swanson, who first introduced me to Phillips because she thought *The Darkest Child* would make a great addition to my dissertation. Even though I was too tired by the end of that grueling process to even consider another chapter, when I did finally read the novel, I knew immediately why you recommended it. Thank you for connecting me to my kindred spirit in Phillips and for all those warm and encouraging "when's that book coming out?" inquiries. You have always been one of my loudest cheerleaders and I love you for that.

Finally, this project would not exist without the brilliance of Delores Faye Phillips, a quiet powerhouse throughout her entire life. Thank you for sharing your brilliance with the world. Even though I never had the privilege to meet you, I thank God that he placed you in my life. I hope this project makes you proud.

Delia Steverson

A Timeless American Treasure

Delores Phillips's Literary Legacy

In the introduction to the 2018 reissue of *The Darkest Child* (2004), novelist Tayari Jones pondered the enigma that was Delores Phillips. The Black writing world is small, she explained, and although she and Phillips were both Black women writers from Georgia, she was saddened that they never crossed paths, nor did anyone seem to know anything about the mysterious author. It seemed that Phillips had gifted the world her "one, brilliant novel . . . a timeless American treasure" and faded into a quiet existence until her death.[1] Filled with regret that she had not met Phillips, Jones "was also weighted down with longing for the other books that she would never write." But what Jones did not realize in 2018, however, was that Phillips's writing career spanned more than just *The Darkest Child* and four chapters of its sequel, *Stumbling Blocks*, which were published at the end of the reissue. Instead, Phillips was an experienced and prolific writer who created multigenre literature throughout her entire lifetime. This volume paints a broader picture of Phillips, not just as a brilliant novelist, but as a skilled poet and short story writer as well, and consequently encourages readers to rethink her literary legacy.

CHILDHOOD AND FAMILY

Delores Faye Phillips was born on September 26, 1950, in Cartersville, Georgia, the second of four children of Lennie Miller and Annie Ruth Banks. Finding it difficult to obtain work in Georgia, Lennie, a bricklayer originally from Pine Log, Georgia, moved to Detroit to support his family from afar. Before her marriage to Lennie, Annie Ruth had worked around the United States, including in Florida, Boston, and Baltimore, laboring domestically in white households. With the birth of her eldest child, Linda Diane, and then Delores, Annie Ruth found work as a washerwoman back in her hometown of Cartersville so she could be a steadier presence for the two girls at the time. Lennie would visit as often as he could, sometimes bringing gifts, like bicycles, to the young girls' excitement.

Annie Ruth Banks (*left*) and
Lennie Miller (*right*) in the 1950s

As a child, Delores was encouraged to read and write by her mother who, as an author in her own right, anonymously published a short story in *True Romance* magazine in the late 1950s.[2] Annie Ruth would read to her children every night, particularly nursery rhymes and Hazel Felleman's *The Best Loved Poems of the American People* (1936). Delores's affinity for poetry in general and rhyming in particular found its beginnings with her mother's performances of the poems. Additionally, her curiosity was piqued once she learned to read: "[I] started with *Dick and Jane* first grade readers. I learned to write. I always wanted to play with words."[3] From age seven, she would write a few rhyming lines, motivated spontaneously by brief encounters she had in her childhood, be that an argument with a friend or even a teacher who inspired her.

The family lived in a shotgun house in an all-Black neighborhood on Beauregard Street. About eight years after Delores was born, they moved to a neighborhood called Summer Hill, another segregated space, but unlike the shotgun house on Beauregard Street, the new place had indoor toilets. Delores and Linda quickly learned the laws of Jim Crow Georgia. They knew never to venture to the white side of town, Granger Hill, lest violence ensue there. As Phillips later remembered, "We were taught to stay in our place. I knew that if I was in a line at the five and dime and a white person came up, I was to step aside. We couldn't go to a restaurant. Period. There was not one in the whole town that we could go to and eat."[4] Although *Brown v. Board of Education* ruled the public education doctrine of "separate but equal" unconstitutional, the Miller children did not feel its ripple effect while living in Georgia. Rather, they were reminded of educational inequalities on their walk to school every morning as they passed the brick school building for white children to attend classes in their dilapidated wooden building for Black children. Nevertheless, through her parents' dedication and community support, Phillips and her siblings not only honed their math, reading, and writing skills, but they were also be exposed to public speaking, classical music, and even basic survivalist skills through camping.

As a youth, Delores was quite shy and often had difficulty making friends. Her older sister, Linda, however, stepped in and became her confidant and best friend. The pair, only thirteen months apart, were inseparable, and Phillips counted her sister as "one of the large pieces that completes my heart."[5] They made jokes, defended each other, and even shared a bed. When the two boys were born, Lennie "Skip" Miller in 1954 and Gregory "Greg" Green in 1961, both sisters "adopted" a younger brother counterpart—Delores embraced Greg and Linda, Skip. Each boy had a big sister to protect them, but also to correct them.

Delores at around thirteen years old

In the summer of 1959, before Greg's birth, tragedy struck the Miller family when Annie Ruth received word that Lennie had been injured on the job. She immediately packed up the family and moved to Detroit to be with him. Lennie had suffered a severe leg injury and by October the leg had become gangrenous. The doctors concluded that Lennie—

even though he was a hemophiliac—needed to have his leg amputated to fight the gangrene. Sadly, he bled to death during surgery. After Lennie's death, Delores and Linda, who by October had already enrolled in school, remained in Detroit and lived with relatives, while Annie Ruth took Skip back to Cartersville to care for her bedridden mother, Hattie Banks. Several years later, in 1967, Annie Ruth suddenly died from pneumonia. Remembering that their mother had told her months before she died to keep the family together, Linda gathered all three of her siblings, ages 6–17, and together, after briefly living with relatives in Georgia, they relocated to Cleveland. There the siblings found

Linda (*top*), Delores (*bottom*), Greg (*left*), and Skip (*right*) in 2010

themselves in an environment that would test the strength of their unity, but, as Phillips would later reveal when she nominated her sister for the Unsung Heroes award featured in the Cleveland newspaper *The Plain Dealer*, Linda's resolve to uphold their mother's charge would prove unyielding: "It is possible that we would never have known the strength of our sister had we not found ourselves motherless and homeless on the streets of Cleveland. . . . We scattered, dropped out of school, and became hostile and rebellious individuals. . . . She reeled us in, one by one, and encouraged us to reach out to each other long after we had forgotten how to touch or feel anything positive."[6] Around this time, Delores temporarily joined the army, but after about three months, disillusioned with the idea of war, she quit.

MARRIAGE AND MOTHERHOOD

After leaving the army, Delores briefly moved back to Cartersville, where she married her first husband, Frederick "Butch" Knox, a childhood friend. Although she noticed many similarities between Georgia and Ohio, she concluded that Cleveland afforded her more opportunities than in the South. Phillips desperately refused to remain in the oppressive Georgia environment she was raised, so, as she put it, "I grabbed me a husband and moved on back" to Cleveland.[7] Phillips would be among several Black women writers who called Ohio home, including Toni Morrison, folklorist and children's book author Virginia Hamilton, and playwright Adrienne Kennedy, who, like Phillips, attended Cleveland public high schools. In December 1970, Knox and Phillips had their first child, Frederick "Ricky" Knox Jr. The pregnancy proved traumatic for Delores, who nearly bled out after giving birth. Knowing that hemophilia ran in her family, she implored doctors not to circumcise Ricky. The doctors performed the circumcision against Phillips's will, and Ricky passed away less than a week after his birth. Even though her first pregnancy ended in tragedy, Delores wanted nothing more than to be a mother, so she prayed fervently to God for another child. Her prayers were soon answered, and she became pregnant with another child that same year. However, the pain and trauma of Ricky's death, coupled with her increasingly tumultuous relationship with Butch, led Phillips to file for divorce in August 1973, one month before their daughter, Shalana, was born.

To support her family, Phillips, following in her sister's footsteps, pursued a career in nursing, graduating from Cleveland's Central School of Practical Nursing in 1979. She would work as a licensed practical nurse for more than forty years. Around the time she was in nursing school and also waitressing, between 1975 and 1976, Delores was introduced to Charles "Butch" Phillips, a friend of Linda's boyfriend at the time. Delores and Butch Phillips fell in love and married in July 1980. The differences between the two Butches were glaring. While Frederick could be physically abusive, Charles was kind and loving. He was jovial, a hard worker, and loved Shalana. Even though Delores and Charles's marriage was significantly more ideal than her previous one, the strength of their relationship was soon tested when the couple adopted a young boy around four years old from a local foster agency. Unaware at the time of the adoption that the child would need nearly twenty-four-hour support, Phillips eventually quit her job to provide her son with the care he needed.

Delores (*seated*) with daughter Shalana (*right*) in 2005

Over time, struggling with her role as a caregiver and feeling unsupported by Charles, Delores began to question their decision. "She lost all of this weight," Shalana remembers, "and it was a highly stressful situation for her." As a result, she and Butch argued over the boy's future in the home. However, the disagreements over the boy's fate were overshadowed by Charles's diagnosis of lymphoma in the spring of 1983. Although he had been ill for months, after the formal diagnosis, Charles's health rapidly declined, and he succumbed to the disease in July of the same year. Shalana vividly remembers her mother's fragile emotional state amid these circumstances: "So here's my mom, now angry at Daddy and grieving over her husband, this kid who's in limbo, this daughter that in hindsight, she's like, 'Did I give her enough attention?' But I didn't need it, I was okay. . . . I look back and say, 'How did my mother handle all of that?' I just want to scream for her that she had to deal with all of that."[8]

Butch's death would haunt Delores for decades, as she wrote in her journal in 2006, "Husband, if you can hear, I beg forgiveness in my loudest voice. I was there when you drew your last breath, but I could not watch you die—not day after day after day of watching you delirious with fever, stretched on a cooling blanket, burning from deep inside where I could not blow a cooling breath to soothe your suffering. I was there when you died."[9] After Charles's death, Linda, who lived in Maryland at the time, rushed to Cleveland to comfort her grieving sister and niece, while the boy was placed with another family. Phillips never remarried but focused much of her energy providing for herself and her daughter.

LATER NURSING CAREER, CONTINUING EDUCATION, AND WRITING INFLUENCES

Although writing was her passion, Delores chiefly relied on her nursing career to support her family. Mental health work and geriatric nursing became her specialities. From 1985 to 1987, she worked at the Cleveland Psychological Institute, and in the aughts, she fulfilled many duties at Northcoast Behavioral Healthcare and Vantage Place, such as dispensing medications and facilitating group therapies. Delores worked at several long-term care facilities in Ohio, including Golden Age Nursing Home from 1987 to 1994 and Lorain County Golden Acres between 1999 and 2001 as a charge nurse on the Alzheimer's unit. As a licensed practical nurse, she not only provided medication and restorative care to the residents but also supervised the nursing assistants, developed patient care plans, and facilitated and supervised individual and group activities.

Throughout her nursing career, she actively expanded her skills to treat chemical dependency, offer legal assistance, and became a women's advocate. Across Ohio, she served as a guardian ad litem for Lorain County Children Services, an HIV/AIDS instructor for the American Red Cross, a chemical dependency counselor, and a women's advocate at the Center for the Prevention of Domestic Violence. All of these varied experiences, often with vulnerable communities, shaped her writing, resulting in diverse characters and a multitude of themes including love, freedom, spirituality and religion, racism and racial violence, voodoo and rootwork, and psychosocial trauma and abuse.

Because of the flexibility of her nursing career, Phillips was able to return to school to obtain an English degree. Beginning at the age of thirty-three, she attended Cuyahoga Community College, where she registered in continuing education courses in mental health, child development, and psychology from 1983 to 1990. She also enrolled in several writing, mass communication, and English courses, including British literature, African American literature, creative writing, and news writing. She transferred to Cleveland State University in 1992 and received her bachelor of arts in 1994. During those years she enrolled in courses on Chaucer, poetry writing, Milton, African American theater, and mass media communication. Delores's secondary schooling would prove to be a period of extraordinary creativity; she not only focused on fiction writing but honed her journalistic skills by crafting articles and several letters to the editor for Cleveland's *The Plain Dealer*.[10]

Like her mother and sister, Phillips was a voracious reader. As she would later impart on aspiring writers at the local Cleveland public library where she offered workshops, "whether fiction or non-fiction, reading makes you aware of the rhythm and pace of stories, and it builds vocabulary . . . essential tools of good writing."[11] She read a variety of genres including African American literature, mysteries, classics, and Greek tragedies. One of her favorite writers was Walter Mosley, and she also enjoyed Toni Morrison and Stephen King.[12] In her response to a set of unknown interview questions she received in 2007, she revealed that although "no book has ever changed my life," there have been several that "inspired and motivated, made me laugh and cry." For example, she found T.S. Eliot's *The Waste Land* to be "brilliant," "beautiful," and skillful, while she named Emma Harte from Barbara Taylor Bradford's *A Woman of Substance* as one of her favorite heroines. Additionally, she recalled that as a child, she treasured Eleanor Estes's *The Hundred Dresses* because "it was the first book I ever read where I realized that children could be cruel in books just as they were in real life."[13] Delores kept a running list of novels, plays, books of poetry, or anything else that piqued her interest, first on steno notebooks and eventually on her computer, some of which include Unoma Azuah's *Sky High Flames*, Marlon James's *John Crow's Devil*, and Markus Zusak's *The Book Thief*.[14] She enlisted the same routine for increasing her vocabulary, cataloging a list of intriguing words and practicing by writing them in a sentence.

Her writing process was consistent and disciplined. She wrote every day, with a cigarette in one hand and a cup of coffee in the other, Shalana jokingly remarked.[15] In an interview, Phillips explained how she generated the ideas for her fiction: "Early morning with a cup of coffee sets the mood for me. I visualize the place and people I want to write about until I can see it all clearly. I imagine that I am walking the streets or roads of a fictional town, watching the characters, and taking note of their surroundings. These are the things that I jot down and work with as I begin a story."[16] Although her mode of writing followed the improvements of technology from typewriter to word processor to computer, Delores always used a steno notebook in some capacity. She then welcomed feedback from Linda, who recognized early on that her sister had a special gift: "As she started to write, I knew that she could write. I knew that you felt her words. I knew that when she read to you, those dimples would come out and she'd have fun. It was just a joy to her to share her work with you."[17] But their relationship was not merely one-sided; Delores also provided feedback for Linda, a writer herself, and encouraged her to nur-

Delores sitting at her nurse's desk, circa 1990s

ture her gifts.[18] Phillips also taught and mentored other aspiring writers by leading writing workshops at public libraries around Cleveland.

ILLNESS AND DEATH

During one spring day in 1998, at her home, Delores suddenly began feeling dizzy and experiencing double vision. She was rushed to the hospital where she was diagnosed with multiple sclerosis, a nerve disease that causes a communication disruption between the brain and the spinal cord. Initially, the symptoms of multiple sclerosis not only affected her writing, but also inhibited her daily functioning. Linda became her constant caregiver, and she remembered how difficult those first few months were: "[Faye] could barely walk. She used a walker and a cane. She could not read but she still wanted me to read to her. She still wanted the word, so I would read to her."[19] In time, Delores eventually regained her ability to see, read, and walk, though, in the last years of her life, she had a noticeable limp. In 2002, less than three years after Delores was diagnosed with multiple sclerosis, she began feeling intense chest pain while she was mowing the lawn at her home. Because of her nursing skills, the symptoms signaled to her that she was experiencing a heart attack, but she did not panic. Instead, she calmly went inside her home, crawled up the steps to the bathroom, washed the grass off her feet, then drove herself to the hospital. She experienced a second heart attack less than four years later.

In March of 2014, while working on *No Ordinary Rain* and *Stumbling Blocks*, Phillips was diagnosed with pancreatic cancer. Months before her diagnosis, she had suffered from pancreatitis, feeling sharp pains daily. Understanding that the pain she was experiencing was not a symptom of her multiple sclerosis nor an indication of a heart attack, she visited the ER several times, insisting to doctors that there had to be a more serious issue. Yet, despite her self-advocacy, she was continuously sent home with only bottles of pain pills. By the time she finally received further testing, the cancer had already ravaged much of her body. In a sharp decline, Delores was moved to hospice care in May of the same year. During this time, she wrote letters to family members, expressing her love and gratitude for them while encouraging them to live life to the fullest once she was gone. Her words to Linda were especially poignant, thanking her sister for her unconditional love: "I can cite more than one occasion when you put your life on hold for me. You did when my husband died and each time I became ill with one of my many medical conditions. This sister that you have has put you through the test, and you have passed with the highest possible grade. I thank God for you and for the time He gave us to express our love for each other."[20] Delores succumbed to the disease at the age of sixty-three, on June 7, 2014, with her sister, daughter, and other loved ones by her side.

At the time of her death, Phillips was mostly remembered for the novel *The Darkest Child*. Throughout the 1990s, Phillips wrote a poem that eventually filled numerous steno notebooks, a five-hundred-page line-to-line rhyming poem she entitled "Gussie Mae Potts." The poem, she explained, "explored what might have happened to battered children in the rural South before there were child protection laws."[21] Just as her own mother read to Delores during her childhood, Phillips would often recite bits of the poem to Shalana at bedtime. Although she insisted that the poem was not inspired by her time working at the Cleveland Psychological Institute, her family notes that it was by no coincidence that this poem emerged around the same time. A letter from Phillips to Linda suggests she had visions for a novel as early as 1997, but she did not transform the poem into *The Darkest Child* until the early 2000s. She would read the manuscript—originally more than eight hundred pages—aloud to her sister, who served as both a listening ear and a sharp editor. As Linda described, "She would write for hours and then she would call me and she would want to read all that she had written. This was every day during the writing process. I don't remember one day that she did not call me when she was writing *The Darkest Child*. But I think hearing it herself, that helped to motivate her to continue. . . . She never got angry with any editing remarks that I would make."[22] Soon, by reading *The Writer's Market*, Phillips began looking for publishing opportunities for first-time authors. In quite an incredible feat, after sending out only one letter of inquiry, she was offered a contract with Soho Press, which published the novel in 2004, upon editing it down to less than half the original length.

The Darkest Child follows a violent mother, Rozelle Quinn, and her ten children as they attempt to survive and escape racism, lynchings, and poverty in Jim Crow Georgia during the 1950s. The story is told through the lens of Tangy Mae—Gussie Mae in the poem—the darkest of all Rozelle's children, who values education as an avenue to flee her abusive household, poverty, and racial and sexual violence. Although the novel was not autobiographical in nature, Phillips's experience growing up in segregated Georgia allowed her to paint her fictional town of Pakersfield with such a vivid, detailed, and engrossing realism. In fact, she admits: "The telling of the story might have been different had I not experienced firsthand the soil, the fields, the attitudes of the era, or the taste of Nehi soda."[23]

Due to the novel's depiction of the harsh realities of Jim Crow Georgia coupled with a colorful cast of characters and a fast-paced plot, the novel was well-received by many critics. *Caribbean Life* called it a "brilliant, unnerving, memorable debut"; *Publishers Weekly* called it a "searing debut."[24] The *Black Book Review* concluded that with Phillips's "bold memorable characters and enough drama to keep you up all night . . . [the book] is a definite firm foundation for a long-lasting career as a great storyteller."[25] Author Randall Kenan wrote in *The New Leader* that although *The Darkest Child* was "one of the harshest novels to arrive in many years," somehow Phillips "gives the reader a sense of hope without belying her gothic vision."[26] Faye Chadwell of *Library Journal* similarly commented on Phillips's ability to depict white racism and violence without falling into spectacle, giving "this work a depth and dimension not often characteristic of a first novel."[27] Yet that same attention to unadulterated scenes of lynching, child abuse, and rape proved alienating for some critics, like *The Commercial Appeal*'s Shirley Sykes, who concluded that although the novel "is compelling reading, for [her] the descriptions of violence were overwhelming."[28] In a 1997 letter Phillips wrote to Linda, she anticipated some of the critics' reactions to such heavy material: "I think I picked a bad subject for my first novel. Domestic violence and race issues are taboo in novels. That was the focus of the 'hit list' for books being removed from library shelves."[29]

Some critics praised her writing as so powerful and emotional that even "the minor characters are well drawn and humming with life," but other reviewers were highly critical of her writing style and character development.[30] Lizzie Skurnick of the *New York Times* called her writing "faux-Dickensian prose," arguing that "Phillips's awkward renderings of accent and erudition make it difficult to concentrate both on the characters and the story."[31] Aligning with this critique, the *Washington Post*'s Lee Martin concluded that "Phillips never permits Tangy to use her promised powers of intellectual and emotional savvy to strip away layers of a complicated world of family abuse and racial tension."[32] The character Rozelle was particularly criticized. *Kirkus Reviews* argued that the novel's fundamental weakness was that Phillips "offers no explanation for [Rozelle's] cruelty," and Martin reasoned that the children's illogical desire to honor their mother despite her being "beyond redemption" was "a feeble, belated attempt to add dimension to the character of Rozelle."[33] Phillips read and kept several copies of every review, yet she seemed to be unfazed by Martin's and Skurnick's reviews: "I knew from the beginning that everybody would not get it, that there were some people who would not understand what the book was about. I concentrate on the comments that let me know I succeeded in what I set out to do—comments like, 'I laughed, I cried, I felt like I was there. I feel like I know these characters personally.'"[34]

Despite some criticism, the novel garnered generous acclaim, winning the Black Caucus of the American Library Association First Novelist Award in 2005. In the same year, she was short-listed for the Hurston/Wright Foundation Legacy Award and nominated for the Female Author of the Year Award by the African American Literature Society. The novel also won the Poets and Writers League of Greater Cleveland Award. Phillips went on extensive book tours to visit colleges and universities, bookstores, libraries, and women's groups across the United States. Linda was always

Delores (*seated*) at a book signing for *The Darkest Child* at Hampton University in 2005

by her side, and as Phillips's agent on tour, she never ceased to be amazed at how her sister, who was naturally shy and had a fear of flying and elevators, would blossom in front of an audience, often laughing, making jokes, and inviting conversation.[35] Because the novel was so "vital and engrossing," in 2018, Soho Press reissued *The Darkest Child* with a new introduction from Tayari Jones and an excerpt from *Stumbling Blocks*.[36]

THEMES AND SIGNIFICANCE

The Darkest Child adopts many themes, from generational trauma, racism and colorism, and physical and sexual abuse to love, family, and motherhood.[37] Yet part of what makes Phillips's novel unique is her ability to illuminate disability and mental health. Phillips employs disability in several ways. She uses it metaphorically, to describe, for example, the Quinn home as "old, crippled, and diseased—an emblem of poverty and neglect" or the children's disabling fear of their mother as a "malignancy."[38] She also used it to illustrate how physical violence produced permanent impairment, as experienced by characters like the Quinn's neighbor Mrs. Long, who was left with "a lazy left eye" after being severely beaten by her husband, and even Tangy Mae, whose knuckles are permanently disfigured after Rozelle breaks her finger.[39] Third, and perhaps most notable, is her development of characters with mental and physical differences, specifically Rozelle and Martha Jean. Rozelle, who sees ghosts, constantly swats at bugs she imagines are crawling on her face, and is ultimately committed to an asylum, labeled "mad" and a "lunatic." There is no justification for Rozelle's mental state, an out Phillips consciously resists throughout the novel. Back then, Black people did not have access to psychiatrists and therapy, Phillips explains: "I did not give her a diagnosis because back then you did not have a diagnosis to go on. . . . We just called people crazy."[40] Phillips's hesitancy in diagnosing Rozelle places more emphasis on the character's individual experience than on objective diagnosis.

Through Martha Jean, Phillips features one of the few representations of literal deafness in African American literature. Phillips strove to imagine the experiences of various children in the Jim Crow South, and that included deaf children. She even enrolled in several sign language courses so "she could better communicate with Martha Jean."[41] Martha Jean's presence in the novel challenges negative and surface-level conceptions of deaf people and deaf-related imagery, where in fiction they have "historically been used as generic symbols for something else rather than as fully realized expressions of their individual selves."[42] In African American literature, for example, both Adrienne Kennedy in her play *She Talks to Beethoven* (1992) and Toni Morrison in her short story "Recitatif" (1983) evoke deafness as a *narrative prosthetic*, which, coined by David Mitchell and Sharon Snyder, is a narrative device that characterizes how disability is often used in literature as a means of propelling the narrative forward. Yet Martha Jean's deafness is not erased, nor is she a marginalized character. Rather, by redefining and reordering her relationship to literacy and education, as well as the labor dynamics of the novel, "Martha Jean constitutes a character of complex embodiment who complicates preconceived notions of Black and deaf people as 'burdens' on society."[43]

Phillips's attention to the varied experiences of Black life, coupled with her vivid imagery and beautiful lyricism, make powerful the harsh realities of life for many Black people in 1950s Georgia. Phillips takes a southern setting in much of her work, providing a rich backdrop to explore issues of lynchings, violence, and anti-Black racism, but also space to privilege poor, Black, rural families as complex characters instead of stereotypes. Tayari Jones suggests that because *The Darkest Child* was released in the late twenty-first century, "Phillips [was] free from drawing characters that represent some fundamental truth about the African American female experience."[44] As I hope this collection shows, Phillips's creation of multidimensional Black characters was not just a staple of her novel work; rather, her attention to creative freedom and realism spanned across her varied literary forms.

Taken together, Delores Phillips's poetry, novels, and short stories showcase the love, dedication, and pure talent she poured into her art. *Stumbling Blocks and Other Unfinished Work* is the result of years of extensive research, intimate collaboration, and frankly, I believe, providential guidance. I was introduced to the novel in 2016 by a friend, and, like Tayari Jones, I began searching for more information on Phillips—to little avail, other than a brief obituary and short biography. In 2018, armed with the names of Phillips's surviving relatives, I reached out to Shalana on a whim through a Facebook message. To my surprise, she was thoroughly excited that someone was interested in "Ma," as she calls her, and months later she invited me and my mother, Carolyn Steverson, to Cleveland, where I met her immediate family and Phillips's two surviving siblings, Linda and Greg. As an invaluable research assistant, my mother aided me in conducting interviews with the family members as I learned more about the woman that I never had the pleasure of meeting. Over the years, we have developed and maintained an immense bond as both Linda and Shalana continued to open their homes and share their memories with me. Over coffee, tea, tuna sandwiches, and Linda's homemade baked goods, we began to assemble what would become Phillips's archive, comprising several hundred pages of typescript documents, magazine clippings, letters from Delores to Linda, artifacts, photographs, college transcripts, journal entries, medical documents, and, incredibly enough, Phillips's computer hard drive, which included drafts of all three of her novels.

This collection, then, is organized strategically. Because Linda was Phillips's sister, editor, and closest confidant, I believe it is only right that the volume opens with her memories of Faye, as she affectionately called her. I am sure Delores would have wanted it no other way. Thereafter, the volume is arranged by genre. Phillips's first love was poetry, and because poetry was the form of her earliest publications, this section appears first.[45] Following the poetry are Phillips's short stories. As she wrote these stories, she began to engage in more formal training and to experiment with plot, character development, and long-form prose. Her novel work ends the collection, because that was the form she was working with most closely at the time of her death. Trudier Harris's afterword offers readers more insightful ruminations on Phillips's repertoire and ongoing legacy. Before each part, I provide a brief essay contextualizing Phillips's work in her larger literary journey and explaining my editorial choices.

Finally, this volume is not named in absolute terms—I refrained from calling it Phillips's "complete works" or "all of Phillips's work" because my research has indicated that there is a high probability that more of Phillips's writings are yet to be recovered or even discovered. Following the paths paved by studies such as Maryemma Graham's project on Margaret Walker and Alice Walker's work on Zora Neale Hurston, this collection serves as a fundamental step in the process of recovery work to increase the visibility of Black women writers who may have fallen through the cracks of American history. It is a testament to the power and complexity of a Black artist whose legacy is, indeed, unfinished.

NOTES

1. Jones, Tayari. Introduction. *The Darkest Child*, by Delores Phillips, Soho Press, 2018.

2. Miller, Linda. Interview. 16 July 2020.

3. *Writer in Residence Lecture: Delores Phillips.* Department of English, Modern Languages, and Mass Communication, Albany State University, 2007. DVD.

4. Marchetti, Donna. "Clevelander Finds Quick Acceptance for Her First Novel." *Plain Dealer*, 13 Feb. 2004, p. E1–E3.

5. Phillips, Delores. Letter to Linda Miller. 30 Nov. 1998.

6. "Linda Miller." *Plain Dealer*, 15 Feb. 1995, p. 12. This piece is available in its entirety on the companion website.

7. *Writer in Residence Lecture.*

8. Harris, Shalana. Personal interview. 16 July 2020.

9. Phillips, Delores. "Husband." 4 Feb. 2006. Delores Phillips Digital Archive.

10. You can read her articles and other journalistic endeavors on the companion website.

11. Lunn, Collier. Interview with Delores Phillips. *Clutch Magazine*, 1 Sept. 2007.

12. Phillips, Delores. "Unknown Interview Answers." Delores Phillips Digital Archive.

13. Phillips, Delores. "Laura." Delores Phillips Digital Archive.

14. Phillips, Delores. "Judging." Delores Phillips Digital Archive.

15. Harris, Shalana. Personal interview. 12 June 2019.

16. Phillips, Delores. "Borders." Delores Phillips Digital Archive.

17. Miller, Linda. Personal interview. 12 June 2019.

18. Phillips writes to Miller in a letter from August 25, 1994, "I'm deep into your novel *Gone*. It is a really good book . . ."

19. Miller, Linda. Personal interview. 12 June 2019.

20. Phillips, Delores. "Dear Sis." Letter to Linda Miller, Delores Phillips Digital Archive.

21. *Writer in Residence Lecture.*

22. Miller, Linda. Personal interview. 12 June 2019.

23. Phillips, Delores. "Interview Questions." Delores Phillips Digital Archive.

24. McKanic, Arlene. "Delores Quinn's Darkest Child Is an Arresting First." *Caribbean Life*, 10 Feb. 2004, 54. Review of *The Darkest Child. Publisher's Weekly*, 26 Jan. 2004.

25. Moore, Jacquie B. "What Mama Has on Her Mind." *Black Book Review*, April 2004.

26. Kenan, Randall. "In the Devil's House." *The New Leader*, Dec. 2003.

27. Chadwell, Faye A. Review of *The Darkest Child. Library Journal*, 1 Oct. 2003.

28. Sykes, Shirley. "Tale of Abusive Mother Abounds with Violence." *The Commercial Appeal*, 18 Apr. 2004.

29. Phillips, Delores. Letter to Linda Miller. 11 Feb. 1997. Delores Phillips Digital Archive.

30. McKanic, "Delores Quinn's Darkest Child."

31. Skurnick, Lizzie. "Song of the South." *New York Times*, 28 March 2004.

32. Martin, Lee. "Cruel and Unusual." *Washington Post*, 11 Jan. 2004.

33. "Review of *The Darkest Child*." *Kirkus Review*, 1 Oct. 2003. Martin, "Cruel and Unusual."

34. Phillips, Delores. "Interview Questions." Delores Phillips Digital Archive.

35. Miller, Linda. Personal interview. 12 June 2019.

36. "Celebrating *The Darkest Child*." *SoHo Press*, 2 Feb. 2021, sohopress.com/celebrating-the-darkest-child/.

37. To my knowledge there has been, sadly, only three secondary articles on the novel. One is Kaila Philo's chapter in *Critical Insights: Civil Rights Literature, Past and Present* (2017), entitled "Agency, Activism, and the Black Domestic Worker in Kathryn Stockett's *The Help* and Delores Phillips' *The Darkest Child*." Trudier Harris's chapter "Image Shatterer: Delores Phillips's *The Darkest Child*" in *Mothers Who Kill* (2021) explores representations of motherhood in the novel. I wrote an article for the *Journal of Literary and Cultural Disability Studies* on representations of deafness in the novel, entitled "'Where's the Dummy?': Deafness, Race, and Labor in Delores Phillips's *The Darkest Child*."

38. Phillips, *The Darkest Child*, pp. 7, 50.

39. Phillips, pp. 112, 189.

40. *Writer in Residence Lecture*. I recognize that Phillips's language choice in this instance is troubling, but I have chosen to retain this reference to maintain the integrity of her voice.

41. *Writer in Residence Lecture*.

42. Mcdonald, Donna M. "Not Silent, Invisible: Literature's Chance Encounters with Deaf Heroes and Heroines." *American Annals of the Deaf*, vol. 154, no. 5, 2010, p. 465. She mentions Singer in Carson McCullers's *The Heart Is a Lonely Hunter* and Wemmick in Charles Dickens's *Great Expectations*.

43. Steverson, Delia. "'Where's the Dummy?': Deafness, Race, and Labor in Delores Phillips's *The Darkest Child*." *Journal of Literary and Cultural Disability Studies*, vol. 15, no. 2, 2021, pp. 187–202.

44. Jones, Introduction.

45. Phillips, Delores. "Albany Trip." *Delores Phillips Digital Archive*.

A NOTE ON EDITING AND THE DIGITAL COMPANION

I have edited this volume to my best ability with respect to Delores Phillips's original intentions. Where obvious, I have corrected misspellings, like *canvass bag* to *canvas bag*; added missing punctuation, for instance, a period at the end of a sentence; corrected punctuation errors, like misplaced commas and apostrophes; and in few circumstances, changed verb tense and point of view to maintain consistency with a paragraph, as in *outgrew* to *outgrow*.

The novel section is the most heavily edited. Phillips repeated multiple chapter numbers in both *Stumbling Blocks* and *No Ordinary Rain*, so I have renumbered the chapters to maintain their sequential order. Moreover, toward the last chapters of *No Ordinary Rain*, Phillips begins shifting Zyma's point of view to first person. I have named those chapters "Zyma" to echo the "Girlie" chapters, which are also told in first person. I have also corrected a few inconsistencies. For example, I changed Thursday to Wednesday to maintain consistency of the day that Mr. Percy brings Miss Francine her groceries. Furthermore, there were rare instances where Phillips left a blank to fill in with an adjective or place. I have respectfully filled in those blanks with a word or place that would best make sense. For instance, the location and name of Martha Jean's teacher is left blank in the 2011 manuscript, but an earlier version named the teacher as Robert Bradford from Smyrna.

Finally, two revisions, where guidance in Phillips's archives was scant or contradictory, required me to use my best judgment to both maintain the novel's integrity and to enhance its readability. First, in chapter 17 of the digital manuscript of *Stumbling Blocks*, Phillips and Tangy Mae enter the kitchen twice for sandwiches and lemonade. I deleted the repetition and added the sentence, "She placed the lemonade and plate of ham sandwiches on the dining table and we both took a seat." The most significant edit was to the plot of *No Ordinary Rain*. In the earliest version of the novel *Tomorrow People*, Phillips wrote that Opal's three boys (who do not exist in *No Ordinary Rain*) killed Mr. Lawrence and were imprisoned, but in *No Ordinary Rain*, Phillips indicates Opal and then Cleo as murder suspects. I have chosen to solidify

Cleo as the possible murderer because Opal could not have attended Lawrence's funeral nor been at Van Ida's home if she was imprisoned.

Although this volume serves as the basis for the recovery project on Phillips, there are materials that, due to spatial constraints, it cannot accommodate. Therefore, I have created a digital resource that serves as an additional accessible, educational, and interactive supplement to enhance readers' experience with this volume. The companion website contains materials that I hope will be of interest to general audiences, students, scholars, and teachers alike: Phillips's earlier version of *No Ordinary Rain*, entitled *Tomorrow People*; a more detailed explanation of my editorial choices with comparisons; an interactive timeline of her life with images; a rare video interview of Phillips and transcripts of other interviews; with Linda's consent, a few personal letters from Phillips to Linda; other writings that did not make it into this volume, specifically her journalistic efforts from Cleveland's *The Plain Dealer* newspaper; and various other documents from Delores's digital archives. Moreover, I have included lesson plans, discussion questions, and a list of selected scholarship to encourage wider teaching and discussion of her works. Throughout this volume, I have indicated in a note if the source is available on the companion website.

STUMBLING BLOCKS
AND OTHER UNFINISHED WORK

Born to Write
Poetry

Even though Delores Phillips is widely known as a novelist, poetry was her earliest form of writing. Self-taught as a child and inspired by her love of rhyming and her mother's animated recitations of various poetry, Phillips had had no formal training when her published poetry appeared across several venues in the 1970s. In fact, Phillips did not receive formal training until her first creative writing class at Cuyahoga Community College in 1990. Like her mother, Annie Ruth, Delores loved performing her poems, particularly for her siblings, Linda and Greg, during their childhood and eventually for her daughter, Shalana. Phillips's dramatic flair would leave a lasting impression on all three. Greg remembers being particularly engrossed in his sister's rendition of "Riding with a Friend," a poem about the effects of psychedelic drugs: "I was about seven or eight years old and at that young age, I didn't know anything about LSD . . . But I was hooked on that poem. I can remember that poem clear as day, even if I can't remember the words. But I can remember her acting it out. She was very animated."[1] Phillips's published and unpublished poetry both vary in theme, tone, and structure. Some poems are funny, others are serious, and several are autobiographical in nature. But collectively, to echo the name of the subsection that her poem "Ashes" appeared under in *Jean's Journal*, Phillips's oeuvre is considerably more of "a potpourri of poetry."[2]

PUBLISHED POETRY

Although Phillips crafted poetry throughout her entire life, her published poems appeared during a short time frame, between 1974 and 1976, under the name Faye Miller Knox—Faye for her middle name, Miller for her father's last name, and Knox for her first husband's last name. Phillips published six poems over these two years in three venues, *Jean's Journal*, *The Crisis*, and *Black Times*. There is no indication in Phillips's archives as to why she chose these periodicals, but one plausible explanation is because all three venues actively accepted the work of Black writers. Phillips's first published poem, "Riding with a Friend," appeared in *Jean's Journal* in May 1974. An independent quarterly literary magazine running from 1961 to the late 1980s, *Jean's Journal* was founded and edited in Kanona, New York, by Jean Calkins, a prolific American poet, most known as an influential editor of American haiku in the 1960s. With nearly five hundred subscribers, *Jean's Journal*, which published as *Jean's Journal of Poems* until the mid-1960s, solicited original poetry from aspiring poets of all ages. Phillips published two more poems in the journal, "Ashes" in August 1975 and "Uncle Sam Needs You" in May 1976. The publication itself was suspended after the May 1976 issue until 1979, possibly due to editorial complications.

Also in May 1976, Phillips's poem "Success" appeared in *Black Times: Voices of the National Community*. Originally established as *Black Times: The National Negro Newspaper* in January 1971, the monthly publication was short-lived and appeared to cease publication after August 1976. Launched in January 1971 in California by a group of six individuals, both Black and non-Black, including journalist and editor Theodore Walker and consultant Eric Bakalinsky, the *Black Times* sought to serve as "a responsible Black newspaper on a national basis for information to Black America about both Black and white America."[3] Throughout its tenure, the newspaper included "individual and group efforts and achievements in the community, national and internal news bearing on Black America, letters from prisoners, Black history, book reviews, short stories, and poetry" aimed at "creating awareness of developments in the Black Community."[4] It reproduced poetry from more established poets like Sherley Anne Williams and published original poetry from up-and-coming artists like Neal Jackson, Vina McEachern, and Caruso Brown. Phillips's second poem in the newspaper, "Shalana," was featured in a set of love poems in June 1976. Right above the poem on the page is an image of a little Black girl; however, it is not a picture of Phillips's daughter, Shalana, but rather a stock photo like those that accompanied many of the poems published in the newspaper.[5] Such is the case with "Success," which features an image of a turtle at the bottom of the poem representing the line, "He said he rode to success / On a turtle's back." The images served as a visual association to the poem.

While the majority of her poetry appeared in these two smaller publication venues, one poem, "Forgive Me Child," landed in *The Crisis* in November 1975. Founded in 1910 by W. E. B. Du Bois as the publication of the National Association for the Advancement of Colored People (NAACP), *The Crisis* is one of the most renowned literary magazines pertaining to African American experiences. During the Harlem Renaissance, it was the nucleus of Black literary creation and helped establish prominent Black writers and poets including Langston Hughes, Countee Cullen, and Jean Toomer. Although the readership of *The Crisis* drastically declined after its heyday during the Harlem Renaissance, in the 1970s it remained dedicated to social justice, civil rights, and African American culture and art. While the 1970s would serve as a period in American history when many African American writers revisited the meanings and purposes of art to effect social, political, and economic change, Delores Phillips's poetry demonstrates the creativity of a Black artist attuned to but not confined by the restrictive forces of the Black Arts Movement. That is not to say that a form of racial consciousness is totally absent from her work—on the contrary, as her later poems "Cousin Nathan" and "Gators Alley" establish. Rather, her poetry demonstrates the freedom and creativity of an artist not beholden to any specific conventions or agendas.

Two poems, "Forgive Me Child" and "Shalana," reveal Phillips's investment in the complexities of familial relationships and the challenges and responsibilities of child rearing. "Shalana," titled after Phillips's only daughter, Shalana, who was nearly three years old at the time of the poem's publication, details a mother's anxiety, fear, and frustration caring for a toddler with an absent father. The poem draws comparisons to Audre Lorde's "What My Child Learns of the Sea" (1963), in which a mother contemplates her daughter's growth throughout the seasons "as her winters fall out of time."[6] Likewise, the mother in "Shalana" laments the time she has sacrificed with her daughter while working two jobs to secure their financial future. Similarly, the parental figure in "Forgive Me Child" pleads forgiveness from their child for past and future mistakes.

While "Forgive Me Child" and "Shalana" reinforce the bond between parent and child, in "Uncle Sam Needs You" the speaker disavows familial kinships claimed through Uncle Sam, the image of nationalist propaganda, to reject the call to join the war effort. Although Phillips does not explicitly condemn U.S. involvement in the Vietnam War, she uses humor and sarcasm to effectively critique the war efforts. Several of Phillips's cousins served in Vietnam and returned stateside with a drug habit. Their experience, Greg believes, served as the inspiration for "Riding with a Friend," in which the speaker illustrates the roller-coaster effect that the drug LSD has on the psyche.[7] The friendship between the speaker and the drug has blissful beginnings, but by the end of the ride, the intensity of the trip leaves the speaker crying for help, declaring, "I hate you, LSD." Another addictive habit, smoking, would later become the subject of one of Phillips's unpublished poems, "One More Smoke."

UNPUBLISHED POETRY

Most of Phillips's unpublished poetry was probably written in the 1980s to late 1990s. It is unknown if she sought to publish any of it. Only two of her unpublished poems, one untitled, which I have called "I Never Thought" for clarity, and "One More Smoke," were written for her Poetry Writing course at Cleveland State and include dates, January 11, 1994, and February 2, 1994, respectively. Either Phillips had been working on this poetry years before and was using the space of her creative writing classes in college to rework them, or they were new poems written specifically for the courses themselves.

The unpublished poems survive through hard copies written on either a typewriter or word processor. Because there is no publication history for these poems, it is difficult to pinpoint a more exact period of writing; however, based on the addresses and phone numbers Phillips often added in the heading of her poems, some approximate dates can be deduced. For example, based on the address in the heading of "Insatiable Death," both it and "Cousin Nathan," which appears on the back of "Insatiable Death," were both probably written in 1998 or 1999. Because Phillips was a prolific poet and since much of her poetry was written before the age of the personal computer, it is highly probable that these poems only represent a fraction of her repertoire.

"Cousin Nathan" is unique: although it was originally written as a stand-alone poem, Phillips renamed it "Uncle Nathan" and included it as part of the narrative in *The Darkest Child*. In the novel, Junior, a young Black boy fighting for African American civil rights, shares the poem with the protagonist, Tangy Mae, as a way of processing and remembering his uncle who was lynched in 1950s Jim Crow Georgia. Other than the name change throughout the poem from "cousin" to "uncle," "Cousin Nathan" and "Uncle Nathan" are identical in content. In its imagery of death—the "severed head," "lifeless body," and "blue-black blood"—"Cousin Nathan" follows a long line of African American poetry illustrating the spectacle of racial violence through lynching, including Paul Laurence Dunbar's "The Haunted Oak" (1913), Claude McKay's "The Lynching" (1922), Richard Wright's "Between the World and Me" (1935) and Robert Hayden's "Night, Death, Mississippi" (1962). Moreover, the poem also bears similarity to Nikki Giovanni's "For Saundra" (1968) where the speaker, after observing chaos and strife in the community amid the civil rights movement, declares that "perhaps these are not poetic times at all."[8]

The violence, chaos, and strife of Jim Crow Georgia is compared to the biblical Sodom and Gomorrah in "Gators Alley." In its rhythm and repetition, the poem draws from the African American blues and jazz tradition. The speaker alludes to Ray Charles's version of "Georgia on My Mind" (1960) to reminisce about the tedious physical labor and lack of formal education African Americans often received in the South. Unlike the speaker in Gladys Knight and the Pips' "Midnight Train to Georgia" (1973), who leaves Los Angeles on a train headed *toward* Georgia, the speaker in "Gators Alley" awaits a train to deliver them *away* from their homeplace—a site of oppression and inequality. Even the speaker in "Riding with a Friend" invokes the carnivalesque to situate Cartersville, Georgia, as "only twenty-two miles from hell." The strangleholds of the Georgian environment would prove a constant in Phillips's work across genres, specifically in her novel writing.

Like "Shalana" and "Forgive Me Child," several of her unpublished poems are also autobiographical. In "One More Smoke," Phillips uses humor to address smoking's addictiveness, a chronic habit she picked up in the army. "Queen of Rub-a-Dub" references Dailey's, a club in Cleveland where she would delight in observing the crowd while dancing to the reggae beat. Other poems, such as "Sister, You Wear It Well," take on a more serious tone to reflect on the vulnerability of children at the hands of abusive relatives. The poem, whose second page is lost, relays the deeply personal and traumatic account of Phillips's sister's sexual abuse and Phillips's feelings of guilt for not knowing.

While "Sister, You Wear It Well," highlights the insidious abuse of children at the hands of relatives, "I Never Thought" emphasizes familial relationships that nurture love, safety, and care. In "Uncle Sam Needs You" the speaker denies the metaphorical kinship that ties individual to country, while in "I Never Thought" the speaker revels in gratitude for kin, specifically an uncle, who cared for them. The poem is dedicated to Anderson Terrel, better known as Uncle T, who was a strong presence in the family's life during their time in Georgia. He became like a father figure to the children while Lennie was away, teaching the children baseball and even taking Phillips's mother, Annie Ruth, to the hospital when she gave birth to Skip. After Annie Ruth died in 1967, Uncle T and his wife, Kate—Annie Ruth's older sister—took in all four children. All four siblings adored Uncle T, a church deacon who was patient, kind, and funny and showed no partiality between any of his nieces and nephews. Phillips exudes a love for her uncle in the poem, for which she received one of the few surviving pieces of feedback from her time at Cleveland State: "Excellent use of form. Simplistic [and] superb. Really touching and natural flow. I love it. It works."

Phillips also engages other literary techniques to explore a combination of death, heartbreak, and personal thoughts in both her published and unpublished works. For example, death is personified in "Insatiable Death" as a sex worker who is expensive, nondiscriminatory, and never satisfied, while the speaker in "Ashes" metaphorically becomes dust after being set ablaze. The speaker in "Success" is directly compared to a sidewalk and a ticket to freedom. Moreover, "Jesters," possibly written around 2003, uses analogy to further explore Phillips's mindset.[9] Phillips evokes the image of the jester as a metaphor for the tension she experienced throughout adulthood between her public personae and her private life. Phillips became fixated on jesters, even having dozens displayed around her home in Cleveland. As several of her journal entries reveal, Phillips struggled to maintain friendships and romantic relationships, often masking her pain and discontent behind a gracious smile or a laugh.

Although her published work appeared only briefly, Phillips's contributions during this time marked the beginning of her professional writing career. Unlike the short stories and novels, poetry is the only form of writing to span Phillips's entire lifetime. The majority of her poetry remained unpublished, including her most ambitious poem, a five-hundred-page rhyming piece titled "Gussie Mae Potts," which would serve as the catalyst for her first novel, *The Darkest Child*.[10] Taken together, Phillips wide-ranging themes and style produced "a potpourri of poetry" that can easily stand on its own.

NOTES

1. Green, Gregory. Personal interview. 12 June 2019.

2. *Jean's Journal*, August 1975, p. 12.

3. *Black Times*, 15 Jan. 1971.

4. *Black Times*, June 1976, p. 20.

5. The image is available on the companion website.

6. Lorde, Audre. "What My Child Learns of the Sea." *The First Cities*, Poets Press, 1968.

7. Green, Greg. Personal interview. 12 June 2019.

8. Giovanni, Nikki. "For Saundra." *Black Judgement*, 1968.

9. I say *possibly* because a handwritten version of the poem is written alongside an entry in her steno notebook that reads "2003."

10. I give more context to this poem in the sections that follow.

Riding with a Friend

My friend made everything nice for me.
We were always going to nice places
Where the colored lights were fun to see,
With beautiful flowers and happy faces
And the rides; those trips were great.
Always on time, my friend; he never showed up late.
I love him.

Then one day he left me on the ferris wheel
And a sign said welcome to Cartersville,
Only twenty-two miles from Hell.
Everything was ugly.

Then knives began to run at me.
They were sticking me and all I could see
For miles and miles was fire,
Running, running faster to catch me
In a whirlpool of flame,
Shouting out, "What's your name?"
And I, in all my pain, had forgotten.

Oh what a trick my friend, you're rotten.
Help me, someone, I cried out; help
Before this flame burns me to death.
But my friend stood back and laughed at me
And I knew then that I hated him, and I told him,
"I hate you, LSD," but he just laughed at me.

Jean's Journal, 1974

Ashes

He lit the fire
And watched the smoke descend
The beauty he craved
In the smothering flames
Hazy, belittling, uncaring,
No longer a need,
He diminishes the fire;
Now ashes am I.

Jean's Journal, 1975

Forgive Me Child

Forgive me child,
If I taught you to hate this world as I do,
And if I've led you astray in any way
                              I'm sorry

Forgive me child
If I taught you to hate white because of long ago
Or said hate Black because it's Black
                              I'm sorry

Forgive me child
If I say don't drink and you catch me drunk,
Or say hate a cop because I'm crooked
                              I'm sorry

Forgive me child
If you see me doing what I've told you was wrong
And keep you out of school because I'm a fool
                              I'm sorry

Forgive me child
If I tell you I'll never go away, yet one day
In this changing world you find me gone
                              I'm sorry

Forgive me child
Because I'm wrong and know I'm wrong, yet know no
Other way, and if I've led you astray in any way
                              I'm sorry child, I'm sorry

The Crisis, 1975

Uncle Sam Needs You

How can you say he needs me?
He's not in my family tree.
Mother only had three brothers
William, Sidney, and Paul.
Father had two sisters but,
No brothers at all.
Aunt Emma married Dennis Slade
And Polly is an old maid.
I'm not being disrespectful Ma'am
But I don't have an Uncle Sam.

Jean's Journal, 1975

Success

He said he rode to success
On a turtle's back
And along the way he was many things.
He was a sidewalk, and today still he bears
The prints of many feet that stepped on him.

He was a ticket to freedom that got lost along
The way. He was many times an envelope lost
In the mail and sometimes returned to sender.

A pair of shoes with a hole in the bottom.
A bottle of milk tipped and spilled.

But today he is a shining light
Hanging high up over the street
That is looked up to, and shines for many.

Black Times, 1976

Shalana

Bad and weeping times are now,
When my man is gone (vanished)
I know and care not where,
And the baby unleashes running tears
That fall across an ebony face
And meet at the chin and drop.
And I feel pain.
Like a ton of weight has fallen upon my heart.

This innocent child grows with a love
She cannot see or feel,
She drifts like the wind from city to city.
From child-cares to babysitters
And I fear she will never know me.
For how can she, when all day I hold two jobs
Working my fingers to the bone?
And false pride has tied a noose around my neck,
And it's choking me to death.

I keep telling myself I can fight the snow,
And the icy cold that chills my soul
Far better than I can the welfare roll.
But in reality this is a bitter lie,
For I fear the day that my work is done
And I no longer have to pay
The smiling lady at the child-care
To give my baby love

. . . .

The love I should have had the time
To give her myself.
As of now she cannot speak.
Too young for anything but a Mother's arms,
But what if, one day, when she can
She should run to me
And ask me who I am?

Black Times, 1976

Cousin Nathan

Why should I write
of teardrops falling
silently obscuring
the timeless craft
of a skillful master
whose fingers traced
stained glass of
some distant morrow
ancient souls foretold
would never come
Would that make sense
to you?

How would you know
I am thinking
of Cousin Nathan
lightning fast
fleeing thunder
of hooded henchmen
spurred on by that
man-god, Dionysus
come from Olympus
in a pickup truck
to show old Nathan
no Black man
will ever be as swift
as the great Achilles?

....

How can I write
of morning glories
lovingly caressed
by dawn's sweet dew
or buds blooming
from April showers
and not remember
the severed head,
protruding eyes,
the lifeless body
beside twisted vines
of morning glories
as torrential rains
washed away the
blue-black blood
that men bleed
when the soft light
of dark midnight
cannot shelter them
from murder
as brutal as that
of Cousin Nathan?

Insatiable Death

Death is a whore.
She wears red high heels with taps on the toes,
black tie, blue collar,
Dockers, FUBU.

He is not silent.
He swaggers and sways, cracks his gum loudly between,
Hey, baby, (crack)
wanna have a good time?

She likes to party,
bungee jump, speed race, mainline, freebase,
striptease, gangbang,
please.

Death is high priced,
two-bit, has a sliding scale,
no gender preference,
does not discriminate.

He has crimson lips,
ginger breath. He smiles and salivates desire
as he sips the very last drip
from a wilting stem of life.

She walks the streets,
hangs on corners, escorts in a limousine.
She will do the thing
your mate will never do.

. . . .

Death plays a game,
pleasure and pain, push and pull,
push and pull, pleasure and pain,
no pimp, no protection.

Death is a whore,
takes on thousands of johns or marys
in a single day or night, and still
Death is never satisfied.

Gators Alley

The chattanooga choo-choo
ran through the heart of town.
I raced along the tracks behind
with hope.
Someday it would deliver me
from Gators Alley,

Georgia, Georgia, Georgia on my mind.

Reading, writing,
learning, growing,
living was taboo.
Georgia, screw you!
Don't ask me to spell it,
spelling was forbidden too,
in Gators Alley
near the Chattahoochee River
below the Altoona Dam.
Take your prick out the dike
and let the waters flow.

Georgia, Georgia, Georgia on my mind.

Confederate flag,
sweet Georgia peach,
flat belly, strong legs, healthy teeth.
No bidders; all takers.
I know why I was born.

Georgia, Georgia, Georgia on my mind.

....

Red dirt beneath my sore bare feet,
yellow clay on my tongue,
black mud rushes through my veins
to clog my aching heart.
My soul was bought
and paid for long ago
when I was born
a Gators Alley child
on a midnight train
on a rainy night
with Georgia on my mind.

Sodom
Gomorrah,
Gators Alley,
Georgia on my mind.

Queen of a Rub-a-Dub

The old mother's gait is unsteady and slow
She hums and mumbles to herself
Her children look on with apprehension
They fear she has slipped far outside
the realms of reality.
She has no time to explain as she drifts
into a past
where every night is reggae night
across the park at Dailey's
and she is queen of rub-a-dub.

On a mantle in the family room
is a black and white snapshot
of a woman pressed tightly against her man
—a vulgar picture, fading with age
much too slow for the children.
The woman wears a dark dress, low cut,
too tight, too far above the knees.
Her eyes stare longingly at her mate,
Her lips are curled upwards in a smile.
She bears a slight resemblance to the mother.

It will be the first thing tossed when she dies.
She is well aware of this.
But until then it remains in the wooden frame
between white candles and crystal swans, and the children
can go on pretending it is the face, the body
of a stranger
and the man beside her did not exist
to father a dozen children and desert them.
They should have known him when he had loved
her with a rhythm
on a crowded dance floor at Dailey's.

. . . .

Deeper she drifts into the past, her back against the wall,
his warm breath on her ear, his cool hands on her thighs,
loving her to a reggae beat in a deep, dark corner
at Dailey's where the volume is high, the rhythm is wild,
and the music never ends.
She dips and sways, then grinds her hips.
Laughter flows from the pit of her belly.
She glides, escorted across the floor as the dancers bow
to the queen of rub-a-dub.

Cries of concern summon her back into the present
where she has no desire to be.
She sees them and wonders, are my old, tired eyes seeing double
Or did I have this many babies?

They kiss her gently, preparing to depart
for lives and children of their own.
She tells them now how she loves them all,
but if she had to do over again,
She would never be a mother,
just the queen of rub-a-dub.
They laugh for surely their mother jests,
but their laughter fades as she drifts away
knowing that she means it.

Sister, You Wear It Well

We thought we knew him
that man
who claimed to love our mother
who bought us candy and bounced us on his knees.
You knew him better, sister.
While I slept in innocence, wrapped in youthful dreams,
that monster slipped in, pounced down on you.
I swear, I never knew.
You wear that memory behind wise, brown eyes
and, sister, you wear it well.

Threats, pain, fear kept you silent
year after year after year.
Six, seven, eight, nine.
Happy birthday, Sister.
I swear, I never knew.

Mother would not have died in her sleep
as he said.
And well he knew
she would have killed for you.
That monster is gone forever now.
Sister, what do you feel?

Me neither.

. . . .

At ten, did you believe
he could hurt you any worse?
He did, and finally you told.
With tiny, trembling hands covered in blood
drawn from between your thighs,
you told Aunt Becky.
So she knew, and said
"Go home and take a bath."
Dignity you took with you,
cloaked yourself in it,[1]

....
1. The rest of this poem is missing.

One More Smoke

Early morning rising
Hot coffee brewing
Three or four smokes
That's breakfast
And I'm leaving

On the sofa resting
Video I'm watching
Three or four smokes
Can of beer
Time for sleeping

At my desk typing
Feet start swelling
Three or four smokes
And I'm fine
Now that I'm lounging

Kidney's not producing
Organs start shaking
Three or four smokes
Cup of coffee
Will get me over

Greasy burger eating
Salty fries licking
Three or four smokes
Chocolate shake
Lunch is over

On the floor paining
Lungs not expanding
One more smoke
Call the doctor
Then I'm leaving

In my car driving
Candy bar snacking
Three or four smokes
Homeward bound
Work is over

Blood's not flowing
Heart's not pumping
One more smoke
All I ask
Before it's over

1994

I Never Thought

I never thought to say thank you then
Or anything else I might have said
And I never wondered what might have been.

I was angry when you took me in.
So young I was and mother was dead
And I never thought to say thank you then.

I took for granted the next of kin
With one more mouth to be fed
And I never wondered what might have been.

I know now how you soothed me when
My heart and mind were filled with dread
And I never thought to say thank you then.

I never noticed loving eyes or an easy grin
There were other things going through my head
And I never wondered what might have been.

So thank you, Uncle, for taking me in
When you could have turned your back instead.
I never thought to say thank you then
But often I wonder what might have been.

1994

Jesters

Do wait for me, Mr. Jester, let me walk beside.
The day is over for us both; let's take it now in stride.

You were great; you brought laughter before the court today,
but now the slump of your shoulders gives you away.
Your painted smile beneath sad eyes seems somehow out of place.
Hold still, and I will paint a teardrop on your face.

We could fill this world with tears if our anguish should erupt.
If we put our pride together, it would fill a thimble up.

So long ago should I have known and taken it as an omen
to suffer a lonely lady instead of the other woman.

Your silence speaks it all. You think that I don't understand,
but I am a fallen woman, and you are a broken man.

Since you have stopped to listen, to you I will confess.
There quivers a broken heart beneath this motley dress.

I've been misused so often, I fake love, wit, and charm.
I consider myself lucky to rest on a strong man's arm.

He abandons his mate so that I can please him for a night.
He gives me gifts of trinkets, then blinks me from his sight.

Yes, mock me if you choose, as I've said, I have no pride.
I think of all the lonely nights I've held myself and cried.

. . . .

I have no cockscomb and no filly collar, but
these trinkets, cheap and showy, if not my bauble, what?

Professional fools we are, Dear Sir, though somehow not the same.
You did not trade your flesh or soul to live like me—in shame.

SHORT STORIES

Transforming Poetry into Prose
Short Stories

In spring 1993 Delores Phillips enrolled in the Workshop in Writing course at Cleveland State University, and it was here that she began formal training in fiction writing, first with the short story. Throughout the quarter, Delores developed her skills in plot, setting, conflict, and character voice. A surviving example of one of her earliest short stories produced in the course reflects Phillips's tenacity and discipline. The story is a folktale narrated by an elderly woman who recounts supernatural events happening in the fictional town of Lostem, Pennsylvania. Phillips's interest in magical realism and the fantastical would later become a staple of *No Ordinary Rain*, one of her two unfinished novels. One of Phillips's classmates praised her knack for storytelling, commenting on the work: "This is the best story I've read in this class so far. It reminds me of Toni Morrison because of the African American storyteller with aspects of surrealism."[1] Phillips wrote at least one other short story in the course that is yet to be recovered.

THE RENWOOD CIRCLE STORIES

Some years after graduating from Cleveland State, Phillips began working on a collection of short stories. Like William Faulkner's Yoknapatawpha County, Randall Kenan's Tims Creek, and Wendell Berry's Port William, all fictional communities, the fictional Cleveland nursing home Renwood Circle serves as the setting for most of Phillips's short stories. Compared to Phillips's poetry and novel writing, less is known about her short stories. Her collection was unnamed, but I have called them the Renwood Circle Stories for convenience. Five stories are published here—"Gardenia Sue" (which I have named because the original is untitled), "Renwood Circle," "Choices," "The Good Side of a Man," and "All Talk." All stories survive in physical typescript only, some with multiple drafts. Phillips compiled all the stories into one document that she wrote in sequential order, and the organization here follows Phillips's own sequential structure. Because the stories survive in print only, it is unclear whether "All Talk" is the final story in the collection or if other stories are yet to be recovered.

There is, however, a known sixth story that is omitted from this volume. This unnamed short story (which I refer to as "Wondrene Barry"), originally sandwiched between "Choices" and "The Good Side of a Man," is Phillips's longest tale, totaling more than fifty pages, but the first dozen pages are missing. The story, both humorous and tragic, follows the growing friendship and adventures of two Renwood Circle residents and roommates, long-term resident Della John and newcomer Wondrene Barry, as they seek men's companionship, campaign for nursing home resident president, and even attempt to win theater tickets by being caller number nine on *Tom Joyner's Morning Show*.

Based on information gathered from addresses in the headings of several stories, the most recent versions of the Renwood Circle Stories were likely written sometime between 1998 and 2001, but some of the earlier drafts could have been composed a few years before. A letter from Phillips to Linda Miller indicates she was at least in the revision stage in November 1998. In this letter, Phillips reveals her frustrations with the writing process: "The writing bug has left me for the moment. I read back over my nursing home stories and realized that I was giving all of my residents the same diagnoses. It was either a heart attack or a stroke. I don't know why. I had to change that, but it makes things a bit more complicated. I think if you don't keep it simple, you have too much explaining to do."[2] Linda would not only be an active listener along Delores's writing journey but would also serve as editor of several of the Renwood Circle Stories, including "Gardenia Sue," "Choices," and "Wondrene Barry." The versions printed in this volume include Miller's revisions, which were mostly minor grammatical changes and word choice edits.[3]

WRITING NURSING EXPERIENCES IN SHORT STORY FORM

Phillips's interest in short story writing was bolstered not only by her creative writing courses but also by researching the publishing field. She and Miller would read newspapers, magazines, and books like *The Writer's Handbook* to examine market trends.[4] Soon she was inspired by writers she read, such as Stephen King, who found major success in the short story genre in the nineties. Phillips framed the Renwood Circle Stories around her real-world experience working in Ohio long-term care facilities. From about 1985 until she retired around 2013, Phillips worked as a licensed practical nurse at psychiatric hospitals and various health-care centers.

Over the years, Phillips sporadically journaled about her nursing experiences in her steno notebooks, on her computer, or in letters to Miller. Nursing proved to be very demanding for Delores, and her ability to handle chaos amid life-or-death situations was constantly tested. One test was trying to save a resident's life at Golden Age Nursing Home in Cleveland: "Today I did CPR on a person for the first time. I didn't save her, but I didn't fall apart either."[5] Such high-stress situations coupled with long hours and tensions with fellow employees led Delores to loathe nursing. As a result, Phillips left nursing and tried to branch out into other career opportunities, but over time, she eventually found herself back in the field. In a letter to Linda from August 25, 1994, Phillips accepted what she felt was defeat: "I had to break down yesterday and apply at a nursing home (I hope they never call). . . . Right now I am bored stiff and I really do want a job; I just don't want it to be in nursing."[6] Even though nursing was far from her passion, she admitted that it allowed her the financial freedom and flexibility to pursue her writing: "I thought I would be a teacher or a social worker, but I never pursued either. I think I am good at what I do, and nursing has been good to me."[7]

Writing was Phillips's catharsis, and the short story proved to be an ideal form to excise the frustrations of her day job. In fact, in a letter to Linda from 1998, Phillips adopted the short story form to recount a particularly miserable week she had endured while working as a charge nurse on an Alzheimer's unit at another nursing home. Delores becomes a character in her own story. Using humor and wit, she narrates the facility's lockdown and quarantine during a scabies scare:

> Delores parked her car in the parking lot and strolled up to the main entrance. She was taken aback by the quarantine sign and thought for a moment of fleeing, but then reasons for being brave clouded her good judgment. They were small, insignificant things, such as paying the rent, and not getting fired. She took a deep breath and entered. The director of nursing was there to greet the incoming employees with a smile and reassurance and a tube of Elimite 5% Cream, a topical scabicidal agent for the treatment of . . . scabies. Available in an off-white, vanishing cream base. HIP HOP HORAY.[8]

The story, which ends with Phillips concluding that "Delores needs to talk to her sister," typifies problems she experienced over her nursing career—facilities were understaffed, the employees were frequently unskilled and ineffectual, the residents were incredibly needy, and she felt overworked and underpaid. Phillips transposed these dismal circumstances into the Renwood Circle Stories.

THEME AND CONTENT OF THE RENWOOD CIRCLE STORIES

Although they are littered with medical jargon, the Renwood Circle Stories convert life into art in a setting that is rarely the central backdrop in American fiction—the nursing home. In her creation of Renwood Circle Nursing Home, Phillips skillfully leverages her firsthand knowledge and creative imagination to address issues within the larger U.S. health-care system. She attends to several aspects of care, especially residents' agency in determining their own mode of support. Such is the case in "Choices," aptly named to describe the choice that Renwood Circle resident Minnie Frost must make to determine which of her four children is best equipped to care for her upon leaving the facility. Moreover, Phillips questions the notion of the nursing home as a viable place of care, even down to its name. Although the building is called Renwood Circle Nursing

SHORT STORIES

Home, signaling a rhetorical and ideological shift of these types of facilities from hospital to home, Minnie Frost exposes the facility's true nature. Despite being camouflaged in pastel colors with a welcome mat in the lobby, she observed, it still "had the feel of an institution." Phillips explores this feeling by strategically utilizing both first- and third-person narrative voice to survey multiple perspectives within the Renwood Circle ecosystem—nurses, patients, administrators, family members, and social workers.

Instances of gross negligence and abuse of the nursing home's residents are par for the course at Renwood Circle. To illustrate, Thomas—a nurse working at Renwood Circle for "a paycheck only"—fails to replace an empty oxygen tank on the emergency cart, which possibly contributes to the death of a resident.[9] Gardenia Sue, one of the nursing directors, experiments on the Alzheimer's residents with the hope that they will become "docile diabetics."[10] Her belief that the experiment will improve the patients' quality of life echoes sentiments that have historically been championed by proponents of eugenics to justify harmful practices like forced sterilizations as a means to control often vulnerable groups of the population deemed unfit for society. Furthermore, the environment among the staff is considerably toxic, with several relationships characterized by verbal abuse (a nurse's intelligence is questioned by her director), backstabbing and plotting (a nurse seduces and then claims sexual harassment to get the director fired), sexism, and even physical violence.

Nevertheless, despite these offenses, Renwood Circle still possesses a few glimmers of hope. Phillips considers the nursing home as a potential site to affirm and foster meaningful human connections through practices of care and compassion. For example, a police officer's kindness in "All Talk" saves the life of Jonerva Geiger, a woman freezing to death while experiencing homelessness in Cleveland who eventually becomes housed at Renwood Circle. In "The Good Side of a Man"—which might serve as a useful comparative text to Alice Munro's short story "The Bear Came over the Mountain" due to its poignant depiction of "love, forgiveness, longevity, and an innate goodness in flawed humanity"—the husband, Danny, grapples with impaired mobility post-stroke while reflecting on his relationship with his wife, who is now his main caregiver.[11]

CONNECTIONS TO THE NOVELS

These themes of flawed humanity and the politics of care became a recurrent feature in all three of Phillips's novels, but there is a specific connection between the Renwood Circle Stories and the novel *No Ordinary Rain* in terms of character development. One of the Renwood Circle residents, Clair Walsh, nicknamed Zyma Root, a marginal character who appears briefly in "Renwood Circle" and "Wondrene Barry," was the inspiration for the child protagonist Zyma Root in *No Ordinary Rain*. In the short stories, staff and residents alike fear the "little albino woman" for her ability to relieve a person's pain and suffering as they die. The hint of magical realism in the short stories—Zyma Root's mysterious pow-ers, Gardenia Sue's conjuring abilities—became more fully realized in *No Ordinary Rain*.

While Zyma Root's evolution from the Renwood Circle Stories to *No Ordinary Rain* pinpoints a major connection between the forms, it is also fruitful to comment on two key differences between the short story collection and the novels. First, the stories take place in the urban midwestern environment of Cleveland as opposed to the rural South, where all three of her novels are set. Yet, unlike the novels, in which the location is essential for framing the particular circumstances of the Jim Crow South, other than a brief descriptor of Cleveland as freezing in the winter months, and a few characters named for Cleveland streets, place seems to be irrelevant in the Renwood Circle Stories. Without the narrators' explicitly naming Cleveland as the location, Renwood Circle might as well be anywhere in the United States. But perhaps that is Phillips's point—that Renwood Circle can stand in as the long-term care facility's Everyman, represent-ing the nation's broken health-care system writ large. Second, while race is crucial to all three novels, in the short stories, Phillips shifts away from race and instead privileges other forms of embodied difference. Race is not erased in the short stories, though; rather, racial signifiers are more inconspicuous. Instead, specifically with the residents, Phillips focuses more on bodily composition and condition to honor how aging, illness, and trauma affect bodily change. For example, because of frostbite Jonerva Geiger had both of her legs amputated, Minnie Frost nurses a fractured hip, and Danny suffered a stroke that affected his speech and mobility. Yet, just as in her portrayal of Martha Jean in *The Darkest Child*, Phillips resists the typical overcoming narrative so prevalent in stories of disability. The residents are not magically restored or returned to a previously more-abled version of themselves. Rather, they simply *are*.

OTHER SHORT STORIES

Although the Renwood Circle Stories account for the vast majority of Phillips's short story career, she wrote at least two other stand-alone tales, "Grand Slam" and "The Turken." "Grand Slam" survives in physical typescript only, which includes several drafts. It was probably written sometime between 2000 and 2005, possibly overlapping with *The Darkest Child*. Throughout the story, Phillips experiments with the form of the short story, as it is not revealed until the end of the story who or what exactly Poppy is. Although her skill should be commended, as Trudier Harris applauds in the afterword, the dialogue and the narration seem forced at times, while Phillips's surface-level char-acterization of the protagonist detracts from the story's success. Whereas in her other fiction Phillips shines in her ability to show rather than tell, in "Grand Slam," other than *telling* the reader that Willis is a thug with a "gangster bravado," Phillips falls short of *showing* what makes him so.

SHORT STORIES

"The Turken" is the only short story that survives from a digital manuscript. Crafted in 2010, it is Phillips's shortest prose piece and her latest short story. The storyteller's informal, rhythmic tone suggests that the sketch is suited for oral performance, much like the folktales collected in Virginia Hamilton's *The People Could Fly*.[12] While Hamilton used humor to capture the wit of African American creativity through tales of the supernatural and mythical, Phillips searches for comedy in an otherwise banal task within an agrarian lifestyle. The adversary in this context is not a vicious slave owner or the devil himself (as generally in other African American folktales) but a milder foe, an aggressive turken. Father and child triumph over the turken, solidifying their bond, which is fostered through labor.

ABANDONING THE ART FORM

The short story became a crucial form for Phillips to learn and experiment with setting, plot, conflict, and character development. A modern Cleveland background, along with a unique institutional setting, laid fertile ground for Phillips to transform her real-world experiences into work that, through multiple character voices, critiqued institutional care models, reevaluated the relationship between age and health, and re-affirmed the human desire for love and companionship. Phillips's short story writing period showcases her early development from poet to prose writer. However, examining more market trends at the turn of the century, Phillips became convinced that short stories no longer sold, so she soon abandoned the form. Nevertheless, by the time *The Darkest Child* appeared in print in 2004, Phillips would be armed with nearly a decade's worth of practice, experimentation, and improved storytelling ability.

NOTES

1. Phillips, Delores. "English 430 Paper." May 1993. Delores Phillips Digital Archive. A draft of this earlier paper is available on the companion website.

2. Phillips, Delores. Letter to Linda Miller. 30 Nov. 1998. Delores Phillips Digital Archive.

3. An example of Miller's edits are available on the companion website.

4. There is at least one surviving physical copy of *The Writer's Handbook* in Phillips's archives.

5. Phillips, Delores. Journal entry. 11 April 1992. Delores Phillips Digital Archive.

6. Phillips, Delores. Letter to Linda Miller. 25 Aug. 1994. Delores Phillips Digital Archive.

7. Lunn, Collier. Interview with Delores Phillips. *Clutch Magazine*, 1 Sept. 2007.

8. Phillips, Delores. Letter to Linda Miller. 1998. Delores Phillips Digital Archive.

9. "Renwood Circle."

10. "Gardenia Sue."

11. Phillips, Delores. "Draft of 'All Talk' 1." Delores Phillips Digital Archive.

12. Hamilton was not the first writer to collect these types of folktales. See Charles Chesnutt's *The Conjure Woman*, Zora Neale Hurston's *Mules and Men*, and Julius Lester's *The Tales of Uncle Remus* for other examples.

Gardenia Sue

She was a box kit blond with gray roots. She had a barrel-shaped torso, made perfectly round by the seemingly three pairs of boobs that fit snugly into one bra, the rolled down to touch her round, protruding abdomen. She stood four feet, eight inches in her size five shoes. She had a double chin that mimicked the movement of her lips. She was quite an attractive woman, somewhere, between her late fifties and early sixties, I would guess. There was a white name tag, high on her left shoulder, with black letters that read: G. S. BOSWORTH, RN.

Miss Bosworth had been hired to work second shift on the second floor Alzheimer's unit. She came to Renwood Circle Nursing Home with thirty-five years' experience, after having worked in nearly every hospital and nursing home in the Cleveland area. Our administrator, Mr. Roth, had prompted us to welcome this good fortune, but we were not impressed.

During her first week with us, we quickly realized that she was unaccustomed to our type of residents. She seemed perplexed, irritated by the noise they made, and troubled by their behaviors.

The assistants on the unit were Clyde, Philip, Rosalind, and I, Casandra Tore. We hid in the residents' rooms and watched the nurse huff and puff her way along the corridor, awed by the sight of her. We were all much too old to be acting so silly.

Clyde, the most assertive of the aides, was twenty-seven and egotistical, with an overactive libido and no respect for women. He refused to consider himself an aide and called himself a tech. He drove a late-model van, probably purchased by some woman, and on his evening breaks, he usually went to the van to have a can of beer and one of the female staff. It was common knowledge.

On a Wednesday evening when we were all on duty and had the residents in bed for the night, Miss Bosworth called us to the nurses' station for an impromptu meeting.

"As of this moment," she began, "excessive breaks will cease. There will be no more visiting on other units while on company time. There are fifty-six residents on this unit. They are here because they require care, and we are here to provide that care. All incontinence will be attended to within five minutes, all call lights answered within two. I realize that you are overworked and probably underpaid, but you are here by choice, and as long as you are on this unit, you

SHORT STORIES

will work. You will address me by my name, Gardenia Sue. Not Nurse, not Miss Bosworth, but Gardenia Sue. I look forward to working with all of you, and if you have no questions, you can get back to work."

An angry twitch that had originated in Clyde's left eye, during the nurse's speech, began to spread and spasm down the left side of his face. He opened his mouth, and his lips curved up on one side and convulsed down on the other. "What the fu . . . "

Philip quickly clamped a hand on Clyde's shoulder. "Come on, man," he said. "Let's get back to work."

Philip was twenty-one, and a college student with no commitment to Renwood Circle. He could afford to be nonchalant. Rosalind, on the other hand, suppressed her nervous giggles until she was down the hall, far from the nurses' station, then she leaned against a wall and let loose the laughter. She was thirty-five, and her only ambition in life was to see her four children grown and gone. She had been an aide for seventeen years and would probably retire an aide. Laughter was her coping mechanism.

I was twenty-three. I had been employed by the home for four years. I had seen many nurses come and go. I decided I would bide my time with Gardenia Sue.

"She's got to go," Clyde mumbled. "She's got to get up outta here."

A month later, she was still there. Those of us whose livelihoods depended solely upon our pay checks were damn near afraid to breathe, and Clyde could come up with no feasible way to get rid of Gardenia Sue.

Our nurse was a pain, for sure, but she wasn't our only pain. We were responsible for physically strong adults with infantile mentalities. There was Mr. Frantz, a former attorney, who now wore diapers, needed to be fed, and held daily counsel with invisible fellows. There was Mr. Bell, who tried to leave every day for Euclid Beach, a place that no longer existed. There was Mr. Unger, a once prominent businessman who was now combative and cried constantly for his mother, and Mrs. Marshall, the biter, who had once been a wedding consultant. From all walks of life, our residents had taken a crooked path that had led them straight to Renwood Circle.

Gardenia Sue had a talent for escaping the noise and redundancy of the unit. She would erect a mental barrier around herself and bask in contented isolation. There in the nurses' station, seated on a shrivel stool that was hidden beneath her bulk, she appeared to float in midair, far above the level of normal conversation. So it was, we learned to reach her in voices raised to screams and shouts.

Rosalind's approach, on the day she found Polly Agora covered from neck to thighs in a mass of pimply pink, was a shriek. Gardenia Sue stepped from her barrier and listened to Rosalind describe the rash, then she loaded her treatment cart and went rolling down the corridor.

My presence was required in the room to help keep Polly from trashing and kicking while Gardenia Sue inserted a straight catheter into the woman's bladder and withdrew a full liter of urine. Rosalind was then sent to the kitchen for a pint of whole milk. When Rosalind returned, the nurse mixed urine, milk, a scalp ointment, an arthritis cream, four drops of earwax remover, and a sprinkle of cornstarch in a specimen cup and stirred it with a tongue blade.

"Here," she said, placing the container in Rosalind's hand. "Cover her body with this, then wrap her in a blanket. And, Rosalind, the next time you approach me, keep the panic from your voice. It stresses me, and I don't function well under stress." She flipped a hand toward Polly's pink, rash-covered body. "This is nothing," she said. "It's petty-wetty stuff, nothing to get excited about."

"Petty-wetty?" Rosalind questioned, arching her brows after the door had closed behind our nurse. Poor Rosalind could not control herself. Tears slid from her eyes as she doubled over with laughter, and I thought for sure she would spill the concoction from the container.

For the rest of the shift, we slipped in and out of rooms, giggling and whispering about our weird nurse, but by the time we made our last rounds for the evening, there was not a single pimple on Polly Agora's body.

Gardenia Sue had a list of intolerances a mile long, and she was death on Clyde. On a day when Clyde had long overstayed a fifteen-minute break, Gardenia Sue went down to the ground-floor lounge and confronted him in front of his coworkers from the first and third floors.

I wasn't there, but they tell me she said, "Clyde, it is my understanding that you are paid a quarter over the minimum wage. Is that right?" When Clyde did not answer her, she continued, "This home is mandated by no union, government agency, or anyone else to pay you that quarter, and as of your next payday, you will see, reflected on your check, a twenty-five-cent deduction in wage. Technically, Clyde, you are AWOL from your unit. You have deserted the residents under your care, which is grounds for immediate termination. But I think, this time, a simple pay cut will suffice."

They say that Clyde, in an effort to maintain his macho image, turned on Gardenia Sue and showered her with the profanities of a 49 brothel on a sailors' night. He verbally attacked areas beneath her clothes, told her what her body needed, and offered to rock her old, tired world. At which point the old nurse accepted his offer and invited him out to his own van.

So determined was Clyde to get Gardenia Sue fired, he went to the administrator's office the next day and accused the nurse of sexual harassment. It backfired on him, but Gardenia Sue was woman enough to let the matter drop.

"You really did it, didn't you, man?" Philip asked Clyde, as we stood in the corridor loading our linen carts, and our nurse moved about in her station. "You really did it. And you could face people in a court and say she harassed you into it? Not in this life."

"Hell no! You know me better than that," Clyde said. "I never touched her."

We turned toward the sound of Gardenia Sue pushing her medication cart out into the corridor. "Clyde," she called sweetly, flashing her triple smiles, "has the pain started yet? It will, you know. It'll start as an irritating little itch, then the pain will bellow and roll through your gut like waves on a stormy sea. Your little petty-wetty is going to swell to the size of your thigh, and there's absolutely nothing you can do about it."

Clyde stared at her in horror. "You're joking. Right?" he asked.

"No, I'm not," she answered. "The swelling will go down in two or three weeks, but until then, oh well . . . That's just the effect I have on men. And, sweetie, you really rocked my world."

Reflexively, Clyde reached for his crotch, and his hand was still groping when he hit the floor in a knee-buckling faint.

Our nurse pulled an ammonia capsule from her cart and passed it under his nose. When he cleared his head and opened his eyes, we were all staring down at him, and Clyde realized that we knew he had been with Gardenia Sue. It was one of those things he would never live down.

Gardenia Sue winked at him, then she moved on, pushing her cart along from room to room, passing pills, and humming to herself.

That was the day Clyde quit.

Because no one wanted to transfer or float to our unit, we were forced to work with a short crew. To our surprise, Gardenia Sue pitched in and helped. She dried the drool from Mr. Watkins's lips and watched as more formed and flowed. She changed a diaper on Mrs. Gerson, and the old woman poked and ripped the absorbent pad to pieces before the nurse could get the last self-adhesive strip in place.

At the residents' dinner time, Gardenia Sue elected to take a feed table of four. We did not warn her that Mrs. Dwyer was a spitter, that Miss Furgerson would not swallow without a gentle massage to the back of her neck, nor that Mr. Diller clawed the hand that fed him. We let her learn the hard way, and she was flustered and wary by the time she reached the fourth resident at the table, Mrs. Stuart.

Gardenia Sue scooped up a spoonful of pureed meat and held it to Mrs. Stuart's lips. The old woman did not spit or claw. She bared her gums and began to chant, "Help me. Help me. Can you help me, please. Please, help me. Help me. Help me. Can you help me, please. Please, help me."

Calmly, Gardenia Sue placed the spoon on the table and rose to her feet. Temporarily defeated, slumped in the shoulders, she trudged her way back to the nurses' station.

Philip made the comment, "Not as easy as she thought."

Nothing was easy. Under the influence of a full moon, and the stress of noisy and restless residents, Rosalind forgot to lift the side rail on Mrs. Hager's bed. Mrs. Hager tumbled over the side and hit the floor. Luckily causing only minor injuries.

Once again, Gardenia Sue was summoned from her blissful isolation. She made it a point to stand beneath the warning sign that hung over Mrs. Hager's bed. "Side rails up at all times," the sign read.

"Can you read, Rosalind?" Gardenia Sue asked.

"Of course I can," Rosalind answered, a hint of indignation in her voice.

"There is no 'of course' about it," Gardenia Sue snapped. "I asked a legitimate question. You strike me as a person of limited intelligence. If it were not for the fact that you are physically strong with those large bones of yours, I would have gotten rid of you long before now. Trust me on that."

Rosalind fled the room, no laughter accompanying her tears this time. Gardenia Sue busied herself with attending to the small scrapes Mrs. Hager had sustained in her fall. I quietly left the room to go in search of Rosalind, and in the corridor, Mrs. Stuart's voice bounced off the walls. "Help me. Help me. Can you help me, please. Please help me."

Thirty minutes before the night shift was due to arrive, Gardenia Sue called us to the nurses' station. We were tired, pissed, and ready to go home, but we stood at attention, avoiding eye contact with the nurse on the swivel stool.

"We have problems on this unit," Gardenia Sue began. "Because I have never worked on an Alzheimer's unit before, the three of you are waiting for me to make a mistake. It won't happen, but if it did, none of you would have enough sense to know it anyway. So stop playing your silly little games with me. While you've been playing, I've been doing research. I've called other facilities. I've studied old and new medical records. I've discovered that our residents are susceptible to every disease known to man, except one. Diabetes. I have concluded that Alzheimer's patients do not get diabetes and diabetics do not get Alzheimer's disease."

She paused for the oohs and aahs that should have followed this revelation, but we said nothing.

"Don't you see?" she asked. "If I'm right, it means we can take the most cantankerous and belligerent few and turn them into docile diabetics by altering their endocrine cells. We can restore some quality of life. The screaming and spitting will cease. Don't you see? The more I think about it, the more I realize we can do it."

"There is no *we*," Philip said. "In all due respect, Gardenia Sue, even if I believed it could be done, I wouldn't help you do it. You can't just take it upon yourself to experiment on human beings. I'd report you before I'd let you get away with something like that."

Gardenia Sue smiled. "Report what you like, and I'll deny it," she said. "Mr. Roth is well aware that all of you have been trying to get rid of me since the day I set foot on this floor. I'm an asset to this facility. Mr. Roth knows it, and you'd do well to recognize it, too." She turned on the stool and stared directly into Philip's eyes. "Have you talked with Clyde lately?" she asked. "The next time you do, ask him about his swelling. I have a way of making tongues swell, too, without ever getting my hands dirty." She winked, and her threat was not lost on the three of us.

"She's a witch," Philip said, when we were in the parking lot. "The question is, is she a dreaming witch or a dangerous witch?"

"It doesn't matter," I answered. "Clyde was right. She's got to go."

"I'm quitting," Rosalind announced. "She frightens me."

"Don't quit," Philip said. "Gardenia Sue can be brought down just like anybody else."

We united to dethrone Gardenia Sue. From the onset, she seemed to know our plan and how to win us over. She demanded and was given float help for the unit. She began to speak to us as equals rather than subordinates. She lessened our workloads, and even went as far as taking on two feed tables in the dining room. She gave us longer and more frequent breaks.

In the confusion of this drastic change, we failed to notice the black leather case Gardenia Sue had begun to carry back and forth to work. Rosalind literally stumbled over the case one evening while in the nurses' station.

It was two days later before we had the chance or the nerve to slip inside the nurses' station and explore the contents of the case. There were syringes, vials of insulin, tubes of instant glucose, lancets, and a glucometer for measuring the level of glucose in the blood. There was also a jar filled with tar-black and glowing yellow capsules, the likes of which none of us had ever seen before.

"She's doing it," Philip said. "She's experimenting on these little old people."

So we knew and excused the knowing. Philip, for his tuition, Rosalind, for her children, and I, for my rent, became guilty, spineless accessories to the fact.

As the weeks passed, we avoided eye contact with each other, and avoided our nurse completely, so absorbed in our own culpable lives that we did not hear when Mrs. Stuart ceased to scream for help. We did not notice when Mr. Frantz began dressing himself and reading the newspaper from front to back. The changes were anything but subtle, yet I did not notice until Mrs. Gerson called me by name and asked for a drink of water.

The months of deceit and witchery had taken a toll on Gardenia Sue, but it was paying off. She celebrated her success by coloring her hair a lighter shade of blonde, but she could do nothing to hide the dark circles beneath her eyes or the slowness of her steps. She became impossible to avoid, and we became her subordinates once more, the targets of a fiery tongue.

When I was able to face Rosalind and Philip again, I could read the message in their eyes: "She's got to go." But our nurse seemed a mountain that could not be moved.

We were near ready to quit, all three of us, when suddenly a mandatory meeting of nurses was called in the first-floor conference room. I wasn't there, of course, but they tell me Mr. Roth opened the meeting with a list of added demands for the nurses. Gardenia Sue listened as Mr. Roth read down a list that included: daily skin grids on problem areas, two additional pages to an already four-page incident report, a weekly update on all care plans, a weekly written report on the condition of each unit, each shift, for the sake of comparisons, and in conjunction with the shift count of narcotics, a count of all insulin vials, syringes, and suppositories.

They say Gardenia Sue allowed him to finish before she bounced up from her seat, tossed her unit keys across the conference table, and said, "You silly little man, you. Who do you think you're talking to? If what you propose is possible to do within an eight-hour shift, along with our other responsibilities, then you do it your damn self. I'm here for the people, not the paper."

Mr. Roth remained calm and in control. "If you intend to work here," he said, "you will do whatever falls within your job description. I am an administrator with responsibilities of my own. I am not a nurse, Miss Bosworth."

"And I am not a fool, Mr. Roth," Gardenia Sue retorted. "I will not have my activities monitored, nor will I remain in an environment where I am not trusted. It has been a pleasure working here, but I think it's time for me to move on."

She extended a hand across the table for him to shake. Reluctantly, but in a show of professionalism, Mr. Roth stood and extended his hand in return.

The swelling, they say, was immediate. It began in his right hand and throbbed the length of his arm, into his neck and face, until his head resembled a lopsided melon. The weight of his head tilted him over onto the conference table. One eye was swollen shut, the other stared out in confusion, and not a single nurse in the room knew what to do for him.

Mr. Roth went on sick leave for a full month for his edema of unknown etiology. In his absence, our nursing director hired a nurse for our unit. We are satisfied with this new nurse. She is easy enough to get along with, and she appears to be normal, although she did mention that she has never seen so many diabetics on an Alzheimer's unit before.

Clyde called the unit today. He said he had quit his job at the nursing home on Euclid. He said he had been working on his unit last week when a barrel-shaped nurse, with fiery red hair and gray roots, had stepped off the elevator and winked at him. He had fled in terror before getting a close look, but now he wanted to know if we thought it could have been Gardenia Sue.

Renwood Circle

An ominous mist, like trouble in the air, fogged the pale blue walls of the corridor. It seeped in from beneath the closed doors of the conference room, growing in density as it circled the violated facility. No corner of the building was left untouched as it eased through the residents' rooms and the employees' lounge.

The housekeepers, tired and overworked, seemed not to notice as the perpetual odor of urine and disinfectant gradually gave way to a putrid stench of frustration and misery as the mist flowed, undetected, up and down the stairways and the elevator shaft until it came to settle on the first floor. There it hovered, like a dark cloud, just below the ceiling of the nurses' station.

Trudy Beal shivered as she made her way along the corridor toward her unit. It was seven minutes after three on a cold February afternoon, and she was late for her shift report. That made it a bad start for a long evening.

Thomas Harding, the day nurse on unit 1, was at the desk in the nurses' station when Trudy entered. His hands trembled noticeably as he shuffled through the stack of papers in front of him, seemingly unaware of the clutter surrounding him.

Bottles of liquid medicines stood atop the medication cart, and portions of their contents had spilled down, leaving sticky spots on the surfaces of the cart. Charts had been removed from their racks and were stacked haphazardly across the desk. A plastic lab container filled with water stood on the edge of the sink, and specimen bottles, which should have been on ice, floated across the water like miniature sail boats.

Opened cans of Jevity and Ensure, spatters of applesauce, and juice-soaked documents covered the top of the file cabinet next to the desk. This was Renwood Circle Nursing Home, and such untidiness, while irritating to Trudy, was not uncommon.

"How's it going, Thomas?" she asked, sliding onto the chair next to his, and refusing to comment on the mess he undoubtedly intended to leave for her.

"Another one of those days," he answered, tossing the papers aside. "My head feels like it's going to explode, my wife can't decide whether she wants to come home or stay gone, and life has a foot up my ass. Nothing new."

Trudy turned slightly on her chair to face him, listening dutifully to the barrage of inconsequential chatter that had become characteristic of Thomas.

When he had first joined the staff of Renwood Circle nearly three years ago, Thomas had made a show of being positive and energetic. Recently, however, things had changed. Not only had his wife left him, but he had burned out, and his goal now was to share his misery with everyone around him.

"I know you won't believe this," he said, "but I'm cold sober today."

He was right; Trudy did not believe it. She could not remember the last time she had seen him with clear eyes and steady hands. She was twenty-seven and judged him to be at least twice her age, or older. His clean-shaven appearance had vanished beneath a straggly beard, his black hair was turning gray at the temples, his shoulders had begun to slump, and he appeared tired most of the time. The only thing that remained of the former Thomas was his deep baritone voice, and even that was frequently affected by hoarseness.

"Don't get me wrong. I don't expect a medal or anything. It's just that the one day I decide to come in here with a clear head, all hell breaks loose. Why is that?" he asked.

Trudy shrugged her shoulders, wishing he would give his shift report and get it over with. He seemed to be in no great hurry, and she was forced to reach deep within herself to summon up the two ounces of patience that she kept in reserve. Patience, she suspected, was the virtue that enabled her to tolerate Thomas.

"Grace Sharpley had a seizure at the breakfast table this morning," Thomas said. "Before I could finish taking care of her, Mr. Peoples took a fall in the shower room."

Trudy scribbled this information down on her report sheet. If she remained silent, maybe Thomas would not realize that he was inadvertently giving report while complaining about his day.

He paused to rub his temples, using a thumb and forefinger. His glasses were on the desk and he picked them up with his free hand. For a few seconds, he just sat there staring at the glasses, then he focused his attention on Trudy as if appraising her.

She was five feet, six inches tall, and the twisted bun atop her head made her appear slightly taller. She was a shade too dark for his taste, but he could live with that—if she would let him. She wasn't pretty; she was graceful, and lovely to watch, but too reserved—too distant—and definitely out of his league, although he didn't know why. He guessed it was because she wanted it that way.

"Damn, my head hurts," he said finally. "It's this damn place; it's driving me nuts. Why, in the name of God, doesn't Nunn hire some nurses? How does she expect us to take care of all these damn people when they're all yelling and screaming and wanting everything at the same time? If Dillman Electric hadn't closed down, I wouldn't be doing this. America is screwed up. Women's rights and all that crap. No decent jobs for men anymore, and now we have to take orders from women who don't know what the hell they're doing. This is not the job for me."

"Look at it as a challenge, Thomas," Trudy said evenly, although offended by his remarks. "Think of the exhilaration you feel following a calmed crisis. And don't tell me you don't feel great when you're able to help one of the residents."

"No, I don't feel great. I feel like they all came here to die and they should get on with it. And the only challenge here is you, challenging the rest of us to work up to your expectations and enjoy this crap. We need some help up in here, and Nunn needs to hire some nurses," he grumbled.

"I think Nunn intends to interview a few nurses this week," Trudy lied in an attempt to pacify him.

Alberta Nunn was the nursing director and a woman who stayed as far from the units as possible, probably to avoid hearing complaints. She was slow to hire, but Trudy attributed that to a tight budget and pressure from administration to use the resources at hand.

"I wish I had Nunn's job," Thomas said. "It can't be that hard to hire a nurse."

Right, Trudy thought. Hiring a nurse was easy, but retaining that nurse was a different matter. The retention rate at Renwood Circle was bottom barrel. Employees were dissatisfied and quitting on a daily basis. Supplies were limited, equipment was obsolete, beds squeaked, mattresses sagged, the elevator broke down weekly, and the building housing this chaos was old and tired and crumbling above their heads.

Thomas was still complaining about staffing when the phone on the desk began to ring. They both stared at it, and after the third ring, Thomas clamped his hand down on the handset, but would not lift it from its cradle.

"Doctor Stevens made rounds today," he said, ignoring the persistent ringing of the phone. "He has orders scribbled all over these charts. I didn't have time to take them off, so I guess that's left up to you."

"What time was he here?" Trudy asked, just as the phone fell silent.

"Ten o'clock this morning, but I told you I had a busy day, so don't start with that 'Thomas, why didn't you do it?' stuff. And did I mention that we've been without heat all day? The boiler broke down, and they only got it working about three hours ago. All that time Nunn was sitting in her office with a space heater. The next time the heat goes out, I'm going out too. To hell with this place. All they ever . . . "

Trudy had to block him out. Right before her eyes, Thomas had turned into a big brown phone, all wired up and ringing too loud. It was hard to ignore, but she knew if she waited long enough, it would fall silent, just like the desk phone.

On the west wing, Trudy could see the day shift nursing assistants steaming towards the time clock, although the shift would not officially be over for another ten minutes. Along the east wing, the afternoon assistants darted from room to room making rounds.

Joan Wiggins, one of the afternoon assistants, crossed the lobby and rushed toward the nurses' station. "Trudy, we've got some problems out here," she said anxiously. "Mr. Jesse is complaining of chest pain. Could be indigestion; I don't know, but I think you'd better come have a look at him. And that's not the worst of it. Zyma Root is sitting at Nannette Fellon's bedside."

Trudy stood, pushed the sphygmomanometer and the stethoscope toward Joan, then pulled the drawer where the emergency equipment was stored. For a moment, it seemed the drawer was jammed, then she realized that it was locked, and Thomas had not turned the unit keys over to her. He had not given report, either, nor had they counted the narcotics. It would have to wait.

"Thomas, bring the emergency box and the Nitrostat," she said, rushing for the door. She had one foot out of the nurses' station when the big brown Thomas phone suddenly disconnected.

"I'm off duty," he said, and dropped the keys on the desk.

Trudy snatched up the keys and collected the emergency box and the oxygen tank. She headed for Mr. Jesse's room, knowing from experience that there was nothing she could do for Mrs. Fellon if Zyma Root was already in the room.

Clair Walsh was the little albino woman who lived on the third floor. Everyone called her Zyma Root because she claimed her power to relieve the pain and shuddering of death had been derived from a zyma root. She had never kept vigil on a single soul who had lived to tell about the experience, but Trudy had to admit that a peaceful expression came onto the faces of the dying when

Zyma Root touched their hands. Mrs. Fellon's time was up and that's all there was to it.

Trudy was nearly out of breath by the time she reached Mr. Jesse's room. She could see him lying on one side of the bed, as if he had been trying to sit up, one balled fist pressed against his chest, his eyes wide with pain and fear.

Mr. Jesse was a large man and his abdomen, bulging beneath a yellow pajama top, rose and fell in quick jerky motions. He was soaked in perspiration, and in obvious respiratory distress. Joan already had the blood pressure cuff wrapped around his arm, but she had not thought to elevate his head.

Trudy raised the head of the bed using a manual crank, then wheeled the oxygen tank around to the left side and began attaching the oxygen tubing.

"We're going to help you, Mr. Jesse. Just hang in there," she said, in an attempt to soothe his mounting anxiety.

"Just give me a minute. I'll be alright," Mr. Jesse managed to say between labored breaths, as perspiration poured from his scalp.

"Trudy," a male voice called.

Trudy glanced up, saw Thomas standing at the foot of the bed, and ignored him. Her priority was to get the oxygen started on Mr. Jesse.

"Trudy," Thomas repeated. "Don't you hear me talking to you? You're making a mistake."

"Pulse is weak and irregular," Joan said. "Couldn't get a blood pressure read. I'll have to try again, or you can see what you get."

Trudy nodded, slipped a nitro tab beneath Mr. Jesse's tongue, passed the nasal cannula to Joan to insert into the man's nostrils, set the flow meter on the oxygen tank, then turned to Thomas. "What are you talking about, Thomas?" she asked.

Thomas placed a hand on her arm and roughly pulled her away from the bed. "The man is a DNR," he whispered.

"As of . . . ?"

"As of ten o'clock this morning. Do not resuscitate. That's what the family wants, and that's what Doctor Stevens wrote. It's right here on the chart."

"No flow from the oxygen," Joan called out. "I think this tank is empty, Trudy."

"Damn," Trudy whispered, seeing the DNR written on the chart and, at the same time, rushing toward the oxygen tank. "Check the supply room for another tank, Thomas," she said. "DNR does not mean we withhold oxygen."

Thomas did not move, but Mr. Jesse did. With Joan's assistance, he struggled into a sitting position. His upper torso swayed, and his head bobbed, seemingly disconnecting from his neck. He began to cough, a hacking cough, as if something had become lodged in his throat, then he slumped back onto the bed.

"He's stopped breathing! He's stopped breathing!" Joan cried, reaching into the emergency box and pulling out the Ambu bag. Mr. Jesse stared up at her, wide-eyed, as if trying to understand what she was saying, then his eyelids fluttered and a deep groan echoed in his throat. He lay perfectly still.

"No CPR, Joan," Trudy said quietly.

Trudy reached for the stethoscope and began a rapid assessment of Mr. Jesse. His skin was warm and damp, an insignificant factor since all heart and lung activities had ceased. It was the moment they should have begun resuscitation. They did nothing—nothing at all.

Trudy fought the impulse to ignore the family's wishes and the doctor's order, but as the seconds ticked on, she knew she could not. She turned to her weeping assistant and said, "Go take a few minutes to pull yourself together."

Joan wiped tears from her eyes and nodded.

"Now what?" Thomas asked, as Joan left the room.

"I don't know," Trudy answered softly. "I just don't know."

"You seem to know everything else," he said. "I just thought . . . "

"Thomas," she snapped, "I thought you were off duty. I thought you had a headache. Why don't you go somewhere and take something or do something? Just leave me alone."

She found it hard to believe that one of the nurses was so incompetent as to leave an empty oxygen tank beside the emergency cart. Would the oxygen have made a difference between life and death for Mr. Jesse? Would they have been able to save him if Thomas had not come along with the chart? She would never know, and she was angry.

"The man was old. It's no great loss, Trudy," Thomas said, making a fist and saluting Mr. Jesse. "Here's to you, Mr. Jesse. You died like a man. That's the way I'm going out. No CPR and all that crap for me. Nobody bouncing up and down on my chest, breaking my ribs. I've already made me a living will that I carry with me at all times, and it's stamped DNR in big red letters."

From the corridor Trudy could hear the sounds of life going on without Mr. Jesse. It seemed inappropriate, as did Thomas's behavior in the room.

"You're changing, Thomas," she said, "and I don't know what to say to you anymore. It's like you've given up on yourself and everybody else. You really need to pull yourself together."

"What I need is a fifth of Canadian Mist." Thomas retorted. "And we're all changing. Everybody, except you. You're the same cool, calm, efficient Nancy nurse you were when I first walked through the doors of this place. You act like you're perfect, but you're not."

He glared at her with an expression of contempt, then asked, "Why don't you let your feelings show, girl? If you want to cry for this dead man, then cry. It won't change a thing, but boo-hoo your damn eyes out if it'll make you feel any better. Just get the fuck off my back."

"You're a cold, cruel man, Thomas," she replied.

"Whatever," he said, shrugging his shoulders. "I'm outta here. In the meantime, you have calls to make, Trudy. Let's see, there's the doctor, the family, the funeral home, and the pharmacy. You have pills to pass, tube feedings to start. Treatments and charting to do, ailments to attend to, complaints to deal with, and forms to fill out. Oh, and don't forget, Zyma Root is in with Mrs. Fellon."

"I guess I'm not perfect; I had forgotten," Trudy said, stepping away from Mr. Jesse's bed, gathering the stethoscope and sphygmomanometer, then turning toward the door. "Pull the privacy curtain around him, Thomas, until Joan and Gayle can come in and take care of the body."

"Ha," Thomas spat. "I'm not pulling anything, I'm not touching anything. I'm off duty, Trudy."

Fuming, Trudy retraced her steps, gripped the edge of the privacy curtain, and yanked it, enclosing Thomas inside the cubicle with Mr. Jesse.

From behind the curtain Thomas's voice fell into a rhythm of singsong taunting, "I'm off duty, Trudy. I'm off duty, Trudy. I'm off duty . . . "

. . . .

He needed a drink in the worst sort of way, and he needed to be far away from this nursing home, but he couldn't seem to leave. He knew precisely what had happened with the oxygen tank. This morning he had exchanged Miss Darcey's empty tank with the emergency tank. It had been too damn cold to go into the supply room, and he had been too damn busy, but he had intended to bring a full tank out once the heat was restored. He had simply forgotten.

A drink would ease his guilt and dull the ache in his head, but Trudy was about to experience the shift from Hell, and he wanted to be there to witness it. He wanted to see her make mistakes, falter under an overabundance of demands from whiny residents, and finally crumble under the stress of it all. Then he wanted to be there to lift her up, dust her off, and comfort her. He set out to follow her.

....

By the time Trudy reached Mrs. Fellon's room, Zyma Root was gone and Mrs. Fellon lay in the contorted fetal position her body had assumed over the years, strapped with tubes of survival. Nasogastric, oxygen, and urethral tubing jutted from the old woman's body, and a suction pump stood on the nightstand at the side of her bed.

Her arms were contracted and pressed against her chest, making it difficult for Trudy to listen for a heartbeat and a struggle to attempt a blood pressure reading, but these were procedures she had to follow before calling the doctor. Mrs. Fellon's body was cool, had been mottling and cooling for days, and Trudy quickly concluded that her slow dying had finally come to a standstill.

The door to the room opened and Thomas came striding in. "How is she?" he asked.

"She's dead," Trudy answered solemnly.

"Well, surprise, surprise, surprise," Thomas twitted in an excellent Gomer Pyle imitation. "Didn't I tell you they come here to die?"

"What about the ones who come here to live?" Trudy asked.

He searched his wit bank for a clever response but came up empty. He was relieved when the door opened and Mrs. Wager, a visitor, barged into the room and drew back the privacy curtain.

"I thought I saw you come in here," she said to Thomas. "My mother needs a bedpan. Do you think you can send one of the girls to the room to help her?"

An amused expression brightened Thomas's face. "I'm off duty, Mrs. Wagner," he said, then tilted his head toward Trudy. "Miss Beal is in charge, now."

"Well, Mrs. Beal, can you send a girl to my mother's room?" Mrs. Wagner asked. "I saw one of them in the day room, but I hate to ask them anything. They get so snappish."

Mrs. Wagner was a plump, pompous woman in her midforties who always scheduled her visits to overlap the day and evening shifts. She seemed to prefer

Thomas over all the other nurses, and he knew it, although his opinion of her was less than complimentary.

With her eyes, Trudy silently pleaded for Thomas to take control of the situation. He stood grinning for a moment, then he relented and escorted Mrs. Wagner from the room.

When he returned, to Trudy's surprise, he gloved his hands and began removing the tubes from Mrs. Fellon's body.

"Why?" Trudy asked, grateful for his help but suspicious of his motive.

"Because you've been covering for me. I would've been fired a long time ago if it hadn't been for you. I never asked for your help; I don't want it, and I wish you'd stop. But all the same you've had my back. Now, go on and start making your calls."

Trudy left the cubicle, and Thomas scolded himself for being such a wimpish hero. He had offered to help too soon, given in too easily, made it all so simple for her. Maybe that was it. Maybe everybody made things simple for her and allowed her to shine like a star over a cesspool. That was how he felt, like he was drowning in the depths of human waste and she was shining above him, just out of reach. Thomas whistled as he worked over Mrs. Fellon's body. He had Trudy's back, but her back wasn't what he wanted.

....

Trudy was off on Tuesday but returned to work on Wednesday to find that a night assistant had been fired for falling asleep in Mr. Jesse's bed. Grace Sharpley had gone into status epilepticus and had been sent out to the hospital. The evening nurse and a day assistant from unit 2 had quit without notice. Thomas, she was told, had collapsed in the day room and it had taken a full five minutes to revive him.

By Friday afternoon, Trudy was dragging from having worked double shifts on Thursday to cover for Thomas. The cold, heavy feeling that had begun on Monday still troubled her, and to make matters worse, Thomas had returned, and she could hear his angry voice even before she reached the time clock to punch in.

Thomas was not in the nurses' station but standing just outside the door. Alberta Nunn leaned against the corridor wall, and Edna Verbisky, the social worker, stood about two feet away, clutching a file folder to her chest.

"I told you, I'm not gonna do it!" Thomas shouted. "And I've just about had it with the both of you."

Trudy punched her timecard, then rushed up the corridor toward the commotion. She focused her attention on Thomas. "What's going on here?" she asked.

"What's going on? I'll tell you what's going on," he bellowed. "This stupid social worker and your director here are conspiring to kill us. That's what's going on."

"No," Edna said. "We're only . . . "

"I told you to shut up!" Thomas barked, pointing a finger at Edna while keeping his gaze on Nunn. "We're getting a new admission, Trudy. A 376-pound paraplegic with a list of meds as long as this hall. There's not one Hoyer lift in this whole damn building. Now, how the hell do they expect us to lift the man?"

"Thomas, we can work this out without making a scene," Trudy pleaded.

"That's right," Nunn quickly agreed. "Maybe we should all calm down and consider our options."

"Consider what you like," Thomas said, turning his back to her and stepping into the nurses' station, "but I'll tell you right now, I'm not gonna lift the man."

He was walking away from a potentially explosive situation, when Edna turned to Nunn and said, "You should fire him. That's insubordination. He shouldn't be allowed to talk to us like that. If you don't fire him right now, I'll turn in my resignation."

Trudy expected Thomas to torn and attack Edna, instead he took a seat at the desk and calmly said, "In order for me to be insubordinate, Edna, you would need to be my superior, and you're nothing but a grungy little social worker."

"And you're nothing but an alcoholic," Edna shot back. "You reek of booze."

"That's enough!" Nunn said sternly.

Being every inch as tall and stout as Thomas, Nunn made a move to keep Thomas away from Edna, but Thomas never budged from his chair.

"Edna, you come with me," Nunn said. "And, Thomas, I'd like to see you in my office in fifteen minutes."

From the window of the nurses' station, Thomas watched the two women walk across the lobby, then he faced Trudy. "Think she'll fire me?" he asked.

"Probably not." Trudy answered, taking a seat at the desk. "I think you handled yourself pretty well."

"Right about now, I don't care whether she fires me or not," he said. "Too many chiefs and not enough Indians in this place. Everybody trying to be superior to everybody else. Even you, Trudy. You undermine me and put me down every chance you get. If I chart nosebleed, you come behind me and chart epistaxis. If I chart vomit, you chart emesis. If I give Tylenol for discomfort, you come along and give a sympathetic ear. How are the rest of us supposed to compete with that? Nobody has time to sit and listen to sob stories from a bunch of weepy old people."

"I do," Trudy said. "I take the time because these old people could be my grandparents or my parents. Sometimes the pain they complain about is just the pain of loneliness, Thomas."

"Spare me the crap," Thomas said. "You're starved for love and afraid of men, Trudy. You get off on the idea that these residents love you, the staff respects you, and the doctors call here asking for you. Renwood Circle is your life. I'm here for a paycheck and a paycheck only."

"So you get your paycheck, and what else do you have? You have nothing, Thomas," she said angrily. "You're a drunk, just like Edna said, and your wife is never coming back."

Trudy had hit below the belt and she knew it. Her lips moved to utter an apology, but she was too angry to form the words.

Thomas closed his eyes and began to massage his temples. He did not have the strength to fight with Trudy. He knew his wife was not coming back; the divorce had been final for months. He just didn't want to face the fact. It seemed to him that he had spent his entire life fighting with women. He wanted to get away from them—away from the likes of Nunn, who felt she had the authority to order him to her office, and Trudy, who covered for him, kept him around, to make herself to look better.

He would go to happy hour at Smitty's, have himself a drink, then go home and go to bed. If he stayed around these women too much longer, he'd go off and clobber one of them, and he was reasonably sure that they didn't have happy hour in jail.

"Uh-oh," Trudy said, interrupting his thoughts. "Here comes Mrs. Wagner, and I know she has something she wants to complain about."

"She'd better tread lightly," Thomas said, glancing up. "I'd hate to have to cold-cock that bitch today."

Trudy hoped he was joking, but he didn't sound like it.

Anita Wagner, daughter of Martha Sheffield, reached the nurses' station clutching a pink denture cup in her delicate, jeweled hands. She eased the angry frown lines from her face when she spotted Thomas.

"Mr. Harding," she said politely, almost flirtatiously, "I'd like to know if you can get one of the girls to come to my mother's room. Her dentures need cleaning. Just take a look at this." She extended the denture cup toward Thomas. "These teeth should be clean and in my mother's mouth at this time of day. There's no excuse for this."

"The girls, as you call them, are all busy right now," Thomas answered wearily.

"Well, can't she do it?" Mrs. Wagner asked, gesturing with her head to indicate Trudy.

"Why can't you do it?" Thomas shot back. "In the time it took you to walk from your mother's room to this nurses' station, you could have cleaned those damn teeth three or four times. What's up with you, anyway? Every day you come in here with a different complaint, and I'm sick and tired of hearing them. 'Who stained the satin slippers that I bought for my mother?'" Thomas mimicked, imitating the woman's overly pleasant voice. "'Get my mother out of bed so she can visit with me.' then fifteen minutes later, 'Put my mother to bed; she looks so tired.' You need to stop tripping, Mrs. Wagner, because nobody's going to cater to your fat little mother."

Beneath the desk, Trudy bumped Thomas's knee to silence him, but frustration and anger had pushed Thomas to the limit and he would not be silenced.

"Let me tell you about your mother's teeth," he said. "Now, we all know that her boo-boos are gold-studded and odorless. Well, today she scooped up some of that gold between her fingers and yum-yum ate it up. The 'girls' had to clean her mouth, hands, and hair. And for your information, that's why her teeth are in soak at this time of day."

Mrs. Wagner's eyes widened and she gasped, stunned by Thomas's words and his manner. "I don't believe you," she said. "I want to see Miss Nunn."

"I'm sorry, but Miss Nunn is busy," Thomas said, with a slight smile. "She really should be at your beck and call since you're paying her salary, but I'm sure you understand just how unreliable the big bosses can be sometimes."

"I intend to report you," Mrs. Wagner snapped, "and I'm going to have my mother transferred out of this place."

"Well, that's good, Mrs. Wagner. I intend to transfer out myself. Maybe we'll bump into each other someplace," he said, then winked at her.

Mrs. Wagner turned in a huff and stormed back across the lobby toward her mother's room, forgetting all about the dentures she had brought to the nurses' station.

Thomas chuckled. "Think they'll fire me now?" he asked.

"Probably," Trudy answered.

Thomas stood, removed the unit keys from his pocket, and placed them on the desk. "Well," he said, "when you see Nunn, tell her I quit."

Had he lingered five minutes more, he could have walked out with Edna Verbisky, who did indeed turn in her resignation.

. . . .

After a month of using agency nurses, Nunn finally hired Miranda Lowen to fill the position vacated by Thomas. Miranda was a tall, young nurse with bouncy red curls. She was young in mind and spirit and, to Trudy's way of thinking, not yet mature enough to cope with the concerns of a geriatric population.

Mr. Roth, the administrator, hired Sidney Unchin as the new social worker. Sidney was also fresh out of college, but he was an administrator's dream come true. He managed to get Edna's obese paraplegic, Mr. Munford, admitted to Renwood Circle despite the time that had lapsed since the initial paperwork.

"We need to keep these beds filled," Sidney said one afternoon at a staff meeting.

"Oh, God," Miranda groaned. "What are we getting now?"

"You're not getting anyone. You work on the first floor, and according to my census report, you have no unoccupied beds, or have I missed something?"

"Fat chance," said Edward, a nurse from the third floor. "We have two empty beds on my unit. What are we getting, Sidney?"

"What is it with you nurses?" Sidney asked. "Why is it always, 'What are we getting?' Why can't you ever ask, 'Who?' You're not getting a thing; you're getting a person."

"What are we getting, Sidney?" Edward repeated, making no attempt to disguise the irritation in his voice.

Sidney lowered his gaze and studied the notepad on the conference room table, then he said, "You're getting a tracheostomy."

"Wait just a minute!" Edward shouted angrily. "Third floor is set up for alert ambulatory and rehabilitation. We can't handle a trach up there."

"Well, make a list of everything you need, and I'll see that you get it," Sidney said. "The woman is coming, and she's coming to unit 3."

Sidney was getting the job done; there was no doubt about it. Trudy, however, remained unimpressed by his efforts until the third week of May, when Vera Andrews, a woman who had lingered throughout the winter with terminal cancer, died at 2:45 one afternoon. At exactly 3:47, a new resident was resting comfortably in Vera's bed.

"I think he keeps them hidden in the basement someplace until a bed becomes available," Miranda said. She had stayed over to pull the medications and break down the chart on Vera, freeing Trudy to begin the assessment and paperwork on the new admission.

"Maybe so," Trudy agreed, "but I think he has friends in high places. Nobody moves that fast without help."

"Speaking of people in high places," Miranda said, "I've spoken to Nunn about transferring up to unit 2. I think I'd like to work with the Alzheimer's residents for a change."

Miranda had not been on staff long enough to transfer to another unit, but Trudy did not mention that for fear Miranda might quit and a new nurse would have to be broken in.

Trudy completed the assessment on the new admission, passed out the four o'clock medications, and was preparing to get two or three of the treatments out of the way before dinner when the intercom crackled and the dietary supervisor's voice filled the building.

"ATTENTION, ALL EMPLOYEES, THE ELEVATOR IS DOWN. PLEASE, FORM A TRAY LINE. I REPEAT, THE ELEVATOR IS DOWN. PLEASE FORM A TRAY LINE."

The nursing assistants began to complain immediately, and Trudy could not blame them. The dietary department was located on the ground floor, and a tray line meant passing 168 trays, one at a time, up the stairway to all three units. She dropped the scissors and tape she had been holding and went to join the line.

The elevator stayed down for more than a week. It was the week that the state inspectors were due to arrive, and the entire staff was busy preparing and hoping to pass. During that week, Miranda did not mention unit 2.

The next week, however, she went to Nunn's office to inquire about her transfer and was told it had been denied. From that moment on, Miranda became an active member of the Renwood Circle complaint club. She was charge nurse on her shift, and her dissatisfaction quickly rubbed off on her staff. The complaints on day shift became unbearable and the call-offs almost intolerable.

"My back is killing me," Miranda told Trudy a few weeks later at the change of shifts. "I've been thinking about turning in my resignation. Why doesn't Nunn hire some people around here? It's a wonder we passed that inspection. There should be two nurses on this unit, and at least eight assistants, instead of four."

Trudy smiled. "Mr. Munford has finally gotten to you, hasn't he?"

"Well, he's pleasant enough, but it takes three of us just to turn him. He weighs close to four hundred pounds."

"Three hundred and seventy-six pounds, to be exact," Trudy corrected.

"You know, I probably shouldn't have come to a nursing home straight out of nursing school," Miranda said. "I feel like I'm still new enough that I should be getting some supervision, and I'm not getting any. I like working with the residents and all, but I can see myself burning out real quick at this rate. The minute you get attached to a resident, they up and die on you. Half the time I don't know what I'm doing. Then you have the visitors, like Mrs. Wagner, who make it hard for me to keep a positive attitude. I'd like to make it through just one shift without hearing a complaint from her."

"Some people complain when they feel helpless," Trudy said. "I think that's her problem, and she feels guilty for having to put her mother in here. Most of us enjoy the work we do, but we complain too, especially when things aren't going our way."

"You're talking about me, aren't you? I never hear you complain. What's your secret, Trudy?"

"I guess I haven't felt completely helpless yet."

"Well, you just may get that funky feeling today," Miranda said. "You're getting a new admission in . . ." She checked her watch. "In about thirty minutes. And I get a feeling that something's up with this one. Nunn brought the papers out, instead of Sidney, and she wants you to page her after the admission arrives."

Trudy was puzzled by this. "What is it?" she asked.

"It's a CVA out of Metro Hospital. Right hemiplegia and aphasia. He's lucky to be alive. According to this printout, he was in a motor vehicle accident while DUI. Bought a pole on West Thirtieth Street. He had left facial lacerations requiring forty-two sutures, and a left enucleation. Had the stroke five days post-op."

"Whew," Trudy whistled. "Anything on mental status?"

"In a stupor, I would imagine. He's going into the male ward until another bed becomes available. He's an African American male, fifty-one years of age, with a history of substance abuse. And from all the whispering between Nunn and Sidney today, I gathered he used to work here. Poor thing."

Trudy's heart lurched and she felt dizzy from the gush of blood that rushed to her brain. "Is his name Thomas?" she asked.

"Wite-out on the printout. No name," Miranda answered.

"It's Thomas," Trudy said with certainty. "I know it's Thomas. Who else could it be? Please, God, don't let it be Thomas. Why isn't the name on the printout? That's odd."

"Yeah, it is odd," Miranda agreed. "Thomas is the nurse I replaced, isn't he? Look, Trudy, do you want me to stay until they bring him in? You don't look like you're going to be able to handle this."

"I'll be alright," Trudy said, making an attempt to steady her trembling hands, knowing that if it was Thomas, she would not be alright.

"Well, at least I can help you set up the area before I leave," Miranda offered. "He's on antibiotic therapy and has an intravenous feeding and an indwelling urinary catheter. He's a suction as needed and get this—there's a DNR order here. It makes no sense. I hope it's not your friend, Trudy."

Despite Trudy's insistence that she could manage things alone, Miranda stayed to help set up the ward. Five minutes after Miranda's departure, Trudy found herself wishing that the other nurse had stayed.

Nearly an hour after the estimated time of arrival, an ambulance pulled up to the rear door of the facility, and two attendants unloaded a gurney with Thomas Harding strapped to it. Trudy directed the attendants to the main ward, called Joan to assist her, then began a thorough assessment of Thomas.

Suture lines formed a distinct pattern on the left side of his face, like triple ladles with the cups encircling his entire jaw area and the handles stretching from scalp to chin, bent by his sightless orbit. His remaining eye stared up at her without recognition, and when he spoke, it was an utterance of meaningless phrases.

"What have you done to yourself, Thomas?" Trudy wondered aloud.

"Paperwork is in your hand, Trudy," Joan said. "I'd like to know, too. I don't think I'm gonna be able to take care of him. How can anybody expect me to bathe Mr. Harding? And why didn't you prepare me for this?"

As curious staff drifted down from the other units to get a glimpse of Thomas, Trudy thought about Joan's question. How does anybody prepare for this? The nurses could always prepare for a diagnosis, and the person behind the diagnosis was secondary—until you knew them. Maybe that had been the reason for Nunn's secrecy.

They would have to care for Thomas the way they cared for the other residents, although everyone seemed to share the same sentiment—it was not right to have brought Thomas to Renwood Circle.

Trudy moved blindly through her shift, possibly making mistakes that would later come back to haunt her. She hoped not, but she found it difficult to concentrate on anything, except Thomas. On every opportunity, she went to the ward to check on him.

Leatha Radshaw, the night nurse, was also stunned by the report that Thomas was a resident. "I still see him as a coworker," she said. "How long has he been gone? Four or five months? How am I supposed to take care of him? Who brought him here, and what were they thinking?"

Trudy had no answers, but she would try to get some. She managed to get through the shift report, then she punched out, doubled back along the corridor, and went to Thomas's room. Space was limited in the ward and she was unable to fit a chair beside his bed, so she stood, watching his one eye open, focus, cloud, and close.

On midnight rounds, Leatha found Trudy leaning over Thomas's bed, holding his hand. "Trudy," she said in surprise, "I thought you were gone. You look beat. Go home and get some rest. He's in capable hands."

Thomas yawned, then opened his eye, and for a moment it seemed to focus on Trudy. Then the gibberish flowed from his tongue.

"Oh, my God!" Leatha exclaimed. "He's babbling."

It was babble, but Trudy thought Thomas might be trying to say, "Let your feelings show, girl. If you want to cry for this dead man, then cry. It won't change a thing, but boo-hoo your damn eyes out if it'll make you feel any better."

Thomas was staring up. As things began to come into focus, he could see a young nurse standing over his bed. He didn't know where he was or what had happened to him, but he knew her. He just couldn't remember her name.

He opened his mouth. "Help me," he said, "I don't want to die. Where am I? Don't let me die here. Help me! Please, don't let me die."

An older nurse came to stand beside the young one, and they both stared down at him. He felt himself sinking beneath something heavy, like an ocean of cold water, and he struggled to breathe. Over and over, he called to them for help, but they seemed not to hear, seemed not to know that he was drowning. They stood there and did nothing—nothing at all.

"He's asleep, now," Leatha said. "He'll be alright, Trudy. Go home. You're off duty."

Choices

Minnie Frost was a weary traveler loitering at a dismal layover between life and death. They called this one Renwood Circle, but that was just another fancy name for a nursing home. They had camouflaged it with pastel colors, mini blinds over the windows, and even a welcome mat in the main lobby, but it still had the feel of an institution, and after ten months of living here, Minnie was ready for departure.

Life had been good to Minnie; she knew it, and she wanted to get on with it. She had known eighty-one years of sound mind and body before a fractured hip, from which she was rapidly recovering, had placed her in this home. She had married a kind and gentle man who had passed on some twenty years ago. To this day, she still longed for his touch. Their union had produced four of the most defective but caring children ever born in Cuyahoga County.

Minnie hobbled along the corridor of the west wing toward the family room where her children were waiting for her. They rose when she entered, stepped forward to kiss her cheeks, then remained standing until she had seated herself. Such love and respect, she thought.

She had named them for Cleveland streets: Superior, Chester, Quincy, and Cedar. Maybe that had been their curse. It was too late to regret or change things now. Her plan was to make her home with one of them. The question was, which one?

"How you doing, Mama?" Quincy asked, staring at her with dull, brown eyes, his thick tongue speaking a message sent down by a sluggish mind. He limped when he walked, and Minnie felt responsible.

She had stayed with him once, for two months, in a duplex on the lower east side. The house was infested with rats. Huge ones. On a day when one had lumbered across the kitchen floor, causing her to shriek, Quincy had come to her rescue, stumbling into the kitchen, gripping the butt of a .38-caliber revolver.

"What is it, Mama?" he'd asked, glancing frantically about the room. "What's the matter?"

Words would not come as she stared at the floor and realized Quincy's clumsy steps had landed him on the tail of a squirming rat. She could only point, and his gaze followed her pointing finger down to the linoleum, across the checkerboard squares, and came to rest at his feet.

When her poor, brave son finally spotted the rat, spittle flew from his mouth, his shoulders stiffened, and his pudgy arms twitched. He aimed the revolver and pulled the trigger, completely missing the rodent, but managing to shatter the bones of his own right foot.

Minnie shook the memory from her mind. "I'm doing alright, Quincy," she said, "but I'm leaving Renwood Circle."

Superior, who believed herself to be just that, leaned back in her chair. "Well," she said, "I'm glad you finally came to your senses. I knew you'd do it sooner or later. That's why I never rented out our upstairs apartment."

Minnie stared at her firstborn and nodded, acknowledgment rather than consent. Superior was wasting away, a bit thinner each time Minnie saw her. Her eyes were like hollow sockets, and Minnie thought she could hear the bony click of mandible against temporal each time her daughter spoke.

"Are you well, Superior?" she asked.

"I'm fine, Mama," Superior clicked. "I'm healthier than I've ever been in my life. I've given up on meat, that's all. You know about the mad cow disease? Well, now they say the farmers are growing chickens with cancerous tumors. They say when you bite into one of those chickens that the tumors bust in our mouth and spread a creamy substance like mayonnaise. I figure if chickens can get cancer, then any animal can."

"She's given up on everything, Mama," Cedar announced, reaching into her purse and pulling out a pack of Kool Milds. "Stanley is gonna leave her. You come on and stay with me. You can't live with Superior. She won't cook anything that she can't grow in a pot on her own front porch."

Superior crossed her legs. "You can't smoke in here, stupid," she said, "and my mother is not going to live with you. Who would? Cedar, you're fifty-two, and you've never had a decent job in your life." Her bones shifted on the chair until she was facing Minnie. "Mama, Cedar told me she had been taking computer training at community college. Right? So I put in a word for her at my job. She came down there and typed nine words with four errors. It was truly embarrassing."

"It was fourteen words with four errors," Cedar corrected.

Chester chuckled softly, then said, "Cedar, some things are best kept to yourself."

"Well," Cedar pouted, "at least I'm not skin and bones. I'm not afraid to eat."

"No, you're not, and it shows," Superior retorted. "Are you still with your boyfriend from the Bugsy Burger?"

Minnie sought to end the bickering between these two old women who were her daughters. "There's nothing wrong with working at a restaurant, Superior," she said. "It's not how much a man makes, but what he does with his money that counts."

"Click, click, click," Superior laughed. "He doesn't work there, Mama. He's a beggar with a droopy eye and bad breath. He doesn't have a change of clothes, and Cedar had the nerve to give him her phone number. That's desperation."

"I got rid of the rats," Quincy said, staring down at the backs of his hands.

"You're jealous, Superior," Cedar said, fishing a cigarette from her pack. "Give me a light, Chester."

"You can't smoke in here, stupid," Superior repeated.

"Stop it!" Chester interjected. "Mama didn't ask us here for this. Me and Marian have a big house with four bedrooms. Our kids are grown. I work every day, and we do eat meat. Mama, you can come live with us."

Minnie gazed into the face of two mild heart attacks and a stroke—still handsome. Chester loved her, but she was on a rung somewhere below his Budweiser and Bacardi. She remembered the time he had awakened from a blackout in a motel room on West Twenty-Fifth Street, silver rings piercing his earlobes, nipples, naval, and the tip of his tongue. He had cried for three days, a grown man doubled over in misery. She had carefully removed each and every ring, and then, because his wife would not, Minnie had called his job and told them truthfully that he was ill. She had never asked him to explain.

"Hell, Mama, I was drunk," Chester had said in explanation anyway, having read the question in her eyes.

Minnie scanned the room at the faces and forms of her offspring. She was blessed to have so many choices. She could stay at Renwood Circle, live and die here, or she could go home with one of her children. Which one?

She fought the fatigue that was slowly creeping through her bones. She remembered Quincy's quiet comment that had fallen softly in the midst of so much conversation. "How did you get rid of the rats, Quincy?" she asked.

For one full minute, Quincy studied the backs of his hands, then he lifted his head, his eyes as lifeless as a porcelain doll's. "Huh? I'm sorry. What'd you say,

Mama?" he asked. "I was trying to listen to both of you." He dropped his head. "But wasn't but one of you talking, was it?"

Minnie stood, and her children rose to kiss her cheeks. She held on to Quincy a moment longer than she did the others. While they had been willing to accept her, he had been preparing for her. The rats were gone. Maybe one day he would aim his revolver at a fly or bee and strike her heart instead. So be it. She pressed his hand and made her choice.

The Good Side of a Man

They had been married for sixty-four years. She had watched him become what he was—a helpless, twisted old man, and he despised her for seeing it. He had never intended this, this binding unity, sharing a single room in a nursing home, never a day away from each other. Where once this oneness may have been his longing, it was now his torment.

She was his view. She teetered about the room in a space between his bed and hers just for the sake of movement, her thin legs knotty and wobbly, her spine curved into an arch.

A framed testimony on the wall portrayed her once stark beauty. He had taken her hand in marriage, delicate hands passed over from a doting father to be cherished and pampered. For all he was worth, he had loved this woman who was his wife.

He had built his home, his whole world around her. He had worked them wealthy until his back was tired and his hands were raw, and she had said, "Enough." She had forced him to face himself, a blessed but aloof and rigid man.

In a changing world, when their children were adolescent, she had packed her bags and left him. Eight months without her, and he had thought he would go insane.

He chuckled at the memory of her return to meet his accusing eyes without a flinch and part sweet, curled lips to say, "I have found that life is hard without you. I have roamed, Danny. Been with another. Do you think you can forgive me?"

Forgiveness had been hers for the asking.

His children, whom he had loved more than life, but not nearly as much as he loved her, were not so eager to forgive. "Look what you've done to Daddy," they accused, in voice and manner.

"No," he had assured them, "your mother has made me a contented man." It was work and worry that had nearly done him in. So many years ago, so much happiness in between, and now this.

She could tell in intricate details of patterns forty years ago but could not tell the day of the week in present time. A stroke had left him hemiplegic, stuck with a worthless left half of a body, and also aphasic, to speak words that were garbled and maimed, that only she could understand. She translated, made his needs known, and he despised her for it.

Each day she pushed his wheelchair down the corridor to the dining room, and he needed to believe that the chair served as her crutch rather than his source of mobility. She was eighty-three, and her hands had not been groomed for labor.

On bad days, when the frustration was more than he could bear, he used his good arm to throw peas from his tray across the table into her face. Primly, she would take her napkin and wipe the peas away, then say to him, "Be a good boy, Danny."

The nursing staff would rush to her defense, separate the two, speak to him as though he were a child, and accuse him of being an abusive mate.

Never. He had used his hands to build a castle, to erect for her a throne. Sometimes he even wondered what else had he done with his life, except to fail to make her happy. It pained him, the things he could no longer do. He had loved and raised three children who had loved him in return, and they had done all they could before placing him in this home. They still came weekly to visit. In a sense, he guessed he was a blessed man.

Hands handled him daily. They dried him, bathed him, got him up each morning, and put him to bed each night. Hands handled him daily, but he needed to be touched. In eighty-five years, he had never once asked for comfort, but his life screamed for it now.

He laid on the bed where hands had placed him and closed his eyes to block a flow of tears. He remembered her the way she used to be, filling his life with joy, and his mind called out her name. Irene, dear sweet Irene.

His body stiffened as a hand touched his shoulder and a teardrop wet his face. He opened his eyes to see her standing there, then felt angry that she could come and look down on him like this. In a garbled voice, harsh and resentful, he yelled at her, "Get away! Why do you trouble me, woman?"

She stood her ground on the good side of her man. "I thought I heard you call my name, and so I came," she said. "I promised you, Danny, that I would never leave you again, and I never will. I love you."

He raised his useful arm with the intent of striking or shoving her away. The arm had only the strength to touch the curvature of her spine and pull her gently onto the single bed. There he held her. There they cried together, and it felt so good.

All Talk

The two policemen standing in the lobby of the Renwood Circle Nursing Home took no notice of Jonerva Geiger, but they should have. She could have told them everything they needed to know. She had witnessed it all, from the initial blow that knocked Ruth Rodman senseless, to the shooting in the rear parking lot.

These cops weren't from the third district. Down there, they had hassled Jonerva enough to know her well, poking at her cardboard housing and paper bedding, and moving her along from doorways and bus shelters.

A policeman had probably saved her life. He had spotted her one early February morning stumbling along an icy Cleveland street, nearly numb from the cold and desperately trying to reach the enclosure of an RTA bus shed. The officer had given her a cup of coffee that she could barely hold, then he had taken her to a hospital instead of a homeless shelter.

At the hospital, they had cut off her toes, then they had stood over her bed talking their jargon, asking if she understood and not waiting for a reply. They had chopped off her legs up to her knees, leaving her half the woman she had once been, then they had shipped her out to this nursing home.

She now lived in a ward on the west wing, room 116, near the time clock and the noisy elevator shaft. It wasn't so bad, though. Not really. She could sit in her wheelchair by the window and watch the staff do things at night that would boggle Jerry Springer's mind.

Jonerva had not been at her window on the Wednesday evening when Ruth Rodman allegedly fell from bed, knocking herself senseless. The reason Jonerva had not been at the window was because of her body. Funny how a half-body caused more trouble than a whole one ever had. It clogged, spewed, or just fell apart with no consent from her.

On that Wednesday evening, her body had clogged. She had wheeled herself to the nurse's station for a dose of Milk of Magnesia. She could have turned on her call light, but it would have been something like four days before anyone responded, and by that time her intestines would have exploded. She had swallowed down the tasteless substance that the nice nurse, Trudy Beal, had given her. On her way back to the ward, she had fallen in behind one of the nurse's aides, Gayle something or other, who didn't seem to like her job very much.

Gayle was trying to get slow, rude Ruthy Rodman out of the corridor and into her bedroom.

Ruthy was being her normal self. She cussed Gayle from head to toe, spit on her, and kept hitting the poor girl's leg with her quad cane.

Jonerva could tell by the twisted expression on the aide's face that something ugly was about to happen, but she never expected Gayle to throw the punch that knocked rude Ruthy across the threshold of room 110, and onto the floor. Ruthy deserved it, but it shouldn't have happened to a dog.

Jonerva had heard Gayle say, "I'll show you how it feels to be spit on, old lady." From inside the room had come the sounds of hawking and spitting, followed by flesh striking flesh.

Before her presence could be detected, Jonerva had rolled her chair around and pumped the wheels with all her strength, grateful for a lightweight chair. The nurses' station had been deserted, and Jonerva had wheeled on until she reached the day room. The nurse had been there with three of the aides.

"Did you need something else, Miss Geiger?" the nurse had asked.

Jonerva had fixed her mouth to tell what was going on in room 110, but before she could speak, there had come the slapping sound of soft shoes moving rapidly toward the day room.

"Miss Beal! Miss Beal!" Gayle had shouted in pseudo panic, blood stains smearing her dingy white uniform. "Ruthy is on the floor. She fell out of bed, and I think she hurt herself pretty bad."

The nursing staff had rushed for room 110, leaving Jonerva to wait for what she considered a respectable length of time before wheeling her chair toward the west wing. As she passed room 110, she saw the nurse examining rude Ruthy, who was still on the floor where she had fallen, not even close to her bed.

Satisfied that the nurse was smart enough to figure out what had happened, Jonerva had wheeled on to her room, hoisted herself onto the bed, and listened to the activity of the staff preparing rude Ruthy for a trip to the hospital.

Morning arrived, and staff conversation in the day room centered around how awful it was that Ruth Rodman, an eighty-year-old woman, had fallen from her bed.

By noon, word buzzed about the facility that Ruth Rodman was not expected to survive her fall. It was then that Jonerva had bypassed the day shift nurse and had gone directly to Alberta Nunn, the nursing director. She had told it all and had a feeling that Miss Nunn did not believe a word of it. However, Gayle had not shown up for work that afternoon, nor the next, nor the one after that. And the gossip had started.

"Did you hear? Nunn fired Gayle."

"What? For what?"

"They say Ruthy didn't fall. They're trying to say that Gayle beat her."

"Are they pressing charges against Gayle?"

"I don't think so. They'll probably try to hush it up. You know those people in the office. They don't want the state up in here investigating. They don't want Ruthy's family to know, either. That could be a lawsuit."

"I don't believe Gayle did it."

"Well, I do."

Jonerva tuned them out and told herself that she had done the right thing by telling. She believed she had until Sunday night, when the telephone in the nurses' station began to ring. Every fifteen minutes it rang and Trudy answered. After the second hour of this, the little nurse was a certifiable mess.

"Gayle keeps calling here," she told Joan, one of the aides. "She's threatening my life. She blames me for getting her fired, and says I had no right to tell Nunn anything I couldn't prove. I've tried telling her that I never suspected nor accused her of anything, but she won't listen."

"Don't answer the phone," Joan advised.

"I have to. This is a business. It could be a doctor or a family member on the other end."

The more the phone rang, the more exasperated and anxious the nurse became. She tried to function normally, but when she approached Jonerva with night medicine, the little cup of pills fell from her hand. Jonerva watched a Colace gelcap roll across the day room floor and beneath the piano, like a small, red ball of anger looking for someplace to hide.

Trudy sighed deeply, abandoned her medication cart, and went to the nurses' station to place a call of her own. Jonerva positioned her chair in the arch between the day room and the lobby to give herself a partial view of the lobby, day room, and nurses' station.

She thought the nurse had probably called the police, but after thirty minutes, she knew she was wrong.

Nobody talked to the police that long. Jonerva gave up her wait for pills and wheeled herself to her room, where her five roommates lay as quiet and still as stuffed blankets, seemingly oblivious to life.

Jonerva sat at her window and watched the night staff pull into the parking lot. She had spent the last seven years of her life on the streets watching cars when there was nothing else to do. Now here she was, doing the same thing again from the safety of her room.

An unfamiliar gray Corsica entered the lot and parked behind the garbage dumpster. *Gayle*, Jonerva thought, then remembered that Gayle drove a blue LeBaron.

She could hear the clanking and groaning of the elevator taking the night staff to the second and third floors and bringing the evening staff down to the time clock. Jonerva continued to stare at the dumpster that hid the gray car. The car remained there until the evening staff had cleared the parking lot, then it pulled away, without headlights.

Ruth Rodman was returned to the facility on Monday morning, purple and blue, an oxygen mask over her thin lips and pointed nose, and an L-shaped suture line over her left eye. To Jonerva, rude Ruthy was the image of death, even as her one good arm rose from the gurney to rip off the oxygen mask.

At a little past noon Jonerva's body decided, on its own, that it would spew. Although she was able to get herself in and out of bed by using a trapeze bar, she could not lift herself onto the toilet. She pulled the call light and waited forty-five minutes before an aide appeared, by which time Jonerva was stump deep in stool.

It took two aides to swing her onto the commode. They gripped her at the armpits, counted to three, then swung her onto the seat. On their way out they complained about the smell. As bad as it was, the spewing went on and on, throughout the day and on into the evening. Back and forth, every hour on the hour, they swung her from the wheelchair to the commode.

She missed the *Jerry Springer Show* because no one would come to take her off the toilet. When they finally came, she found out that Miss Beal had the day off. A relief nurse popped a Lomotil into Jonerva's mouth to quiet the runs and told the aides to put a diaper on her.

That night as Jonerva sat by the window, her armpits sore, and her rear end aching so bad that she wished the doctors at the hospital had chopped it off, too, she cursed the policeman who had saved her life. Her head was barely above an ocean of self-pity when she spotted the gray Corsica, and an uneasiness replaced the pity.

Jonerva awakened on Tuesday morning to find that nothing had happened or changed except that for once her body was cooperating. She listened to the day staff gossip about Trudy Beal, accusing the young nurse of things that Jonerva thought her incapable of doing. They talked about Gayle, and they talked about rude Ruthy, saying how her fall had made her even more belligerent and demanding than before. They talked about Miss Nunn, then they talked about each other.

Trudy arrived for her evening shift, looking refreshed and relaxed. Her hand did not tremble when she gave Jonerva the little cup of Zoloft and Colace, and all evening she made no mention of Gayle.

That night the gray car was back. Jonerva saw it pull in behind the dumpster. She considered wheeling herself around to the day room to tell the staff, then realized that she had probably already told too much.

She watched the night staff arrive and listened to the noise of the elevator moving up and down. Just as the evening staff was preparing to leave, an old, blue LeBaron passed Jonerva's window. She saw Gayle step out of the idling car with a gun in her hand. Gayle was so close that Jonerva could have reached through her window and touched the poor, dumb creature.

"Where is she?" Gayle screamed, then fired the gun once, as a barrage of profanities rolled from her tongue. "I'm gonna kill her. Come on out of there, Trudy Beal." She fired again with no sighted target.

Bodies dove for cover, some spilling from the hallway over into Jonerva's room. Someone, crouched beside her bed, yelled for her to move away from the window, but she couldn't. A bullet smashed a window on one of the upper floors, and a scream rang out in Jonerva's room. She couldn't blame them for being afraid; the bullets weren't meant for them but hiding as they were did not allow them to see what was happening in the parking lot.

It was like a movie at the old Hippodrome Theatre. Two villains moved through darkness, between parked cars, and toward the heroine, Gayle. The villains were armed, and poor, witless Gayle never knew they were there until the one with the mustache tapped her empty skull with the butt of his gun. Gayle swayed, then slumped to the ground, and the villain stood back and let her. The other one, young and handsome, aimed his gun toward the sky and began firing off rounds.

Out in the distance, the mysterious gray car pulled slowly from behind the dumpster. A third man, short and stocky, emerged from the car, opened the trunk, and helped the first villain to life Gayle inside. Young and handsome continued to fire his gun into the air. When they had closed the trunk on Gayle, the short one and the young one got into the gray car. The one with the mustache got behind the wheel of Gayle's car, then the two cars rolled off of the lot—no rush about it.

The two policemen standing in the lobby of the Renwood Circle Nursing Home were getting assumptions. Everyone assumed that Gayle had fired more than a dozen rounds in a failed attempt to kill Trudy Beal. That wasn't true. The policemen assumed they would pick Gayle up at her residence. That wasn't true, either.

Jonerva could have told them the truth, but nobody was paying her any attention, except the night nurse who had told her twice to go to bed. Twice Jonerva had pretended not to hear. She stole a glance at Trudy, and the young nurse seemed to glow with complacence.

The lobby was packed with night staff and detained evening staff. The nursing director and the administrator made a late entrance after being summoned by the police. It was all so exciting to Jonerva.

She parted the crowd and wheeled herself down the corridor to room 110, intending to tell Ruthy that Gayle would not be back to harm her again. Flipping the wall switch, she turned on the overhead light and saw that Ruth Rodman was awake and propped up on the bed. The oxygen mask had been removed.

"Get out!" Ruthy shrieked when her eyes focused on Jonerva. "Get out! I know who you are. You're the street woman. They've put you up in the poor people's room. Get out! Don't come bringing your nasty street germs in here."

Rude Ruthy was right; Jonerva was from the streets. She had seen and done things that would boggle Jerry Springer's mind. An event that had frightened so many others had excited her to the point of entering rude Ruthy's domain. Dumb. She began to think that maybe Gayle wasn't so bad after all. Age did not give Ruth Rodman the right to be so rude, and maybe somebody should do something about it.

Jonerva stared at the old woman's rage-twisted face, then her gaze came to rest on the wrinkled, throbbing throat.

"Chop-chop," Jonerva whispered, before flicking the wall switch and throwing the room into total darkness.

Grand Slam

Willis had known, even before she came in from work, that his mother's first words would be, "Where's Poppy?"

He had no idea.

"When was the last time you saw him?" his mother asked. "Did you feed him, give him water?"

Willis nodded, hoped she wouldn't know he was lying.

"How'd he get past you?"

"I don't know," Willis answered, whining like a baby. He was nine, almost ten, and she was making him feel like a two-year-old.

"You get up, go find him! It'll be dark soon. Go on now, check the neighborhood."

Willis wanted to cry, but he was too old, too tough. It was 7:55, possibly an hour before dark, definitely five minutes before game time. All day he had waited for the televised game between the Indians and the White Sox. Now he was going to miss it.

He left the house and walked south on Jarred Street without a clue where to begin his search. It was his own fault. He hadn't stayed home like he'd been told to do but had spent the day in the corner lot playing baseball with his friends. He hadn't given Poppy a second thought. He didn't know whether he should be angry with himself or his mother. As he turned the corner onto Pine Avenue, he decided it should be her.

Two days ago, she had brought Poppy into the house and announced that he would be Willis's companion while she was at work. "You'll learn responsibility," she'd said, "and he'll keep you off the streets and out of trouble."

What a joke, Willis thought as he peered between the houses along Pine Avenue. Wasn't he in trouble and on the streets now? He passed a drug house that had been raided and boarded up by the police. His mother had freaked when that happened. A dozen people arrested, and all she could say was, "That's right around the corner."

If Poppy had wandered into that house, he could stay there. Willis knew the gang that had taken over the place. They never bothered him, but the things his mother said about them frightened him. Gangs had taken over everything, and nothing his mother did was going to protect him, not unless she brought home an Uzi. Now that would be neat . . . Nah, maybe not. If he'd had an Uzi yesterday, he probably would have smoked Poppy. Who needed a companion that wet all over everything, then curled up and slept the day away? What in the world had his mother been thinking?

Willis left Pine Avenue, trudged the long stretch across Sixty-Fifth to Bennes Street, passed a corner store, and headed east toward the laundromat. An RTA bus came to a stop beside him, and he glanced through the windows at the side profiles of frowning faces. He thought they somehow knew that he had lost Poppy.

Two teenage girls climbed onto the bus, and the bus pulled away from the curb. Willis slowed his pace, allowed the bus to get far ahead of him. It was going in the wrong direction, anyway. It should have been headed toward downtown and Jacobs Field. Didn't people know that Sabathia was pitching tonight? He was thinking about the game when his gaze swept past the object of his mother's most recent concern—Poppy.

Willis quickly devised a plan whereby he would sneak up on Poppy, seize him, and drag him home. As he moved stealthily up the sidewalk sidestepping pedestrians, a car backfired out on the avenue. He saw Poppy shudder with fright, then hobble down from the curb right in front of the bus, and on out into the traffic. Mindless of blaring horns and screeching brakes, Poppy reached the safety of the sidewalk, then stared back at the traffic as though he had no idea what all the commotion had been about.

By the time the light changed and Willis was able to cross, Poppy was shuffling past a Citgo station. Willis stared at the pathetic creature ahead of him and fought the impulse to turn for home. He could lie to his mother, tell her he'd searched everywhere and hadn't seen Poppy. He estimated that the game was in the fourth or fifth inning by now, and if he didn't get home soon, he'd miss the whole damn game.

"Stop fooling yourself," he said aloud. He knew he could grab the old, toothless pain in the neck in four giant steps if he wanted to. He was close enough now to see filth clinging to Poppy, as though he had rolled in dirt and eaten from a garbage can.

His mother was going to have a fit. Suppose she was searching the hood at this very minute, telling people how she had brought home a buddy for him.

He'd never live it down. Among his friends, Willis had a reputation of being tough. He couldn't allow his mother to spoil that.

He turned his attention back to Poppy, only there was no Poppy to be seen. Willis began to jog, to search the doorways again. One more block, then he'd go home. He crossed the old trolley tracks to the Avenue Bar and Grill. There he saw Poppy panting so fast that it seemed his ribs were sucking up his flesh. Several men were leaning against the bar front, and one of them began to pour beer from a bottle into Poppy's mouth while the others laughed.

Knowing he had to do something, Willis stepped closer and called out, "Poppy!"

Poppy slowly turned in Willis's direction with only a hint of recognition in his one good eye. A permanent scar on his skull and the yellow slime oozing from his bad eye sickened Willis.

"Come on, Poppy," Willis coaxed. He moved forward, stared down at his hands. His hands had handled garbage, had even carried a dead mouse from the basement once, but those things had not seemed as repulsive as having to touch Poppy.

Willis sighed, extended a hand, and grabbed a hold of Poppy. Dragging his captive along, he took every shortcut he knew of from Bennes to Jarred, thanking God for the fading daylight.

From her position on the front porch, his mother spotted them coming. She eased down to the yard, wrapped Poppy in her arms, and began to cry. After what seemed an eternity, she released Poppy and took a long look at him, then she turned to Willis.

"Where'd you find him?" she asked. When Willis told her, her eyes narrowed and grew as dark as the night sky. "And you brought him all the way home like this? You couldn't even pull his pants up around his waist?"

"Humph," Willis grunted with contempt, forgetting for just a second that she was his mother. "I wasn't about to put my hands on those . . . "

She clutched his collar, choked his words off, and he felt a moment of terror before she shoved him away. "Get out of my sight, boy!" she said with cool anger—the worst kind.

Willis scampered up the steps, into the living room where he buried himself in the cushions of the sofa. He chewed on his crumpled collar as his short life came roaring in on itself. In the real world, he could hear his mother fussing over Poppy, bathing and feeding him. Willis blinked, tried to make it back to his mother's world, where he could run to her and apologize. Of course, he couldn't do that—not if he intended to maintain his thug bravado—but he wanted to.

She came to him, spoke softly. "Poppy is my father, Willis, and I love him. You need to understand that. He's been sick for a long time, been in a nursing home, and the doctors say he'll never get any better. There are things I hope you never remember, but I wish you could remember when Poppy was strong and healthy, and the way he loved you so much."

She moved away, leaving Willis remembering, biting his collar to keep from crying. He remembered the men coming to the house with guns, looking for his dad—a face he could no longer recall. One man had threatened to shoot Willis if his mother did not pay the debt his dad owed. She couldn't do it. Poppy had been there. He had grabbed Willis, thrown him out of the line of fire. Poppy had been shot in the head. That had been six or seven years ago.

"Damn," Willis whispered, and increased the volume on the television to drown out those awful memories. The game was over—thirteen to six—with a Cleveland win. He heard the commentator's energized recap of Lawton's fourth-inning grand slam. He had missed it. That was enough to make a thug cry, wasn't it? He stared at the screen as his tears flowed freely.

The Turken

I can remember when I was about eleven years old and my father asked me to go gather eggs from the henhouse. It was a chore I complained about because of our rooster. The rooster was actually called a turken—half turkey, half chicken. He stood about two feet tall and was as mean as could be. My dad called it his seed because when they reproduced, they were bigger than regular chickens—more meat to eat.

Well, back to my story.

Every time I went to get the eggs that turken would attack me and make me break the eggs. I told my dad, but I didn't think he believed me. My dad even made a trapdoor on the henhouse. The way it worked was, I would go to the coop and throw corn through the fence, then shut the trapdoor by pulling a rope. I could then step into the coop and gather the eggs. After the eggs were gathered, I would wrap up the rope and the trapdoor would go up.

One day, I didn't know it, but my dad was watching me from the bathroom window of our house. I fed the chickens, pulled the trapdoor, gathered the eggs, then went to wrap up the rope. I could see the turken's feet at the trapdoor. I knew he was waiting on me to open the door, so I decided that if I did it real fast, he wouldn't get me. I hurried, but that turken was coming right at me. He jumped up, kicked me, and knocked the basket out of my hands. The eggs burst and I started to cry. I slammed the door shut, sat on the ground, and cried.

My dad came down the hill laughing. He said, "I watched that crazy turken from the bathroom window. It's okay."

We both laughed and walked away. That evening my dad killed that turken. I told him, "But Dad, that was your seed."

"It's okay," he said. "I have more seeds."

That was the best tasting turken I ever ate!!!

NOVELS

Mastering the Art of Storytelling
Novels

During the last decade or so of her life, Delores Phillips transformed her writing into the genre she is most well known for today—the novel. *The Darkest Child*, published in 2004, was the only novel published in her lifetime. At the time of her death, however, she was working on two additional novels, *Stumbling Blocks*, a sequel to *The Darkest Child*, and *No Ordinary Rain*, a standalone novel inspired by the Renwood Circle Stories. Her novel work features a beautiful harmony of the talents and skills she perfected through her poetry and short story fiction. The lyricism, imagery, and rhythm of her poetry coupled with the humor, vivid character descriptions, and keen storytelling of her short stories combine in her novels to create, as Randall Kenan praises, "a depth of characterization worthy of Chekhov, pitch-perfect dialogue."[1] Like Charles Dickens's *The Mystery of Edwin Drood* and Jane Austin's *Sanditon*, both *Stumbling Blocks* and *No Ordinary Rain* are unfinished, but this should not detract from their literary merit. If anything, the open ending of the novels invites readers to focus less on closure or finality, challenging them to find pleasure and aesthetic value in the literary process itself.

STUMBLING BLOCKS

Although she originally had no intention of writing a sequel, after the success of *The Darkest Child*, Delores Phillips received so much feedback from people invested in the Quinn family that she began to imagine their lives beyond the ending of the novel. And thus, around two years after the publication of *The Darkest Child*, the sequel, *Stumbling Blocks*, was born. The story begins three years after the end of *The Darkest Child*, in 1961, with seventeen-year-old protagonist Tangy Mae Quinn and her younger sister, Laura, as they catch a bus to Tennessee to escape their mother Rozelle's abuse and to pursue more educational and economic opportunities. Following their older sister Tarabelle's death at Rozelle's hand at the end of *The Darkest Child* and Rozelle's commitment to an asylum, Tangy Mae kidnaps one of her sisters and begins a journey toward familial love, safety, and care. In *Stumbling Blocks* Phillips descriptively places the reader in the fictional African American community of Roanoke Pike, outside of Knoxville, Tennessee. Tangy Mae's and Laura's escape from Pakersfield propels them to an extended stay with Tangy Mae's paternal grandmother, Miss Francine Yardley. Tangy Mae also reunites with her father, Clarence Otis Yardley, better known as Crow, who first appears in *The Darkest Child* when he reconnects with his then-fourteen-year-old daughter after having been largely absent from her life. Unlike in *The Darkest Child*, threats of lynching, rape, and domestic abuse are absent from *Stumbling Blocks*; rather, those obstacles are replaced with milder conflicts, such as the threat of Tangy Mae and Laura's being sent back to their abusive mother and the Booster Street residents' being forced out of their homes in Roanoke Pike to make way for a housing project.

Phillips's digital archive suggests that she began working on the sequel in 2006 and had a draft of the first eighteen chapters by 2010. There are two versions of *Stumbling Blocks*—one dated July 2010 and a later one, printed here, from September 2011. Four chapters from the 2011 version comprised the excerpt in Soho's 2018 reissue of *The Darkest Child*. Both the 2010 and 2011 versions end abruptly midsentence in chapter 18, indicating that there was more left to be written. A comparison of the two reveals more than six hundred revisions Phillips undertook, ranging from rewriting or reordering the novel's events to smaller edits like word choice changes and minor grammatical issues. Barring the prologue, which remains relatively the same, the major edits occur in the first five chapters of *Stumbling Blocks*, while the other chapters are identical. This contrast suggests that Phillips's revision process was in progress but incomplete.

One of the most significant changes is a complete rewriting and reorganization of chapter 1. In the 2010 version of the sequel, for example, Phillips delays detailing Laura and Tangy Mae's troubled past until the third chapter and sets the action in a bus station waiting room. The *Stumbling Blocks* draft published here instead centers both the travel to Tennessee and the events related in *The Darkest Child*. This chapter 1 begins with dialogue from Laura, demanding that she be allowed to "get off th[e] bus" headed to Tennessee as she and Tangy Mae remember their sisters' traumatic deaths in *The Darkest Child*. By initially privileging Laura's voice in the chapter, Phillips makes her character development, lacking in *The Darkest Child* and in the first draft a central element of the sequel.

Stumbling Blocks' new cast of characters is as colorful and lively as those in *The Darkest Child*. Particularly, the introduction of Miss Francine adds to a long lineage of Black matriarchs in African American literature. After an accident falling over the neighborhood cat, Miss Francine, who owns a local restaurant, now spends her days self-confined to her home nursing her injured leg. As a "dark, large-boned woman" who commands obedience, Miss Francine is reminiscent of the *strong Black woman* literary archetype. The myth of the strong Black woman in African American literature appeared in response to historical representations of Black women in the American popular imagination as promiscuous and unvirtuous. Examples of the strong Black woman archetype include Mama Lena Younger in Lorraine Hansberry's *A Raisin in the Sun* (1959) and Miss Emma and Tante Lou in Ernest J. Gaines's *A Lesson before Dying* (1993) who are self-sacrificial, morally unwavering, extremely hardworking, and never in need of care or protection.

In her domineering encounters with her granddaughters, neighbors, and even her lover, Mr. Percy, Miss Francine surely fits the archetype. Much of the way Miss Francine establishes her authority is through food. She insists on teaching Tangy Mae to cook *her* way, scolding Tan for making the smallest mistakes, whether it be holding the knife the wrong way or watching eggs boil or adding too much or not enough seasoning to a dish. Miss Francine forces on Tangy Mae the domestic work Tan had so desperately sought to escape in *The Darkest Child*. Historically, cooking has been a way for Black women to express their creativity, yet Miss Francine weaponizes the act to assert power over Tan. While Miss Francine tries to use the space of the kitchen to bond with her granddaughter and learn more about her mysterious past, Tangy Mae views Miss Francine's acts as "fake, strained with impatience," and sometimes even triggering.

At times, Miss Francine's strict rule proves harmful for those closest to her, but the instances when Tangy Mae observes her crying alone in her room cracks the veneer of her grandmother's unwavering strength. Miss Francine is trapped in what Trudier Harris identifies as a state of "suprahumanity," in which Black women are expected to suffer in silence, swallow their pain, and persist despite adversity. Such suprahuman characters are "denied the 'luxuries' of failure, nervous breakdowns, leisured existences, or anything else," which often leads to a mere surface-level conception, devoid of depth.[2] However, by representing Miss Francine as a Black woman with impaired mobility, Phillips makes room to conceive of a character with a depth beyond the surface. Even though Miss Francine still rules her home from her living room chair, her limited mobility requires that she begrudgingly acquiesces to receiving care from those around her, thus threatening her ability to maintain the facade of superstrength.

As in *The Darkest Child*, Phillips explores a variation of human experiences by centralizing disability in *Stumbling Blocks*. Phillips situates Miss Francine in a unique position to highlight the novel's racial, class, and gender dynamics alongside labor. For instance, Miss Francine's lack of proper medical assistance illustrates the unequal access to care citizens have in segregated towns like Roanoke Pike. Because there is no doctor in the community, Miss Francine can only watch her leg fester while she treats the side effects with pain pills. Because her leg is not healing, she cannot return to her physically demanding job, which leaves her financially strained. Furthermore, the injury affects her relationships with Mr. Percy and other neighbors who, not understanding why her leg will not heal, try to authenticate her pain, constantly debating whether she is simply faking it. While Miss Francine's injury places financial pressure on her household and strains her relationships, it is this same impaired mobility that provides her a unique mode of resistance. Namely, while other community members are selling their homes to make way for the housing project, legend has it—as one of the neighborhood children Willie Mae tells Tangy Mae—that Miss Francine, who refuses to be forced out, strategically employs her impaired mobility as a conscious way to remain planted, stable, and unmovable in her home.

NO ORDINARY RAIN

While *Stumbling Blocks* is a novel written to sate popular demand and is based on a world readers will already be familiar with, *No Ordinary Rain* invites fans of Phillips into a different setting—one imbued in magical realism. Based on Phillips's short story "Wondrene Barry"—whose first several pages are missing—the narrative details the fantastical powers of Renwood Circle Nursing Home resident Clair Walsh, a.k.a. Zyma Root, whose touch relieves the pain of her fellow nursing home residents on their deathbed.[3] She claims these powers derive from a magical herb, a zyma root. Over the years, however, Phillips decided to turn the short story into a novel that became *No Ordinary Rain*. While in "Wondrene Barry" Zyma Root is an elderly woman living in an early nineties Cleveland nursing home, in *No Ordinary Rain* she is transformed into a mysterious young child growing up in 1930s Butcher County, Georgia. In an overview of the novel, Phillips writes that the child, Zyma Root, would have the same powers as her elderly literary predecessor: "This is the story of a child—Zyma—who is able to purge the deepest guilt from a dying person. She is drawn to the fading spirit by smells and breaths. The story begins with events leading to the child's birth, then moves on to the family who is left to raise her after her mother's death. They live in a place where superstitions are prevalent, where roots are used for healing and harming, and where it is frowned upon not the share the beliefs of the majority."[4] Indeed, superstitions pervade southern, rural Butcher County and help propel the plot.

No Ordinary Rain shares with *The Darkest Child* and *Stumbling Blocks* Phillips's keen dialect writing and her focus on poor, Black, rural, southern familial units. *No Ordinary Rain* departs from *Stumbling Blocks*'s quest in favor of a community drama highlighting the daily lives of the Butcher County residents. Smart, witty, and funny, *No Ordinary Rain* demonstrates Phillips's mastery of visualizing Black folk life. Whereas *The Darkest Child* and *Stumbling Blocks* feature mainly first-person narration from protagonist Tangy Mae's perspective, Phillips shifts narration in *No Ordinary Rain* to the third person, allowing the reader insight into all of the characters' inner thoughts. Interspersed throughout the novel are first-person chapters entitled "Zyma" and "Girlie," and the chapters written from Girlie's perspective, as communal ancestor, give historical background of the sharecropping community, while Zyma tells the present-day story as representative of the youngest generation.

The novel reflects Phillips's flair for humor and her burgeoning experimentation with magical realism. The supernatural is foundational to the story, as Phillips herself observed: "In a county where superstitions abound and evil omens are a given, both the animate and inanimate are suspect. It can be said that one's destiny rests on being a firm believer or nonbeliever. There is no middle ground."[5] Indeed, some characters approach snakes with the caution demanded by such supernatural beliefs. For instance, before she dies giving birth to Zyma, Mildred Wheaton sees a snake and recognizes it as a bad sign. Even chickens are not immune from the web of superstition Phillips weaves. Cleophus Bender's chickens, for example, are cursed—eating one would cause imminent death. Furthermore, the townspeople spread rumors that Van Ida's skin disfiguration is actually scales, proving that she had certainly been hatched from an alligator's egg in the swamp.

Superstition is foregrounded in all three versions of No Ordinary Rain. The first, which Phillips titled Tomorrow People, is a 223-page draft of the novel from February 2010, but her digital archives suggests she began envisioning the story in late 2003.[6] The second version, entitled Night Bloom, is a reworking of Tomorrow People coauthored with her sister, Linda Miller. Phillips had always envisioned writing with her sister, as she remarked: "Our styles are different, but she has the vocabulary and I enjoy playing with words."[7] The version printed here, No Ordinary Rain, is Phillips's latest draft from July 2010, but like Stumbling Blocks it is also unfinished. Night Bloom is a more succinct rendering of the July 2010 version's first six chapters. According to Miller, the collaboration was soon abandoned due to their diverging visions about the direction of the novel. In the five months that Phillips transformed Tomorrow People into No Ordinary Rain, the novel changed drastically, including the order of the events and the fates of several characters. The evidence from her archives suggests that she had intended No Ordinary Rain to be her second novel, as it was not until 2006 that she began to consider a sequel to The Darkest Child. In an interview with Clutch Magazine in 2007, she hinted toward this trajectory when asked about her plans for future novels following the success of The Darkest Child: "Right now I am stuck in mud in another Georgia town. If I am ever able to dig my way out, I hope to have another novel completed soon."[8]

In its theme and content, No Ordinary Rain draws comparisons to several African American literary predecessors. For instance, in its description of omens and its feature of a strange girl-child whom the community fears, No Ordinary Rain echoes Toni Morrison's Sula (1973). Just as the townspeople in the Bottom of Ohio are afraid of Sula

Peace because she brings bad omens and causes much chaos in the town, so the residents of Cranston are fearful of young Zyma Root because they believe she is a witch who brings death. Additionally, the conjurer Girlie adds to the historiography of conjure women as a literary trope in African American literature, following Aunt Peggy in Charles W. Chesnutt's *The Conjure Woman* (1899), Hattie in Zora Neale Hurston's *Jonah's Gourd Vine* (1934), and Mama Day in Gloria Naylor's *Mama Day* (1988), among others. As an umbrella term that includes healing and spirit work, the conjurer, scholar Kameelah Martin explains, "served as the spiritual adviser and doctor during the centuries of chattel slavery in the Americas and has since advanced into a type of hero recalled in the folktales, personal narratives, fiction, and visual representations of the African diaspora."[9] Even though Girlie is physically located on the margins of the community, in *No Ordinary Rain* she occupies a central role in the Georgia town as doctor, spiritual adviser, and preserver of Butcher County's history.

Additionally, familial relationships in *No Ordinary Rain* are often fragile and fluid, which places the novel among other African American literary predecessors that feature southern Black families one or two generations removed from slavery. Much like Janie Crawford and Logan Killicks in Hurston's *Their Eyes Were Watching God* (1937), Alabama Wheaton, Zyma's grandfather, marries local outsider Van Ida out of convenience and necessity rather than love. While Alabama remarks that he has no love for Van Ida because he considers her extremely unattractive, Alabama needs someone who can help raise his two sons and daughter, work in the cotton fields, and cook and clean for him after Alabama's first wife, Katie, abandoned the family with no warning. Van Ida is not romantically interested in Alabama either, observing that they are "just folks passin' each other in the same house ever'day," and over time they learn to coexist and tolerate each other for mutual survival. This need for mutual companionship considerably mirrors Vyry Dutton and Innis Brown's early relationship in Margaret Walker's *Jubilee* (1966) before it grew into romantic love. Their arrangement is also reminiscent of Alice Walker's portrayal of southern, rural Black spousal relationships in two of her novels, *The Third Life of Grange Copeland* (1970) and *The Color Purple* (1982). While Alabama is less physically abusive than Brownfield is to Mem or Mister is to Celie, he shares with Brownfield and Mister his explicitly disparaging remarks about his wife's appearance and her branding in the town as the "gator woman." In Alabama's eyes, Van Ida represents the opposite of femininity—tall, ugly, and unkempt. Like Mister, who has an affair with the lighter-skinned, more "feminine" Shug Avery, Alabama harvests his repulsion of Van Ida as an excuse to have an affair with Wondrene Barry, who he believes is the epitome of desire, possessing qualities that Van Ida lacks—youth, style, ginger complexion, and naturally wavy hair.

Alabama's disrespect and abuse does not deter Van Ida from nurturing and caring for Alabama's sons and Zyma Root. After Mildred dies, Van Ida becomes a surrogate mother for Zyma, or what Patricia Hill Collins identifies as an "othermother"—blood-related or non-blood-related Black women who provide care for Black children when the blood mother cannot or will not.[10] She nurtures Zyma and comforts her when the townspeople ostracize the young girl. This practice of othermothering is not only present in *No Ordinary Rain*; Miss Francine serves as an othermother for Tangy Mae and Laura in *Stumbling Blocks*. Although Miss Francine rules her house with an iron fist, not allowing the girls to leave the house without a dress on and forcing them to cook and clean while criticizing their efforts, she still provides more care for the sisters than Rozelle. Phillips's emphasis on motherhood in both *No Ordinary Rain* and *Stumbling Blocks* highlights her attention to care work and Black women's labor politics that often go undervalued in an ableist and capitalist society.

GEORGIA AND LEGACIES OF SLAVERY

Stumbling Blocks and *No Ordinary Rain* not only share connection with their emphasis on care work, but they also take place in distinctive southern communities. Both novels are set in Georgia, where Phillips spent much of her childhood. There is something about the South in general, and Georgia in particular, that her protagonists cannot escape. Even Tangy Mae, who makes it as far as Tennessee, is forced to return to her roots in Pakersfield at the end of the unfinished novel. This emphasis on Georgia is no coincidence. In an interview with Joyce Cherry, Phillips exclaimed, "I always go back to the Georgia landscape—the climate, the entire feel of Georgia, the people, everything."[11] As with *Jubilee*, *The Third Life of Grange Copeland*, and *The Color Purple*, which also all take place in Georgia, Phillips's setting for her novels demonstrates Georgia's unique place in the creative imagination of several Black women writers. The legacies of slavery, sharecropping, and Jim Crow in Georgia provide rich content for writers like Phillips to explore a wide range of themes, from survival, trauma, labor politics, and anti-Black racism to love, motherhood, Black communal relationships, and perseverance.

NOTES

1. Kenan, Randall. "In the Devil's House." *The New Leader*, vol. 86, Nov. 2003.
2. Harris, Trudier. *Saints, Sinners, Saviors: Strong Black Women in African American Literature*. Palgrave, 2001, p. 12.
3. The original title of this short story is unknown, but I have named it "Wondrene Barry" for sake of clarity. You can read more about this story in the short story section and on the companion website.
4. Phillips, Delores. "Birth of Zyma." Delores Phillips Digital Archive.
5. Phillips, Delores. "Pearl." Delores Phillips Digital Archive.

6. The manuscript of *Tomorrow People* is available on the companion website.

7. Phillips, Delores. "Interview Questions." Delores Phillips Digital Archive.

8. Lunn, Collier. Interview with Delores Phillips. *Clutch Magazine*, 1 Sept. 2007.

9. Martin, Kameelah. *Conjuring Moments in African American Literature: Spirit Work, and Other Such Hoodoo*. Palgrave Macmillan, 2013, p. 2.

10. Hill Collins, Patricia. *Black Feminist Thought: Knowledge, Consciousness, and the Politics of Empowerment*. Routledge, 2009, p. 178.

11. *Writer in Residence Lecture: Delores Phillips*. Department of English, Modern Languages, and Mass Communication, Albany State University, 2007. DVD.

STUMBLING BLOCKS

Horrible things had happened at our house. Over the years it deteriorated in weeping wounds with each wail of a child, whirr of a strap, snap of a bone. Left standing there old and alone on a hill, that house must have felt our abandonment as deeply as it had felt our sorrows. The dwelling, though already leaning and falling apart, might have stood on that hill for years had not our mother struck a match supplied by an angry and vindictive daughter. Once the fire was ignited, that poor old house conceded the inevitable, collapsed upon itself. Too late the tin roof that had compressed raging storms within sent distress signals in waves of smoke across Pakersfield.

Our mother whirled in a cascade of embers that drifted down and around her. Like dancing in a spring rain with her arms uplifted, she appeared child-like, lively, carefree. She swayed in a dance of joy while the house fell down and took my sister, Tarabelle, with it.

I had come to loathe my mother long before that moment. During my seventeen years of life I had become well acquainted with her capacity for cruelty. On impulse, she might reach out and harm any one of her children. Judy, six months old and defenseless, had been thrown from a high porch and down into a gully. That old house had sagged a little more when Judy died, then it had taken in a strengthening breath and stood sentry around her coffin. There was nothing it could do for Tarabelle, except go down with her.

There were ten children born to our mother, and we had known, maybe since birth, that our reason for breathing was to honor and obey her. Tarabelle had shunned that commandment, raised a hand against Mama, and admittedly secured a seat to Hell.

As an obedient and fearful child, I doubted that I could ever physically harm my mother. I had dreamed of revenge, but I wasn't truly committed to it. Space was what I needed to put between us. I wanted to live to reach an old age, to die a natural death. I did not trust my mother to let that happen.

My three brothers had found the courage to strike out on their own. My deaf sister, Martha Jean, was married, and the now youngest of my mother's children, Edna, had been unceremoniously turned over to Frank and Pearl Garrison. Mushy, my mother's eldest child, was resourceful and a survivor. She would endure any hardships that life sent her way. My concern had to be for myself and my nine-year-old sister, Laura. Following a revelation that my burden was lighter and stumbling blocks had been removed from my path, I did something that was frightening and uncharacteristic of me. In the middle of the night, I awakened Laura, and took her with me as I slipped out of Mushy's house on Echo Road. By 5:30 we were runaways on a Greyhound bus headed out of Georgia.

On the route up Market Street toward the four-lane highway, the bus yielded at the railroad tracks that ran through the middle of our town. Over Laura's head, through the dirty bus window, I could see our mother. She was pacing the ground in front of the platform of the train depot—an indisputable lunatic. Her arms were folded across her chest as she marched back and forth, seemingly without purpose. She stopped, glanced at the bus, straight up at the window where we were seated. I was sure she could not see us, yet it seemed she could. I did not want Laura to see the crazed woman outside the window and take that and other memories with her. I placed a hand on my sister's knee, and quickly asked, "Laura, do you remember where I was born?"

She nodded. "Yeah. You was born in a paradise beneath the sp- sp- sprawling branches of a live oak tree."

The bus rattled across the tracks. "What else?" I asked.

"Your first remembered sight was morning glories climbing the boards of a white picket fence. Your first remembered sound was the melody of Mama's voice singing a lullaby." She paused. "I was born there, too. Wadn't I, Tangy?"

I nodded.

Of course there was no truth to the words she recited. It was just a fairytale paradise, a place I had described to my sister so often that she could now repeat it verbatim. Had our world been serene like a paradise, there would have been no reason to escape. I would not have been pressed against my seat expecting the Triacy County sheriff to flag the bus down and drag us off. Mushy's first failed attempt at leaving had resulted in her being beaten and tied to a back porch railing for a week, and that was before Mama had escalated to her current level of madness.

Oblivious to my anxiety, Laura increased the tempo of her recital. "We rolled down grassy slopes over sweetgrass and four-leaf clovers." She lifted a foot and propped it on the back of the seat in front of her. "We ran barefoot over earth as soft as sand, chased butterflies under a golden sun and fireflies under a silver moon."

Her recital did little to ease my distress. My heart raced, and an ache inside my head intensified each time I glanced from the window. I placed a hand over my mouth, tried to suppress my weary sighs. We needed to be quiet, not bring attention to ourselves until we were miles and miles away from Georgia. I eased Laura's foot down, asked her to lower her voice. Over the noise of the bus engine, I could still hear her soft, whispering song. The bus reached the end of Market Street and turned onto the four-lane highway.

". . . a pond with crystal clear water," Laura sang. "Water so clear we could see to the bottom. Violet, emerald, and ruby rocks sparkled in the sun."

No, I thought, but did not say. We have known darkness. There was no sunshine over crystal clear water, Laura, only the gloom of teardrops and rain.

CHAPTER 1

. . . .

"I wanna get off this bus." Laura, restless from miles of riding, eased forward in her seat as though preparing to stand.

"Sit back!" I said. "The driver's not gonna stop to let you off, and where would you go anyway?"

She blew a long dissatisfied sigh, then slowly leaned back and once again stared from the window. After a few seconds of watching her, I closed my eyes and tried to get some much-needed sleep. I couldn't remember the last time I had slept, and I felt drained. I was nodding off when Laura's voice and words startled me.

"Is Tara my fault, Tangy?" she asked. "Is I'm the reason she dead?"

I opened my eyes. "No, Laura," I answered. "She died in a fire, and it wasn't your fault."

"But I told," she said. "I told 'bout her havin' the matches."

At the back of a nearly empty bus I reached out to touch my sister's arm, silently prayed that her grief, guilt, whatever she was feeling would wait for a better time and place. Several seats in front of us somebody struck a match, lit a cigarette, and I thought their timing could not have been worse.

"Tara was mad at me. She called me a thief, but I didn't take nothin' outta her basket," Laura said.

"She knew that, and I don't think she was angry with you. I'm sure Tara had forgotten all about it by the time she reached Penyon Road."

"I don't know," Laura said doubtfully as tears oozed from her eyes and slid down her face. "She called me a thief."

"I know," I said, and allowed my hand to gently stroke her arm.

She tensed, then jerked her arm away from me. Her tears flowed freely, but I thought I saw more anger than sadness on her face.

"It'll be alright," I soothed.

She cried in silence for a while, then leaned her head against the bus window and closed her eyes. A copper-colored complexion made Laura one of our mother's Indian children, as Tara had been. Laura and Tara had never been close, and Tara's last words to her had been spoken in anger. I watched Laura through the vision of tired eyes. Her side profile revealed slightly parted lips, a small narrow nose, almond-shaped eyes, and dark satiny lashes that were now resting just above her cheeks. It was hard to believe that her hair had grown to its present length when she had been nearly bald a year ago, but it had, and I would need to comb it before we reached Knoxville.

Laura was a thief just as Tara had said. I didn't like it, but she was what she was. Mama had taught her to shoplift from the stores in Pakersfield, and Laura had learned it well. I think she'd had to prove that she could do something to please our mother. At first she had stolen out of necessity under Mama's watchful eyes, but I think it gradually became a game to her, a challenge of sorts. She had wet her pallet until she was six years old but had finally stopped. I had to believe that she would eventually stop stealing. I reached out and touched her while she slept, while I could, then I dropped my hand onto my lap and closed my eyes again.

The motion of the bus and the weariness of my body had me shifting myself for a comfortable position. I could not find one, and sleep eluded me. Bits of conversations drifted back to me, but I closed them out and tried to imagine how life would be with a grandmother that I had never seen. It had been inevitable that I would flee Pakersfield, but I questioned whether I had been right to snatch Laura and bring her along. I assured myself that there had been no other options. Sometimes solving a problem was as simple as moving from one place to another. I envisioned our move as playing a game of checkers, moving pieces diagonally, trying to avoid being captured, trying to avoid crowning an opponent a king. I never wanted anybody to rule over my life again.

I was no longer a child, and although I was not yet considered a full-grown woman, I was close—very close. Like most girls my age, I had no idea what awaited me when I crossed the line from adolescence to adulthood, but I knew it had to be better than the life that I was putting behind me. Mushy hadn't been much older than I when she set off for Ohio. She had managed to find a job and a place to live, and I did not doubt that I could do the same. Being full-grown would bring many changes. It would mean that I could make my own decisions, like the one that had placed me on the bus. It would mean that I could move about freely, take control of my own life. In eight months I would be eighteen, and although it was somewhat frightening, I was grateful to be free of Pakersfield, free of my mother.

It was my birthright to bear some of my mother's traits. I did not inherit her beauty or cruelty, and I have prayed to never be marked by her insanity. At her best, melodious laughter flowed from her like spring in perfection, giving life to everything within its reach. At her worst, her soft hands turned violent against her children, spiteful words spilled from her tongue like the harsh coldness of winter, and her dark side manifested as hallucinations. Bugs that no one else could see would crawl all over her. She would scrape her skin raw and still could not rid her body of those bugs.

With a solemn expression, and in a dry tone, Tara had once said, "They ain't bugs. They men. Them is men crawling all over Mama. And she can't pull 'em off, and she can't wash 'em off. There's too many of 'em, and they been crawling on her for too many years. She ain't never gon' get 'em off."

For sure there had been plenty of men in my mother's life, and in my own as well. Although nothing was crawling on me, I was sure my blurred vision had caught the sight of ghosts. For a short while they rode on the bus with us. I don't know where along the highway we were when they first appeared and began to float down the aisle and hover overhead. They were my sisters, Tarabelle and Judy, both murdered by our mother's hands.

Judy seemed to purposely plummet toward my seat. I stretched my hands out to catch her, but she was like a gentle breeze barely grazing my fingertips as she passed by. And Tarabelle—sad, confused Tarabelle—stared down at me with dead black eyes. She never parted her lips, and still I heard her say, "You always been silly, Tangy Mae. You can't catch Judy now. You shoulda caught her when Mama threw her off that damn porch."

I couldn't, Tara. It all happened so fast. I couldn't.

"Humph," Tarabelle snorted, and then she was gone. My ghosts vanished and were replaced by guilt.

Laura had turned in sleep to rest her head against my shoulder. She, at least, was real, and I needed her close to me. That was not why I had brought her along, though. I had brought her to keep her safe, and because I could not bear the thought of leaving her behind to be passed from man to man at the farmhouse. It had happened to me and to my sisters before me. It was not by choice, but by our mother's will. I could not stop her.

Sometimes I think I am at fault for all of the horrible things that happened in our lives. Culpability must be realized so that I do not repeat my past mistakes. I am not the oldest of my mother's children, nor do I know much about life, other than what I learned from books. I was valedictorian of my graduation class, while none of my siblings had made it past the sixth grade. Intelligence countered by defenselessness offers no rewards, though, and I have always been weak. Had I been stronger, more vigilant, Tarabelle and Judy might still be alive. I should have screamed to the world from the high porch of our house on Penyon Road, "Help us! There is something terribly wrong with our mother. She is going to kill us all." Instead, I did nothing.

Rozelle Quinn. Often I have rolled my mother's name across my tongue trying to get a taste of what she is, a feel for who she is. She is a beautiful woman with a cream-colored complexion, high cheekbones, and gray eyes. Her beauty attracted the men who planted their seeds and moved on before the harvest. Ten children my mother had, and I wonder if she can pinpoint the fathers, say without a doubt, "This is your child."

I was fourteen when I first met my father, Crow. That was three years ago, back in 1958. It was nighttime in the center of a dirt road. He loomed out of and blended into the darkness. He was a tall, muscular man with a broad nose and a matchstick dangling from a corner of smiling lips. He said I had his mother's hair, and he called me a queen. I was happy that somebody as dark as I had come along to claim me. He believed he was my father, and I knew for certain that I was his child. To this day I don't think my mother knows or cares that his real name is Clarence Otis Yardley. All she knows him by is Crow.

People often say that a man spit a child out when the child looks so much like him. Foolishly, I had studied the faces of the men in Pakersfield, trying to determine the fathers of my siblings. When I was young, I searched for a man who could not hear with the intention of making him Martha Jean's father. No face would have ever divulged paternity because no man spit her out. She is the spitting image of our mother with her dimples, gray eyes, and light complexion. She came into this world deaf, eleven months before me.

I imagine it must have baffled Mama—what to do with a damaged creature who could not hear the storms raging beneath our roof. Every child has to learn, and so Mama taught her. She taught Martha Jean obedience by embedding an ice pick in her hand, and once again I did nothing. I was six at the time—only six—but that's a feeble excuse. Mama sold Martha Jean to a man by the name of Velman Cooper, and I resented it because I thought he should have bought me. I stole a kiss from him once and tried to fool myself into believing that it was for the sake of my sister. She could not, but I could, voice a love for him. He called me "little sister," though, and made it clear that that was all I'd ever be.

My list of transgressions is long. It is my fault that Mushy returned from Ohio to Georgia. She came back to help me, and now I have left her there in Pakersfield. Mushy asked the question one day, "How long I gotta pay for being born first in this damn family?" I had no reply then, but I should have said, "We've all paid a high price." It would not have answered her question, but it would have been a way of letting her know that I understood.

Mushy, whose real name is Elizabeth Ann, had not been there when Mama wrapped a leather belt around my head and bent my finger to the point of breaking. She had not been there when Mama had taken me to the farmhouse where I swallowed the semen of men while they swallowed my spirit. Mushy is eight years older than I, so I had not been there for her when her young body had been bartered for cash in haylofts and back rooms. I think Mushy was serious when she told me one day, in a joking tone, "If it's one thing I learned from my mama, it's how to pay the rent." Maybe that was how Mama got Mushy started. I don't know what she said or did to Tara, but she forced me into pleasing men under the pretense of getting my brother, Sam, out of jail. If I ever see Sam again, I will say, "Sam, you look white because you are the son of a white man." I think he needs to know that the man who locked him away, stole nearly a year of his life, is his father. I found that out one night by eavesdropping on the sheriff and my mother.

I have slipped away from Pakersfield with memories, a shopping bag of belongings, and the determination that Laura's childhood will never be like mine. If my grandmother doesn't want us, my backup plan is to at least get her to tell me where to find my father. In the past, Crow had been free to travel anywhere he pleased. Now, since he killed a man for me, he cannot return to Pakersfield. "A murderer is a murderer whether he kills one or one hundred," Crow had told me, "and I'd kill a thousand for you." It is no wonder that I've seen ghosts. I am the progeny of murderous parents. At this point in my life I just want to find Crow and let him be a father to me before I totally outgrow the need for one.

CHAPTER 2

The near-empty bus that we had started out on was almost full by the time the driver finally announced our arrival in Knoxville. As soon as we were off the bus, I right away searched for a pay telephone. I had memorized my grandmother's telephone number, but, tucked down in the shopping bag, I also had the paper that Crow had given me. It didn't matter how slowly I repeated the digits to the operator as I had her recheck the number after several tries with no answer. The number was right, the telephone was ringing in the house on Booster Street, but nobody was answering. We slid onto the back seat of a taxi in front of the Knoxville bus depot. "Where to," the driver asked, and I gave him my grandmother's address. He turned on the front seat to glance back at me. "That's up in Roanoke Pike," he said. "I'll tell you before we start, the fare is extra to go up there."

"No," I said, certain that he had misunderstood me. "We'd like to go to Booster Street right here in Knoxville."

"The only Booster Street I know is in Roanoke Pike," he responded in a friendly manner. "I can take you or you can find another driver who'll tell you the same thing."

Already I had called my grandmother's telephone number from inside the bus depot. She hadn't answered, and I told myself that there could be any number of reasons for that. Maybe she was out in her yard, or visiting a neighbor, out on an errand, or taking a bath. Whatever the reason, I knew that I would rather wait on Booster Street than at the bus depot with so many strangers. "Take us," I said.

Our journey took us across a bridge, through numerous turns, and up a steep, rutted hill that was overcrowded with a variety of trees. I was observant of the landscape along the route even as I listened to the driver grumble and swear as rocks kicked up underneath the car. Our driver reached the crest of a hill, drove along the smooth surface of asphalt, and turned left at a boarded-up corner building. Old signs of cigarette and cold drink advertisements were dangling but still attached to the building. As we turned the corner, I glimpsed my first signs of life in Roanoke Pike. An old man was cutting grass in the yard of a white house, and a woman observed him from the porch. The sound of the lawnmower faded in the distance, and finally our driver said, "This is it. This is Booster Street."

Green paint gave way to brown, or vice versa, on the exterior walls of the single-story house where he stopped. The house had a screen-in front porch and twin rose bushes at each corner. As I paid the driver and stepped from the taxi, the first thing I noticed was the lack of sidewalks and driveways along the street. Dust hung high and gravel crunched beneath our feet as the taxi pulled away and we headed for the house.

Laura summed up the paint situation, clarified it. "Somebody ran outta green paint," she said with a frown. "We gon' be stayin' here?"

I didn't want to bring up Penyon Road, the fire, or Tarabelle again, but I thought the house before us was remarkable in comparison to where we had begun our lives. A graveled path led us to the steps where the sound of a television traveled through the walls and out into the yard. I knocked, waited, then knocked again even harder. After several knocks with no response, I took Laura with me and ventured around to the back of the house. A gray cat was stretched on the top step. It watched us, showed no fear, and did not move until we were nearly upon it. I peered through a window in the door, saw no signs of activity, but knocked anyway.

"I know somebody in there," Laura grumbled as we moved back along the side of the house to the front.

Laura was hungry, thirsty, and wanted to go home. "Try to be patient, Laura," I said. "She can't have gone too far or the television wouldn't be on. She's old. Maybe she's taking a bath or something and can't get to the door right away."

Across the street were two vacant houses. To our left was another empty house with grass growing high in the yard and up through the gravel walkway, but in the house to our right a little girl stood at a window looking out at us. When I waved to her, she disappeared from the window, but at least I knew that somebody lived in and was at home in that particular house.

Each time I crossed the front porch to knock at my grandmother's door, I would tell myself that it was the last time, but it never was. We sat for hours on the front steps as bees drifted out from twin rosebushes and buzzed around our heads. Early on I had been comforted by the fragrance of the freshly mowed lawn and the presence of a pickup truck out on the street. They and the little girl next door indicated that we were not isolated on the street, but I wondered about the lack of traffic and pedestrians. It's the heat and the time of day, I told myself as I watched my sister swat at a bee that was hovering near her face.

Our salvation came in the form of the elderly man we had earlier seen cutting grass. He wore overalls and a plaid shirt with hanging threads from where the sleeves had been ripped off. He had a cinnamon-colored complexion, and thin, wavy salt-and-pepper hair. He hoisted the lawnmower onto the back of the pickup truck, then he turned toward my grandmother's house. "Hey," he called out to us. "Where y'all come from? I just cut this grass 'bout a hour ago, and y'all wadn't here."

As hours go, he was badly mistaken. We had been on those steps long enough to watch the sun shift in the Tennessee sky, long enough to think that my grandmother must surely have caught sight of us by now.

"We're looking for Francine Yardley," I said.

The man glanced at the shopping bag beside my feet. "Y'all got somethin' there for her?"

"No, sir. I'm her granddaughter."

"Her granddaughter? Well, I'll say." He came up to the steps. "Did y'all knock?"

"Yes, sir. Several times."

"A hundred times," Laura mumbled.

"I'm Percy Hudson, a friend of Francine's," the man said as he mounted the steps between me and Laura. "Y'all come on."

He pushed the door open without knocking while I held onto Laura and remained on the porch. Darkness and desperation might have prompted me to try opening the door as he had done, but I doubted it. Barging in as a stranger just didn't seem the proper thing to do. From the doorway I saw the old man turn the television off, and the emitted sounds that had been both a comfort and an annoyance were finally silenced. Over and over he called out my grandmother's name, and I was thinking that she must be dead in there. Finally, Mr. Percy Hudson called out for us to come inside.

More than anything I had wanted to look presentable when my grandmother saw me for the first time. I had worn my best dress—a yellow one with short sleeves—and a pair of white pumps, but wind blowing through the open window of the taxi had wrestled with my hair, the bus seat had wrinkled my dress, and I knew that my face was shiny with perspiration. I held onto our shopping bag with one hand, used the other to smooth down my hair, then drew in a deep breath to calm myself.

Laura and I entered the house to see a dark, large-boned woman dead or asleep on a blue flower-patterned couch. Her head was on an armrest and her legs were stretched across the cushions. Her left leg, from ankle to knee, was wrapped in an opaque bandage and she wore a floral-printed purple dress that clashed with the pattern of the couch. On the coffee table in front of her were a cane and an empty water glass.

Mr. Percy stood between the coffee table and couch. "Francine!" he shouted as he leaned forward to shake her. After several shakes he straightened his back, then turned to face us. "She'll be awright when she wakes up if y'all wanna wait that long. It's them darn pills the doctor give her for pain. They ain't no good for her."

I was listening to him, but I was also watching my grandmother. Her eyelids fluttered and opened a crack. "Earlene?" she questioned drowsily. "Is that you, Earlene?"

"Wake up, Francine," Mr. Percy said. "It ain't Earlene. These girls say they yo' grandchillun. Wake up now!"

"I'm woke," she mumbled, then smoothed her dress down over her knees as if to prove it. She made the full opening of her eyes suspenseful, like something that might never happen. Her head turned slowly back and forth against the armrest, toward the window and away from the window. Her eyelids tightened, fluttered, smoothed out, tightened again, and finally opened.

"Ma'am," I said before her eyes could close again, "I'm Crow's daughter. My name is Tangy Mae, and this is my sister Laura."

"Lord, have mercy," she whispered in a hoarse voice. "What'd you say, child?"

I repeated myself and watched as she continued to struggle toward alertness, knew she was almost there when she croaked, "Percy, get me a drink of water."

Mr. Percy picked up the empty glass from the coffee table and stepped from the room. When he came back, he had a glass of water and a wet face cloth. "Here, Francine. Wash yo' face. You need to wake up. You been takin' them darn pills again, ain't you?"

She ran the cloth across her face, took a sip of water, then cleared her throat. "Where y'all come from?" she asked.

"Pakersfield, Georgia," I answered. "Crow gave me your address and telephone number."

"Lord, have mercy," she repeated softly, and shifted until her back was against the armrest. "If he gave you all that, how come you didn't let me know you were coming? Y'all done caught me looking a mess. Let me get up from here." She slowly maneuvered her body into a sitting position and lowered her legs. The fabric of the armrest had left indentations in her face, and light from the window made the lines appear deep. "You say you Clarence's child?"

"Yes, ma'am."

She had a round face, Crow's broad nose, and thick, graying hair braided like a crown around her head. Strands of hair were sticking up in places, and her eyes were puffy from sleep. She did indeed look a mess. Squinting through puffy eyes made her appear angry as she leaned forward for a better look at me. "All anybody gotta do is look to see," she said. "Don't you see it, Percy?"

"Yeah, Francine. I seen it when she was out in the yard. That's how come I brought 'em on in here."

I stood beside the coffee table and watched my grandmother as she slipped her feet into a pair of black loafers. She picked up her cane and Mr. Percy helped her to stand. Moving slowly with the cane clicking the distance against the hardwood floor, she made her way to a straight-back chair beside a telephone table. She squeezed the bridge of her nose, closed her eyes, and for a moment sat there doing nothing.

"Wake up, Francine!" Mr. Percy shook her shoulder until she raised a hand to brush his away.

Finally, she placed a person to person call to Detroit, Michigan. After a brief pause, I heard her say, "Hey, Clarence, it's your mama. Ain't nothing wrong. I just called to let you know your Tangy Mae is here with me. Didn't call or nothing; just showed up. Hold on and I'll let you speak to her, but don't stay on too long."

"Hey, Crow," I said as soon as the receiver was turned over to me.

"Hey, sugar. What you doin' in Knoxville?"

"Looking for you. I wanna see you, Crow."

"I wanna see you, too, but I just left there. It's gon' be a few weeks befo' I get back. How you talk Rozelle into lettin' you go to Knoxville?"

"I didn't," I answered softly.

"What you mean, you didn't? Do Rozelle know where you at?"

"You're my daddy, Crow. You know where I am," I said.

"Listen to me, sugar. Don't tell Mama that Rozelle don't know where you at. She don't go for that kinda stuff, and I ain't too keen on it myself," he said just before my grandmother's hand reached out and took the receiver from me.

"Do that sound like your Tangy Mae?" she asked into the telephone.

Crow must have answered in the affirmative because my grandmother nodded her head. She pressed the receiver more firmly to her ear, listened for a minute, then said her goodbye. "When it's long distance, you get on, say what you gotta say, and you get off," she informed me. "Long distance calls cost too much, but he's gonna call you from his end either this Sunday or next. While we're at it, I guess I should let you call your mama."

"Her telephone's been disconnected," I responded.

My grandmother nodded as though she understood. "There's a lotta people don't have telephones. They get them, then they start making long distance calls without thinking that they have to pay the bill later."

"Francine, I got two mo' yards to cut, then I'll be back," Mr. Percy said.

My grandmother gave an exasperated sigh. "Percy, you know you ought not be out there cutting grass at this time of day. How many times I gotta tell you that?"

Mr. Percy smiled. "Girl, stop worryin' 'bout me. How you know what time a day it is when you been layin' up in here sleep?"

She waved a hand in his direction. "Since you're looking for something to do, just gotta have something to do, why don't you run on down to the restaurant and get these children something to eat?"

"Well, awright then," Mr. Percy said. "You want me to help you back over to the couch or you gon' sit there 'til I get back?"

"I'm too tired right now to make it back over there," she said. "I'm gon' sit right here and talk to my granddaughter."

Mr. Percy left out, and my grandmother dropped her hands onto her lap, closed her eyes, and fell asleep again right there in the straight-back chair. *Welcome to Knoxville that's not really Knoxville at all*, I thought to myself as Laura and I sat quietly on the couch and watched my grandmother sleep.

CHAPTER 3

Mr. Percy lived down in Knoxville, but every day he came up to my grand-mother's house. She said that he was a neighbor man who cut grass for people and tinkered with anything that had bolts and screws, whether it was broken or not. He ran errands for her and did her grocery shopping on Wednesdays. Laura and I both liked him.

My grandmother had put us in the rear bedroom that belonged to my father. It was an awkward step down from the kitchen to enter the small room that had no door. There was a single window with venetian blinds, a dresser, the bed, and a small closet. Photographs were all over the house and the bedroom was no exception. There was a picture of Crow in a frame on the dresser. He was wear-ing an army uniform and leaning against a truck. I'd never known that he was in the army. Every night I would study that picture while acknowledging that I knew little to nothing about the man I so readily called my father. I figured that I would get to know him better through his mother.

In clearing a spot in the dresser to place our clothes, I had come across a top drawer of neatly folded shirts that I sniffed for the scent of my father. The second drawer held patterns, scissors, threads, and scraps of material. It was a catch-all dresser, and I had to shift things around before we were able to put our clothes away in the bottom drawer.

Miss Francine had told us to do whatever we needed to do to make the room our own. "If I had known y'all were coming, I woulda had Maggie's girl clean out those drawers," she'd said.

It was obvious that my grandmother couldn't do much. She nursed her in-jured leg and kept it wrapped in a bandage. Although her room was near the front of the house, just off the living room, I would sometimes hear her crying at night. Since I had thought myself the one most capable of getting meals on the table, I right away familiarized myself with the kitchen. I made the mistake of taking breakfast to my grandmother's bedside on my first morning with her. She told me that a bedroom was no place to eat for a person capable of getting up. After that, I began to wait until I heard her stirring in her room before I'd fix her a plate. Slowly but surely, she would make her way to the table to either frown at, eat, or toss out the meals that I set before her. She never complained; she'd either eat or not eat.

"It was hard on me moving around this kitchen when I first came home with

NOVELS

Stumbling Blocks   103

that cast on my leg," she said to me one morning, "but nasty people will make you get up and do what you gotta do. Maggie from next door used to come over, but I couldn't eat her cooking. I'd have to remind her all the time to wash her hands, then she'd get snippy and storm outta my house."

"I always wash my hands, Miss Francine," I told her.

With a slight nod of her head, she said. "I know. I'm not saying you're nasty, Tangy Mae, but most of the time your food doesn't have any flavor, no taste to it at all. I've owned a restaurant for years, and I know what food is supposed to taste like, how it's supposed to be prepared. You have to use seasonings when it's called for."

She was quick to tell people over the telephone that her granddaughter was visiting with her, but untimely she would hang up, turn to me, and say, "Tell me a little more about yourself, Tangy Mae."

It wasn't that we didn't talk. We talked all the time, but never about ourselves. She talked about Mr. Percy and a host of dead people that included her sister, Earlene, and her husband, Jim. She would hold a photograph in her hand for hours while she reminisced about some event, and I guessed that was her way of imparting small images of her past. I shared with her the joyful things in my life, like singing in the church choir and graduating from high school. To give her a true picture of my life meant that I would have to wade through garbage, pick out the bits and pieces that could be brushed off or hosed down. I wasn't ready or willing to do that.

My grandmother had pictures in shoe boxes, in bags, and in bundles tied together with ribbons. "Family is everything," she would say when she stared at the picture of her sister, Earlene, that hung on the front room wall, then she would move on to the subject of her son. Those were the moments that I so patiently waited for. "You can't call him when you wanna tell him something, but you can write to him," she told me. When she tried to get me to write a letter to my mother, I told her in all honesty that my mother could not read. Her response was to tell me to write one anyway, that somebody else could read it to her. I didn't do it, and I hoped that with time she would forget about it.

She seldom asked Laura anything, and maybe that was because Laura outwardly expressed her boredom of the house, the photographs, and even my grandmother. While I sat on the couch one day looking at pictures and evading my grandmother's many questions, Laura took the initiative to go out into the backyard. Miss Francine watched her departure, then said, "I don't think she likes it here."

"She's never been away from home before," I said, "but she'll be alright."

Rather than mentioning any more about my sister, my grandmother concentrated on her own. "Tangy Mae, do you think you can climb up on a chair and wipe off that glass in them frames? I'd have you take 'em down and clean the wall behind, but you probably wouldn't be able to hang 'em back up there right."

I brought a kitchen chair into the front room where I stood to wipe off the glass that trapped my great-aunt Earlene and my grandfather inside their frames. After finishing the task, I stepped down from the chair. "I'm done, Miss Francine."

"From here it looks like you left a streak of dust running across Earlene's face. Climb back up there and see can't you wipe it off." She watched while I wiped at a nonexistent streak, then she said, "Earlene had a big heart, a good heart, but then her heart just gave out one day."

"I'm sorry," I said. "I can tell you miss her a lot."

She nodded. "It's been years, but sometimes it seems like yesterday."

When she was satisfied that dust no longer obscured her sister's face, she suggested we go out to the kitchen. "Laura doesn't seem happy unless she's eating," she said. "Why don't you fix something that she likes."

It was a hot day, and after scanning the kitchen shelves I decided to make tuna salad. Had my grandmother remained in the front room, the task would have been much easier and I would have been more relaxed. She commented on the way I held the knife to chop the onions and celery. "You'll cut your fingers off holding a knife like that." Because she was watching me so intently, I remained at the stove with my back to her while the eggs boiled.

"There's a way to cook most things where you don't need to stand over the stove," she said. "You put it on and time it, then you go back and check on it. Child, your standing there won't make those eggs boil one second faster. Why don't you move on away from that stove and show me your diploma again?"

My grandmother was trying to bond with me, trying to teach me. Somehow, though, it came out fake, strained with impatience. I went into the bedroom to get the diploma while all the time asking myself what I could do to please her.

"I know your mama was happy when you got this," she said when I handed her the diploma. "Clarence didn't make it all the way through. He just kept fighting and failing until I threw my hands up. He went off to the army, and after I got done crying about that, I started to pray. I still pray every day for that boy." She studied the diploma and I moved back to the stove. "I wish they had put Tangy Mae Yardley on this diploma instead of Tangy Mae Quinn. Why didn't you tell 'em you were a Yardley?"

For most of my life I hadn't even known that I was a Yardley, so I smiled, shrugged my shoulders, and said, "The eggs are ready."

My grandmother glanced up. "Put this back," she said. "I wouldn't want you to spill anything on it."

I put the diploma back in the drawer, then I hurriedly mixed the tuna in a bowl while she watched me. At home I would have made a sandwich and placed it in Laura's hand, but in my grandmother's house I had to more or less set the table. She insisted that juice and vegetable soup accompany the sandwich. When I had everything in place, I called Laura inside.

"Those eggs are still too hot. You should chill that tuna before you feed it to that child," my grandmother remarked.

I involuntarily blew a sigh. "We like it like this, Miss Francine."

"Well, don't bother about giving me any. It's got too much mayonnaise in it anyway. I'll just take a bowl of that soup."

I ate the warm tuna in silence and stole occasional glances at my grandmother, saw her slurp down a spoon of soup, and then try on one of her fake smiles, which I had come to associate with her need to pry.

"Last time my boy was home all he could talk about was his Tangy Mae," she finally said. "I thought he made you up to shut me up. I guess I should've known better, though, 'cause most men would've said they had a son instead of a daughter. I knew your name, but not your face, 'cause the only picture he had was old and wrinkled from being in his billfold. You were just a baby and I couldn't make out what you looked like at all, but all anybody gotta do is look to see."

She had said that before, so I assumed it was true. I was still waiting for some strong feeling to accentuate our kinship, but so far I felt nothing. She had allowed me to take on numerous responsibilities in her household, and I guessed it was her way of making me feel at home.

"If I didn't have this busted leg, I'd more than likely be jumping for joy," she said. "Call me Granny, Tangy Mae." She glanced at Laura. "Both of y'all. I wanna hear how it sounds. You can't be walking around here calling me Miss Francine when you're my grandchild."

She didn't have to accept Laura as a grandchild, but she did. It was at that moment that I decided she was going to be alright, I was going to make myself like her.

"How old are you?" she asked for probably the tenth time since my arrival.

"Seventeen."

"That's a lotta years we've missed out on getting to know each other. I'm not sure how I feel about that. All those years that boy didn't mentioned nothing about having no child, then all of a sudden he couldn't stop talking about you. It was after I broke my leg that he mentioned you for the first time and showed me that picture. I was on him to settle down and get married. That's when he told me, and like I said, I thought he was just saying something to shut me up. I asked him, 'If you got a daughter, why aren't you married to her mother?'" She shook her head and gave a short laugh. "He told me, 'Mama, every woman I meet don't wanna marry me.' And I guess they don't, but every woman he meet don't have his child."

I imagined Crow in this house being encouraged by his mother to marry mine. How could he tell her that he had tried and failed for no other reason than the color of his skin? Maybe there were other reasons, but if there were, he hadn't told me. It troubled me, though, that he had gone for years without mentioning me to his own mother.

"It's good to have friends," she was saying. "I don't know what I would've done when that boy left here if I hadn't had friends. You think your children are gonna be with you forever, but then they wanna leave, and I guess you gotta let 'em go. Now, if that boy had married and settled down right here in Knoxville, I would've known my grandchild long before now, and I'd have a daughter-in-law to help me out."

Laura finished her soup, took a few bites of her tuna sandwich, then held up what remained. "Can I feed this to the cat?" she asked.

What my grandmother gave her was more of a scowl than a glance. "Is it a fat, gray cat?"

Laura nodded her head. "Yes, ma'am. It's out there on the steps."

"Here's what I want you to do, sugar." Granny lifted her cane from beside her chair and extended it toward Laura. "You take this stick, go out there and whack that damn cat upside his head. Get him all the way outta my yard."

Laura looked to me for guidance. I could tell by the expression on her face that she did not want to hit the cat, but still she reached for the cane. Sometimes

I thought that if there was a queen of timid, it would be me. I did not want to offend my grandmother, but still I said, "She doesn't wanna do that."

The deepening scowl line in my grandmother's forehead, the narrowing of her eyes, and the tone of her voice all amounted to anger. "Let her speak for herself, and you butt out!" she said to me. "That damn cat is the very reason I'm laid up here with a busted leg. It ain't even my cat. Belongs to Maggie's children and thinks it's gotta stay over here all night and day. Who ever heard of a cat named Fred, anyway? That cat was balled up on my step when I tripped over it one morning. A cat with any sense at all woulda heard me coming and moved, but not that one. The way I fell down those steps, it's a wonder I didn't break my neck instead of my leg."

"I don't wanna hit him," Laura said as soon as Granny paused for breath.

Granny stared at her, then took the cane back and propped it beside her chair. "Well, you don't have to hit him," she said in a softer tone. "Just keep him away from my steps. I've been trying to keep Fred away from over here ever since I got back on my feet. That's the stubbornest, most ornery cat I ever saw in my life."

I was up and clearing the table when my grandmother said, "Let your sister do that! I want you to sit here and talk to me for a while longer. How long y'all gon' be here with me?"

"I'd like to see Crow before I leave," I answered evasively. It wasn't the time to tell her that I had no plans of leaving any time soon.

"Clarence," she stressed. "His name is Clarence. He's been running back and forth from Detroit ever since I broke my leg. I guess y'all might be with me most of the summer 'cause he just left here, and he ain't gon' want you to leave before he sees you, either."

Laura returned to her seat and didn't move to clear the table, so I continued with the task. Granny didn't speak again until after I had finished washing the few dishes, then she said, "You got good manners, Tangy Mae. Somebody taught you well, and I reckon it was your mama. My boy ain't gon' stay put long enough to teach nobody nothing. Was it that Quinn man that took my boy's place as a daddy and raised you up?"

"No, ma'am," I answered as I reached for the towel to dry my hands. "We were raised by our mother."

"So it's just you, and your mother, and your little sister here?"

Laura propped her elbows on the table, raised her hands, and spread her fingers apart. "Our mama had ten children," she said, "but we ain't never had no daddy."

My grandmother was momentarily stunned. Her gaze shifted from Laura to me. "Is that right? Your mama got ten children and ain't never been married?"

"She's never been married," I mumbled.

"My God! Ten children and never no husband? Maggie next door got twins. Were some of y'all twins?"

"No, ma'am. No twins."

CHAPTER 4

It was Mr. Percy who introduced us to Maggie Gearing and her girls from next door. He brought them in through Granny's back door late one evening. The girls were twelve-year-old Willie Mae and the six-year-old twins, Angela and Angel. Although the twins were not identical, they were both chubby little girls with shoulder-length hair. Willie Mae resembled her mother. She was tall and thin with short hair and the first signs of acne dotting her face. The twins had befriended Laura several days ago over the backyard fence, and now that proper introduction had been made, they took her over to their yard to play. Willie Mae propped herself against Granny's wringer-washer and said nothing. Not that it was a problem because Miss Maggie talked enough for all of us.

"Miss Francine, did you see Ralph when he passed by here yesterday?" she asked. "That's the saddest man you ever gon' see. He still living on one end of Locust Street while his wife living on the other end of the same street wit' her new man."

Mr. Percy settled himself on a chair beside Granny. From my seat at the table I watched Willie Mae from the corner of my eye. She was stealing glances into our bedroom, and I wondered what she was trying to see. Miss Maggie kept pacing, and all of a sudden Granny's kitchen had gotten a little too busy for me.

"I don't even hardly speak to Elaine no mo' 'cause of the way she did po' Ralph. He got his letter, and he say he leavin' Knoxville. It's the best thing for 'im, don't you think, Miss Francine?" Miss Maggie asked.

She reminded me of a sound, a snap in fact. Everything about her was quick—the way she spoke, the way her hands moved, and the way her eyes darted from person to person, briefly taking us all in. "Miss Francine, why don't you let 'em go to church wit' us on Sunday?"

Granny took a moment before answering, being deliberately slow to counteract Miss Maggie's upbeat tempo, I assumed. She tilted her head to look up at the other woman, then said, "Maggie, y'all go to a Presbyterian church. These girls are Baptist like me. They can wait and go with me when I'm back on my feet."

"They souls'll rot in hell waitin' on you," Miss Maggie said with a slight laugh. "I could break my back and it wouldn't take as long to heal as yo' leg takin'."

Granny raised her cane. "I can break it for you, Maggie."

"That ain't no way to play, Francine," Mr. Percy admonished as he reached out to lower the cane.

Miss Maggie skitter-scattered toward the back door. "Don't worry 'bout it, Mr. Percy. She ain't gon' hit nobody. She just in one of her sour moods today. I'm gon' head on home and get Leon's supper on the table."

For somebody who didn't believe that she was about to be struck, Miss Maggie took a rather hasty exit. Willie Mae giggled and pushed herself away from the washer. "You wanna go outside?" she asked me.

I followed her outside, and as we reached the bottom step she said, "Mama and Miss Francine act like that all the time. My mama don't hardly come over here no mo', but she wanted to see y'all when Mr. Percy told her y'all was Mr. Crow's children."

Out in Granny's backyard was an apple tree that stood a few feet from her clotheslines. A short wooden fence separated Granny's yard from the Gearings' and standing against the fence was a green lawn chair. Willie Mae and I walked toward the fence, and I was able to look over into her yard. Both twins were swinging on a gym set, and Laura was sitting on the lip of the sliding board watching them. Willie Mae and I stood in awkward silence until finally she said, "I used to come over here and help Miss Francine out when she first broke her leg, but she didn't like the way I did things. I guess you'll be helpin' her out now. I can tell you right now that she ain't gon' like nothin' you do."

"She hasn't complained about anything so far," I lied.

"That's 'cause you ain't been here long enough, but you just wait. You'll see. She'll probably make you work at her restaurant since she won't go down there no mo'. My mama wanted to work down there, but Miss Francine wouldn't hire her. My mama say Miss Francine is selfish."

It amazed me that Willie Mae was at ease in talking about my grandmother. Apparently, she saw nothing wrong with it, or I struck her as a person slow to anger. When I glanced over at her, saw the look of daring in her eyes, I thought she was challenging me. She spoke again, and I knew that I was right.

"My mama say Miss Francine go for bad. Yo' daddy go for bad, too, but my daddy ain't scared of 'im."

"Well, that's good, Willie Mae. Nobody should be scared of anybody," I said. "I'd rather we talk about something else, or not talk at all."

We were midway down a gravel-lined street when Willie Mae pointed and said, "That's Juanita right there. Mama want me to ask her when she can do the twins' hair. They gon' be turnin' seven next month."

I was guilty of expectations. Marigold Lane was such a lovely name for a street that I had visualized beauty. Instead, dust hung high and Marigold Lane crunched beneath our feet. We crossed a yard to a small shabby house that was covered in a gray siding. It was barely a step up from our old house on Penyon Road. A girl was sitting on a warped board that served as a porch with her feet dangling in the spot where steps had once been. She was a short, thin girl with a small nose, a nice smile, hair that reached the center of her neck, and a complexion almost as dark as mine.

Willie Mae made introductions and informed the girl that we were Miss Francine's grandchildren. When Juanita invited us to join her on the porch, I stood for a moment considering how I could gracefully get up on there with a dress on. To get up on the porch meant that I would have to turn backwards, brace my palms against the board, and heave myself up. Willie Mae managed with one athletic leap, but then she was wearing shorts. I was a little peeved with Granny for insisting I wear a dress, but with my new acquaintance looking on, I turned and pulled myself up.

"Juanita, Mama wanna know if you can do the twins' hair," Willie Mae said.

"When she want it done?"

Willie Mae shrugged. "I don't know. Sometime befo' they birthday next month."

"Yeah. Tell her I'll come around there and do it."

As the younger girls wandered off to sit on a tree stump near the footpath, Juanita began a conversation by apologizing for the lack of grass in their yard. "We're gonna be moving soon anyway."

"We moved earlier this year," I said. "It wasn't a big move, just in with my sister."

"I got two older brothers," she said. "They're both grown. I wouldn't wanna move in with either of them."

Her ease into conversation relaxed me, but I was still concerned about my dress picking up dirt from the porch. "I have two grown brothers, too," I said when I glanced up to see Juanita looking at me. "I wouldn't wanna move in with them, either, but my sister is okay."

Juanita reached over and touched my hair. "I'd like to take a hot comb to your hair. It's thick, and I bet it would hang halfway down your back if it was straightened out. I'd have to charge you four dollars 'cause you got more hair that Miss Maggie's girls." She smiled. "I can do it for less if you don't have four dollars. I know Miss Francine broke her leg and ain't been able to work."

I made no comment, but I was wondering just how bad my hair looked. I was reaching up to touch it when two boys walked along the footpath on the opposite side of the street.

"Hey, Larry," Willie Mae sang out.

The boys stopped, and they both waved before they continued on their way. Words were exchanged between them that did not clearly reach across the street. They playfully slapped at each other as they moved along.

"You and Larry liking each other?" Juanita asked.

"Nah. He just a boy from school." Willie Mae hung her head for a moment, but it didn't stay down long before she was once again staring after the boys.

"That 'hey' had a little sugar on it," Juanita teased. "I'm gon' have to tell Miss Maggie to keep her eyes on you."

The boys passed two more houses before they turned and started back. "He's coming back to get another look at you," Juanita said. "You want me to call him over here?"

"For what?" Willie Mae asked in annoyance. "I told you I don't like that boy."

When the boys were directly across from us, Juanita called out, "Hey, Larry, come here for a minute."

"Why you do that?" Willie Mae whispered angrily as the boys made their way across the street. Either self-consciously or purposely she ran a hand across her hair. It was obvious that she liked the boy.

I waited to hear what Juanita would say, just how far she would take her teasing. I was beginning to empathize with Willie Mae, although at the age of twelve I had never found myself in her current predicament.

The boy named Larry was small in stature with ears that he would need to grow into, and hair that hadn't been cut or combed lately. He wore cut-off pants and a dirty white T-shirt. He appeared uncomfortable as he stared at the ground and kicked a foot out against the porch foundation. He and his friend waited to hear what Juanita wanted.

"Y'all found a place yet?" she asked.

"Nah, not yet," he answered. "We still lookin'."

"Well, you tell your mama that when she gets ready to move, I'll come around there and do her hair. Tell her it ain't gon' cost her much 'cause I know people gotta hold on to their money when they tryin' to move and all. You tell her what I said, Larry, 'cause I know she don't wanna move to a new neighborhood with a nappy head."

"I'll tell her," he said, then he and his friend moved out of the yard and crossed the street.

"Now that didn't hurt a bit, did it?" Juanita asked.

Out in the yard Laura and the twins were drawing lines in the dirt around the stump with chunks of gravel. Willie Mae was silent. Rather than allowing Juanita to resume her teasing, I asked, "Do you do everybody's hair around here?"

"Most of 'em. I've been doing hair since I was fourteen. I wanna go to school and learn all the different styles, how to cut hair and all that." She worked her fingers like scissors to demonstrate.

"I think it's good that you already know what you wanna do," I said. "My oldest sister thinks I should be a nurse, but I don't know yet. I just graduated from high school earlier this month."

Willie Mae jumped down from the porch and wandered out into the yard. She looked like a little boy with her slim frame and short hair.

"I didn't know it was gon' bother her that much or I wouldn't have called Larry over," Juanita said. "I remember when I was her age. I never did have no trouble talkin' to boys, though."

"Do you have a boyfriend?" I asked.

"Yeah. His name is Jerome," she said. "He'll be over here after while. How about you? You got a boyfriend?

There was nobody to dispute my words, so I embellished, reached back into my past and pulled up Jeff Stallings, a boy I had gone to a prom with once. I presented him to Juanita, and added, "He's in college. I don't get to see him as much as I'd like to."

Larry and his friend came back down the road and engaged Willie Mae in a ball game, and as we watched Juanita pointed to a vacant house across the road. "My friend Geraldine used to live over there," she said, "but her family moved in April."

"Why is everybody moving?" I asked.

"Because we have to. I think they're gonna build a housing project up here. Everybody on this side of Roanoke Pike has to move."

"My grandmother, too?" I asked.

Juanita nodded. "Everybody."

CHAPTER 5

We had stumbled into the confusion of eminent domain. That knowledge shed light on the bleak condition of Roanoke Pike. Granny had made no mention of it, and she was making no efforts to move or even find a place.

"How come you got a daddy and I don't?" Laura asked as she watched me comb my hair. "Edna got a daddy, too, and another mama, but I ain't got nothin'. How come?"

"Everybody has a daddy," I said. "You just haven't met him yet. I was older than you when I first met Crow."

"It ain't fair," she said. "The twins got a daddy, and that girl we went over to house today, she got a daddy, too."

"Well, you can share Crow with me if you want."

"I don't want to. I ain't dark like y'all, and everybody'll know he ain't really my daddy. I want my own."

"I can't do anything about that, Laura."

"I know," she said as she rested her head on the pillow and turned her back to me. "You can't do nothin' 'bout nothin'. I don't know why we came here."

It was easier to fall into a world of make-believe where everything was perfect than try to explain to Laura the nothing that I knew about her paternity. For the longest time I spoke to her back, recited the old familiar paradise fairytale. When I knew that she was asleep, I went to study my reflection in the bathroom mirror. I was almost grown, had never been a pretty child to start with, and I was wondering if allowing Juanita to straighten my hair would improve my appearance.

Mr. Percy was leaving out when I turned off the light and stepped out of the bathroom. I heard my grandmother lock the door behind him, then her cane clicked across the front room floor and on into her bedroom. I wasn't sleepy, but there was nothing to do except go to bed.

I dropped down on the bed beside Laura, and almost immediately I heard the settling of the house—Granny was crying again. I didn't know if Mr. Percy had said or done something to her, or if her leg was hurting. I did know that I could not keep pretending that I didn't hear it. Rather than turning on lights I let my hands guide me along through the kitchen and front room until I reached my grandmother's room. Standing just outside her door, I called out to her, "Granny, are you alright? Can I do anything for you?"

She didn't answer me right away. Her crying changed to sniffles, she blew her nose, then said, "Gon' back to bed, Tangy Mae."

"Would it help if I rub your leg?" I asked.

"You can't help me," she said, and the crying started anew.

. . . .

Granny had a mop and wax day, an ironing day, and a baseboards day that thankfully did not come every week. On Saturdays the wringer-washer was pulled from the corner and rolled over to the sink. Because Granny was limited in movement, she would sit on her couch to dust her tables. All of the other household chores had been delegated. Willie Mae had done some of the work for her before I came, and now it was my turn.

Washing down the baseboards meant moving furniture away from the walls and dragging, pushing, or carrying it to the center of the floor. Laura wasn't much help, although she had been delighted to find a quarter under the couch the first time. After the couch was moved and no coins were spotted this time, she abandoned the task and went outside.

For longer than it should have taken, I remained behind the couch washing the baseboard beneath the front window. Granny had moved to the armchair that was now almost touching the couch. I thought that she could only see the top of my head, but somehow she managed to supervise my task. She knew each spot that I missed, and even when I didn't satisfactorily clean between the small areas where the boards had separated from the walls. Granny's house was old, but it didn't really show its age to me until baseboards day.

"I've tried my best to leave you alone," she said to me from the armchair, "but you haven't said anything more about writing to your mother. She's probably worried sick not knowing how y'all doing. I'm wondering why she hasn't called or gotten somebody to write to you yet."

"She doesn't have a telephone," I said, knowing that I had already informed my grandmother of this.

"That's not a good enough reason," Granny persisted. "Clarence has friends down there in Pakersfield. Next time I talk to him I'll tell him to give me some-body's number. You can call somebody to give your mother a message if you don't talk too long."

"Miss Pearl got a telephone."

I popped my head up, glanced over the back of the couch, and saw my sister standing in the kitchen doorway.

"I thought you went to play with the twins," I said.

"They playin' wit' that ol' stupid jump rope. I don't wanna play that. You gon' call Miss Pearl, Tangy? I wanna talk to Edna if you do."

"Miss Pearl is at work," I answered.

"Well, where Edna at then?"

"I don't know, Laura," I answered slowly, hoping that she would get the hint that I didn't want to talk about Edna, Miss Pearl, or anybody else in Pakersfield.

Granny patted the arm of her chair. "Come on over here, Laura, and tell me all about Edna and Miss Pearl."

Laura took a few steps into the room where mostly everything was in a heap at the center of the floor. "Miss Pearl is fat," she said.

"Yeah?" Granny encouraged.

"Real fat." Laura said. "Edna ain't fat. She used to be my sister, but she say Miss Pearl her mama now. I ain't got no new mama."

"Oh, God," I groaned. "Laura, go outside and play or do something."

"I had a sister, too," Granny said in an attempt to keep Laura talking. "That's a picture of her right up there on the wall."

"I know," Laura said disinterestedly. "I done seen them pictures a whole lotta times. I don't wanna see no mo' pictures. I'm goin' back outside."

I thought that if the frown in my grandmother's forehead got any deeper it might gouge her brain. "That child is something else," she said to me. "Did you see the way she was twisting her little behind when she left outta here? Y'all say you got the same mother, but ain't nothing about the two of y'all that's alike. I've noticed how you try to be careful with your words, but that Laura don't care what she say or how she say it. I might have to straighten her out."

"I'd better go check on her," I said as I thought of how Granny's constant references to her sister had possibly stirred memories of Tarabelle for Laura. We hadn't really talked about the guilt that Laura had expressed on the bus.

"Wait a minute, Tangy Mae. Sit down!"

Sometimes I wished I could switch scruples with Laura, but I was older and knew that I couldn't. Pleasing my grandmother was a priority for me that fell only a rung below my need for privacy. I crawled away from the baseboard and settled myself on the floor beside the couch.

"Tell me about your mother," she said. "What kinda woman is she?"

I had known this moment was coming. I wasn't so naive as to think that I could just enter into my grandmother's life without a past. Easing around Granny's curiosity might have been possible if Laura hadn't blurted about Mama having ten children with no husband.

"There's not much to tell. She's just my mother," I said, trying to come up with some pleasant memories that I could share with my grandmother. Every time I thought of my mother, though, I would see her angry gray eyes, her balled fist, her standing on the high porch swinging Judy toward the gully. It was hard, but finally I said, "She likes to laugh." It was a pitiful answer, but it was the best I could do at the moment.

"I didn't ask you what she likes. I wanna know what kinda mother she been to you girls, and what kinda woman she been to my boy. I always wanted a daughter-in-law, so what kinda daughter would she be to me?"

"That's a hard question to answer," I said. "I've never pictured her married, so I can't imagine her being anybody's daughter-in-law. What does Crow say about her?"

"Nothing. Clarence doesn't tell me much of anything that goes on outside this house. Look how long it took him to tell me about you."

It wasn't fair to her, but "nothing" was just what I intended to tell her, too. Crow might have had a reason for staying silent. Until I found out what that reason was, I was going to keep my mouth closed. "I really need to go check on Laura," I said, and pulled myself up from the floor.

"Push the couch back and dump that bucket before you leave out," she said. "And see if the mailman's been here yet."

Because I was already in the front room, I pushed the couch back, then stepped outside to the check the mailbox. Mr. Percy's light blue Plymouth was parked in front of the house, and he was making his way along the gravel path toward the house.

"Where's your truck today?" I called out to him.

"Parked. It needs a new muffler."

Laura was sitting on the bottom step staring toward the fence. Fred was on her lap, and she was rubbing his fur. I eased my way down. The back steps of Granny's house were narrow and there were no rails on either side to hold on to. I imagined how her accident might have happened. She had probably reached out for something to break her fall only to find her hands flailing in the air, or maybe she had bumped across each step on her way to the ground.

At the bottom of the steps was a garbage can that was old and banged up just like my grandmother. I felt bad for her. Although she denied it, I thought her pain was so deep that it took all day to run the course of her body. At night, when the world was still and there were no distractions, it made its presence known and she would cry. That was the way I saw it, and I didn't know how many nights had passed with her suffering in silence, without the tears.

Fat, lazy cat, I thought as I sat down beside Laura. I saw Fred as the culprit of my grandmother's misery, and I wanted him to go back across the fence. "Let go of that cat!" I said. "You know Granny doesn't want him over here."

"He don't like it over there," Laura said as she eased the cat to the ground. Fred started his slow cat-walk across the lawn, stopped once to glance back at us, then continued on toward the lawn chair.

Over in the Gearings' backyard, a group of children, mostly girls, were singing in cadence as they jumped rope. Willie Mae popped her head up on the other side of the fence as though she were about to take a turn. She spotted us, waved, then came around to Granny's yard. There was a comb sticking from the back of her hair, and she was wearing a shirt with horizontal stripes, and a pair of red shorts.

"Hey," she said in greeting.

"Hey."

"What's wrong wit' Laura today?" she asked me, despite the fact that Laura was sitting right beside me.

"Nothing. She doesn't like to jump."

Willie Mae giggled. "Everybody over there ain't jumpin'. Mama make me come out and watch 'em when it get to be too many in the yard. It's seven of 'em over there. I wish they'd go home so I can go back in the house. Them Benham boys like to fight, and if I wadn't out here, they'd be done hit somebody by now."

"Why don't you send them home?"

"They mama and my mama is friends, and nobody else for 'em to play wit'."

I looked across the fence at the two little boys. "How old are they?"

"Seven and eight, but they cuss like grown folks. I can send 'em home if they start cussin'."

She started back toward her yard and was near the fence when I asked, "Willie Mae, are there any stores or a library anywhere around here?"

"What kinda store?"

"A place where I can buy a dress."

"Not over here," she said, "and you have to go all the way down the hill to Vine to get to the library."

"Is that far from here?"

She nodded. "It's too far to walk. Ain't nothin' over here in Roanoke Pike, but we can go back over to Juanita's if you want to."

I thought about it for a minute, then shook my head. "Nah. I'd have to put on a dress, and it's too hot right now for that."

"Why you gotta put on a dress? You look alright."

"Granny wants me to wear a dress when I leave the house."

Her annoying giggles briefly filled the yard. "Miss Francine is so old-fashion," she said.

Willie Mae returned to her yard, and I sat with Laura until the rope game ended and several of the children left. Laura got up and went around the fence. but I stayed on the step for a few minutes longer wondering how she had felt watching the others play. It seemed to me that the Gearing twins eagerly accepted Laura's friendship, but they weren't willing to sacrifice their game to placate her. I didn't think I would have, either.

Granny was sitting beside the telephone when I went back inside. "I hope you ain't been out there telling Maggie how your mama had all them babies with no husband," she said. "Are you the oldest?"

"No, ma'am." I answered. "I was her sixth child."

"So what kinda woman is your mama? I can't even imagine my boy chasin' after some woman that already had five babies."

My mother had some strange ways, but that wasn't something I wanted to share with my grandmother. If I stood still in front of Granny long enough, she might see through me the horrors of my childhood. She might pay attention to the brand on my leg, the deformity of a broken finger, the anger inside of me. I shifted uneasily. "My mother is beautiful," I finally answered. "Everybody thinks so, including Crow. I know you can't tell it by looking at me, but she *is* beautiful. She has gray eyes and red hair, and it's not her fault if all the men like her."

"Humph," Granny snorted. "So if some boy say he like you, you gon' go out and get a baby with him?"

"No, ma'am."

Her gaze held steady on me, and I thought I saw in her eyes that old cliché, *apple don't fall far from the tree*. I was more determined than ever not to tell my grandmother anything more about my mother, but I could tell by the way she looked at me that she was not going to let it rest. With her watching me, I returned to my task of washing down the baseboards.

CHAPTER 6

. . . .

Children have disagreements over petty things, and it didn't take Laura long to have one with the twins. She didn't like it that Angel always wanted to play jump rope. Angel would never understand that Laura associated a jump rope with the death of her sister. Laura had been jumping rope in the yard on that day when Mama threw Judy from the porch, and she had not played with one since. It was something that I didn't truly understand myself, so I couldn't explain it, and I stayed out of their spat.

The few children from the neighborhood usually came to the Gearing's yard to play, but to Laura's way of thinking, there was no one to play with if she couldn't play with the twins. When the rope twirled high and looped low in the Gearing's yard, Laura would come home, sit on the back steps, and wait for the game to end. One morning the twins found their jump rope in two pieces, draped over the fence. They may have suspected Laura; I know I did, but nobody outright accused her.

I watched my sister as she stood on Granny's side of the fence, hands on her hips. "I saw Fred chewin' on that rope yesterday," she said. "He musta chewed it in half when y'all was in the house."

"Fred didn't do this," Willie Mae said, and for once she wasn't giggling. "Somebody cut this rope." She turned to her sister. "Don't cry about it, Angel. We'll get Daddy to buy you another one. This one was gettin' old anyway."

As children will do, they forgot about the rope and were soon playing other games. Granny had told Laura not to eat anything from next door. "Maggie is a nasty woman. She don't clean her house, and I doubt if she washes her hands before she cooks. She's raising those girls up to be just like her."

I worried that Laura would repeat Granny's words in the wrong place and at the wrong time. Granny didn't seem worried at all, although she had seen for herself how Laura would say inappropriate things when we least expected. There was no reason for me to go inside Miss Maggie's house, so I accepted Granny's word that the house was nasty. Sometimes I would sit on their front porch or on their backyard lawn chair to talk with Willie Mae, but that was as far as I had gone.

One day in the backyard, Willie Mae said to me, "Ain't nothin' wrong wit' them shorts you got on. We oughta sneak 'round to Juanita's. Miss Francine can't come lookin' for you 'cause she ain't gon' leave the house."

"Sneaking is for children. I don't have to sneak to do anything," I informed her.

"Well, my mama say you gon' be up in that house all summer if somebody don't get you outta there. She say Miss Francine's leg oughta be well by now."

"How does she know?" I asked.

Willie Mae shrugged. "I don't know, but when Johnny Scott broke his leg, he went wherever he wanted to go. Mama say Miss Francine actin' like that leg hurt 'cause she scared to leave the house. She scared somebody gon' come take it while she gone. She even had my mama watch that house when she went to the doctor."

"That makes no sense," I said.

Willie Mae giggled. "Lotta things don't make sense. My daddy say Fred wouldn't stay over there so much if Miss Francine stop feedin' 'im."

"I don't think she feeds that cat," I said as I moved toward Granny's yard.

"You ain't gotta tell Miss Francine what I said." Willie Mae seemed worried, possibly realized she had been talking too much.

"I won't, but you shouldn't be talking about things that you know nothing about," I said, and left her standing in the yard.

Granny's friend Miss Daisy had been visiting and was getting ready to leave when I went inside. Her son was already out front in the car waiting for her to come out. She came over sometimes to drop off a covered dish and to up-date Granny on what was going on with their different clubs, organizations, and friends. Often I would sit with them and listen. It gave me a hint of what my grandmother's life had been like before she fell down the steps. She had kept herself busy. Occasionally, somebody would knock at the door and ask to use the telephone, but other than that it was just the television, the telephone, the pictures, and me to keep Granny company until Mr. Percy arrived in the evenings.

Miss Daisy left out, but a few seconds later she was back standing in the doorway. "Francine, I forgot my blue bowl," she said. "If I keep this up, all my dishes gon' be at your house."

Granny sent me to the kitchen to get the bowl. "It's the one with the yellow flower on the side," she said. "Don't fool around and get one of mine."

When I returned to the front room Miss Daisy was standing by the door waiting. "Francine, why don't you send your granddaughter on down there?" she asked. "You say Betty need help, and she's right here."

"Daisy, that's my business. Tangy Mae is here to visit with me. She didn't come here to work."

Miss Daisy took the bowl from me. "Well, I just thought . . . I mean, she's here, Francine, and you need help. Why can't she do both, work and visit with you?"

"Betty's taking care of that," Granny said with such finality that I thought I could see the big fat period at the end. Miss Daisy must have seen it, too, because she left on out with her bowl, and without saying another word.

That period had been for Miss Daisy, though. She had created an opening and I dived right into it. "I'd like to go to work," I said. "I'm not doing anything else."

Granny sat there frowning. Finally, she said, "You ever worked in a restaurant before?"

"No ma'am," I answered, "but I can learn."

I could tell that she was considering it. "I'll have to talk to Betty about it. I'll call her in a minute," she said, "but I don't want you telling nobody that you came to visit me and I put you to work."

For two days Granny did not mention the restaurant again, and I thought that was the end of it, that I would have to find my own job. The same questions kept coming to mind when I thought about going to work. What was I qualified to do, and how would I get there? I was stuck on Roanoke Pike unless I called a taxi everyday, and I didn't know how long my money would last if I had to pay extra for riding over rough roads. I couldn't let it rest, so I asked Willie Mae again, "How far is it to the restaurant from here?"

"You talkin' 'bout Miss Francine's Place?"

"Yeah."

"It's right at the bottom of Moon Road, right where Knoxville and Roanoke Pike meet together," she said.

"Can I walk there?"

"Shoot," she said. "Ain't nobody gon' walk that far. What you wanna go down there for? It's Miss Francine's restaurant, and she don't even go down there no mo'."

. . . .

It was around four o'clock on Wednesday when Mr. Percy carried some of the grocery bags into the house and asked me to help him get the rest. I was standing in the kitchen putting the things away when I heard him tell Granny that he had doubled up on her groceries. "I gotta help Dan Andersons move next Wednesday, Francine, so I won't be able to go shoppin' for you. Dan got that last house on Sutton Street. Good-size house, too. You need to go in there and see what I bought, let me know if I forgot anything."

"Don't worry about it. We'll make do with whatever you brought," she said.

"Well, alright then. What you eatin' today?"

"Percy, sometime I think the only reason you come over here is to eat, or just to see if you can get on my last nerve."

"How I'm gettin' on yo' nerves?"

"Last house on Sutton Street. Humph," she grunted.

"Well, it was, Francine."

"You can leave if all you got to talk to me about is some old house," she said.

They were quiet after that, and I was tempted to look into the front room to see if she was angry with him. The tone of her voice gave that impression, but it was hard to tell since they so often teased each other in voices that suggested anger. I was done putting away the groceries, and there was nothing to detain me, but I lingered in the kitchen.

"You want me to talk?" Mr. Percy asked. "Well, I could talk . . ." He paused as though thinking. "I can talk 'bout how fat you gettin' 'round yo' waist. Come on! Let's go outside, look at yo' rosebushes or somethin'."

"Shit!" Granny swore. "I ain't goin' out there for no bee to sting me."

"That's just what you need. I bet one of them darn bees light on yo' behind, you'd get movin." Mr. Percy said with laughter in his voice. "Oh, you'd take off down the street, forget all about that cane."

Silently, I urged her to get up, go outside, breathe in some fresh air, but it didn't happen.

CHAPTER 7

Sometimes my grandmother would sit in the silence of the front room, rock her head from side to side, and smile to herself. It always reminded me of somebody in church who was deep into and feeling the spirit. I expected her to come out of it and shout, "Amen!" but she never did.

She glanced up at me one morning with a sad expression on her face, and I was on my way to feeling sorry for her, but then she asked, "Did your 'beautiful' mama teach you how to cook anything else besides breakfast and spaghetti?"

I couldn't feel sorry for Granny. The way she said *beautiful* irked me, mainly because there was something ugly in the way she said it. My mother had taught me little, but then my father had taught me nothing at all. I thought it strange that Granny never asked about my relationship with Crow. As much as I resented my mother, I didn't want Granny to think bad things about her because it ultimately reflected on me. I knew how to cook, and Granny knew that I knew how. She had practically turned her kitchen over to me on my second day with her.

"Granny, you know I can cook," I said.

"I don't know no such thing. You go in there and get skimpy with the food, don't give it no flavor, and most time you giving me something that Daisy brought over."

Sure, sometimes I would take out a dish that had been brought over by her friend, and sometimes Mr. Percy would bring food from the restaurant. On those days I didn't cook anything. Granny had extra mouths to feed now, and nobody in the house was working.

"You can make a meatloaf while I mix up a cornbread," she said.

She left the cane behind as she held on to the wall and hobbled off to the kitchen. The ugly side of her personality had just shown itself. I had seen it before, and usually it did not stay out for long. I lagged a little behind her and thought about what Willie Mae had said. *She ain't gon' like nothin' you do.*

We were going to have a heavy meal for a hot summer day because she was already talking about peeling potatoes and snapping string beans. "I haven't been cooking lately because of my leg," she said, "but I figure with your help we oughta be able to cook Percy a decent meal today."

That was what she said just before she turned around and left me alone in the kitchen to do it all. She returned to the front room, sat on the chair beside the telephone, and stared out the front window. Sometimes I wondered if we were a burden to Granny. June was almost over, Crow had not made his promised call, and I realized that I had not taken control of my own life. I had no job, hadn't been to church, and didn't even know how to get to the library.

The beans were on the stove, and I was peeling an onion to go in the meatloaf when Granny called me into the front room. "I think the mailman done came and went," she said. "Reach out the door and get the mail."

I gave her the mail, and was on my way back to the kitchen when she asked "What's your mama's name anyway? You ain't even told me that."

Laura and I had both told her our mother's name, and I knew that this was Granny's way of getting back on the subject my mother. To my way of thinking, the older a person gets, the more respect they're entitled. I couldn't say that I loved my grandmother, but I respected her, so it surprised me when my words came out a little too loud, a little too snippy. "I've told you before that her name is Rozelle. Crow should have told you my mother's name by now."

Either the start of a smile or a grimace quivered on her lips as she dropped her mail onto the telephone table. "You 'bout to let the real you come on outta there, ain't you?" she asked. "If you hadn't shown me some spunk soon, I was gon' tell Clarence he made a mistake, that you ain't none of his."

"I'm sorry, Granny," I said and meant it.

She nodded her head. "Why'd you come here? You say you want us to get to know each other, but so far it's been me doing all the telling, and you clamming up like you got something to hide. Everyday I've been showing you my pictures and telling you all about my family, your family, too. Now you wanna get mad just 'cause I ask you your mama's name?"

I sighed, then turned from the doorway and walked over to the armchair. She had told me plenty about other people, but not much about herself, and still that was more than I had told her about anything. What could I tell her that would not shame me?

"My mother's name is Rozelle," I said in a more civil tone. "Most people call her Rosie. She had ten children, but there are only eight of us now. Two of my sisters died. Up until she got sick, my mother cleaned houses and taught me to do the same."

The average person would have inquired about the death of my sisters, but Granny did not. "Your mama's sick?" she asked.

"She was. She was in the hospital, but she's home now."

"That's good, 'cause I wouldn't wanna think you came to visit me and left your mama home sick."

Of course, because what would that say about me? If I had waited for Mama to get well, I might have been in Pakersfield for the rest of her life. I couldn't tell my grandmother that, so I said, "I'd do anything for her. That's the way I was raised."

Granny nodded. "That's the way it oughta be. You don't get but one mother in this life. You may get one or two husbands and a bunch of babies, but that's all a maybe. A mother is for sure." She paused, brought her hands together on her lap, then said, "So she's beautiful, she works, and she's raised ten children all by herself. How come she never got married?"

"Crow never married anybody, either," I said defensively.

"Yeah, but Clarence is a man. Ain't nobody gon' think nothing about it if he make little bastard children all the way from here to Detroit."

She was beginning to annoy me. I looked straight into her eyes so she could see that I wasn't a child. I was grown enough to feel the impact of her words. "Is that how you see me, Granny?" I asked. "Am I just some bastard he made between here and Detroit?"

She sat there with her mouth agape, like maybe she was just realizing what she had said. As I passed her on my way back to the kitchen, she reached out and touched my arm. "Child, you a Yardley through and through. I wasn't calling you a bastard. I was just telling you what a man can do that a woman can't."

I had known for some time what men could do that women could not. If I got on that subject, I would more than likely send my grandmother into shock. I closed my mouth and let my silence speak for me. Granny had been all alone in her little house until we showed up at her door uninvited. Maybe she had been content to crack her blinds, take her pills, and spend the days sleeping on her couch. We had changed all of that, but we had also provided her an audience for her pictures.

Tears stung my eyes as I stepped back into the kitchen, not from her words, but from smoke rising up from the pot of beans on the stove. The water had boiled away while I was in the front room, and the smell was strong even before I lifted the lid to check. I salvaged what I could, then used my hands to fan the lingering smoke through the back screen door. Alone in the kitchen, I tried to put myself in my grandmother's place. How curious would I be about the mother of my grandchild? She had a right to know, I decided, but I wasn't going to tell her. That knowledge would destroy our relationship before it had a chance to develop.

As my anger subsided, loneliness crept into the kitchen and got in my way. At home, on a summer day like this, I could have walked over to Martha Jean's, or read a book, or just strolled through town where I knew everybody and everybody knew me. At home I would have been going to church on Sundays, and I might have even gotten my job back cleaning house for the Whitmans. No matter how pleasant a picture I painted, I knew that home was not a safe place for me, but I felt like I was standing still, torn between remembrance and expectations.

Miss Maggie had offered to take us to church, but Granny wanted us to wait until she was able to go herself. It didn't look as though Granny was ever going to make a move to go anywhere. When I had asked for my father's telephone number, she had told me, "He'll call when he gets ready." I didn't know why Crow hadn't called, but I wasn't surprised by it.

I finished up with supper, made sure to turn the stove off, then eased my way back into the front room. Granny had moved over to sink herself deep into the couch cushions. She was wearing her purple dress again. Her eyes were closed and her head rocked as if to a beat. For more than an hour, she hadn't spoken a single word to me. I stood just inside the doorway and watched her while I worked up the nerve to say what was on my mind. I wanted to go to work. Laura was already spending most of her time next door, and I could pay Miss Maggie or Willie Mae to keep a watch on her.

"Granny, did anybody take that job at the restaurant?" I asked

She opened her eyes. "Yeah. Betty got her daughter helping her out."

"Oh," barely escaped my lips. I was too disappointed to say much more.

"Clarence bought that place for me when he got out of the army." She reached for her stack of pictures from the end table. "Let me show you what it used to look like before I fixed it up." She rifled through the pictures and held one up for me to see. I guess disappointment was still on my face because she looked up at me and said, "I'm still gon' send you on down there, Tangy Mae, but you say you've never worked in a restaurant, and I want you to know a little something about what you're doing."

....

Laura must have been hungry because she gave me no argument when I called her in. She bounced around the fence and came toward me. In her hand was a cap pistol that she pointed and snapped. "We was playin' cowboys and Indians," she said.

"Take the cap pistol back over there," I told her.

Without complaint, she went back and gave the toy to one of the Benham brothers. She was dirty and sweaty from romping around in the yard. I loved her so much, and if nothing else had come out of our trip to Knoxville, it had freed Laura, turned her into a child who was able to laugh and play without restraint.

We entered the kitchen together where I thought only a faint smell of the scorched beans remained, but as soon as Mr. Percy arrived at the house, he asked, "What's burnin?"

"Nothin," Granny said as she glanced up at him and placed her pictures on the coffee table.

"Yeah, it is. I know I smell somethin' burnin'. Y'all come on! Let's get on outta here."

Laura's face lit up, and I was sure mine did, too. We were both ready to see something else besides abandoned homes and children playing in a yard.

"I ain't going nowhere," Granny said. "This ol' leg ain't feeling so good today, and I think it's gonna rain."

"Francine, it's too hot to be sittin' up in this house," Mr. Percy coaxed. "It ain't gon' hurt you to at least go outside and catch some fresh air. It ain't gon' rain, and that leg ain't gon' get no better just 'cause you wrap it up in a rag."

"Percy, don't you think I know what's best for my own leg?" she asked.

"Nah, I don't think you do. Ever' time yo' boy come home, you just get downright lazy. Ain't moved a muscle since he left, and now yo' granddaughter makin' you even lazier."

Granny glared at him, and I thought, *uh-oh*, but then she smiled. "You want something to eat?"

"What you got that ain't burnt?"

When Granny didn't answer him, he went out to the kitchen to see for himself. Granny told Laura, "Go wash your hands and fix him a plate."

"I just washed my hands," Laura said. "Why I gotta wash 'em again?"

It was not an unreasonable question. Laura had just washed her hands, and I saw no need to sour her mood by asking her to do it again. "I'll fix him a plate," I said and rose from the armchair.

"Nah." Granny shook her head. "She old enough to do just what I told her to do. You gotta stop babying her so much."

I did not understand my grandmother. How could she complain about me babying my sister when she was busy babying a leg? Even her neighbors and Mr. Percy thought that she should have been up and about by now. Laura looked at me and waited for me to say something. When I said nothing, she turned for the kitchen. I knew this time that she would barely get her hands wet, and what difference did it make?

"Ain't nobody eatin' 'cept me?" Mr. Percy called out to the front room.

Granny was trying to get up from the couch. I watched her, watched the way she pressed one hand against the armrest, watched the way her dress rose above her knees as she inched herself forward. Her knees were thick, and round, and extremely dark against the opaque bandage. Crow had said that I had her hair, and that was alright, but I never wanted knees like that. Those knees drew closer to the coffee table with each scoot and grunt of straining until one knee bumped the stack of pictures that was close to the edge of the table. The pictures fell to the floor as a whole, like they were glued together the way a family should be. It was that thought that made me move to help her.

I gathered the pictures and placed them on an endtable, then I helped my grandmother up. We entered the kitchen together, and right away I saw the plate that Laura had given to Mr. Percy. It was heaped with meatloaf, scorched green beans, potatoes, and cornbread that had no rise to it at all. I watched as Mr. Percy tested the cornbread against his plate—thump, thump, thump—like a fat knuckle drawing attention through a windowpane. Granny looked at me and slowly shook her head. I was thinking that the bread shouldn't have sounded that hard. And then I was thinking that Granny should have made it herself. That was something she could have done sitting down. I had to give Mr. Percy credit for trying to eat the food. He managed to swallow down a bite of the meatloaf, glanced at the beans, then dropped his fork.

"Francine tell y'all she ain't worked since sometime last year?" he asked.

"Mind your own business," she snapped. "Yeah, I told 'em."

Mr. Percy stared down at his plate, then stood up. "If you ain't goin' nowhere, Francine, I'm gon' run on down to the restaurant to eat. I'm gon' mind my own business just like you tol' me, but you done got so lazy that you done forgot how to cook. You keep sittin' on yo' behind, you gon' forget how to strut yo' stuff."

"Percy, you get on outta here," Granny said playfully. "You gon' down there and eat with Betty. Tomorrow I'm gon' show you that I ain't forgot how to cook. And I ain't never gon' forget how to strut my stuff."

We could hear Mr. Percy laughing all the way across the front porch and even out into the yard. When his laughter faded, Granny looked at me and said, "Sugar, don't never tell nobody you can do something you can't do. You can't cook. I could make better bread than that when I was three years old. First thing in the morning, I'm gon' teach you something."

"Why didn't you tell him that I was the one who cooked?" I asked.

"He already knew that. But he wasn't laughing at you, Tangy Mae. That's just Percy's way. He's trying to shame me into doing what he wants me to do, but I ain't that easy to shame."

I made sandwiches, and put the inedible meal in the refrigerator, thinking that maybe I could still salvage something from it later. After clearing the table, I went into our bedroom, pulled five dollars from the shirt drawer, and took it to Granny. "This is to pay for the food I wasted," I said.

She wouldn't take it. "I don't want your money," she said. "I want you to learn how to cook. Every young lady oughta know how to make bread."

I bet that when you go in there to cook nobody is calling you for something every fifteen minutes. I bet nobody called you a bastard or asked about your mother. I bet I can cook just as good as you.

I tried to justify the mess I had made in the kitchen by blaming Granny. There were too many holes in my version for it to stand firm, so I let her off easy. She was just an old woman with a broken leg who meant well. There was enough daylight remaining for me to take a walk over to Juanita's, and that was what I did. I intended to tell her about the disaster that I had made in my grandmother's kitchen, and then maybe she would tell me about something terrible she had done. We would laugh about it, and I would feel better.

When I reached Juanita's house she was sitting on the porch with her boyfriend, Jerome, and his friend Troy. She seemed happy to see me, or just happy because that was the kind of girl she was. "We've found a place, and we're moving next month," she said. "We'll be just three streets over from Jerome." I glanced at Jerome, who didn't seem at all excited by her news.

After hearing that news, I didn't stay long with Juanita and her friends. It was hard to join in their conversation when all I could think about was Granny and her house. Why hadn't she told me? Why wasn't she making preparations?

Laura was angry with me when I reached the house. "I thought you wadn't comin' back," she said.

"I wouldn't leave you. I'll always come back, Laura," I said.

I ended my day by washing Laura's dirty clothes at the bathroom sink and hanging them on a kitchen chair to dry. I thought she was asleep, but as I slid into bed beside her, she said, "I wanna go home."

I kissed her cheek. "It's gonna be alright, Laura. You'll see. Aren't you having fun with the twins?"

"But they ain't Edna," she said.

CHAPTER 8

It was still dark outside when Granny woke us up to get supper on the stove. I rolled out of bed, stretched and yawned. "Cook supper this early in the morning?" I asked.

"Child, after that mess you made yesterday, we probably shoulda started at midnight. I done brought out some recipes for you to see. And later on I'm gonna get Percy to bring my sewing machine to the front room. I bet you don't even know how to sew."

"I can sew in a hem, but I've never used a sewing machine," I said.

Granny frowned. "My God. What do girls learn down there in Georgia? You can't cook, you can't sew. What the hell can you do?"

Laura and I took turns in the bathroom, changed out of our nightclothes, then joined Granny again in the kitchen. "I'm sorry," Granny apologized, "but you're seventeen, almost grown, and you don't know how to do much of nothing. If you'd been here with me all these years, it'd be a whole different story."

She pointed me toward the recipe cards on the table, then called Laura over to stove and got her busy cooking grits. "Watch what you doin!" I heard her warn Laura as I rifled through recipe cards. "You gotta be careful. Grits bubble up and kiss the fingers that stir 'em, and you ain't never gon' find a kiss hotter than that of some grits."

Laura was dressed in the shorts that I had washed the night before. Cooking was new for her, but she didn't seem to be worried about getting burned as she stirred the grits.

"Just look at that. I knew you could do it," Granny praised, and Laura beamed.

I found a recipe that interested me, pulled it from the stack, and placed it on the table. Across the room, Laura could barely contain her excitement. She kept peering into the pot of grits even as Granny dropped sausage into a frying pan. Granny turned the sausage and gave Laura another warning. "Laura, you must be one of them that don't believe fire will burn."

Granny was leaning heavily on her cane, but at least she was up and doing something. She finally turned the stove off, and I got up, put the food in bowls and on plates, then allowed Laura to carry them over to the table. Before any of us had a chance to taste, Laura began seeking praise.

"These better than Martha Jean's, ain't they?" she asked me.

"They're probably just as good," I said. "I haven't tasted them yet. They're still too hot."

Granny right away wanted to know about Martha Jean, and Laura, still bubbly with pleasure, was more than willing to tell her. "She can't hear and talk, but Mama say she gon' have a whole bunch of babies. She already got two."

Granny picked up her fork and speared a piece of sausage. "Martha Jean got a husband?" she asked.

"Yes," I answered at the same time that Laura said, "Velman."

Granny nodded her head, said to Laura, "It's alright for her to have two babies long as she got a husband."

The telephone rang and clouded Laura's shinning moment, took the attention away from her. Her face fell as Granny moved to get up from the table.

"That can't be nobody but Betty calling this early in the morning."

"Do you want me to answer it?" I asked.

"Nah. It can ring 'til I get there. She probably wanna know when I'm gon' send you down there. I told her last night that I'd let you work two or three days a week if I can satisfy myself that you know what to do."

Beside me, Laura had grown sullen, but she picked up her spoon and began to eat. We had been with Granny long enough for us to know that the chair facing the tall windows was hers. She always sat there, and even Mr. Percy would take another chair when he came over. Laura had chosen the one across from Granny, so no matter where I sat it always placed me next to my sister.

I took a bite of the grits, then said, "I think these are better than Martha Jean's."

Laura didn't even look up, and I thought my compliment was too slow in coming. From the front room I could hear Granny saying, "I'll get Percy to bring her down there today." She paused, listened, then said, "I don't know what time, Betty. Maybe this afternoon. Don't worry about it. Tangy Mae is seventeen. That oughta be old enough to help with something, just don't let her near the kitchen right away."

A prayer had been answered and I was going to work. I was wearing shorts and my blue canvas shoes. As the sun rose, I stared through one of the windows and thought how it would be nice if I could go shopping to buy us another change of clothes. I also needed some personal items that I didn't feel comfortable asking Mr. Percy to get, and I wanted a watch. There was only one clock in the house that I knew of and it was in Granny's room, so it was hard for me to keep track of time.

Granny hung up the telephone, and I could hear her shifting on her chair, preparing to stand. "Alright, Tangy Mae, let's get supper on the stove," she said. "You've got a lot to learn, and I don't know what all I can teach you before you go down there. Laura, you finish up eating and wash the dishes while me and Tangy Mae go through those recipes."

Laura tapped her spoon against her bowl. "I ain't washin' no dishes," she said. "Miss Maggie say I'm too young for that. I wanna look at the recipes, too."

"Little girl, get up and wash them dishes! And get 'em clean," Granny said as she reached the doorway. "I ain't gon' baby you like your sister do. When I tell you to do something, I mean for you to get up and do it."

I glanced back to see my grandmother taking quick, unsteady steps with her cane. "We gotta get you ready to go to work," she said to me as she stepped through the doorway. "I wanna make sure you can sift, grate, strain, make bread, and a whole lot of other things. You won't be doing it right away, but you my grandchild and I want Betty to think you know a little something about cooking." When she reached the kitchen, she stood at the center of the floor, glanced from the stove to the table as though trying to decide what to do next. "Y'all can't sit there all day," she said. "We got too much to do."

Laura was in no way intimidated by Granny, and why should she be? I had promised to care for her and to protect her. She gave Granny a rebellious look, then resumed tapping her bowl.

"I'll wash the dishes," I said. "It won't take but a minute."

Granny's response was unexpected and reminiscent of home. She turned awkwardly, raised the cane, and took one staggering step toward us. Her cane struck the table so fast and hard that it broke a bowl and the plate beneath it, sent recipe cards and grits flying in all directions. She winced, dropped the cane, and grabbed her wrist. She was off balance even before the cane clattered against the floor, and then she was falling, reaching out for the table and going down fast. I was already up from my chair and moving toward her. By the time I reached my grandmother, she was sprawled on the floor some distance away from the table with one leg outstretched and the other bent at the knee and twisted at an odd angle.

"Oh my God, Granny!" I dropped down beside her, saw a face shrouded in bewilderment. The thought of another broken leg, a mass of broken bones, brought out my tears. I touched the bandaged leg and felt it jerk beneath my palm. "Who should I call?"

She was just lying there staring up. "Stop crying, child, and help me get up from here," she said. "I ain't hurt, and I don't want you to call nobody."

Unlike the crying that I had heard from her, my tears were silent. I crawled around to her head, slid my hands beneath her shoulders. She moaned as she straightened the bent leg, then finally allowed me to help her into a sitting position. Around us the floor was shiny and slippery with butter, grits, sausage, eggs, and shards of a broken china. I could see particles of grits clinging to her bandage. "I need to clean the floor before we get you up," I said.

Granny shook her head. "Nah. You get me up from here right now. Help me over to the sink and I'll pull myself up."

I tugged on her, and she used her left hand and foot to inch along with me, pushing a smeared path through the mess on the floor. I told Laura to bring a chair over, and while she was doing so, Granny tried to get to her knees. She gave another moan that faded into loud breaths of exhaustion. She was hurt and I knew it. "Should I get Miss Maggie?" I asked.

Granny gripped the seat of the chair and began to pull herself up. I moved in to help her, and it wasn't easy. The chair shifted, and I had to get Laura to hold it steady. By the time Granny was up, we were both breathing heavily. She rested her elbow on the edge of the sink, tested the strength of her right wrist while she caught her breath. "Get my pills off that table in my room," she said.

I rushed through the house, snatched up the bottle of pills, then returned to the kitchen. Granny was rubbing the knee of her already injured leg, and Laura was back at the table eating food that had to be cold by now. I gave Granny the pills, and although she was right at the sink, she dumped some onto her palm and swallowed them down dry, then sat with her eyes closed.

"I should call Crow," I said as I glanced down at her knee.

Granny opened her eyes. "Call him for what? You gon' tell him that I sat down on the floor? 'Cause that's all I did."

"Granny, you fell, and it was a pretty hard fall."

"Don't be trying to use me to get Clarence home. He'll just come down here and try to get me to move to where he is. That's what he did when I broke my leg, but I ain't going to no Detroit. And you stop crying, child!"

I wasn't able to halt my tears, but I slowed them as I pulled out the broom and mop to clean the floor. It was a waste of time trying to ascribe blame because we were all equally at fault. Laura should have done as she was told, I should have kept my mouth closed, and Granny should have better controlled her temper.

Laura was watching me, probably wondering how I could protect her from anything when I was such a crybaby. "It'll be alright, Laura," I said.

She shrugged indifferently. "I know. She said she ain't hurt."

Granny kept denying pain that was obvious in her posture, the way she tried to hold her body stiff as tremors shook her shoulders. Although I assumed that she was in great pain, she sat there and began to talk like nothing at all was wrong. "I want you to throw that meatloaf out, Tangy Mae," she said. "I'm gon' bake a chicken and cook some more beans. Then you gon' make us a cornbread that we can eat. It ain't gon' be hard like that one yesterday. Matter of fact, you throw that . . . that whatever it was out with the meatloaf."

The pills, as they began to take effect, lowered the volume of her voice. She began to mumble, and I wondered just how hard she had hit her head even as I leaned close to hear her words. She went from rigid to wobbly on the chair, tried to stand. I braced my hands against her shoulders and told Laura to hand me the cane. If Granny insisted on moving, I wanted to make sure that she didn't fall again. There was no way that she could get up and start the cooking that she was talking about, but I wasn't sure that she knew it. She stood, held onto the sink, and looked like she was going down again. I lowered my hand to the small of her back and gripped her left elbow, but as she stood swaying, I knew I couldn't manage her by myself. "Laura, go next door and get Willie Mae or Miss Maggie to come help me," I said.

Granny let go of the sink and took her first step. The cane was useless, and all of her weight fell against me. I put the whole of my strength into holding her up. I didn't know where she wanted to go or what she wanted to do, but I guided her toward the front room and the couch. We had barely reached the telephone table when all of the Gearing females came back with Laura. Miss Maggie immediately got on Granny's right side and told Willie Mae to move the coffee table. Granny was still mumbling about meatloaf and beans when we dropped her onto the couch. I lifted her legs up onto the cushions, then I went into her bedroom for a sheet to cover her legs.

"Laura say she fell," Miss Maggie said as I draped the sheet over Granny. "How in the world did you get her up?"

"She got herself up," I answered.

"Is she drunk or somethin'?" one of the twins asked, and I ignored her.

Granny mumbled a few more unintelligible words, and then just stopped, stopped trying to talk or move. She was lying on her back with both hands resting on her abdomen.

Miss Maggie, barefoot, and wearing a dark blue housecoat, looked down at Granny and sighed. "What next?" she asked. "First a broke leg, and now this. Did she break anything this time?"

"I don't think so. She may have hurt her wrist and her knee, but she was able to get up and walk," I said.

"That didn't look much like walkin' to me, but if you sure she didn't break nothin', I gon' get on back home. If you need anything, just yell out the back door or send Laura over."

"Miss Maggie, do you think I should call a doctor?"

"Ain't no doctor gon' come up here to Roanoke Pike. Why don't you just wait 'til she wakes up? She'll let you know if she wants to go to the doctor."

Miss Maggie and her girls left, and I sat on the floor beside the couch, watched the rise and fall of my grandmother's chest. Laura was anxious to go next door to play, but it was much too early for that, and I made her stay with me. Granny could open her eyes at any time, and I'd rather she not catch me sitting there doing nothing. "I need you to sit with her while I wash the dishes," I said, "and I'll have to get supper started."

Laura grumbled until I told her that I would sit with Granny and she could wash the dishes. "Okay. I'll stay wit' her," she offered apathetically, "but I'm gon' turn the television on."

I didn't know if it was necessary for either of us to sit with Granny, but I kept thinking that she might turn on the couch and roll off onto the floor. I could probably push the coffee table against the couch, but what if she rolled over and cracked her head on the table? Finally, I decided that it would be best for one of us to stay with her. I wanted her to sleep because if she woke up and tried to get up, I knew I couldn't support her weight again.

I went into the kitchen and washed the dishes. For somebody anxious to be grown, I wasn't getting off to a very good start. I had imagined that a person might go to bed one night at seventeen and wake up the next morning an adult of eighteen who knew everything there was to know about life. Adults knew what to do for the young and old, the sick and the injured. They knew what to do and say at births and funerals. I didn't think Granny was going to die, but the realization that I knew nothing about being grown came settling down on me as a cold, heavy depression.

Poor Granny, I thought as I wiped the stains from the recipe cards and set to work mixing the bread. Of all the things that I had heard her mention, the bread was the one thing that I knew I had to get right. Periodically, I would glance into the front room to see Granny lying just the way I had left her, and Laura sitting on the floor beside the couch. Maybe Granny would be alright when she woke up.

Granny wanted baked chicken, and I knew I could manage that. I threw out everything from yesterday's supper. Today I wanted to cook a perfect meal for Granny. *You pay for your mistakes*, I thought as I stacked yesterday's pots and pans in the sink. The bread pan was the hardest to clean, but I managed because I had to use it again today. Another hot day, another heavy meal. I took the chicken out, put collard greens in to soak, and started on a potato salad.

I was cracking boiled eggs at the sink when two things happened at once. Miss Maggie came in through the back door with a cup in her hand, and a lawn-mower started up in the front yard to drown out the sound of the television.

Miss Maggie went over to the doorway and looked in on Granny. "I see she still sleep. I ain't gon' bother her. I just came over to borrow a little sugar." She filled her cup with sugar, then opened the refrigerator. All one-handed, she went through Granny's meats and came away with a package wrapped in white paper.

They were neighbors, and I didn't know what was and was not allowed, but I didn't think this was right. "Laura, see if that's Mr. Percy cutting the grass," I called into the front room, and turned my back to Miss Maggie to hide the disapproval that was surely on my face.

"Laura?" Miss Maggie questioned. "Child, Laura been over at my house for the last hour or so."

I abandoned the eggs and went into the front room to see for myself. The television was still on, the front door was standing open, and Laura was no-where to be seen. Granny had turned her face to the back of the couch with one arm resting against her side. At some point she had lost the sheet, and it was lying on the floor. Forgetting all about Miss Maggie, I pushed the coffee table up against the couch, covered my grandmother again, and turned the television off.

Through the front window I could see Mr. Percy mowing the lawn. Today he had on a white T-shirt under his overalls and a straw hat on his head. I went and stood outside the screen door on the top step until he was on the upside of the rolling lawn, then I waved my hands to get his attention. He nodded his head in greeting, then started back down the lawn. He couldn't hear me over the noise of the mower, so I went back inside to wait until he was finished.

Miss Maggie was gone, and I wondered what else she might have taken from Granny's kitchen. What she had done bothered me because I had never seen her come over and take anything while Granny was awake. Mr. Percy had told us that Granny hadn't worked since sometime last year, and already I had wasted a lot of her food. Miss Maggie had a husband who worked every day, and Granny had Miss Daisy and Mr. Percy. Nobody was going to go hungry, and still I was bothered.

I moved the coffee table and sat down on the floor beside the couch, as close as I could get to my grandmother. I imagined her going to work every day, then dragging herself back home in the evenings. It angered me. Miss Maggie was half Granny's age, and she didn't work anywhere. I didn't want to be angry, but I couldn't help it. I was angry with Laura for slipping out of the house, angry with Granny for falling on the damn floor, and angry with Miss Maggie for stealing from my grandmother. Mostly, I was angry with myself for not knowing what to do about anything.

Leaning my head against Granny's back, I tried to get and give comfort. Through her back, I could hear each breath as it entered her lungs, the beating of her heart. She was too deep into sleep to even know that I was there. Granny's comfort came from old pictures of people long gone from this life, and she probably didn't want anything from me, except answers to her questions. I sat there, sighed, waited for Mr. Percy to finish the lawn, and wondered how bad Granny had hurt herself. The telephone rang, and Granny didn't even stir. I got up, answered it, and told the woman on the line that my grandmother was asleep.

"Is this Tangy Mae?" the woman asked.

"Yes, ma'am," I answered.

"This is Betty. You coming down here today?" she asked. "Francine told me she was gon' get Mr. Percy to bring you down here to meet me."

"Her leg is hurting today," I said.

"That ol' leg again, huh?" The woman said. "Well, you tell her Betty called. Maybe Mr. Percy can still bring you when he gets there."

"Yes, ma'am. I'll tell her you called when she wakes up."

Mr. Percy had come in and was standing in the doorway looking over at Granny. "What's wrong wit' her?" He asked. "She been takin' them pills again?"

I nodded. "She fell this morning in the kitchen."

"How bad is she hurt?"

"I don't know. Miss Maggie helped me get her on the couch."

He walked over to the couch, and I watched as he touched my grandmother. He turned her onto her back, then lifted her arms one at a time. He was gentle with her, but he wasn't a doctor. It wasn't until after he removed the sheet from her legs that I spoke up. "What are you doing, Mr. Percy?"

"Trying to see if she broke anything," he answered. "Did you check to see?"

I let him get on with it, and I didn't answer. The bandage on my grandmother's leg was embarrassing to me. It was grimy from the mess on the floor, and I hadn't even thought to remove it. Mr. Percy brought in a chair from the kitchen, set it next to the couch, and began to rub his hands along Granny's legs.

"Go out there and push my lawnmower 'round to the side of the house," he said as he began to remove Granny 's bandage.

"Mr. Percy, do you have Crow's telephone number? Do you think I should call him?"

"Nah. We'll see what needs to be done when she wakes up. Them darn pills the doctor give her is like some kinda dope. She tol' 'im this leg gettin' worst when it oughta be gettin' better, and he give her some stronger pills. Them things ain't no good for Francine."

I went outside, moved the lawnmower to the side of the house, then went over to Miss Maggie's to get my sister. Laura wasn't there. "I gave 'em all a nickel," Miss Maggie said. "They went down to Walt's place to buy some candy. She'll be back in a minute and I'll send her on home."

One of the good things about Roanoke Pike was that there weren't any stores, or so I had thought. I hadn't had to worry about Laura stealing, and now Miss

Maggie was telling me that Laura had gone some place where she might be tempted to steal.

"Is Walt's place a store?" I asked.

She laughed. "Nah, child. It's just that house right down there at the end of the street. Mr. Walt sell penny candy and Popsicles outta his back door. They'll be right back."

"Miss Maggie, don't let Laura go anywhere without letting me or Granny know first," I said.

The smile faded from Miss Maggie's face. "Shoot! Ain't nobody payin' me to watch her. If you don't want her to go wit' my girls, you better keep her over there wit' you."

Laura, when she finally came in, had a yellow sucker in her mouth. Mr. Percy was still sitting with Granny, and I pulled Laura into our bedroom. "Don't ever leave here without telling me where you're going," I scolded.

"Everybody else was goin'," she said.

Although I was tempted to, I did not check her pockets. I wanted to trust her, and if the man was selling candy out of his house, the chances were that Laura could not get her hands on anything. "Just don't do it again," I warned.

Mr. Percy stayed to do what he could, like putting an ice pack on Granny's knee. I hadn't thought to do that. In the evening he awakened Granny and tried to get her to eat. She wouldn't do it, couldn't. He troubled her enough for us to get her to the bathroom. I stood uncomfortably in the small bathroom with her until she was finished. Together we managed to get her to her bed, then I was left alone to get her into a clean nightgown. From the moment Mr. Percy had walked into the house, I had allowed him to take over the care of my grandmother, had been relieved to have a competent person with me, but now it was time for me to take over. I sighed and moved toward my grandmother's dresser.

Her top drawer was filled with papers, receipts, and ledgers. The second drawer was where I found her gowns, underwear, and about half a dozen of the bandages she used for her leg. I took out a white flannel gown, then pulled Granny up into a sitting position.

She was heavy and limp—dead weight—and her head flopped to the side as I pulled her up by her arms. It was a tedious task to get the dress off and the gown on, but I succeeded. According to the clock on her dresser, it had taken me fifteen minutes to do it. When I had her stretched back on the bed, I examined the area where Mr. Percy had removed the bandage. The lower leg was soft and discolored like it had been too long immersed in water, but the knee was swollen, the skin taut and shiny. It looked painful. I couldn't bring myself to touch the knee, but I tried to rub some color back into the leg before I wrapped it in a clean bandage.

Her bottle of pills was still in the kitchen. I thought I should put them within her reach along with a glass of water, just in case her pain returned during the night. I went out to the kitchen, looked all along the sink, and did not see the pills. I searched the floor where they might have fallen and rolled before calling out for Laura to come help me search.

"You ain't gon' find them pills," Mr. Percy said from the front room. "I got 'em in my pocket, and I ain't puttin' 'em back."

He was making me feel like an intruder, a stranger, totally in the way. When I stepped back into the front room, he had in his hands the sheet that had earlier covered Granny. I watched as he carefully folded the sheet, then I stuck out my hand. "I'll take that," I said. "It needs to go in the dirty clothes basket."

"Nah. I'll keep it," he said. "I might need to cover my shoulders durin' the night. I'll be right out here on the couch in case she needs anything."

"You don't need to stay, Mr. Percy. I'll hear her if she calls out for anything. I can take care of her," I insisted.

He sat down on the couch and placed the folded sheet on his lap. "I don't doubt you can," he said, "but wadn't you gon' give her them pills again when we can both see they ain't no good for her? Well, alright, then. I'll be right out here on the couch."

I slept with anger, with a man in the house, with worry on my mind, but I did sleep. I knew that because a nightmare came and brought Crow along with it. He stepped in through the bedroom window with Granny's butcher knife in his hand. "What'd you do to my mama?" he asked. I was trying to answer him and scream at the same time. One got in the way of the other. The scream swelled in my throat, and the answer never came. Laura saved me by pummeling my body with her fist and calling out my name.

"I don't wanna sleep in this bed wit' you no mo'," she said. "You was kickin' me."

"I'm sorry. I had a nightmare."

"About what?"

"It doesn't matter. It won't happen again. Go back to sleep," I said.

It wouldn't happen again because I was going to stay awake for the rest of the night. The nightmare was like a premonition of danger to come in the form of my father. I wished Crow were here, but the last thing I wanted to do was explain to him how I had allowed his mother to fall.

CHAPTER 9

Granny remained in bed for another day before finally getting up and telling Mr. Percy to go home. "Go cut grass or do something, go tinker with your lawn-mowers, Percy. You can't sit up under me all day." She tried to convince him that she was no longer in pain. He looked at her swollen knee, watched her walk and wince, and refused to leave. At a time when I thought she should have been crying the most, she hadn't cried once. In the room without a door, I had waited and hoped that she would call out for me, instead of Mr. Percy, but she never did.

"How long he gon' stay here?" Laura wanted to know that night.

"I don't know. I guess until Granny gets better."

Laura popped her knees together while she sang, "Oh, Mister Moon, bright shiny moon, you're hiding behind a high, high tree." I joined in and she stopped. "Tell me a story, Tan," she said.

I thought about it for a minute, thought that she was getting a little too old for bedtime stories. It would have been nice to read a book to her, or to get her interested in reading one on her own. I began to tell her a story about an old man who walked across a bridge every morning with a coal sack slung over his shoulder. Laura blew a sigh that sprayed me with spittle and made me laugh.

"You didn't give me a chance to tell you what was in the sack," I said.

"I don't wanna hear nothin' like that," she said. "Tell me about the paradise."

I blew a sigh of my own. "I don't wanna talk about that paradise anymore."

"Just the part about Mama's hands," she begged, holding her hands up in the moonlight as thought I needed a reminder of what hands were. "And when we rolled over the grass."

And so I did. "Mama's hands were soft and had the fragrance of Jergens lo-tion." I expanded on the hands, made them larger than life, as soft as a clouds, gentle and safe, then I started on the things that most of Roanoke Pike was sorely missing. "We rolled over sweetgrass and four-leaf clovers. We ran bare-foot on earth as soft as sand, chased butterflies under a golden sun and fireflies under a silver moon."

On and on I talked until Laura was asleep, then I lay awake until I heard Mr. Percy leave. He had driven his truck over instead of his car, and I was sure that the entire skeleton of a neighborhood heard the catch, stall, and catch again before the engine finally caught and he drove away.

Today Mr. Percy was gone, and Granny had propped herself on a kitchen chair and was pointing with her cane to the cabinets, the stove, the refrigerator, wherever she wanted me to be. I kept trying to get a glimpse of her knee, but the dress she had on covered her knees and most of her lower leg, although the edge of her bandage was clearly visible. When she caught me looking, she tugged at the dress to pull it down even farther like she had something to hide. She had me preparing enough food to feed an army, getting me ready, she said, to go to the restaurant.

Of all the people I had met in Roanoke Pike, people looking for places to live, and those already packed and ready to go, Granny was the least prepared to make a move. She hadn't mentioned anything about moving, and I made the mistake of asking her about it. For the longest time she said nothing, and I turned from the stove to look at her.

"I ain't moving nowhere," she stated angrily, glaring at me as though eminent domain was solely my creation. "This is my house and ain't nobody got the right to tell me I gotta move."

"But, Granny, everybody's talking about moving."

"You ain't heard me say nothing about it."

"No, ma'am, but how are you exempt if everybody else has to go?"

"Exempt?" she echoed harshly. "What you mean 'exempt'? You leave outta here a few times then come back thinking you got a right to get in my business. Tangy Mae, you ain't been here long enough to know what's going on." Her nostrils flared with anger, but she slowly calmed herself, shook her head, and gave an apologetic chuckle. "Child, don't pay me no mind, but somebody wanting to take my house ain't something I wanna talk about. Dip me up some of that macaroni and cheese. I wanna taste it."

I scooped up a good-sized helping and took a plate over to her, then sat down, not quite ready to drop the subject of her moving. "I like your house, and I'm not trying to get into your business. I hope you never have to move, but I don't want you to be up here on this hill all by yourself, and it seems that everybody else is moving."

She tasted her food, nodded her satisfaction, then said, "I been right here for more than fifty years. Clarence was born in this house. When me and Jim first bought it, it was just them two rooms up front and this kitchen. The bathroom was outside on the porch. Jim closed in the bathroom and made it part of the house, then when Clarence was born, he built that room where you and Laura sleeping. Before I got the restaurant, I used to serve suppers right here outta this house." She gave her first true smile of the day. "People would come and eat and didn't never wanna go home. Them was some good times."

I waited for her to continue, but when she spoke again it was to tell me to hand her a bowl and all of the ingredients for a pound cake. Sitting on her chair more relaxed than I had seen her in days, she mixed her cake and talked. We both talked.

"Since you walked through my door, I guess I've been trying to make time stand still," she said. "I knew you'd have to leave 'cause everybody leaves sooner or later, but I wanna hold on to you long as I can."

"I don't have to leave, Granny. I can stay as long as you want."

"You mama is maybe missing you and Laura by now even more than I miss Clarence," she said. "Y'all so young to be away from home. I think Laura is homesick, but I don't know what to say about you. You remind me so much of Earlene. She was dead before you was born, and still you talk just like her, or the way I remember the sound of her voice. It's been a lotta years, but sometimes I sit there in my front room and I can hear her whispering to me through my walls." She gave a short laugh. "I know that probably sounds crazy to you, but it's true. Percy say I live in the past, through my memories and my pictures, but I didn't have much else 'til you walked through that door with my sister's face and some of my boy's ways. You didn't even know me yet, but you showed concern for me soon as you got here."

She finished mixing the cake, lined her pan, and told me to lock the back door to keep the children from running in and making her cake fall. I placed the cake inside the oven, then we went into the front room to wait.

"Granny, I've never seen you drink coffee," I started as I settled on the couch beside her. "You don't even buy it, do you?"

"I can get Percy to pick some up if you want some," she said. "I drink it at the restaurant sometimes, but it ain't a taste that I'm crazy about."

"I don't drink it, either. I was just thinking of my mother. She always wanted coffee as soon as she woke up."

Granny nodded her head. I think she knew that I was about to open up to her, and for the first time she wasn't rushing me. Mr. Percy's opening the windows had brought fresh air into the house. For that I was grateful, but I knew they would be closed again as soon as Granny caught a chill.

"All of my older sisters and brothers dropped out of school," I said, but quickly added, "They all know how to read and write, though. I think I did well in school to compensate for everybody else. My teacher, Mr. Pace, thought I could have gotten a scholarship, but at the time I didn't think I could leave home. Now that I'm here and a college is close by, I think about it all the time."

"Can you still get that scholarship?" she asked.

"I don't know. I'm not in school anymore, so I think that's an opportunity that I missed out on. If I go to work at your restaurant, I can probably save up enough to go."

My grandmother laughed at that. "Child, you'd be working forever. I can't pay you that much, and the few pennies you'll get in tips won't add up to nothing. If you really wanna go to college, we'll figure out something."

"I do wanna go, Granny."

"What you gon' study when you go? Can't be wasting money on no silliness."

I liked the way she put that, like it was a given. "Maybe a nurse or a social worker," I answered. "I'd really like to be a lawyer, but I know that's ridiculous."

"Why is that ridiculous?"

"Well, Granny, I'm a colored woman, and I haven't even met a colored man that's a lawyer."

"There're some right here in Knoxville, and I'm gon' introduce you to one when I get back on my feet. Leonard Pruitt's been a lawyer for years. He comes in my restaurant all the time. Course, he can't do nothing about this eminent domain, but I bet you could if you were a lawyer. You'd probably save this house for your ol' granny."

"I'd try," I said, although I doubted that I would ever go to law school, and if by chance I accomplished it, Granny's house would be just another memory. She had not squashed my hopes and dreams, and I allowed her to hold on to hers for a while longer.

In trying to decide how much to drop our guards, I spoke of safe subjects, the insignificant. She learned from me that Pakersfield was an extremely prejudiced place to live and because of that my brothers and their friends were troubled and dissatisfied. I told her about the woods behind our old house where I would go sometimes to read or just think. Through her eyes, I was able to see my father as a young boy, learned that he was forty-four years old and had been born on an unseasonably warm day in February. I learned what Booster Street had been like in the twenties, and how it had changed over the decades. I even imagined that I could see my grandfather coming home from work and stepping through the back door.

"Jim was the kinda man who liked to wash up, then sit down and eat before he did anything else," she explained. "Always came in through the back door because it was closer to the table. Ain't too many joys in the world better than having your man sit down at the table and show you just how much he enjoys your cooking."

"I think that someday I'd like to have a husband just like my grandfather," I said.

"You'll be lucky if you can find one like him. After all these years I still miss him sometimes." She leaned back on the couch, closed her eyes, and smiled.

She's lost in another memory, I thought. This time I knew she was thinking of her husband. Her eyes opened abruptly to catch me staring.

"Tangy Mae, I don't know what all your mama taught you, but having ten babies with no husband ain't a good thing. You need to know that. Are you still a virgin?"

Where in the world had that come from? Did I give indications that I was not? I wasn't, hadn't been for some time now. I felt embarrassment crawling across my body like I imagined my mother's bugs had crawled over her. Maybe I reached out to scratch or snatch, or maybe I lied with a barely perceptible nod of my head.

"You ever gave yourself to some little boy?" she asked as she leaned forward again, her face so close to mine that I could see my reflection in her eyes.

I was able to honestly say that I had not, had never freely given myself. "No."

She must have seen something in my face that made her lie to me. "Sugar, you're a virgin 'til you give your body to some man or little boy. You gotta stay one if you wanna find yourself a husband like my Jim."

CHAPTER 10

At Granny's request, Mr. Percy came on a Monday morning to drive me down to the restaurant. He tried to get her to ride with us. "It'll do you good to get outta this house, Francine, and I'll bring you right straight back," he said.

"I ain't going. We'd have to drag Laura along with us. By the time she gets dressed half the morning'll be gone."

As subtle as they tried to be about their relationship, I had known for some time that there was something intimate between them. Mr. Percy looked at Granny in the same way that Velman looked at my sister Martha Jean. He wasn't just some man who cut the grass and ran errands as Granny had said, and I knew it.

"Francine tell you her place is open from six in the mornin' 'til seven at night?" He asked as he stopped the car in front of a white brick building. The restaurant was situated between a wooden structure and another white brick building, but they were still in the dark at this early hour.

"Yes, sir. But she said I don't have to stay all day today."

"I didn't think so," he said. "I'll come back and pick you up right after lunch."

A girl unlocked the door of the restaurant after peering through the window at us. She stepped back just enough to allow us entrance, and Mr. Percy said, "Pam, this is Francine's granddaughter, Tangy Mae."

"I know," she said, then turned to face me. "You're from Georgia, right? I called some of my friends and told them to stop by today to meet you."

It was Mr. Percy who informed her that I wouldn't be staying all day. While they talked, I glanced around the place. The floor was covered in a red and white checkerboard linoleum, and I could see where moving chairs back and forth had scraped and torn the linoleum in places. There were six tables with four chairs each, no tablecloths. Left of the entrance door was a counter with six red-top stools.

Pam was wearing a white dress with a white apron tied around her waist. She was a stout girl with the same cinnamon complexion as Mr. Percy, and medium-length hair that was pressed and tightly curled. I noticed that she had on lipstick, and black pencil lining around her eyes. She led me to the back kitchen area and introduced me to her mother, Betty, then she returned to the front, where Mr. Percy had seated himself on a stool.

I stood in the kitchen doorway while Miss Betty sized me up. She was a short, plump woman with a ruddy complexion. Her hair was brushed flat against her scalp, and she was wearing a flimsy hair net.

"You ever waited tables before?" she asked.

"No, ma'am," I answered, and knew that she was just making conversation because I had heard Granny tell her over the telephone that I had never worked in a restaurant.

She gave me a quick tour of the kitchen. "This area right here belongs to me while Miss Francine is on the mend. I do all the cooking, and I fill the orders that you'll give me through this window here." She touched the base of a square opening. "When you clear the tables, you'll have to bring the dishes in though that door where you're standing."

She handed me an apron, then told me that we would be opening in about fifteen minutes. "Breakfast around here goes pretty fast," she said. "Pam will help you get started, but don't let that girl talk you to death. I've gotta get back to this stove."

When I turned around, I could see most of the space behind the front counter. Pam was busy filling salt and pepper shakers. There were two trays of glasses and two trays of cups beneath the counter where she worked. A large coffee pot stood on a thick ledge beneath a hanging chalkboard menu, and a cash register was located at the entrance end of the shelf.

I tied the apron around the waist of the dress that Granny and I had sewn. It was a light green A-line dress with no collar or sleeves, just right for the summer weather. Granny had told me to wear my canvas shoes until we could get me another pair, but the pumps were better suited for the dress, and I had wanted to look nice. Mr. Percy was preparing to leave when I stepped back into the dinning area. "I'll be back to get you right after lunch," he said. "You take it easy now."

In my mind, working in a restaurant had to be easier than cleaning some-body's house, and I was ready to get started. At six o'clock, Pam unlocked the door, and five minutes later the first two customers were seated at a table. Two hours into my first day, I learned that Pam and I paid for any mistakes made by Miss Betty. Customers would send us back to the window for things she had forgotten to put on their plates, or if things were not cooked to their satisfaction. Each time I went to the pickup window, Miss Betty would tell me that I was doing a good job, although she really didn't know how I was doing. Not once had she been out of the kitchen. From noticing how busy she stayed, I could see why it would be a while before Granny would be able to come back.

It was not an easy day for me. Just as the lunch customers started coming in, I bumped a table and knocked over one of the glass dispensers of sugar. The metal top had not been screwed on properly and most of the sugar spilled out onto the floor. I didn't know where the broom and dustpan were kept. Instead of telling me, Pam decided to show me. She locked arms with me as she led me through the kitchen and to a back closet.

"You gon' stay and eat lunch here?" Miss Betty asked as we passed through her area.

"No, ma'am. Mr. Percy is coming to pick me up."

"How come you don't stay all day?" Pam asked. "You'll catch on quicker if you stay."

"You didn't stay all day when you first started," Miss Betty reminded her.

"Yeah, Mama, but I got my friends coming to meet her." Pam turned to me. "Can't you just wait until they come?"

I felt like I was letting her down, but I hadn't expected my feet to hurt so bad, and I really needed to sit down and not get back up for a while. Because it was my first day, I was given the responsibility of washing both the breakfast and lunch dishes. There were times during the day when every seat in the restaurant was occupied, and there were times when we did not have a single customer. Still, we were on our feet constantly, restocking, sweeping, mopping up spills, washing dishes. By a quarter to one, I was already sneaking peeks through the front window to see if Mr. Percy was out front waiting for me.

Miss Betty called me into the kitchen to ask how my first day had been. Before I could answer her, she said, "Mix that batter while I season these greens."

A large bowl stood on a counter and was filled nearly to the top with batter. I picked up a large wooden spoon and began to stir the thick mixture. I was doing alright until she told me to add a half cup of milk and two more eggs. I let go of the spoon and it stood straight up in the bowl. Granny's comment about my cooking came rushing back to me.

"I can't add anything, Miss Betty," I said. "Granny doesn't even want me in the kitchen right away."

Miss Betty laughed. "Child, Miss Francine did me the same way when I first started working here. Gon' and add that stuff. Ain't no way you can mess it up. It ain't nothing but batter."

I was getting ready to do it, but I must have been moving too slow.

"Get out the way," Miss Betty said with a touch of humor in her voice. She added the milk and eggs into the mixture. "You actin' just like your daddy. He a grown man and he still do whatever Miss Francine tell him to do. She can't send you to work and not expect you to help out."

"I am helping out," I protested. "She just doesn't want me to cook."

"And you ain't cooked nothing. Have you? All I asked you to do was add some milk. How hard can that be?"

Had she spoken in a harsh manner, I would have taken offense, but she hadn't. I think she was teasing with me. After she had finished mixing the batter, she slid the bowl across the counter. "Let's see if you can pour this into those pans over there," she said.

I did it, then moved toward the kitchen door. I didn't want Mr. Percy to have to wait too long for me.

"Crow comin' back this summer?" Miss Betty asked.

"He said he was."

"That's another thing," she said. "Miss Francine don't want nobody to call him Crow, but everybody do it. Folks done called him that all his life. His daddy started it. Mr. Jim was somethin' else. Miss Francine couldn't do nothin' with that man. She do a lot better with Mr. Percy."

I was waiting by one of the front windows with my tip money when Mr. Percy pulled up. He was laughing at me when I reached the car. "You limpin' 'bout bad as Francine," he teased. "How'd it go?"

"Alright, I guess." I opened my hand so he could see my tip money.

"How much you got there?"

"Fifty-seven cents."

"I guess that's awright for half of a first day," he said. "Close to the weekend it'll be a lot better."

I appreciated the way Mr. Percy had taken the time out in his day to drive me back and forth to work. Granny had told me that he spent his days fixing lawnmowers, washing machines, and anything mechanical except cars. When he wasn't doing that he cut grass and ran errands for people. Rather than taking me straight home, he showed me the area and the businesses near the restaurant. I saw in daylight the hand-printed sign over the restaurant that read Francine's Place. He drove along the same main road that the taxi had taken on my first day, and I knew that I was leaving Roanoke Pike and going into Knoxville. Mr. Percy took me to see his house on Henley Street, and he showed me the church that he and Granny attended on Patton. I knew I wouldn't remember the names of all the streets that he pointed out to me, but I would remember his little one-bedroom house with the tall wooden fence that was practically leaning over the handles of old lawnmowers, mostly push mowers. The lawnmowers were lined up in a row as though they had been purposely placed there to keep the fence from falling.

This ride back to Granny's house with Mr. Percy was much different from my first trip by taxi. This time the roads didn't appear as narrow, nor the hills as steep. Rocks kicked up under the car, but Mr. Percy didn't swear the way the taxi driver had done. It seemed to take no time at all to reach Booster Street. "Is my grandmother your girlfriend?" I asked Mr. Percy as he turned onto Granny's street.

He laughed. "Somethin' like that, I guess. But don't you ever let her hear you say it. She'd have a fit."

He stopped the car in front of the house. "Francine gon' lose business if she keep stayin' home 'cause of her leg," he said reflectively. "I done fell a lotta times and ain't never been laid up for months on account of it. She needs to get movin' again. Betty can't cook near 'bout as good as Francine."

We went in together, and I headed straight for the backyard to check on Laura. I didn't see the twins, but I saw my sister sitting on a step with Fred on her lap. She was stroking the cat's fur and talking to him.

"Did you have lunch yet?" I asked.

My voice startled her. She released Fred, turned to face me, and nodded her head. "I had a sandwich."

"Where're your friends today?"

"They went some place wit' they mama," she said. "I'm invited to they birthday party."

Laura seemed so fragile sitting on the shaded step all alone. She was barefoot and her skinny legs stuck out from the pair of pink shorts. Her hair needed combing, and although she was able to comb it, most often she would not. I decided that was what I'd do after I took a bath. As I turned from the door, I heard Mr. Percy tell Granny that I would need better shoes if I was going to be walking around all day.

"I told that girl not to wear those damn shoes," Granny said. "She gon' have to learn the hard way."

Mr. Percy laughed. "I think she done already learned. You oughta seen the way she come limpin' outta that restaurant today."

I did not go to the restaurant on Tuesday, but on Wednesday I wore my canvas shoes and I stayed all day. Pam had a few of her friends drop by to meet me—three boys and a girl. They were friendly enough, but I didn't have much time to get to know them. I worked all day, ended it with three dollars in tips.

I had Thursday morning free, and that was the day Mr. Percy took me and Laura shopping. We got our first look at the stores in Knoxville, and we got some dos and don'ts from Mr. Percy, which amounted to segregation in Knoxville being just as prevalent as in Pakersfield. On the outside looking in, though, it was totally different. The Negroes in Knoxville had their own movie theater and they owned businesses when I never would have dreamed it was possible. There were Negro firemen and policemen, and nobody moved off of the sidewalk for anybody else.

"Don't let that fool you, though," Mr. Percy said when I commented on my observations. "We still can't do halfa what they can. You go over to the Alcoa plant, you gon' see mosta the colored men workin' in the pot room. That's the hardest and most dangerous work they got."

"But at least they're working," I said. "My brothers couldn't even find a decent job in Pakersfield. They had to work the fields, and the women do housework for whites."

"You'll find the same thing here," he said. "We got them college students that wanna march up the streets talkin' 'bout change, but they ain't gon' get it like that."

Inside the stores, I kept Laura at my side to curtail her from trying to pocket anything. I bought two gifts for her to take to the twins' birthday party. I bought a plain white dress to wear to the restaurant, and a pair of flat, white shoes. I also splurged and bought myself a Timex wristwatch.

"Mr. Percy, do you think you can teach me to drive?" I asked on our way home.

"Yeah, I can teach you if it's alright wit' Francine."

"I'll ask her," I said excitedly, "and maybe you can start teaching me tomorrow. I don't have to work tomorrow."

He glanced over at me. "You don't have to work tomorrow? Tomorrow is Friday. It's the busiest day at the restaurant: it's payday for most of the people 'round here, and you'll get mo' tips than any other day of the week."

I nodded. I wasn't thinking about tips. I wanted to learn to drive, and I needed to spend some time with Laura. She hadn't mentioned wanting to go back to Pakersfield lately, and I wanted to keep it that way.

When I brought up the subject of learning to drive, Granny accused Mr. Percy of putting silly notions in my head. "You ain't nobody's daddy, Percy," she said. "She can wait 'til Clarence gets here. He can teach her to drive if he wants her to learn."

"Nah, I ain't nobody's daddy," Mr. Percy agreed, "but Tangy Mae ain't nobody's baby, neither. You gotta cut her loose, Francine, befo' she bust loose on you."

There would be no driving lessons, and I wasn't going to bust loose on Granny—whatever that meant. I watched Mr. Percy in his spotted T-shirt and gray pants as he crossed the kitchen floor to stand beside Granny's chair. It looked as though he had worked with something oily before coming over and had managed to get oil all over his clothes. I had fixed a hearty breakfast for him, but as of yet he had not sat down to eat.

"I'm gettin' you outta here today," he said to Granny. "Stayin' up in this house all the time is makin' you mean."

She shook her head and looked frightened when he gripped her hand. "I ain't going nowhere."

"You can't stay up in here forever," he told her before releasing her hand.

I could see in his face, tell by the way his voice had taken on a gentle tone that there was something more he wanted to say to her.

"Come on, Laura," I said. "Let's go for a walk."

"No!" Granny shouted at me. "Look at this kitchen. You can't leave out of here and leave this mess."

"Let her go, Francine. If this kitchen is that important to you, I'll wash the dishes, sweep, mop, do whatever you want done. All I want is that you get outta this house. Walk around the yard, go out to the back fence. Take a ride down to yo' restaurant. You ain't even gotta get out the car."

Granny gave a sigh that did not have enough breath behind it to blow back her tears. Her hands covered her face, her shoulders shook, and she cried right there in front of all of us.

Instead of offering her soothing words, Mr. Percy placed his hands on her shoulders, then he leaned down and kissed the back of her neck—a tiny little peck like a bird plucking a seed from grass. "Time don't stand still," he said. "You oughta know that."

Laura was slowly eating her breakfast and hanging on to their every word. They needed to be alone, so I allowed my sister a few more bites before coaxing her away from the table. "Come into the bedroom with me," I said. "I have something for you."

To prolong our stay in the bedroom, I placed my tip money on the bed and told Laura to separate and stack the coins by denomination. There was no door to close out or muffle the voices coming from the kitchen, and although I wasn't trying to hear them, it was impossible not to. I wondered if Mr. Percy ever won an argument with Granny, why he was so patient with her, and why she was so stubborn.

Laura would have had more money if she had chosen the quarters, but she chose the dimes because the stack stood taller. We heard Granny get her last word in and we heard Mr. Percy leave out. He could have saved himself the argument if he had called before coming over. I would have told him that there would be no driving lessons.

By the time we came out of the bedroom Granny's eyes were dry and she tried to give us a smile. Maybe she was embarrassed by the way she had acted. "I'm gonna bake Percy a peach cobbler today," she said as though that excused everything.

And so our day progressed with Granny sitting and Laura counting, stacking, and recounting dimes. I went to sit beside the telephone where I willed Crow to call. Granny watched me from her kitchen chair.

"Laura told me the other day that y'all got an older sister who likes to drink," Granny said out of the blue. "You don't fool around with whiskey, do you, Tangy Mae?"

Oh, my God! What all has Laura told her?

"Why were y'all talking about whiskey?" I asked.

"I reckon she saw a bottle over at Leon's house. He and Maggie like to drink sometimes. But you didn't answer my question. Do you drink whiskey?"

"No, ma'am. I don't even like the way it smells."

"Laura said your mama drinks, too. So if your mama and sister both drink whiskey, it's a reasonable question to ask you."

Laura and Granny were sitting in their usual spots across the table from each other. I took a seat with my back to the front room and watched Laura fumble with the dimes. "I don't know what all Laura has told you, but she gets things mixed up sometimes."

"Nah, I don't," Laura said and rolled her eyes at me. "Mama do drink, and she say Wallace done put a voodoo on her. He had some dead woman's pee in a bottle that he was gon' pour on her."

"Laura, be quiet or I'll take those dimes back," I threatened.

Laura got up from her seat and began to shove the dimes into the pocket of her shorts. She dropped one and it rolled under the table. Just as she located the dime and picked it up, the back door opened and the twins stepped into the kitchen. Thick, shiny, bouncing curls flowed over their shoulders, and they were both grinning from ear to ear.

"Oh, just look at that pretty hair," Granny exclaimed in one of those sweet voices reserved for children.

"Juanita came over and did it," Angela said. She brought a hand up to pat her curls, then turned so Granny could see the back. Angel did the same.

Laura eased around to Granny's side of the table, closer to the twins as she admired their hair. "I want my hair like that," she said.

Looking at the soft, silky texture of Laura's hair, I knew a hot comb was out of the question. "You can't get it like that," I said, "but I'll put your hair a different way."

"I don't want it a different way," she yelled at me. "I want it like that."

"Child, didn't you hear your sister tell you that you can't get it like that?" Granny asked.

"She ain't my sister," Laura shouted angrily. "She just a mean ol' darkie."

Granny nearly fell off her chair as she reached out for Laura. It was such a swift movement that my sister had no time to move. Granny seized Laura's arm with one hand. With her other hand, she gave one loud swat to Laura's bottom. The lick wasn't hard enough to bring tears, but it was a definite warning that Granny meant business.

As soon as Laura's arm was released, she backed toward the door and stood between the twins while keeping her gaze on Granny. When she had put a safe distance between herself and Granny, she dropped her arms to her sides. I know it didn't happen, but for a minute Laura's eyes seemed to be spinning. They were definitely pooling with tears. "She a mean ol' tar baby darkie," she said. "My mama say I ain't gotta call her my sister if I don't want to."

"Bring her here!" Granny demanded.

"Granny, I—I don't . . ." I stammered.

"I said bring her here!"

Hesitantly, I started after my sister, but Laura shoved the twins aside and ran out the back door. The twins momentarily impeded my progress, and by the time I was outside, Laura had run around to the front of the house. I chased her up Booster Street until I lost sight of her when she reached the corner and turned onto another street. I ran faster. She hadn't run in the direction of Juanita's house, and I couldn't imagine where she might be going. I followed the street that she had taken. Scanning the entire street, I slowed my pace because I had to, because the weight of my emotions was too heavy to run with any longer. When I reached the next corner and still did not see her, I began to call out her name.

She never answered me, but I spotted her sitting on a dirt curb in front of an abandoned house. As I neared her, she wouldn't even look at me. I dropped down beside her to catch my breath.

"I can't believe the way you're acting," I finally said. "You'll have to apologize to Granny."

"Why? She's mean, and I don't like her," Laura said. "She wanted me to hurt Fred. I like Fred better than I do her."

"Laura, listen to me. We're staying in Granny's house. She's an adult, and you know better than to disrespect her."

"If she hits me again, I'm gon' hit her back."

I would have laughed at that if I'd had the energy. I got up, then helped my sister to her feet. We walked in silence, and as we neared the house, Laura asked, "Is she my grandmother, too?"

I shook my head. "No."

"I didn't think so. She don't like me."

"Granny likes you. What makes you think that she doesn't?"

"I don't know, but I ain't gon' call her Granny no mo'. I'm gon' call her Miss Francine."

It did not matter to me what Laura called her as long as she respected her. I had started a job, and for the first time had been leaving the two alone. I hadn't thought to ask how they got along with each other. I asked it now. "Is Granny mean to you when I'm not there?"

"Nah. All she do is sit on the couch and watch the television and look at them pictures. I could push her down the steps, and everybody would think she tripped over Fred again."

I was horrified that she would say such a thing. "Laura, don't you dare put your hands on Granny to push, hit, or anything else," I warned. "They have jails for children. Do you wanna go to jail?"

"I wanna go home and be wit' Edna," she said. "I don't like it here."

When we were back at the house, Granny sat on the couch while Laura stood all the way over by the television. I nudged Laura, and she said, "I'm sorry, Miss Francine."

"You don't sound like you're sorry," Granny said, "but that's alright. You ain't goin' to that birthday party."

"I hate it here," Laura screamed as she rushed off to the bedroom to sulk, cry, scheme. I really had no idea what she would do, but I knew I had to give my grandmother a subtle warning about Laura. I sat down beside her on the couch.

"Granny, does Laura give you a hard time when I'm not here?" I asked.

"Nah, child. Mostly she stays outside and plays with the twins. I ain't never seen her act like this before. Why in the world did she call you a darkie?"

Maybe Granny had failed to notice that both she and I were dark people, and that was reason enough. In defense of my sister, I placed the blame where it rightfully belonged. I told Granny about our mother, how she labeled her children according to our skin tones. "Mama calls me a darkie. That's where Laura got it," I explained.

"Oh, my God," Granny said. "That's the most ridiculous thing I ever heard of." She reached out to touch me as though I needed consoling.

I did not need sympathy, but I allowed her to hold me, rock me against her bosom. While I rested my head, I kept thinking of Granny going to the door to call Laura in for lunch, and Laura hiding some place, shoving Granny down the steps. I shuddered.

"It's alright, child," Granny soothed, taking my shudder as distress.

As I pictured the scene taking place, I realized that it couldn't happen. There was no place for Laura to hide on Granny's back steps. The space was too small, and Granny never went down the steps, but still I worried. I drew away from my grandmother so that I could see her face. "Granny, don't go near the steps when I'm not here," I said. "Don't call Laura in for lunch. If she gets hungry, she'll come in on her own."

Granny stared at me. She didn't ask why; she just nodded her head and said, "Let's get out to the kitchen and make that peach cobbler for Percy."

. . . .

Before I left out for work on Saturday, I suggested taking Laura with me, but Granny said no. "How you gon' do your work with her tagging along behind you?"

Most of the restaurant's business for Saturdays was takeout, and during a slow period, I used the wall telephone to call Granny. It took eleven rings before she answered.

"Is everything alright there, Granny?" I asked.

She sighed. "Your sister went on over to that birthday party."

"You changed your mind?"

"Nah, child. I couldn't catch her. She probably would've stayed all day if Maggie hadn't sent Willie Mae over here to borrow some sugar. I had Willie Mae bring her on back over here along with a hickory switch. I stung them little legs good. Spare the rod, spoil the child. And that one sho'nuff spoiled rotten."

I hung up feeling fortunate that business was slow. I couldn't much concentrate on anything except Laura and Granny. I feared Granny was going to push my sister into an act of revenge, and I had no idea what Laura might do. Whether I wanted to admit it or not, we had come from a violent family.

Near closing time, my already bad mood took a turn for the worse when a young man entered the restaurant and placed a ridiculous order. It wasn't hot dogs or hamburgers that he wanted. He took a seat at the counter, and said, "Give me the liver and onions on rice with gravy and put a little broccoli on the side."

"That's not on the menu today," I said as I pointed to the erased menu board.

He was neatly dressed, had a tan-colored complexion and a quite pleasant smile. "It's always on the menu for me," he said. "Tell the cook that Troy is out here requesting his usual."

"I can tell Miss Betty what you want, but I don't think you'll get it," I said.

He winked at me. "I think I will. Where's Pam? I thought she was working here for the summer."

"She's off today," I answered as I moved toward the kitchen to tell Miss Betty about the arrogant young man.[1]

"Mr. Percy picks me up. I thought I already told you that," I said.

"Yeah, you did, but it's Saturday night. Don't you wanna do something else besides go home?"

....

1. Both versions of *Stumbling Blocks* contain an abrupt scene jump here.

I shook my head. "No."

"Come on," he pleaded. "I won't keep you out late, and maybe we can go dancing or something."

I explained to him that I was tired and I wasn't dressed for dancing or anything else. He lingered at the restaurant until Mr. Percy arrived, and all I could think was how lonely Troy must be.

Laura was lying quietly on the bed when I entered our bedroom. "I hear you went to the birthday party?" I said.

"Yeah. Gran—Miss Francine didn't let me stay over there."

"That's because you weren't supposed to go."

"I know," she said. "I got one little ol' piece of cake, and that's all. They got a lotta stuff for they birthday, Tangy."

"Did you give them their presents?"

"Miss Francine hit me," she said, ignoring my question, "and that ol' ugly Willie Mae pulled my arm."

I said nothing.

"You gotta get 'em for that," Laura said as she looked at me through half-closed eyes. "Mama said if anybody hit Edna, I'd have to get 'em, and if anybody hit me, you or Wallace would have to get 'em. So you gotta get 'em."

I laughed. "Laura, go on to sleep. Forget about it. I am not going to hit my grandmother."

. . . .

We missed another Sunday of church, and I feared that the longer I stayed away, the harder it would be for me to return, but Granny was unwavering in her decision.

On Monday morning, Mr. Percy asked why I was looking so tired. "Didn't you get enough sleep?"

"I'm alright," I said. "Mr. Percy, does Granny ever complain about watching Laura?"

"I ain't never heard her complain," he said. "I think she glad the chile is there to keep her company."

"I don't think so," I said. "Laura spends most of the day playing outside, and Granny watches the television. That's what they told me, so how can one be company for the other?"

"Company can be just knowin' the other person is there," Mr. Percy explained. "I done seen 'em laughin' and talkin' together, havin' a good time."

"I guess you're right."

"Sho' I am. Now, you ready to get behind the wheel of this car, try yo' hand at drivin'?"

"Granny said I couldn't."

"If you don't tell her, I won't," he said. "Just don't hit nothin' or get in no wreck."

We didn't have much time, but after explaining about the brake and accelerator pedals, he allowed me to drive until we reached the rutted stretch.

After the first few days, Mr. Percy would take the passenger seat and let me drive myself back and forth to work. The car still weaved a little, but mostly I was able to stay in my lane. It didn't matter much about the lanes because there was hardly ever any traffic coming toward Roanoke Pike. I followed Mr. Percy's instructions on driving, and I also heeded his warning about the restaurant and made sure I worked the following Friday. I saw what he meant about the tips. Friday's tips were nearly triple that of any other day.

....

On the Sunday that Granny decided it was time for her to get out of the house and go to church, I asked if I could call Crow before we left. She was in a rush. "It's been months since I went to church, and I don't wanna be late," she said. "You can call Clarence when we get back. He don't talk with good sense this early in the morning no way."

My grandmother was dressed like it was Easter Sunday and she was the star of the Easter parade. She wore a light blue tailored suit with three-quarter-length sleeves and a skirt that fit snugly against her hips. There was nothing old-fashioned about her outfit today. She had on a white hat with a light blue band, white beads and earrings, and she was carrying a white pocketbook. The only things that stopped her from being picture perfect were her flat black shoes, but I was sure people would overlook them considering she was recuperating from a broken leg. More and more often she was walking around the house without her cane, but she had it with her today.

Mr. Percy held on to Granny's arm as we made our way out the door and down the graveled walkway. We were very close to the car when Granny stopped and shook her head. "I can't make it," she said sadly. "This ol' leg don't wanna carry me."

I could see the disappointment on Mr. Percy's face, but he neither encouraged her nor argued with her. He just turned around and escorted her back inside. "I'm goin on, Francine," he said. "I didn't put on this suit for nothin'. The girls can come wit' me if they want to."

Laura went on with Mr. Percy, but I stayed with Granny. Nothing but sighs of frustration came from Granny as she sat on the couch. I knew how much she had been looking forward to going to church.

"You'll make it next Sunday," I told her.

"I don't know," she said, "but I know I ain't goin' back to work tomorrow like I planned. Ain't no way I can stand up in that kitchen all day."

"How about half the day?" I suggested.

She chuckled dryly. "I don't know about all of that. Percy might drop me off and leave me there all day. I ain't never seen no man so ready to see a woman go to work."

I did not respond to that. She knew as well as I did that Mr. Percy was concerned about her.

"You shoulda went on with them, Tangy Mae. It ain't right for you to miss all these Sundays of church fooling around with an old woman," she said. "Go on and call your daddy if you want. His number is taped underneath the telephone."

"Maybe later," I said.

At that moment I wanted to stay beside my grandmother, hold her against my bosom the way she had held me, tell her that everything was going to be alright, but I didn't. As the long awkward minutes passed with her sighing and me feeling her disappointment, I just held her hand. I thought about her restaurant and knew there was nothing I could say to make things better. Her discontent would probably last until she was able to go back to work. Maybe that was why she cried at night.

I got up, went to the door, and looked at the dirt paths that served as sidewalks along both sides of the street. Most of the houses had the same gravel passageway across their lawns to their steps as Granny's. It was no wonder that Mr. Percy was constantly repairing lawnmowers. It made sense that people would want somebody else to mow their lawns. I knew I wouldn't want to be out there with gravel being slung by rotating blades. Mr. Percy was lucky to still have both of his eyes. I turned back to face my grandmother.

"Your leg wasn't hurting until you started down the walkway," I said. "I think it was walking across that gravel that made it hurt."

"It was hurting before that, just not as bad," she said. "Look in my room and hand me them pills."

I was on my way to her bedroom when I remembered that there weren't any pills. Mr. Percy had gotten rid of them. We sat for nearly an hour before she was able to get up and change out of her suit, then she sat with me while I put supper on the stove. Granny had a way of tilting her head and looking at people as though she could read their minds, or like they were supposed to read hers and answer whatever question she had in mind. She was looking at me like that now.

"How come you call my boy Crow?" she asked.

"That's how he was introduced to me."

"But you call me Granny."

"You told me to," I said. "Crow never told me to call him anything else."

She sat at the table, stared through the tall windows. "Tell me about your mama, Tangy Mae. Tell me what kinda woman would call her own child a darkie?"

"She didn't call me that all the time."

"She shouldn't have never called you that. I know what kinda man would call his boy Crow. One that wouldn't let no woman tell him what to do. When Jim seen our baby, the first thing out his mouth was, 'He look just like a little crow, Francine.' It hurt me when he said that, but he never said it with meanness. He'd come in the house every day, proud as could be. 'How's our little crow today?' he'd ask. I couldn't get him to stop it, and soon everybody on the street was calling him Crow. I never did. I named him after my daddy, and he always been Clarence to me."

"I'll be glad when he gets here." I said.

"Me, too," Granny admitted. "You still wanna call him?"

I placed the call, but when a woman answered on the other end, she told me that he wasn't home and she didn't know where he was or when he'd be back. I dared to hope that he was on his way to Knoxville.

Shortly after I hung up the telephone, Mr. Percy's car pulled up in front of the house. Laura got out and slowly made her way inside, but Mr. Percy drove off. I watched my grandmother's face fall with disappointment. "Is he coming back?" she asked Laura.

Laura shrugged and went into the bedroom.

Granny limped to the front door without her cane. She stared out at the street, her head turning one way and then the other to take in the whole. When she turned from the door, her eyes were teary. "He's getting tired of me," she said.

CHAPTER 12

. . . .

Mr. Percy began staying away from Granny's house. She speculated that it was because he was upset with her that her leg wasn't healing faster. Miss Pearl has once told me that there was no fool like an old fool. She had been talking about her husband, Mr. Frank, but I guessed it applied to all old people. I watched my grandmother swallow her pride instead of the meals that I placed on the table for her. Everyday she would call Mr. Percy on the telephone, and everyday she practiced walking without the cane. If she really, really needed anything, Mr. Percy would bring it to her. He still brought her groceries over on Wednesdays, but he no longer lingered to talk or show concern. He no longer chatted with me on the drive to the restaurant, either, but at least he still drove me back and forth, and he still allowed me to drive sometimes.

In no way that I could see was I a part of their discord, but I felt the strain of it just the same. One morning I asked him if my grandmother had offended him in some way.

"Nah," he answered. "It's just that I'm tryin' to get caught up on some of that work I got piled up in my yard."

He wasn't a very good liar, and he concentrated too much on a road that he could have driven blindfolded. "She misses you," I said.

He shook his head sadly. "That's my girl. Maybe I'll see her tonight."

He didn't see her that night, nor the night that followed. I stopped mentioning my grandmother to him, but every morning when he picked me up, he would ask how she was doing. Although he allowed me to drive myself to work, it wasn't the same now as when he had been talkative and friendlier. I pulled up to the restaurant, and he didn't ask if it was my long or short day.

"I'll be here all day today, Mr. Percy," I said as he shifted over to the driver's seat.

So solemn was the expression on his face that I wondered if he even cared, but I thought I saw him nod his head before he pulled off.

Pam was angry when I entered the restaurant. She was standing at the counter filling salt and pepper shakers, and she barely glanced at me. "I ain't lazy, Mama," she shouted toward the kitchen. "I just wanna have some fun before school starts back. I ain't done nothing all summer but work in this restaurant."

"Yeah, but you been spending money 'bout fast as you make it," Miss Betty retorted. "You ain't bought not one piece of school clothes. And what about school supplies? You got the money for that?"

Pam looked at me and mouthed, "She makes me sick." Aloud she said, "Mama, you told me you wanted me to help out 'til Miss Francine comes back. When she coming back? Y'all better hire somebody 'cause I ain't gon' keep doing this."

Even as I put on my apron and unlocked the door for the day, they continued to argue back and forth. If I had yelled at my mother the way Pam was doing, chances are I wouldn't be standing here today. The one time I had dared to raise my voice and point a finger at my mother, she had broken that finger and silenced me.

Like mother, like daughter did not apply here. Pam was able to quiet her anger, put on a smile, and wait on customers. Miss Betty, on the other hand, kept a sour face all morning as she slammed pots and pans in the kitchen.

I was washing the breakfast dishes when Pam stuck her head in the kitchen and announced, "I'm leaving at one o'clock today."

Miss Betty didn't say anything, but I left the sink, joined Pam in the dining area, and asked, "Are you coming back tomorrow?"

She took a seat at a table. "I don't know. Don't you wanna have some fun, Tangy? All we do is stay up in this restaurant."

"I like having a job," I said. I wanted to sit with her, but I didn't want Miss Betty to bring her anger into the dining area and accuse us both of putting all the work off on her. She would say that sometimes even when she wasn't angry and we were busy working. "I'd better get back in there and finish those dishes."

"Wait!" Pam said. "We're getting together over at Charlene's house tonight. Why don't you join us?"

"I'll ask Granny," I said.

"Good. I'd help you finish up the dishes, but I don't wanna go in there with Mama," Pam said. "She been fussing with me all day, even before we left home."

"Are you gonna quit?" I asked.

She shrugged. "I don't know. If I don't do it now, I'll have to do it in a few weeks. School's gonna start soon. I'm gonna be a senior this year, and I ain't spending all my time at this restaurant. I don't care what Mama say."

Pam had been working most of the summer, but apparently she wasn't managing her money to Miss Betty's satisfaction. That was between them, but I had let them know that I was willing to work more days. I thought about what Pam had said about school. It was past time for me to start asking questions about getting Laura registered.

Miss Betty was quiet and peeling potatoes at a counter. Already she had two pots on the stove harmonizing a bubble and simmer and sending steam up toward the ceiling. She looked frazzled from the heat and maybe from the anger she had carried all day. I went back to the sink to finish washing the dishes. If I had my way, Granny probably would go broke because I would have hired a dishwasher.

"Hand me that pot," Miss Betty said, and I took it over to the counter where she stood.

"I don't know how much Miss Francine has told you about me," she said.

"Just that you've worked here for years, and she doesn't know what she would have done without you," I answered.

Miss Betty nodded. "Yeah, it's been some years." She dropped a potato into the pot and began peeling another one. "I got a son and a daughter. Pam is my baby."

I waited for her to elaborate on her children, but when she said nothing more I returned to the sink.

"When Crow comes home, he spends most of his time with me," she finally said. "The last time he was here, he had to take care of Miss Francine. I understood that. We been together since Pam was in second grade. My boy ain't never had no problem with it, but Pam can't figure why I wanna spend my time on a man that's gone more than he's here."

"You two are courting?" I asked.

"Courting? Yeah, I guess you can say we're courting. How do you feel about that?"

It didn't matter to me one way or the other. People, including Granny, assumed that because Crow was my father that I had some sort of special relationship with him. I didn't really know the man. I knew that I had bumped into him once at a whorehouse in Pakersfield, and he hadn't even known who I was. He had been wrapped around a woman named Leona Wright, and as far as I could tell Miss Betty was definitely a step up.

"It doesn't bother me," I said.

She abandoned the potatoes, placed her knife on the counter, and straightened her back. He lips twitched slightly at one corner before she spoke again. "Miss Francine likes to tell folks that Crow is an insurance man," she said. "Policy man don't mean insurance man. Crow 'bout crooked as the day is long, and he always got money."

I iked hearing things about my father, about his younger days, but I did not want to hear about him being crooked. I turned back to the remaining dishes. Throughout the afternoon and on into the evening, Miss Betty kept trying to get me to talk about Crow when I thought I had made it clear that I did not want to. When the last of the customers were gone for the day, she closed up the kitchen and took a seat on one of the stools. I was mopping the floor when she said, "You know, Crow . . ."

The minute she said his name, I changed the subject. "Miss Betty, do you have anybody in mind that you'd like to hire if Pam quits?" I asked.

She scoffed at my lack of subtlety, then said, "Nah. I guess we can put a help wanted sign in the window."

"We're spending about thirteen hours a day here with cleanup time," I said. "I think we need somebody who can relieve you sometimes."

"You trying to get rid of me just because I told you about me and your daddy?" she asked.

"No, ma'am, Miss Betty. But you're in the restaurant all day, every day. You must be tired."

Even Pam had commented on how tired her mother looked. Miss Betty was slowing down, making numerous mistakes, and the customers had begun to complain.

"You're right," she said in a salty manner. "I'm tired. I'm going home. You can lock this place up yourself."

She walked out of the door mumbling, left me alone with my mop and bucket. It didn't matter, though, because I knew Mr. Percy would be coming soon. I had a key and I knew how to lock up.

. . . .

Pam worked another two weeks before quitting. Her departure left me working every day from opening to closing, and Granny knew that it was too much. Juanita had moved away from Roanoke Pike, but she often came to the restaurant to see me. I tried to talk Granny into hiring Juanita, and she discussed it with Miss Betty one night. When she got off of the telephone, she said, "We don't wanna hire no more young people. Juanita would probably quit like Pam did."

"You'll be back soon," I said, "and I could help Miss Betty if we had Juanita to help wait tables."

Laura was always asleep when I left for work and tired by the time I came home. I needed to find a way to spend more time with my sister. Granny was reluctant, but I was persistent. Finally, she told Miss Betty to just go on and hire somebody, anybody.

It wasn't Juanita that Miss Betty hired. It was a woman named Gwen from Aiken, South Carolina. Gwen was in her midthirties, and she had worked in a school cafeteria before moving to Knoxville. "This ain't nothin'," she told Miss Betty. "It's a breeze after foolin' wit' children every day."

Gwen was sociable, and better prepared than I had been when I first started. Her presence shifted hours and responsibilities at the restaurant. It allowed Miss Betty to come in later two mornings each week, and on those day I got off earlier. I had chosen to get off early on Wednesdays to help Mr. Percy unload the groceries and so that he would not have to double back to pick me up.

It was on a Wednesday in August that Mr. Percy made his routine trip from the supermarket to the restaurant to pick me up, then on up Moon Road to Roanoke Pike. At Granny's house, I got out of the car wondering if I would have to cook supper today. I walked ahead of Mr. Percy as he carried two of the bags and I carried the other two. We found Laura and Granny sitting on the couch clinging to each other, both in tears.

"What happened?" I asked in alarm as I put my bags down and knelt beside my sister to check her for injury. "Are you alright, Laura? What's wrong?"

Mr. Percy had also placed his bags on the floor. He was checking Granny for injury. "Did you hurt yo' leg again? Did something happen to yo' boy, Francine? What the hell done happened?"

As anxious as we were for an explanation, we had to wait until Granny eased Laura's head from her bosom, then she used her fingers to wipe away her own tears. "I barely was able to save this child from Maggie," Granny finally said. "It scared me something awful, Percy. I ain't never seen Maggie act like that before. Look like to me she intended to kill this child."

My first thought was that Laura had stolen something from the Gearings' house. I knew my sister was a thief, and I had failed to warn my grandmother. I had hoped that new surroundings would end her need to steal.

"What did you steal, Laura?" I asked.

"Steal?" Granny questioned as she looked down at me. "She didn't steal nothing. Maggie wouldn't kill nobody for stealing. This child done went and cut the hair off little Angel's head."

"We was playing," Laura explained in a trembling voice. "It'll grow back. Mine grew back when Mama cut mine off. We was just playing, Tangy."

In the midst of all the crying. I rose from the floor and went into Granny's room to get her a handkerchief for her eyes. I heard her tell Percy, "I can see we got a little liar on our hands. I don't know what's wrong with this child, but I know good and damn well her mama ain't cut her hair off."

But Mama had. She had cut hair from the heads of all her children and hid it in a box under the floorboards in her room. During a moment of anger, when she thought I had run off, she had cut Laura's and Edna's hair to the point of bleeding scalps. Our mother had believed that if she held on to our hair we would stay with her in Pakersfield forever.

When I returned to the front room, Mr. Percy was patting Granny's back. "Stop cryin' now, Francine. It'll be awright."

"I don't know that it's gon' be alright," she said. "I ain't never seen Maggie that mad before. She came charging through the back door chasing after this child with murder in her eyes. It was all I could do to stop her. Thank God this one had sense enough to lock herself in the bathroom 'til I was able to get up off this couch. You might need to fix that bathroom door, Percy, before you leave." It was not in me to soothe or baby Laura at that moment. I felt that she was old enough to have known better than to cut somebody's hair. She should have remembered how she felt with no hair; after all, it hadn't been that long ago. Fear was bouncing about in my body. I was thinking that Miss Maggie might call the police and cause us more problems than we could handle.

"I hit Maggie hard as I could with this cane, mighta broke her shoulder," Granny said, "but she oughta knew she couldn't run up in my house."

Mr. Percy drew away from Granny, rose to his feet, and stared down at her.

"Don't look at me like that, Percy," she said. "What was I supposed to do? I couldn't fight her with a bad leg, and if she had got her hands on this child, it's likely we'd be making funeral arrangements right now."

Not another sister, Lord! I can not bear to lose another sister.

Poor Mr. Percy stood in the room with three sobbing females, and I think I was crying the hardest. Granny reached across the coffee table to touch me, and I cried even harder. Mr. Percy came to stand behind me. He placed his hands on my shoulders and gently squeezed, but it was Granny who said, "Tangy Mae, it's gon' be alright."

"What should I do about Angel, Granny?" I asked.

Granny slowly shook her head. "Nothing right now. I think we gon' have to give Maggie time to cool off. I don't know how long that's gon' take, and I don't know how bad she's hurt."

Granny passed her handkerchief over to me, but it was too damp to use. I wiped my tears away with the backs of my hands, then I stood up from my crouched position beside the coffee table.

"I need to call Crow, Granny," I said.

"What can he do?" she asked.

"I just need to call him."

She nodded her head, and I moved over to the telephone while Mr. Percy settled himself on the armchair. If I could have called Mushy, I knew she would have said, "Yeah, that's pretty damn bad, Tan, but it ain't the end of the world." She would have found me a way out of this mess. I had no idea what Crow would say. I glanced at my watch while I waited for Crow's landlady to get him to the telephone. It was 2:33 in the afternoon when the landlady answered, 2:35 when Crow came on the line and said, "Hello."

"Hey, Crow. It's me. Tangy Mae."

"Hey, sugar. Everything awright?"

"No," I answered. "Granny's okay, but I have a problem."

My tears resurfaced, and I was sure he could hear worry in my voice.

"What is it?" he asked.

"Laura cut Angel Gearing's hair, and then Granny hit Miss Maggie with a cane. Granny thinks Miss Maggie might call the police."

"Damn!" Crow swore. "Laura's wit' you, Tangy Mae? Why in hell didn't y'all tell me this befo' now?"

His anger was so loud and fierce that it came through the telephone. Granny and Mr. Percy stared in my direction.

"I thought Granny told you," I whispered, hoping that he would stop shouting at me.

"She didn't. Don't look like y'all been tellin' me much of nothin'. Got me up here thinkin' everything is awright when it ain't. Put Mama on this damn telephone."

"I will," I said, "but I want you to tell me what I should do, Crow."

"Go next do," he said. "See if Maggie is hurt and see how bad the girl's hair is cut."

"What if Miss Maggie is still angry?" I asked.

"You damn right. She probably mad as hell, but you gon' have to face this, Tangy Mae," he said.

"I don't have to face it," I said. "I didn't do anything. It was Laura."

I realized how immature I sounded as soon as the words were out, and Crow realized it, too. "So you plannin' on hidin' out?"

"I'm not hiding, Crow. I just don't know what to do."

He was silent for a moment, then he said, "Didn't you tell me Rozelle don't know where you at?"

"She doesn't."

"So she don't know where Laura is, neither. Damn, Tangy Mae, you done got us in a lotta trouble. Let me speak to Mama!" he said.

I called Granny to the telephone, and I said nothing more to Crow as she made her way over. She never said hello. She said, "Boy, what in hell is wrong with you? Don't be cussin' at this child like that. You yellin' so loud I could hear you halfway cross the room."

She listened for a minute, then said, "I thought Tangy Mae told you."

She listened again. "I don't want the police to come, but if they come, I'll talk to 'em."

Her face drained of anger and filled with worry as she listened to Crow. "What? What you say, Clarence?" She glanced over at me. I could see that her hands were trembling. "Lord, have mercy," she said, and this time there was no doubt that it was a sincere plea. "Lord, have mercy!"

When she hung up, she told Mr. Percy that Clarence would be home on Friday, but for right now she and I were going next door to set things straight. "Can't have the police coming. You stay with Laura 'til we get back, Percy."

Mr. Percy shook his head. "Nope. Uh-uh," he said. "I'd rather go over there myself. C'mom, Tangy Mae. Let's go next do', get this over wit."

CHAPTER 13

. . . .

The house was lived in. It wasn't as neat as Granny's, but it wasn't what I would call nasty. We stood because Maggie Gearing did not offer us a seat. She was angry and had no time to waste on hospitality. I guess we were lucky that she was even willing to speak with us.

"When I think about what coulda happened, Mr. Percy, I get all upset again," Miss Maggie said. "That child ain't had no business out there wit' no scissors. One of them children coulda fell on 'em, or she coulda cut Angel real bad."

Mr. Percy nodded. "How's yo' shoulder, Maggie? I'm kinda worried 'bout that."

Miss Maggie had not touched her shoulder until he said that, now she began to gently rub it. "It's awright. Miss Francine ain't got the strength she used to have. And I was wrong, anyway, goin' up in her house like that. I ain't even worried 'bout that, Percy. I'm mo' worried 'bout Angel's hair."

"She ain't cut or nothin', is she?" Mr. Percy asked.

"Nah, but you tell Miss Francine my girls ain't comin' back over there 'til that child is gone, and I don't want her back over here."

I had allowed Mr. Percy to do the talking, but he wasn't apologizing the way I felt he should have been. "Miss Maggie, I'm so sorry this happened," I said. "I'll do anything I can to make it up to Angel."

"What you gon' do?" Miss Maggie glared at me. "I thought y'all was decent girls, but y'all fooled me. I done caught that Laura twice tryin' to steal things outta my house."

"Why didn't you tell us?" I asked.

"What you gon' do?" Miss Maggie asked for the second time. "I told Miss Francine, and she didn't do nothin'. She too old to be tryin' to watch out for that bad child."

I suspected that Miss Maggie was the type of person who would go out and spread rumors about us, and now she had reason. I had entered her house apprehensive and contrite, but she had managed to alter my feelings with the hateful words that flew from her mouth.

"Laura is not bad!" I shouted.

"Shiiiit," Miss Maggie hissed. "It runs in the family. You make excuses for her like Miss Francine always made for Crow. I know no good when I see it, and that child ain't no good."

I was thinking that if I had Granny's cane, I would hit Miss Maggie across her head with it. I did take a step toward her, and she met that step.

"You wanna fight me? Come on!" she barked.

Mr. Percy stepped between us. "We didn't come to fight. We here to try to make things right, Maggie."

"Angel! Angel, come here for a minute," Miss Maggie called out.

All three of her girls came silently into the room, and I gasped when I saw Angel's head.

"Can you make this right, Mr. Percy?" Miss Maggie asked as she placed her hands on her daughter's shoulders. "Her daddy gon' have a fit when he get home."

The bulk of Angel's hair was gone. The little that remained stood up on her head like fur on a startled cat. She wasn't exactly scalped, but her hair had been cut very close to the roots. For sure Miss Maggie would not be able to braid it, but I thought it could be worked with. The sight of the girl's hair sobered me.

"I'm sorry," I said, more to Angel than to Miss Maggie.

"Just get on outta here," Miss Maggie said with the wave of a hand. "Just go."

When Mr. Percy and I reached Granny's walkway, I said, "Laura's just a little girl. I love her, and even I get angry with her sometimes. But other people don't seem to like her. I hate that, Mr. Percy, because I don't know what to do to make people treat her better. Even you. You don't like her."

He said nothing until we reached the steps. He sat down and asked me to join him. "It ain't that I don't like Laura," he said.

"You don't," I replied. "You're always nice to me, and you don't say two words to Laura. You did when we first got here, but you've changed."

He turned his face away from me, looked back toward the Gearings' house. "You remember the Sunday I took her to church?" he asked.

"Yeah. That was the last time you were nice to her."

Mr. Percy dropped his head, looked down at his lap. He pressed his calloused hands together, shifted slightly on the step. The sunshine on his eyes showed lines at the corners. He glanced nervously over his shoulder toward Granny's screen door. "I don't want Francine to ever get word of this," he said when he faced me again. "Laura stole money from the collection plate. I made her put it back, and when we was comin' home, I tol' her I'd have to tell Francine what she done. That chile tol' me, 'You better not tell nobody, Mr. Percy.' The way she said it felt like somebody had done po'd cold water down my back."

I must have sighed or given an anguished groan, something that made Mr. Percy glance at me with pity through eyes that were already weary with age. "Don't beat yo'self up," he said. "I know you mean well by yo' sister, but I don't know that you or Francine gon' be able to do much wit' her."

"What do we need to do with her?" I asked. "All children do foolish things. I know I did, and you probably did, too."

He cleared his throat, and still his voice was low and hoarse when he spoke. I had to lean toward him to hear his words. "Comin' back from church that day, she reached over, tried to unzip my pants and get to my privates. Tol' me she'd make me feel good if I didn't tell 'bout her stealin'. I pushed her away, then I stopped the car, made her get in the back seat. It's been gnawin' at me ever since."

"No. You must have misunderstood," I said.

"I wish I had, Tangy Mae. I wish I had."

Horrified, I could only stare at him. Because of his relationship with my grandmother, I had trusted this man. I had allowed my sister to go off alone with him. It was possible that he had tried to bother Laura, and she had fought him off. A lie could be his way of discrediting her story should she ever decide to tell, but she had mentioned nothing about it. It had to be a lie, though, because what would a nine-year-old girl know about making some man feel good? What I had to do was talk to Laura.

"Less of a man than me could spell trouble," Mr. Percy said.

I nodded because that was all I could manage.

We entered Granny's front room, and I stared long and hard at Laura to see if there was some change in her that I had been too busy to notice. She was sitting beside Granny on the couch, and I joined them. Mr. Percy took a seat in the armchair. "Maggie ain't hurt, Francine," he said. "She didn't mention nothin' 'bout callin' no police. Said somethin' 'bout Leon bein' upset when he get home."

"I'd be surprised if he wasn't upset," Granny said.

Laura rested her head on my grandmother's shoulder, a sure sign that she wanted to be babied and protected. As I watched my sister, I wanted to hate Mr. Percy, but I couldn't. He hadn't bothered Laura; he had told me the truth. I thought Mr. Percy needed Granny's shoulder more than Laura at that moment, and Granny probably needed his.

"Come on, Laura," I said.

I intended to take her from the room, but she clung to Granny and glared at Mr. Percy as though she sensed the truth had surfaced and that I now knew what she had done. Under her stare, Mr. Percy uprooted himself from the chair. "I got one mo' bag in the car," he said. "I'm gon' bring it in, then I'm goin' home to get some rest. You call me if you need me, Francine."

"I'll get that bag, Mr. Percy," I said and followed him out.

The bag was heavy with cans, and I stood on the lawn with my arms wrapped around the bulky bag, allowing the weight of it to anchor me as Mr. Percy drove off. Growing up was not easy. I had to face that fact before I could take another step. I had taken Laura away from all that was familiar to her. When I thought about the way our summer was going with me spending long hours at the restaurant and leaving her alone with virtual strangers, I knew I had to make some changes.

After supper, I had planned to take Laura to the backyard and talk to her, but Granny told me that she needed to talk to me. She waited until Laura was in bed, then she called me into the front room.

"You done brought trouble to my house?" she asked.

"No, ma'am. I wouldn't do that, Granny."

"Don't sit there and lie to me, Tangy Mae. Clarence told me that you run off from home and don't nobody know where you at. I thought you came to visit for the summer. He say the police could be looking for you. And you seemed like such a nice child when you first got here."

"I am," I said. We were sitting on the couch, and I kept my gaze focused on the surface of the coffee table, could not look at her. "I had to get out of Pakersfield."

"What kinda child are you that you run off and don't say nothing to your own mama?" she asked. "Clarence is a grown man, but he always make sure I know where he is."

"Yes, ma'am," I said.

"You go back there to that telephone and call your mama right now! Call a neighbor. Call somebody. I don't care how long it takes her to get to the telephone. I'll pay for it, but you've gotta talk to your mama." she demanded.

I glanced up when she said that. "Granny, I can't. I'll leave your house if you want me to, but I can't call my mother."

She sat there breathing heavily, staring at me. Finally, she gave a loud sigh. "I don't want you to leave. We ain't gon' do nothing 'til Clarence gets here."

CHAPTER 14

The house was already clean. Everything with the slightest speck of dirt had gone into the wringer-washer yesterday. We had swept, mopped, and waxed floors, polished every table leg and top, washed and rewashed dishes. While Laura and I cleaned over clean surfaces, Granny cooked up a feast for her son.

"Don't look like y'all washed down these baseboards," Granny said as she entered the front room.

We had, but I thought no amount of cleaning would be enough for Granny. She wanted things perfect for Crow, and she was determined not to use her cane during his visit. I couldn't see that happening. To me her cane was tantamount to a necessary appendage.

When a shiny black Thunderbird pulled up in front of Granny's house at two o'clock in the afternoon, she went out to the porch to greet her son. I stood against the wall of knickknacks and waited with my arms crisscrossed against my chest, my fingers gently touching the pulse in my neck. All of my tiredness had evaporated. I felt light, like I could float out into his arms.

No hat, no suit, but still he was the same man that I had met in Pakersfield— tall, dark, and my protector. He wore a light blue shirt tucked into the waist of gray pants. There was a matchstick between his lips that he removed before leaning down to kiss Granny. She was all hands, touching her son, patting his back, rubbing his thick arms, placing her hands on his broad shoulders.

When she released him and they stepped in from the porch, Laura said, "Hey, Crow. We been waitin' on you all day."

"Hey, Laura." He smiled at her. "I wadn't sho' you'd remember me."

I just stared at him. He stared back, and after what seemed a full minute, he stretched his arms toward me. We met beside the coffee table, and he drew my body to his, my head to his chest. What must have seemed an embrace to Granny and Laura was actually Crow inconspicuously rubbing his hands across the scars on my back.

Releasing me, he took a seat on the couch beside Granny. For a minute he glanced from me to Laura, then he let out a long, weary breath. I stood alone at the center of the room and watched him. Before my eyes, his face slowly clouded over with something resembling disappointment or worry. I wasn't sure which, but neither was what I had expected.

"I got your bed made up for you," Granny said. "I know you gotta be tired after driving all this way. You wanna eat first?"

"I'm gon' take a bath first, Mama. Let me get my things out the car."

After he had bathed, the four of us settled at the kitchen table for the feast that Granny had prepared. "Mama, we gon' have to open that back do'," Crow said. "I can't be up in here wit' all this heat."

"I been keeping it shut in case Maggie decide she wanna come over here again," Granny said.

"I'm home now, Mama," Crow said. "You can open yo' do'. Maggie and nobody else ain't gon' come in here and bother you."

I was still waiting on Crow to tell me how much he had missed me and how much he loved me, but I guess he had other things on his mind. I took the initiative and said, "I'm so glad you're here."

He smiled and winked at me before filling his mouth with food.

"When you get done eating, Clarence, I want you to go in there and get some rest," Granny said. "One of the girls can sleep with me tonight and the other one can sleep on the couch."

It was hours before bedtime, but when Crow was done with his meal, he heeded his mother's advice and went into the bedroom. I took Laura out back to the steps so she would not make noise and wake him. We sat in Fred's shade between the two walls. Laura wanted to play, but there was no one to play with.

The Gearings were still angry over the loss of Angel's hair. The girls, including Willie Mae, clung to their front porch or backyard everyday and watched Granny's house from a safe distance. They were the sentinels who protected the neighborhood children from Laura, stopped the other children in their tracks and turned them around. They even tried to keep Fred out of Granny's yard, but it didn't work.

"Laura, I need to talk to you about something," I said.

She sighed impatiently. "I don't wanna talk; I wanna play."

After my initial failed attempt, I had purposely put off talking to my sister about Mr. Percy until Crow arrived. Now I could do it. If it turned out that Mr. Percy had bothered Laura, which I seriously doubted, Crow would take care of it. I had known that I could not mention it to Granny.

"When you went to church with Mr. Percy that Sunday, did you take money from the collection plate?" I asked.

She glanced over at me. "I put it back."

"I know," I said, "but what else did you do? What did you do on the ride home?"

She made a move to get up, but I stretched an arm across her chest and blocked her. "What did you do to Mr. Percy, Laura?"

"Nothin.'"

"So when he told me that you unzipped his pants, he was telling a lie?"

Her lips quivered. She stared out at the yard and would not look at me. "I don't like Mr. Percy," she finally said.

"Is he lying on you?" I asked.

"It's yo' fault." She turned angry eyes in my direction. "You the one said we was crossin' the Georgia state line."

"And we did," I said, not knowing what one thing had to do with the other.

"Mama—" She paused. "Mama would put me and Edna in her car. She always said we was crossin' the Georgia state line, be we knew we wadn't. After the first time, we knew the men was gon' be there."

"What men?"

She shrugged. "The men."

"Laura, what men are you talking about?"

"Edna cried," she said, "but I didn't. Mama said I was a big girl, and I wadn't s'pose to tell nobody what we did."

Chills in the summer heat. I hoped she was not saying what I thought because no amount of money was worth it. How could they have endured the pain of it? An unpleasant, weightless sensation rushed to my head, and I thought I was going to faint. I placed my elbows on my knees, my face against my palms.

"What's wrong?" Laura asked. "You want me to get Granny?"

Touched by her concern for me, I lifted my head, held back my tears, and asked the dreaded question in as delicate manner as I could manage. "Laura, did some man put his privates between your legs?"

Bright, clear eyes stared out from an innocent face as she shook her head in denial. "No. That's nasty, Tan," she said.

I sighed with relief. "Thank God!" I whispered.

"Just in my mouth," she said.

A cry that I could not contain filled the space between the walls. It frightened Laura, and she moved away from me, got up from the steps. My cry brought Granny to the back door. "Girl, what in the world is wrong with you?" she asked.

"I thought I saw a rat, Granny," I lied.

"Turn 'round here and look at me," she said. "That didn't sound like no scared scream to me. Sound like you mad about something. I thought Maggie had done come over here and hemmed you up."

"No, ma'am. I guess it was just a squirrel."

"Your daddy trying to get some sleep. If you gon' be out there carrying on like that, then you need to move on out in the yard," she said.

I waited until she had moved away from the door, then I joined Laura in the yard. I gripped her shoulders, made her look at me. "Don't you know that putting a man's privates in your mouth is a bad thing to do?" I scolded.

She shook herself loose from my grip, kept her gaze on my face. "Nah, it ain't," she said, and all innocence gave way to a smirk. "Mama said you do it, too. And Tarabelle, and Mushy."

"I don't, I don't, I don't," I repeated, my voice getting louder each time I said it. "I don't, Laura."

"Yes, you do."

I scooped up a fallen apple from the ground and flung it at the tree. "I don't."

Laura mimicked me as though she thought I had suddenly decided to play a game with her. We gathered fallen apples from beneath the tree, then threw them and watched them smash into apple sauce against the tree trunk. Throwing apples gave my hands something to do that I wouldn't later regret.

....

Crow, when he woke up, led me out back to the lawn chair beside the fence. He reached over and lifted the chair from the Gearings' yard that he said belonged to his mother. I had seen it before, and it was identical to the one I was sitting in. I watched the sun set as a gentle breeze stirred in the space between me and my father. He asked questions and I explained my arrival at his mother's door.

"You know you gotta go back, don't you?" he asked just as the sun faded completely from the Tennessee sky. At the house next door, someone turned on their back porch light, and I wished they hadn't done it.

"Tarabelle is dead," I said. "Our house on Penyon Road burned to the ground. They sent Mama off to an insane asylum right after you left. She's back home, but I don't think she's well. There's nothing in Pakersfield for me to go back to."

There was no order to the way I explained things to Crow, but I needed to get everything out in a hurry. I needed for him to know why I could not go back.

"What happened to Tarabelle?" he asked. "She wadn't sick or nothin' when I left."

"Mama killed her, Crow. She set fire to our house with Tarabelle inside. She said Tara was trying to kill her. She may have been telling the truth since it was Tara who took the matches and gasoline out to the house."

"Damn," Crow said softly. "I'm sorry to hear that. Where y'all been stayin'?"

"With Mushy on Echo Road," I answered. "When Mama came home, she moved in with us. I had to get away from her. That's why I came looking for you."

"You can't stay here," he responded tenderly. "You ain't grown yet, and I can't have nobody comin' 'round here lookin' for you."

"I'm almost grown, and I wanna go to college, Crow." My voice was low and pleading. "Don't try to make me go back. I won't do it. If I can't stay here, I'll just go some place else."

He leaned forward on his chair. "I love you, sugar," he said. "I wish you could stay here wit' Mama, and go to college here, if that's what you wanna do. If you hadn't brought yo' sister, we wouldn't even be havin' this conversation."

Right away I got defensive, and it didn't matter that he had finally said he loved me. "What's Laura got to do with anything?" I asked.

"Everything. First of all, you kidnapped her. You tol' me don't nobody know where you at. You didn't bother to tell Rozelle that you was leavin', or that you was takin' Laura wit' you. That's kidnappin'. If the law lookin' for you, you done led 'em straight to my mama's house. If they catch me here, they gon' send me to the electric chair."

"Nobody knows it was you," I said.

"Rozelle looked me dead in my eyes when I cut that man's throat. Don't fool yo'self into thinkin' she done forgot it, or that she ain't gon' tell. If you stay here, you gon' start missin' yo' brothers and sisters. You gon' write 'em or call 'em or somethin', and we both know it. Wake up one mornin', and the law be standin' here ready to drag my ass back to Georgia. I gotta stay here a while, gotta get Mama moved off this hill. Mr. Percy say she cry all the time 'bout losin this house. It mean ever'thing to her. Mama gettin' old, sugar, and I have to let her know where I be. They'd get it out of her."

"Granny would die before she let anybody hurt you," I said.

"Yeah, but I don't want her to die. Ain't no way you can get Laura or yo'self in school here wit'out sendin' to Pakersfield for records."

What Crow said made sense. He had the winning argument, but I wasn't ready to give up. "Maybe I can change Laura's name and start her over in first grade. That way nobody will have to send for records," I said.

Crow chuckled and shook his head the same way Granny does when somebody says something ridiculous. "You'd need records, too, Tangy Mae. How you gon' go to college wit' no records?"

I dropped my head in defeat and thought of all the things that had happened to get us to this point. "If you had it to do over, would you still kill Chadlow?" I asked.

"Yeah," he said without hesitation. "I don't feel bad 'bout that. I left you safe."

He probably thought that he had left me safe, and I had to love him for that, but I also had to straighten him out. "You didn't leave me safe. You left me with Mama. You left me with a woman who lit a match and burned her own child up."

"Wait a minute," he said evenly. "You said yo'self that Tarabelle is the one had the matches. As much as I love you, sugar, I wouldn't stand still and let you set me on fire. What was Rozelle s'pose to do?"

"You still love her," I accused.

Deny it! Please, deny it.

"This ain't got nothin' to do wit' me lovin' yo' mama," he said. "This is 'bout me lovin' mine. I ain't tol' her nothin' 'bout what happened in Georgia, but I know I'm gon' have to sooner or later."

"I haven't, either," I said. "I know how to keep things to myself."

He shook his head. "Uh-uh, you don't. You know how to keep yo' mouth shut, but yo' face tells the tale. How you think I knew 'bout yo' feelins for yo' brother-in-law?"

Neither of us had noticed Fred until he leapt down from the fence beside Crow's chair. Crow hissed at the cat and stomped a foot against the ground, but Fred did not run. He turned his head and looked at Crow. Crow hissed and stomped again, and Fred finally ran off toward the vacant house.

"Shit!" Crow swore. "We put this chair in Leon's yard thinkin' it would keep that cat on the other side of the fence, but I see it ain't workin'."

I had no more interest in Fred than he had in me. He was just a gray shadow moving through the night, minding his own business. Heavy on my mind was this rejection by my father. I was sure he did not understand what he was asking of me. I thought for a minute that I should be like Fred. Nothing anybody did kept him away from Granny's house. If I could be sneaky like the cat and clever enough, I might be able to get Granny to come up with a plan that would allow me to stay.

"Being in Knoxville has kept me away from Velman," I said. "If I go back, I might fall in love with him all over again. Or I might turn out like Mama. I might go out to the farmhouse and screw every man that's got a dollar."

"I don't think you that big a fool," Crow said.

I had managed to anger him, and little else. He got up and started toward the house. As he reached the door, I called out to him, "How long can we stay?"

"I'm puttin' you on a bus first thing Monday mornin'," he answered.

CHAPTER 15

Saturday morning I awakened with the secure feeling that I had spent my first night ever under the same roof with my father. Crow wasn't there, though, and Granny said he had probably stayed the night with Betty. He should have stayed with me, been the first face I saw this morning and the last I would see tonight. He and Granny had already told me that I would not be returning to the restaurant. That felt like loss, as did everything else. I sat at the breakfast table with Laura and Granny and voiced my disappointment.

"Clarence don't see things the same way you do," Granny said. "He think he's doing the right thing. Maybe he is, maybe he ain't. I don't know."

"Can't you do something, Granny?" I asked.

"It ain't up to me," she said. "You shoulda called your mama when you first got here."

"She doesn't listen to me," I said. "She doesn't listen to anybody. She's a horrible woman. You don't know because you've never met her, but Crow can tell you. Ask him! He'll tell you. There's something wrong with her."

These were things I should have told my grandmother when I first arrived, and I had not. Now my words were weightless, had the ring of a child who had done wrong and did not want to face her punishment.

"I've never heard Clarence say one bad thing about your mama," Granny said.

"That's because he hasn't told you anything," I responded. Frustration had me out of my chair and pacing across the kitchen floor. My own grandmother doubted what I was saying. "Ask Laura. She'll tell you how bad our mother is."

"Tangy Mae, you settle yourself down. I ain't gon' try to get this child to say nothing against her mother," Granny said.

I felt like throwing my hands up, but instead I went into the bedroom and began packing our clothes into a suitcase that Granny had given me last night. I heard Granny ask Laura about Pakersfield. There were things I did not want Granny or anyone else to know, and honestly, I did not know if there was a way to explain some of it without telling it all. If I told her about the farmhouse, the men, would I suddenly become a whore in her eyes? If I told her that we had been forced to steal, would I lose her trust? I held a folded pair of shorts against my chest and listened to my own words come back to haunt me.

"We was born in a paradise," Laura said.

There was skepticism in Granny's voice when she asked, "A paradise?"

"Yes, ma'am. We rolled down grassy slopes over sweetgrass and four-leaf clovers."

"So it's a nice place there with your mother?" Granny asked.

Okay, this is it, I thought. Laura is going to tell her how awful our mother is. She's going to tell Granny that she's afraid of Mama.

Laura was silent for a moment, then she said, "My first remembered sound was the melody of Mama's voice singing a lullaby."

I had to put a stop to the lies. I stepped back into the kitchen and glared at my sister. She was sitting there swinging her legs back and forth, looking small and innocent. "What about Judy?" I asked. "Tell her about Judy."

Laura shifted her gaze from Granny to me. Her eyes filled with tears, and, with heartbreaking sincerity, she said, "Judy fell off the porch, and Mama cried."

Granny stretched her arms out to Laura. "Come here, baby," she said. "You poor child."

Laura rose and went into the outstretched arms.

"Granny, something is wrong with Laura," I said. "She's lying to you. Judy didn't fall off that porch; Mama threw her off."

Granny released Laura and stood. She took slow steps toward me. I was so used to being hit that I did not flinch as I stood there waiting for a blow. "Don't say things like that in front of this child," she said in a soft, admonishing tone. "You're old enough to know better. Tell me how come it is that there's something wrong with everybody, except you."

"There's something wrong with me, too," I said, "or you wouldn't be sending me back."

Stepping away from her, I went back to the bedroom, wished there was a door I could close. She followed and sat on the bed beside me. This time it was me that she held in her arms. I allowed it because I desperately needed some gesture of love.

"Tangy Mae, I know I got a way of saying things that people don't like," she said. "I don't mean to hurt your feelings, but what you did, sugar, just wasn't right. I know y'all didn't come from no paradise. You wouldn't be so on your head to stay here if things were good there. When I look at you, I see a lovely young lady that's got a lot inside she just can't talk about. That's alright. I got stuff in me that I can't talk about, either."

With my head resting against her chest, I listened to her words hum against my ear. Her dress smelled of fresh air and Tide laundry soap, like a garment straight off the clothesline. The tears that slide from my eyes, crisscrossed in a mixture of rejection and acceptance.

"I love you, Granny," I said.

I felt her chin bob against my head. She knew I was speaking the truth.

"Your sister is a troubled child," she said. "I knew that even before she cut Angel's hair. But if she can see something good in Pakersfield, you gotta be able to do the same thing. It can't be all that bad or you wouldn't have turned out this nice."

I said it again. "I love you, Granny. Please talk to Crow. Don't let him send me back."

CHAPTER 16

"Boy, I don't think you slept a wink all night," Granny grumbled. "You troubled about sending that child back? 'Cause you know you don't have to do it."

In the early morning stillness, her voice carried from the front room to the rear of the house. She and Crow were stirring about, and I was lying on his bed awaiting daylight, dreading the day ahead. Crow had spent the night on the couch, allowed me and Laura to keep the bed.

"Mama, if there was another way to do it, I'd keep Tangy Mae here forever," he said.

The two of them entered the kitchen. I could not see what was taking place, but I had become familiar with the sounds of the house. I heard the squeak of the bathroom door and utensils being pulled out in the kitchen. Granny hummed a church hymn until the bathroom door squeaked again, then she picked up the conversation right where they had left off.

"She's your child, and I don't see why you can't let her stay. I've gotten used to having a grandchild, and I want her to stay here."

A chair scraped against the floor, and I guessed it was Crow taking a seat at the table. "I ain't got no choice, Mama," he said.

"You always got a choice. Until the day you die, you always got a choice. You understand?" Granny asked.

Unless he nodded, shook his head, or made some other silent gesture, Crow did not respond. The refrigerator door opened and closed, water was turned on at the sink, eggs were cracked against a bowl, and finally Crow spoke.

"Mama," he said.

"What?" she asked. "You want toast or biscuits this morning?"

"Mama," Crow repeated. "How would you handle it if I went to jail?"

He was sugar-coating the situation for Granny. Jail was not his worry. Being put to death was.

"Jail?" Granny asked in alarm. "You talking about 'cause Tangy Mae brought Laura here without telling anybody? Just tell the police you didn't know—'cause you didn't."

"That ain't it," Crow said. "That's bad enough, but it's worse than that. S'pose some man hurt Tangy Mae? S'pose he hurt her real bad? It ain't like that cat that made you break yo' leg. A man got sense enough to know when he hurtin' somebody."

"Yeah," Granny agreed cautiously, "but Tangy Mae ain't got no broke leg. Ain't nobody hurt that child, Clarence."

"Yes, ma'am, somebody did."

The chair scraped against the floor again, and then I heard Crow's footsteps coming toward the bedroom. "Tangy Mae!" he called out. "Tangy Mae, wake up! I need you to come out here."

I wondered if I should feign sleep. Crow was talking about jail, and that could mean only one thing. He was about to dig up the dead, and Granny would have to smell the stench of something long ago buried. I did not close my eyes, but I lay still and silent hoping he would go away, go back to Miss Betty before he fooled around and said something that we would all regret.

Crow stood in the doorway. "Tangy Mae, I need you to come out here."

I rose from the bed and did not bother with shoes as I stepped through the doorway past him. Still wearing her nightgown, Granny stood with one hip against the edge of the sink. She held a wooden bowl in one hand as she watched my approach.

"Sugar, I want you to show Mama yo' back," Crow said as he took the bowl from her hand.

Granny reached out to retrieve it. "Boy, you better give me that bowl if you intend to eat this morning. You done forgot I'm goin to church? I gotta start gettin dressed."

Crow gave a disheartened sigh which caused Granny to frown. "What is it?" she asked nervously.

"Go 'head, sugar," Crow said to me, and after a moment's hesitation, I turned around, reached back, and lifted my pajama top. The gasp that escaped Granny was not surprising. I had heard the same intake of breath from nearly everyone who had seen the condition of my back.

"A man did this to her, Mama," Crow said. "A white man beat my child like this."

"Oh, my God," Granny groaned as she came to stand beside me. I felt her hand move across the rough, knotty scars on my back. Tears welled in her eyes as she grasped both of my hands in her own. She turned to face Crow. "Did you get him?" she asked.

"Yes, ma'am, I did."

The seriousness of Crow's dilemma registered in her eyes. "A white man? Is that why you're talking about jail?"

Crow nodded.

Granny took a seat at the table. I could see her hands trembling. She reached up, pinched the bridge of her nose to stanch her flow of tears. "Come over here, child," she said to me.

I took a seat beside her, and she slipped a hand beneath my top and once again fingered my scars. "Look like you was horse whipped," she said. "It ain't keloids, I don't think, but them some nasty looking scars."

"Yes, ma'am," I agreed. I had tried looking over my shoulder into a mirror once, but what I saw sickened me and I hadn't tried again. "It doesn't hurt anymore," I said. "This happened nearly a year ago."

"What happened?' Granny asked.

I looked into Crow's eyes for some indication of how much he wanted me to tell. He wasn't looking at me, though. He was staring down at the floor, holding a bowl that he had probably forgotten about. I thought he was miles away, maybe back in Pakersfield.

"There was this man named Chadlow, Granny," I started. "He thought I was disrespecting him."

"So he beat you?"

I nodded, then drifted into the telling while knowing that it would undoubtedly shake the foundation of our relationship, but I was finally ready for Granny to know. I told her of the things Chadlow had done to me before the night of the beating. He had been a powerful man in Pakersfield. He had been a friend of our sheriff, Angus Betts, and without any authority whatsoever, he had made himself the law that patrolled the Negro sections of our town.

It was last August. I had been designated by my mother to accompany Chadlow to the farmhouse. He drove us out and barely glanced at Miss Frances, the woman who ran the place, as we entered her kitchen. He was sullen and distant—characteristics I had never witnessed in him before. In an upstairs bedroom with the door closed, he pressed my head against his chest, and must have felt my recoil because he stepped back and spun me around so that I was facing the bed. To hasten the inevitable, I disrobed and took my place between dingy white sheets, where I transformed timidity and humiliation into emotional numbness.

Chadlow momentarily stood in the spot where I had left him. His eyes scanned the room and came to settle on the nightstand, where a lamp stood on a lacy, oblong doily. But when he moved, it was not toward the nightstand or the bed, but to the chair where I had placed my clothes. He rummaged through my possessions and lifted a single white sock from the pile, then came to stand over the bed. Fully dressed, Chadlow straddled my chest and pinned my arms to the mattress with his knees, stuffed my sock in my mouth, snatched up the doily from the nightstand and tied it over my lips.

Panic gripped me. I was used to doing whatever the men commanded of me, but this was different. The faraway look in Chadlow's eyes was terrifying. It was as though he no longer recognized me. I struggled against him, but his weight on my chest restricted my movements and rapidly exhausted me. I gagged as I tried to breathe around the sock in my mouth, then my nostrils took over.

Chadlow eased off my chest, then I felt rough hands on my body as he flipped me over. With my nose pressed against the mattress and my mouth stuffed, suffocation seemed imminent. I desperately tried to shift my body, slowly realizing that my arms, caught in a human vise, were extended awkwardly behind my back. My feet, the only mobile part of my body, kicked against the mattress, then cold metal clicked in place around my wrists.

"Rozelle's been telling me all about you," Chadlow said. He was winded from his struggle with me, and that gave me a smidgen of satisfaction. "Rozelle says you've been giving her a rough time, and that you're lazy, you won't help out at the house. You've been disrespectful, back-talking your own mother. Now she tells me you think you're better than everybody else, think you're better than me. Are you?"

With the sock shoved halfway down my throat, I couldn't answer him, but I managed to shake my head.

"You oughta be thrilled that I pay you any attention at all," he went on, "but Rozelle tells me that you don't want me to touch you. Is that right?" He paused, as though waiting for me to answer, then said, "I told your mother I would help her straighten you out. And I will, by God, I will."

It was pure rawhide that cut into my backside, and Chadlow brandished the weapon with expertise. Someone downstairs must have heard the whirr, hiss, crack of the strap as it struck my defenseless body, but if they heard, no one came to investigate. I closed my eyes, twitched and moaned with each excruciating blow, dug my toes into the mattress and tried to fade away. An inferno roared through my arms, legs, buttocks, and back.

After what seemed an eternity, Chadlow ended the beating. He had straight-

ened me out for sure, to the point where—if I survived this—I would say one last thing to my mother concerning Chadlow, then I would never mention his name to her again. Chadlow removed the sock and the handcuffs, and I plunged into darkness.

Miss Frances was sitting in a chair beside the bed when I opened my eyes. She was washing my back from a basin that stood on the nightstand. She spoke to Chadlow as she worked. "It's a shame you beat this child like this. For what?" she asked. "What she do? These sheets ain't never gon' be no mo' good. Blood don't wash out that easy. I'm gon' have to throw 'em away."

I ended my story on that note, putting emphasis on "blood" and "throw 'em away." Like a black granite statue, Crow stood there without making a sound. It took a while before he remembered the bowl of eggs in his hand. He placed it on the table as he started from the kitchen. "I don't want no breakfast this mornin," he said, "and, Tangy Mae, ain't nobody throwin' you away."

Granny reached out and grabbed his arm as he started past her chair. She looked up into his face. "You killed him, didn't you?" she asked in the most solemn voice I had ever heard.

Crow leaned down, kissed her forehead. "I know what you thinkin', Mama. You thinkin' we can't send her back to that. But I done took care of it. She ain't gon' have that problem no mo."

"Don't try to explain it to me," Granny said. "Clarence, my conscience would eat me alive if I sent this child back to a place like that."

My heart leaped for joy. Finally, I thought, compassion and common sense are taking control. Miss Betty had said that Crow always did whatever Granny wanted. I waited for him to succumb to her appeal on my behalf.

"She can't stay, Mama, and that's all there is to it," he said. "I know a little somethin' 'bout the law. You'd be in a world of trouble if they found Tangy Mae and Laura hidin' here in yo' house. They'd send me to the electric chair for what I done down there in Georgia, and we can't do Tangy Mae no good if you in jail and I'm dead."

"We can't do her no good if she dead, either," Granny said.

"I'm sorry, Mama, but I don't know what else to do."

"What kinda man are you?" Granny asked. "You can look at them scars and send her back to that town?"

"I took care of that. Ain't nobody gon' hurt her no mo."

Granny gave a grunt and a nod, then rose from her chair. She retreated to her room, and Crow called after her, "Mama, I'll be waitin on the porch when you ready to go to church."

"Nah, you go get dressed, too," she called back. "We're all going. We're going as a family."

CHAPTER 17

Nothing of significance ever changes in Pakersfield—or so it seemed to me. It is a stagnant little town with a railroad track running through the center of the business district. The same office buildings, stores, and shops have stood in the same locations for as long as anybody can remember. Forced, but limited, modernization came about thanks to my brother, Sam, and a few of his friends, who ignited fires on both sides of the tracks. Those structures have been replaced, and their newness only served to make the old look even more ancient.

From the bus station, all along Market Street, to Echo Road, I glanced the familiar from the back seat of a taxicab. Echo Road is located in a Negro section of town known as the flats, and it lies parallel to the tracks. Once again, I will have to accustom myself to the noise of trains and the way they make Mushy's little house vibrate. My solace comes from knowing that it is only temporary.

A heavyweight wasp was hovering in front of Mushy's screen door when we stepped up onto her porch. She had apparently been looking out for us because she pushed the door open and rushed us inside.

"That damn wasp been getting on my nerves for the last hour," she said. "I ain't never understood why something so free would wanna fly up in a house. All he gon' do is get trapped in here, and I ain't gon' rest 'til I kill 'im."

Same old Mushy, I thought. I dropped the suitcase and reached out to embrace her. After we released each other, she picked up the suitcase and took it into the bedroom that Laura and I had been sharing before we fled.

Mushy was sober. I hadn't smelled alcohol on her breath and her speech was clear. All the same, I scanned the coffee table for her treasured Mason jar of corn whiskey or bottle of liquor. The room had changed in my absence. Her two wing-back chairs were gone, as were her table lamps. Pictures on the walls, the record player, and the old rust-colored vinyl couch were all that remained.

Laura, standing quietly beside me, surveyed the room, then gave me a questioning glance. As soon as Mushy returned, Laura asked, "Where all yo' stuff, Mushy?"

"Richard took it. He went on back to his wife. For good this time." She answered Laura, but her eyes challenged me. "And don't ask me how I'm paying my rent, Tan, 'cause I ain't screwing nobody to do it. I'm working for the Munfords."

"Oh," I said in surprise. "You took Tarabelle's job?"

It was an innocent remark that she immediately took as snide. "You can't get in this house good befo' you start judging me," she snapped. "It ain't like Tara coming back for that damn job. It ain't like she wanted it in the first place."

I could see that I was going to have to earn forgiveness. The last thing I wanted to do was fight with Mushy. I wasn't good at it. While Laura watched the wasp through the screen door, I silently counted to ten, then made my way over to the couch.

"Where's Mama?" I asked.

Mushy shrugged, then sat down beside me. "I don't know. She was already gone when I came in from work. Hard to keep up wit' her anymore since she got that insurance money on Tara. They didn't wanna pay her 'cause they said she hadn't paid the policy for months. She wanted to know how she was supposed to pay 'em when she was in the hospital."

Although I had watched my mother scrape nickels and dimes together for years to pay the insurance policies on us, I felt she shouldn't have gotten one thin dime after murdering Tara. I kept my thoughts to myself.

"You know folks saying we drove Mama crazy," Mushy said, "like we the ones made her have ten babies. Mama hit the insurance man wit' her fist, and when she seen that that wadn't hurting 'im, she ran in the kitchen and got a skillet. I had to stop her from killing 'im."

Laura drew our attention by opening the screen door. "That bee gone now," she said. "I'm going 'round to Martha Jean's."

Granny had said it wasn't proper for girls to travel in shorts, so Laura was wearing a sleeveless beige dress with a sash tied in back. I knew she wasn't hungry because Granny had packed us a lunch. I wanted Laura to change into a pair of shorts, she didn't want to, and Mushy said, "Let her go."

The changing of the guards came easy for Laura. She simply went along with the sister who was more inclined to agree with her. I did not protest because Martha Jean lived only two streets over, and I knew Laura was anxious to see familiar faces again. Tomorrow I would take her into Stump Town to see Edna.

"You hungry?" Mushy asked. "I got some ham sandwiches and lemonade in the kitchen."

She was already up and moving. I followed her into the kitchen although I wasn't hungry.

"We got a lot to catch up on," she said as she took a pitcher of lemonade from the refrigerator and uncovered a plate of sandwiches. "What you done was wrong, Tan. You coulda left a note, or called, or something."

"I know," I mumbled. "I'm sorry."

"You took Laura, and didn't nobody know where y'all went," she said. "You left me here wit' a dead sister and a crazy mother. You probably never even wondered how I was gon' handle all of it."

I didn't think Mushy wanted to be angry with me, but she had been holding it in since I left and was ready to let it out. I sat there dutifully contrite as she kept throwing *you* at me as though everything was my fault.

"You selfish. You probably been off having fun while I been here seeing after Mama."

I was guilty of some things, but if Mushy hadn't been passed out drunk when I left, she would have seen me go. I would never say that to her, but I was ready to put a stop to the finger pointing.

"Why didn't you tell the sheriff that Mama killed Tara?" I asked.

"Why didn't you?" she countered.

"I couldn't."

"I did. That fat face bastard didn't believe a word I said. Pretty people like Mama don't lie, and they can't do no wrong. That's how the sheriff see her. He always did."

"You're pretty, too, Mushy," I said because she was. She was one of my mother's white children, and everything about her was well proportioned—from her facial features to her body. She had a personality to be envied whenever she wasn't drunk or angry.

A smile momentarily brightened her face. "I know," she said, "but I ain't screwing him."

With my own eyes I had watched pretty negate insanity and a lot more. The sheriff had seen Mama at her worst, in a catatonic state even. He had a wife, children, and a job to think about. I couldn't imagine him risking it all to fool around with Mama. The last time I had seen the two of them together he had been trying to interrogate her about the murder of Chadlow. Maybe he still was. That thought made me uneasy because one day she might remember and tell it all.

"How's Mama doing?" I asked.

"You'll see for yo'self when she gets here. After she went at that insurance man, the sheriff took her back to the hospital. They didn't keep her, but they gave her some pills. Sometimes she take 'em, sometimes she don't. She say she don't need 'em."

"Tell me about Sam," I said.

"After you tell me where you been and what you been doing all summer."

I drew my knees up onto the couch, faced my sister, and began to tell feasible half-truths. "I went to Knoxville to find my father, but he wasn't there. I spent the summer working in a restaurant and staying with the woman who owned it. Now I'm back. That's all there is to it."

"You coulda called."

All I could do was agree, apologize, and try to change the subject. "Tell me about Sam, Mushy."

"Wadn't nobody looking for Sam," she said. "'Bout a week after you left, Mama went to the sheriff to get him to find y'all. She wanted you to go to jail, but she wanted Laura back." Mushy chuckled as though she found the memory of it amusing. "Mama is a funny kinda crazy. One night she got up out that kitchen chair and went and got in the bed. Not the bed Harvey bought for her, but the one you and Laura had been sleeping in. I think she was sleeping in that chair 'cause she didn't wanna be in the room wit y'all."

Mushy was digressing, staring at me, but seeing a place where I was not. "Sam," I prompted to get her back on track.

"Wadn't nobody looking for Sam. Another week went by and the sheriff still hadn't found y'all. Mama told 'im she was going to the police 'cause she didn't think he knew what he was doing. He didn't. He was spreading word all over town that he was looking for y'all. One day somebody from the courthouse told him they hadn't heard nothing 'bout no Tangy Mae Quinn, but last year an army recruiter had sent a request for a birth certificate on a Samuel Quinn. Would that help?"

Now Mushy was laughing uncontrollably. One hand waved in the air, and she was leaning forward. The sight of her made me laugh, too, although I had yet to hear anything hilarious.

"Dumb, dumb, dumb," she said as she fought to restrain her laughter. "I don't know how that man ever got to be sheriff of this town. He was sitting right there where you sitting now, Tan, when he told Mama 'bout Sam. She come up outta her deep crazy, forgot all about y'all, and start talking 'bout her Sam."

"So where is he?"

"In the army some place in South Carolina. Sheriff went down there, come back talking 'bout some jude—jude—juderision."

"Jurisdiction," I said.

"Yeah, that's it." She poured us both a glass of lemonade. "Come on! Let's eat," she said, transferring the ham sandwiches and lemonade to the dining table, where we both took a seat. "I was gon' have everybody over tonight," she said, "but I ain't got no place for 'em to sit. That damn Richard took everything."

Richard Mackey had been seeing Mushy since she came back from Cleveland and had moved her into this house. Sometimes he would go home to his wife, but he always returned. Mushy would talk about him—his big feet, his slow speech—but I thought she loved him. Otherwise, why would she fight his wife over him?

I picked up a sandwich and began to nibble. Mushy obviously did not intend to talk about Sam. I let it go because other thoughts in my head were scrambling for attention. Already I knew that I was going to buy chairs and lamps for Mushy, but I also knew that I would have to stash my money with Martha Jean. I couldn't trust keeping it here with Laura in the house. I wondered if I should tell Mushy about Laura's behavior in Knoxville. Maybe later. I also wondered if I was in trouble with the law for taking Laura away from Pakersfield. Who would come after me? The sheriff or the police? What would Mama's reaction be when we came face to face? What would my reaction be?

Mushy, sitting across from me, seemed lost in thoughts of her own. She hadn't touched her sandwich or lemonade. She had propped her elbow on the table and was resting her forehead against her palm. She glanced over at me and tried to smile. It was a quick little twitch of the lips without the energy to sustain it.

"How come love always gotta be so hard?" she asked. "Harvey still beating on Carol Sue, and Velman talking 'bout leaving Martha Jean. He shoulda knew he was gon' have some problems when he married a girl that can't talk. He was doing the same thing to me that he used to do to you, always coming 'round here trying to get me to sign things to her. You know how depressing that is, sitting up in the middle of a fight, yo' sister crying and you ain't got no signs to make her feel better?"

Mushy was bringing me up to date on all the things she deemed important, and none of it was good. I realized how hard things must have been for her with all the problems and no one to discuss them with. She glanced around the kitchen, and I could see in her face what she wanted even before she raised a thumb and forefinger. She held them up, slightly apart to indicate a measuring of less than an inch.

"Just this much," she said. "If I could just get this much gin I'd feel a whole lot better." She gave a weary sigh as though blowing the thought away. "I'm seeing Matt now, but he don't want me to drink. Sometime I sneak and have one or two when I know he ain't coming over here. I like him a lot, but I been thinking he might have to go on 'bout his business and leave me alone."

"Who is Matt?" I asked, glad in a way that she had dropped the subject of family.

"You know him, Tan. Matthew." She said trying to jar my memory. "Matthew Pace."

"You can't mean my teacher, Mr. Pace."

"He ain't yo' teacher no mo'. I wish he'd loosen up some, have a drink every once in a while, have some fun."

Mushy was twenty-five years old. She liked flirting, having a good time, and alleviating her problems with alcohol. She wasn't above getting rowdy and combative in the face of a competitor, as Brenda Mackey could attest. Mr. Pace, on the other hand, was the epitome of sophistication. He was about ten years older than Mushy, and he had a protruding forehead that made his eyes appear sunken in his face. I had once thought his head was shaped like that to keep all of the knowledge from spilling out. If he was courting Mushy, then he wasn't nearly as intelligent as I had thought. I could only imagine the epithets she came up with for him after hearing all of the things she had called Richard.

I finished my sandwich and the lemonade that needed a little more sugar. Since I hadn't been hungry to start with, I didn't know if the heavy feeling in the pit of my stomach came from overeating or from dread. Wasp or no wasp, I got up from the table and went out to the front porch. Staying in Pakersfield was not something that I wanted to consider, but I didn't know how I could possibly leave Laura with Mushy, who seemed to be carrying the weight of our entire family on her shoulders already.

Mushy left me alone for just a short while before coming outside. She sat beside me on the step and almost immediately began to complain about mosquitoes. Children ran back and forth along the street, always slowing to speak to us as they passed by. A group got together in front of Miss Mable's house and decided to play a game of Hide and Seek. As dusk slowly crept over Echo Road, we watched the children scatter for hiding places. Marsha Crothers held a finger to her lips to hold us in secret as she found a hiding place beside Mushy's house. Little Jerome Daniels, the youngest in the game, passed the house three times searching for hidden players. Because he was having such a hard time of it, I gave Marsha up. I pointed a finger toward the side of the house, and Jerome found his first hider—only seven more to go if my count was right.

"Why'd you do that?" Mushy playfully chided.

"He'd be out here all night trying to find somebody," I said. "At least now he has somebody to help him."

Mushy slapped then flicked a mosquito from her thigh. "I coulda used somebody to help me," she said. "Wallace and Edna the only two I didn't have to worry 'bout all summer." She gave a final slap to her thigh, then stood up. "I'm going back inside. These damn mosquitoes 'bout to eat me up."

"I'm gonna walk around to Martha Jean's to get Laura," I said.

"No need. Here she comes now."

Laura was slowly making her way toward the house. She stopped to talk with Marsha and several of the other children. It surprised me that Martha Jean had allowed Laura to walk home alone; after all, it was dark now. It also occurred to me that Laura may not have gone to Martha Jean's house. I called out for her to come on home, but she waved a hand at me and said, "I'll be there in a minute."

The minute we stepped inside Mushy began to talk about Martha Jean and Velman. "He didn't know what to do," she said. "He came over here five days in a row asking me if I could talk to her. I realized them old signs I made up when she was a little girl just wadn't working no more. I went up to Mr. Hewitt's house to ask him if he could teach Martha Jean something. He said it might be too late, that he told Mama a long time ago to send Martha Jean to a school for deaf children in North Carolina. She wouldn't do it, and he couldn't make her."

Mr. Hewitt was the principal at the Plymouth School for Negroes. I already knew about the school for deaf children, but Martha Jean was no longer a child. Mama had objected to sending her to the school because it would have meant staying there for most of the year. Now Martha Jean was a grown woman with two daughters and a husband that she was having trouble communicating with.

"Mr. Hewitt sent me to Matt," Mushy continued. "Matt got a friend, Robert Bradford, a teacher live in Smyrna. He been teaching 'em to use signs. Twice a week he teach 'em. He come to Pakersfield on Tuesdays, and they go to Smyrna on Fridays. Sometimes I go with 'em. It's gon' be a long time before they be able to use them signs to talk to each other, but at least now Velman know how hard it is for me to make Martha Jean understand everything he want her to know."

All of those years of watching the rest of us go to school, and now Martha Jean was finally getting her chance. Mushy had made that happen, and I loved her for it. I wondered what our lives would have been like if she had stayed in Pakersfield instead of running off to Cleveland all those years ago. Even if she did drink a little too much, Mushy was still the backbone of our family.

"I love you, Mushy," I said. "You've always known how to get things done."

She smiled. "Tomorrow I'm gon' show you how to sign your alphabets, Tan, but right now I'm going to bed." She paused at her bedroom door and asked, "Did Matt always correct you when you talk?"

"Yeah, he always did," I admitted.

"That's what he try to do to me, but I think I'm catching on to them signs a whole lot faster than him."

She went to bed, and I went back outside to get Laura. We were home and still we had not seen Mama. It felt natural, though, because I had already begun to put an emotional distance between myself and the woman who called herself my mother.

CHAPTER 18

She made a quiet entrance like one more ghost floating into my life. The bedroom light came on, and even through closed lids the glare of the bare bulb irritated my eyes. It took several seconds of squinting before I was able to focus on anything in the room. Standing in the doorway, wearing a light blue summer dress, was my mother. Her hair was swept to one side and hung in curls at the front of her right shoulder.

My first thought, as my eyes adjusted, was how I'd like to change the color on her lips. They are so heavily coated with lipstick that her mouth looked bloody. Those lips had been painted by the unsteady hands of intoxication. I knew she had been drinking even before the whiff of alcohol reached my nostrils. She was staring at me, and I wondered if she could see the fear and loathing inside of me.

"Hey, Mama," I croaked in a voice heavy with sleep.

"Get out my damn bed!" she said without a single slur to her words.

While I pulled myself up to stand between the two beds, Mama stepped into the room and looked down at Laura, who was using the sheet to block the light from her eyes.

"My baby," Mama said as she pulled the sheet away. "My baby. I thought you was gone for good. I thought I'd lost you." She sat on the edge of the bed, drew Laura into her arms, and painted my sister's face with lipstick kisses. Keeping her eyes closed, Laura pressed her face closer against Mama's chest and accepted the kisses.

I dropped down onto the smaller bed and sat there watching my mother shower Laura with affection. The need for sleep gradually left my body like a warning that I would be in danger if I closed my eyes. It was a cramped room with the two beds and a dresser, no space to run if the need arose. The small bed was pushed against the wall and the only window in the room. My mother's presence seemed to still the night air that had been drifting in through the open window. The aura in the room became oppressive, and I suddenly felt trapped and claustrophobic.

Mama didn't bother to remove her dress as she laid on the bed, kicked off her shoes, and draped an arm protectively across Laura. "Turn that light out!" she said. Although she did not speak my name or turn to face me, I knew her words were meant for me.

Forever the obedient child, I got up to turn the light off, squeezed my way between the two beds. My watch, which I had taken off before going to bed, was laying atop the dresser that stood at the foot of the beds. I paused long enough to pick it up and check the time. It was a little after midnight, too many hours to go before daybreak. I turned off the light and kept walking until I reached the front room, where I could breathe freely. I did not trust my mother and I did not want to be hemmed up in the room with her.

As I stretched on the couch, I knew that I was not going to sleep, and I was thinking that I should not have left Laura in the room with Mama. If I tried to move her, though, I was sure it would make Mama angry. So far she had shown no threatening behavior, but I knew from experience that she had a way of striking out when it was least expected. I intended to keep my guard up.

For as long as I could, I stayed awake, stared into the darkness, and tried to plan my next move. If Mama was taking her pills and getting better, then Laura would be alright staying with her. It was not what I wanted, but I didn't have many choices. Martha Jean had a husband and two daughters of her own. I couldn't even trust myself around her husband, and God only knew what Laura might do if she was thrown into that household. All of the rest, except Mushy, would need permission from someone else to take Laura in. Wallace lived with Mr. Grodin, Harvey was married to Carol Sue, and Sam was away somewhere in the army. It all came down to me or Mushy unless I could get Miss Pearl to raise Laura along with Edna.

Too much thinking and trying to stay awake had given me a slight headache. I found myself nodding off, jerking awake, then nodding off again. Maybe if there had been some sounds in the house, I could have concentrated on that and stayed awake. I felt a little foolish trying to fight off sleep while worrying about things that were more or less out of my control.

I finally fell asleep with pleasant thoughts of my grandmother. There were no dreams or nightmares to bring on a feeling of suffocation, and yet I could not breathe. Each time I tried to suck in air, the flow was stanched by weighty darkness. So heavy was the weight being pressed against my face that I could not turn my head. Panic caused my arms and legs to flail. My hands went up to free my face, and my hands touched soft hands. Death was heavy on my chest. I could not scream, but I kicked until one foot bumped against the coffee table. I kicked again and again, felt the table shift, then heard it toppled to the floor.

I was free and gasping for breath. What I was able to see through the infant light of dawn was Laura standing in the bedroom doorway. Beside the overturned coffee table was a bed pillow, and on the floor Mama and Mushy were struggling with each other. Mushy had the upper hand. She was sitting on Mama and holding onto her arms.

"Come on, Tan!" she managed to say between breaths. "Help me hold her down."

Mama was kicking and straining to free her arms from Mushy's grip while spittle and profanities flew from her mouth. Still shaken and trying to recover from near suffocation, I dropped to the floor and sat all of my weight across Mama's legs. The strength of her struggle bounced me up and down, but I held on.

"Forget her legs," Mushy shouted. "Come get one of her arms."

We were surely going to Hell. I knew that even as I shifted from Mama's legs to her arm. Along the way something went wrong. Either Mushy released the arm too fast or I wasn't holding on tight enough. Mama managed to free one arm, and the second it was free, she reached out and clawed into my sister's arm. Mushy drew her hand back, then slapped Mama across the face with a cracking sound that seemed to echo across the entire front room. My eyes followed the sound of the echo, and I saw Laura standing in the doorway of the bedroom watching us.

"Can you hold her down while I get her pills?" Mushy asked.

"You know I can't handle her by myself," I said.

"You gon' have to or we'll be here all day," Mushy said as she lifted her weight from Mama and rose from the floor.

. . . .
1. Both versions of *Stumbling Blocks* contain an abrupt scene jump here.

NO ORDINARY RAIN

CHAPTER 1

Alabama Wheaton wondered how so many troubles could befall one man. Every time he thought that life was giving him a break it would turn around and treat him like a twig, try to break him in half. He was a strong man, though, and he wouldn't let poverty, last year's drought, or a pregnant daughter wear him down. Anger had boiled in him for several months now, ever since he'd been made aware of his daughter's condition. What enraged him most was her refusal to tell him whose seed she was carrying. He had never spared the rod with his two sons, but he had never known quite what to do with a girl-child. He had chastised her enough times to teach her right from wrong, had warned her not to be a fool long before she even knew what a fool was.

Heavy with child and a child herself, his daughter, Mildred, lagged behind him in a Georgia cotton field. It was May of 1933, and the fields of Butcher County were sprouting little more than weeds and regrets. The region had endured a prolonged drought where the crops and livestock suffered and the water receded in the river. April had brought a few light showers that did not completely satisfy the soil. Mildred's family didn't have much, didn't ask for much, but today, as they glanced up at a changing sky, they grew excited by the prospect of rain.

"I done seen this kinda sky befo'," her daddy said. "It don't mean nothin'. Don't y'all be gettin' yo' hopes up 'bout somethin' might never happen."

While Mildred, her mama, and her two brothers returned to their work, her daddy, Alabama Wheaton, studied the sky. They all glanced up and around as the clouds came together and darkened the field. Her daddy dropped to his knees and began to pray aloud. He asked God for enough rain to keep them working for the season. He told God things that God already knew—how the well was running dry, how no vegetables were growing in their garden plot. He told God that the fields and even the animals needed water. He admitted to being a sinner-man who was now carrying the sins of his daughter.

Mildred wished that he would be quiet or at least pray in a whisper that only God could hear. She was sure that people in the other fields could hear him. He daddy desperately wanted rain, though, and his voice grew louder in the stillness of the earth. "Lord, tell me what you want me to do, and I'll do it," he prayed. "Maybe a little rain will help wash our sins away, and we'll be better for it. Please, God, send us some rain."

The first drops, when they came, fell like a tease. We might soak the soil or we might blow over, the clouds seemed to suggest as they parted, gathered again, then hovered over Blevins Stretch. Mildred saw her daddy rise from the ground, glance toward the sky, then nod his head as though he and God had reached an agreement. Without warning, the wind howled, the clouds opened, and the land was blessed with a downpour.

Tears mixed with rain on Mildred's face. Last night and all this morning she had been burdened with an ache in her back. It wasn't a pain that she couldn't endure, but it was a worrisome throb in her lower back that hoeing weeds hadn't helped. She stumbled toward her brother Ruben. "I think I saw lightnin'," she said.

"I didn't see nothin'. I don't think Daddy saw nothin', neither. He don't seem to be in no rush," Ruben responded.

"Daddy's talkin' to God and pointin' a finger at me," Mildred said, "Let's go, Ruben! We can't work in this rain. It's comin' down too hard."

Reaching home for the Wheatons meant walking into the face of an escalating wind. Mildred's oldest brother, James, came up beside her and took the hoe from her hand. Together the three Wheaton children trudged across the field in the direction of home. Because she wanted it to be so, Mildred imagined that their daddy was supporting their mama, holding her arm to keep her from blowing over. When she actually glanced back, she witnessed her mama struggling across the field on her own. "James, go back and help Mama," she bellowed into the wind. "I'll be awright holdin' onto Ruben."

The discomfort of being drenched, wind-tossed, and rain-slapped made Mildred ignore the pain in her back as they rushed along. Lightning was dazzling a distant sky by the time they reached their yard, and Ruben fought his way through the blowing rain to make sure the chickens were secured. Mildred entered the house alone. She stepped out of her shoes just inside the door, went into her space, and pulled the curtain across the rope. She heard the footsteps of her family as they crossed the threshold. James questioned how long it might rain, and she heard her daddy say, "Just be glad we finally got it."

Throughout the house came the sounds of wet clothes being removed and the rumple of dry clothes replacing them. Mildred's brothers shared the area just beyond her curtain and her parents had the bedroom at the rear of the house.

Nobody bothered her in her space as long as she kept her curtain drawn. She intended to keep it that way until everybody was asleep for the night.

Another pain, a different kind, ran through her back, and she gritted her teeth. As the pain eased she removed her wet britches and for a moment stood touching her abdomen. Neither she nor Jonathan had been particularly proud of making a baby, but alone in the woods they had discussed whether it should be a boy or a girl. Even if Mildred had wanted to be happy, her daddy's anger wouldn't have allowed it.

From behind the curtain she could hear her daddy and brothers talking in low voices at the kitchen table. As a family they respected storms and everything else God sent their way, so it surprised Mildred that they were engaged in conversation. There was excitement in her daddy's voice that she hadn't heard for a long time. She was sure the rain had done that, had washed away some of his gloom if nothing else.

"If I knew for sho' that Mr. Blevins was gon' let us stay, we could work on gettin' us a cow," he told his sons. "Then maybe later we can get a mule."

"Daddy, can't we work on gettin' me a pair of boots befo' we start on a cow?" James asked. "Them I been wearin' ain't gon' hold up much longer."

"You go into Cranston when you leave work on Saturday afternoon, James. See can't you get Charlie Watkins to fix them shoes," her daddy responded. "How yours holdin' up, Ruben?"

"I reckon they'll last 'til winter," Ruben answered. "Daddy, why can't we keep gettin' our milk from Mr. Jack? A cow take a lotta money to feed and keep healthy."

"Sometimes, Ruben, you just gotta have your own," their daddy replied. "I figure we'll get out there in that field and work toward gettin' us a cow, and then we'll work on gettin' a mule and our own land. We gon' have to work even harder than we been doin'. Mr. Taylor told me last week how Mr. Blevins talkin' 'bout gettin' one of them new irrigation systems. I reckon that's why he lettin' folks go, so he can pay for it. Let me see them boots, James. See if I can't do somethin' wit' 'em 'cause it look like we gon' be workin' a wet field come mornin'."

No, Mildred thought, I can't do it. That rain is giving my daddy hope like that's money falling from them clouds. If Jonathan don't marry me soon, I'm gon' tell my daddy this his baby. I don't mind the work; I'm used to it, but this baby can't take it.

Outside, the wind gave a howl that shook the house. Inside, Mildred sat waiting for a break in the weather. It didn't have to stop raining, just slow down long enough for her to meet Jonathan at the forest of pines. Jonathan was smart and he worked at a store over in Mays Spur. He said that money was slow in coming, but his boss was going to pay him soon, and he'd have enough for them to get married. Sometimes they would stretch out side by side in the forest and Jonathan would tell her to close her eyes and step into his dreams with him. He had dreams of wealth, of a better life, of moving away from Butcher County, of owning his own store some day. As hard as she tried to picture his dreams beneath her closed lids she could never see them.

Beside her bed was a wooden box that her daddy had made for her one year for her birthday. The only things inside were a comb, two white buttons, and Jonathan's lucky coin. Mildred took the coin from the box and rubbed it between her fingers. It was a flattened beau dollar that Jonathan's daddy had given to him. Jonathan had told her to hold onto it until they were married. If she were lucky enough, Jonathan would marry her come Saturday. She would never have to return to the field, and she would no longer have to hold on to their secret.

She replaced the coin and tried to think of something other than Jonathan, but she couldn't. At the age of sixteen Jonathan was a handsome young man. On his tan-colored face was a shadowing of fine hair that initiated him into manhood. He had made it all the way through eighth grade over at the school in Mays Spur, and then he had been smart enough to get a job at the Dupree's store while other young men were looking for work. Once again Mildred closed her eyes and tried to bring forth the dreams that he wanted her to see. They weren't there.

CHAPTER 2

So fierce was the storm that rain formed a swirling pool in the space between Morgan's Mortuary and Dupree's General Trading Store. Jonathan had rushed out of the store only to be halted by the ominous weather. He murmured his entire vocabulary of profanities as he witnessed what was taking place around him. He needed to be on the run, but the wind was too high for that. It would carry him, slam him into a tree, house, fence, anything in its path. He knew without a doubt that the storm was retribution for what he had just done. He had stolen from his boss, and he was going to get caught. It hadn't been planned, but the opportunity had presented itself and he had taken advantage.

Andrew, the boss's nephew, had been sorting through the inventory when a rodent frightened him from the center room. Inventory was unclaimed articles left too long at the store, and Mr. Dupree had plenty of it. There were rows of shelves heaped with the wealth of people fallen on hard times—jewelry, broaches, watches, and rings. Jonathan had stuffed as much as he could into his pockets before fleeing the store. He had even snatched a pocket watch from a hook on the top shelf.

As he stood on the walkway where an overhanging roof provided moderate shelter, he was torn between the fear of moving forward into the storm or backward into the store. He had the feeling that he was being watched, only who could see the guilt on his face through the pouring rain? On the opposite side of the street was a pencil factory, and the wind was playing with a corner of the roof, lifting it and slapping it back in place. Farther down was a residential area with three of the oldest and most stately houses in town. The largest one belonged to Miss Dora Cranston, the wealthiest and most respected woman in Butcher County. Jonathan thought the mortuary had been built in the perfect place since death from old age would soon place the Lowell Street residents before the mortician. He had never had a fondness for old things or old people. He especially disliked the old man he worked for.

Mason Dupree had never been a good boss, and he hadn't paid Jonathan over the last five months. In lieu of pay he offered "eat by today or rot by tomorrow" potatoes from a bin or something else that was going bad in the store. Jonathan had told him, "I need my pay, Mr. Dupree. I can grow my own potatoes."

"Then maybe that's what you oughta do," had been Mr. Dupree's response. "There's a hundred boys just like you would take this job and be glad to have it."

Jonathan's mother had taken him to work with her at the Blevinses' fields, and when that hadn't worked out, she had made a deal with Mason Dupree. Without consulting him, they had decided that Jonathan would work without pay for a week to prove his worth. If his work was satisfactory, Mr. Dupree would hire him. Jonathan thought it was a bad plan and an idea that his mother should have kept to herself. She had opened a door whereby Mr. Dupree could keep getting men on a trial basis, get the work done, and never have to hire anybody.

He had hired Jonathan, though, and had paid on a regular basis at first. Even after his pay dwindled and finally dried up, Jonathan had held on to the job with the hope that things would get better. The job consisted mostly of running errands, lifting boxes, moving barrels, keeping the store clean, and killing rats. Dupree's General Trading Store, three rooms long and stretching the entire length of the walkway, had only one door open to customers. That door was up front where groceries and tobacco were sold. There was hardly anything, except maybe livestock, that Mr. Dupree and his nephew, Andrew, wouldn't barter over. They had a tall, sturdy cabinet where guns were tagged and locked away, and another where small items were locked away at night. If a customer had not reclaimed his property by the allotted time, the items were placed in the center room to be sold.

A gust of wind blew across the walkway, and Jonathan grabbed hold of a porch post to steady himself against falling. Soggy debris and clattering cans were rolling all along Lowell Street, and he thought he heard the bray of a mule near the feed store. He glanced in that direction, saw nothing but sheets of rain. He wondered if the overhang would endure the storm and if the roof would hold on the pencil factory across the street. He wondered why neither of the Dupree men had come to the door to glance out. They probably assumed he was closing down the shutters since that was one of his responsibilities, but maybe they had discovered the theft. He had to get away from Lowell Street, only he didn't know how when even the wind had turned against him.

Rain had widened gaps in the overhang all along the walkway, and the widest one was right over his head. He stood like an idiot braced against a post to keep from being carried like debris. If his luck hadn't been bad already, he might have blamed it on the black cat that darted across his path last week. He had always had an arm for throwing, and that was just what he did. He'd picked up the largest stone on the road, flung it at the cat, and caught it midair in a leap toward Tarlo Medfield's fence. Even before he'd spotted the cat, bad luck had been with him, was all he'd ever had. Mildred was still nagging him to marry her, and Mr. Dupree still wasn't paying.

He gave Mildred rock candy and promises, and he despised Mr. Dupree a little more each day. Every night at closing Jonathan would cover the barrels and food supply with heavy canvas to deter the rats. Sometimes he would sit on a barrel in the storeroom and just wait for a rat to sneak in from under a board. All he had to do was be quiet and wait with something heavy in his hand. The last time he had spotted a fat, sluggish rat that had probably gotten hold of poison, he pretended it was Mr. Dupree. He beat the thing to a pulp and didn't notice that blood had splattered all over the canvas until the next morning.

The sound of thunder was close. Jonathan had seen no lightning yet, but it was coming. The thunder alone frightened him enough to let go of the post. Wind carried him back against the store's wall, where he dropped and covered his head with both hands. *Of all the days I could have stole, why today?* he wondered. *Nobody's gonna buy this stuff. It's like Mr. Dupree said, "Ain't nobody got no money."*

He didn't know have long he stayed huddled on the walkway, but it was long enough to dampen his clothes. Three times he had thought about stashing his loot in the alley beside the mortuary. Three times he had thought about putting it back before it was missed. In between all of the wavering, he thought about his father, and of how a man could be respected one day and ridiculed the next. No one would respect him when they found out he was working for nothing.

As the wind began to die down and the rain slackened, he pulled himself to his feet. He told himself, "Don't run and look guilty, don't give back what you've already got, and don't get caught."

Girlie : Opal Lester got a reason to cry. Today the sky's 'bout dull and gray as that ol' quilt threw 'cross my bed, but the rain done stopped for a spell. Sun tried to break through earlier, just couldn't make it all the way. I'd be willin' to bet it's quiet and still like this all over Georgia. Last night the win' made one hell of a racket. I sat here lookin' out my window, watched the smallest of the trees bend all the way over, nearly touch the ground, then rise back up and sway the way thangs do when a good win' is blowin' bad.

This mornin' three canned jars of gumbo was waitin' on my porch. Somebody's way of thankin' me for the rain, I reckon, but I didn't have nothin' to do wit' that. Whenever somethin' happens 'round these parts, good or bad, folks say, "Girlie Shrugs, the voodoo woman, had her han's in it." I don't know nothin' 'bout no voodoo. If I did, I'd probably rid myself of a whole lotta trouble. Knowin' 'bout roots don't make me no voodoo woman.

This house I live in didn't cost me not one penny. I been right here ever since 1885. It's three rooms they told me used to be a overseer's house. My heart start thumpin' real fast when I look outside the back do' and seen a big ol' field. I thought Mr. Henry Cranston might change his mind and plant cotton, and he'd done put me right here so if I step out my back do', I'd be in that field.

"Mr. Henry," I say, "you gon' plant yo' fields in cotton?"

He shake his head, give a li'l laugh. "No. I want trees, Girlie. I intend to plant thousands of trees out there."

That was good 'cause I didn't wanna thank I'd done left the Jepson place just to come here to pick mo' cotton. I'm here 'cause I tend Mr. Henry's daughter when she come down wit' a fever out at the Jepson plantation the year befo' they move me here. Mr. Henry had done brought both his chilluns wit' 'im out there, but the boy didn't come down wit' nothin', and I didn't, neither. You'd'a thought the world was comin' to a end when that girl took sick, and she wadn't no young girl, neither. She was older than me. The way they carried on was somethin' to see. They sent for the doctor all the way over in Mays Spur, and they sent for one of the ol' slave mothers to tend her 'til the doctor could get out there.

The girl, Miss Dora, was delirious wit' fever and she was screamin', had done knocked a cup of tea outta Mama Nina's hand. Mama Nina was 'round 'bout seventy, I reckon, and I was just sixteen. So it wound up me carin' for that girl befo' the doctor got there and long after he left. She was awright wit' me long as she was layin' there quiet and full of Mama Nina's root tea, but when she got a li'l color back in her cheeks, she was meaner than a rattlesnake. All day long I'd bathe that girl's fever away and po' horehound tea down her throat. I'd give her them quinine tablets that the doctor left and some of Mama Nina's tea, then I'd bathe her some mo'. She come up outta that fever one mornin', wanna know where she at and what a Negra doin' beside her bed?

I say, "Miss Dora, you done died from the fever, honey. This here is heaven you in now."

That was just the devil in me talkin' 'cause I didn't like the way she'd done Mama Nina. Her daddy was tryin' to buy some land from Mr. Jepson, and he was tryin' to get her married off. Even wit' all his money I knew he was gon' have a hard time findin' her a husband. She was nice and plump the way men like 'em, but she wadn't no pretty girl.

Her daddy bought this ol' plantation from Mr. Jepson, and when they was ready to go, Miss Dora want me to come wit' 'em. She tell her daddy how she still need lookin' after. That's how I wound up here. I had a man, but that didn't mean nothin' 'cause I hear Mr. Henry Cranston tell Mr. Jepson how he don't think the land he bought is right for plantin' no cotton. So I say to Jesse, "I love you, but I'm goin' on wit' 'em."

Mr. Henry hire one of the stable boys name Tarlo, and we head on off to our new home. Ooh wee, it was a fallin' down mess. Fields that hadn't been planted in years, and mo' trees in one place than I ever seen in my life. The big house had two flo's, but I'd'a been scared to put my foot on one of them steps. Nobody ask me to. The land had li'l shanties scattered all over the place wit' the roofs all caved in, and I reckon the only place they could put me was in this overseer's house. Them Cranstons unload me and Tarlo out here, then they head on off to they house in Mays Spur. Wadn't long tho' befo' Mr. Henry come back wit' dogs, horses, supplies, and men to patch up and paint his big house. They didn't put no paint on mine.

I wanna know what my job was gon' be.

Mr. Henry say, "Dora wants you close in case her health fails her again. We can't always count on the doctor to be nearby."

Nah, I thank to myself, it's mo' to it than that. And it was. Mr. Henry want me to cook his meals and clean his house whenever he bring men over in here to go huntin' through the woods and fishin' in the creek. So I done it after they'd done fix them steps. I seen right off that this land was just play fun for Mr. Henry, just somethin' else he could say he own.

Tarlo was just a young boy back then, and it was his job to see after Mr. Henry's dogs and horses. They give him a li'l one-room house out yonder close to the main road. We was all the company each other had, and sometimes loneliness would creep in on me and I'd wanna go back to the Jepson plantation to see Jesse.

Tarlo say, "Girlie, ain't nobody out here to stop you from ridin' one of them horses to go see Jesse."

"How I get there?" I ask.

"You just go twelve or twenty miles back up that road we come down. You bound to see it sooner or later."

It was mo' to it than that, and I knew it. Still, I was willin' to try anythin' 'cause I couldn't take it no mo'. Miss Dora had done sent for me once, so I got a chance to see Mays Spur. That made me feel lonelier than I was befo'. I tell Tarlo one day, "Alright, I'm goin' to see Jesse today. If I can find my way, I'm gon' show 'im how to get here."

Didn't make it that day 'cause I couldn't ride no horse. Wadn't as easy as it looked. Tarlo tried to make me a wagon outta some wood he found over yonder by that row of houses near the pines. The wheels was damn near square, and he tried to hitch it to that horse. Lawd, have mercy! That doggone horse bucked, splintered the wood to pieces, and near 'bout kill Tarlo. Took a lotta days to mend 'im back to walkin' and thankin' straight.

Mr. Henry and a bunch of men would come in here to hunt, and ever now and then I'd hear 'em out there shootin' them guns. Sometimes a cold feelin' would run up and down my spine 'cause I'd thank they'd done shot Tarlo, but a day or so later he'd show up at my do'. Mr. Henry would show up sometimes, too, wit' a man done been cut wit' a huntin' knife or one that broke a bone, and I'd fix 'em up.

Them Cranstons was 'bout the richest folks in Butcher County. Mr. Henry had two wives, and he outlived 'em both. He had Miss Dora wit' his first wife, and Mr. Marshall wit' that second one. They owned mosta Mays Spur, the lumber mill, a pencil factory, and a whole lotta other stuff in other places. Mr. Henry's pride and joy, though, was this land he'd bought over here. He'd make me and Tarlo stand in his yard while he talk 'bout his house and his land. "Just look around you," he'd say. "Seventy-five hundred acres of the best woodland in Georgia."

It mighta been, but to my way of thankin' it wadn't nothin' but wilderness. He didn't even live over here, didn't never plant nothin' but some trees. He had another plantation over in Albany, but I ain't never seen that one. Mr. Henry loved this land, didn't want it cleared, neither, just wanted it planted in trees. Sometimes his face would be all trancelike when he look at his land. I reckon he'd be thinkin' 'bout all the trees that hadda come down in other places for his lumber mills. He tell Miss Dora that when he die he want her to bury him at the peak of the hill so he can look down at his beautiful land. He died in 1898 from a snake bite, and Miss Dora buried him at the foot of that hill. Two days later she sold all his dogs and horses, then she come to me sayin' how her daddy's ghost kept watchin' her, kept tellin' her not to cut down his trees and not to sell his land. She want me and Tarlo to dig 'im up, turn 'im 'round so he'd stop pesterin' her.

"No, ma'am, Miss Dora," I say. "I ain't gon' be troublin' Mr. Henry. Let 'im rest."

She wanna know if I can do somethin' wit' my roots. "Just to give my daddy some peace," she say.

"Roots don't work on the dead," I tell her, then I give Tarlo one of my cross-eyed looks 'cause I know he'd been tellin' her stuff 'bout my roots that she didn't need to know.

Miss Dora oughta know better. If Mr. Henry wanna be buried at the top of that hill, then that's where she oughta put 'im. She say there wadn't no way to get 'im up that high, but I say she was in a hurry to get 'im in the ground. She made it clear that she didn't care nothin' 'bout this land, say she had no intention of bein' over here wit' two ol' Negras and a multitude of snakes.

I couldn't figure how one or two snakes ever' ow and then had done got to be a multitude. "Miss Dora, I coulda saved yo' daddy," I say, "but them men wouldn't bring 'im to me."

"Well, he's dead now," she say wit' the wave of her han' like she just didn't care.

It was hard on me what happen to Mr. Henry—how they rode 'im all the way to the doctor in Mays Spur when I was right here. I don't know what kinda snake got 'im, but they say he was dead befo' they reach the doctor's house, and the doctor wadn't even home. I was a li'l bit sad 'cause the world lost a good man when Mr. Henry died. When Mr. Marshall come of age he had his daddy dug up and buried again over in Mays Spur. The bottom of that hill just wadn't no good place for no grave. In a good rain like we had last night, mud would wash down that hill and bury Mr. Henry all over again.

A year or so after her daddy died Miss Dora married Mr. George Philpot, who was the Butcher County sheriff at the time. Then she start wearin' a jail key pinned to her clothes. She say Cranston money built that jail, and she had ever' right to a key. When Mr. George wadn't the sheriff no mo', he start sellin' Miss Dora's land. By the time Mr. Marshall come in from Albany to put a stop to it, Miss Dora had maybe less than half them acres left. Mr. George had even sold her daddy's house out yonder to a colored man from Atlanta— Neville Sloan. Neville say he owned a business in Atlanta befo' the riots come, and he wanna start a business in Mays Spur. Didn't take him long to find out that a Negro ain't never gon' have no business in Mays Spur. Finally, he start makin' moonshine and sellin' it outta Mr. Henry's ol' barn. Even befo' the Prohibition come that stuff wadn't legal, but Mr. George let 'im sell it anyway.

Mr. George died in 1929, and I thought like ever'body else that

Miss Dora killed 'im. She'da been in her right to do it. He'd done let all sorts of folks move in here so he could charge 'em rent. Whether folks had a tent or a shanty, they hadda pay Mr. George to be on this land. He tell Tarlo to keep a head count over here and make sho' we don't cause nobody no trouble.

Just about ever'body live on this land come here from one of the farms or plantations, or else they wandered in from the county road and decided to stay. They all come wit' they own beliefs and ideas of how thangs oughta be, and it ain't never all the same. There's railroad tracks a few miles south of here. A whistle blows when the train start slowin' down for Mays Spur. Sometimes I can tell by the sound of that whistle, just like the sound of the win', whether we in for hard times or easy livin'.

Right now we havin' some pretty hard times. Folks say they ain't never seen it this bad befo'. Folks hop down from them boxcars when they see the trees 'round here. I reckon Cranston looks kinda peaceful peekin' from a train, but sometimes it ain't all that peaceful. Some folks hop back on them trains jus' as fast as they hopped off, get on outta here. I sit in my house and wait 'cause I know that befo' long whatever happens out there is gonna make its way to my do'.

CHAPTER 3

· ·

The trees stood colossal and sturdy, did not bow to console their brethren that had fallen to crude dwellings for human inhabitants. There were plenty of children, but no school—a stable and barn, but no horses or hay. There was a Baptist church on Marshall Road that welcomed everybody. It was a community that had shrunk in acreage as it gradually grew in population over the years. Heading west toward the farmland, oak trees gave shade at intervals along the two-mile hike between Marshall Road and Blevins Stretch. Small, isolated cabins could be reached by leaving dirt roads and following foot-worn paths through the trees and shrubbery. A towering hill stood to the east and separated the flat land of Cranston from the town of Mays Spur. As bleak as Cranston was, it was lively in comparison to Blevins Stretch.

Mildred wore a yellow gingham dress that Miss Nadine had given to her nearly a year ago. She had outgrown it and her flesh protruded through busted seams. The yellow fabric against her honey-brown complexion gave the appearance of a sunflower springing up in the center of the road. She was a child of thirteen when she entered Cranston on that cool May evening, but the weight of uncertainty and a baby growing in her womb made her feel she was a woman.

Pain and worry had kept her awake most of the night, and then this morning her daddy had insisted that they all go out to a soggy field to work. The sun, as a taunt, had popped out for a few seconds to peer down at the sodden land and give a glimmer of hope. It hadn't stayed long enough to dry the land or warm the cold feeling that seeped into Mildred's heart. She had worked well into the afternoon before slipping away under the pretense of emptying her bladder. She knew that she would be missed, and still she had hurried home and changed into her yellow dress. Now she was on her way to Jonathan.

"Don't tell nobody 'bout me," he had warned her. "Yo' daddy will kill me."

Although she hadn't really expected him to be there, she was disappointed when she reached the forest of pines and didn't see him, but they had so many other secret places. They had shared beds of leaves and of hard earth hidden away from the eyes of the world. They had even been together inside the abandoned Philpot store.

Jonathan had come to Blevins Stretch once to work in one of the neighboring fields during the picking season, but it hadn't worked out for him. He was more mischievous than productive, and it was clear to everybody, including his mother, that he wouldn't last long at the fields. Mildred was a hardworking girl as her daddy expected her to be, but that hadn't stopped her from following her brothers as they gravitated towards the edge of the adjoining fields where Jonathan sat to eat his lunch.

James was the same age as Jonathan, but James had never been to school. Ruben had been on the rare occasions when the field did not require his sweat. Mildred had been given the opportunity, and she had messed it up when she met Jonathan. That day, as she sat between her brothers listening to their laughter, she hadn't known that a baby was already growing in her womb. She had known, though, that the boy she loved wasn't looking at or speaking to her. By the time Jonathan was let go by the field boss, Mr. Taylor, and told not to come back, they were meeting each other as often as they could.

Standing behind a pine tree, Mildred peered out into the clearing. She saw a few people coming and going along the distant roads, saw Mr. Tarlo open his door and dump a basin of water into his yard. She held her breath when Miss Nadine passed on her way home from her job in Mays Spur. Far-off voices, small creatures scurrying across pine needles, and the infrequent suction of boots in mud invaded Mildred's solitude. She glanced up to see a flock of birds far above the tips of the pines. They were free and she was hiding away like a criminal. As she stood glancing up, she wondered, where do birds go when the storms come? How do they know to get out of the rain, or do they just keep flying? If she could be a bird, she would fly over to Hangling Road, swoop Jonathan up, and carry him away with her. She didn't know where they would go since she had never been beyond the boundaries of Butcher County.

Even as the last gray streaks of daylight faded into dusk, Mildred remained where she was. She pondered the worst that could happen if Miss Opal found out she was carrying Jonathan's baby. She had once asked Jonathan why his mother hated her.

"Mama think girls oughta be clean," he had said. "And she say sharecroppers is some nasty folks."

It was the only time Mildred had ever been angry with him. "We ain't no sharecroppers no mo," she had yelled at him. "My mama and daddy work the same fields yo' mama work."

A smile had appeared on Jonathan's lips, a smile that made his face so hand-some to her. "What it matter who don't like you long as I do?" he'd asked as he drew her into his arms, allowed his words to drift over her head. "You know you ain't the cleanest girl 'round here, Mildred, but I like you just fine."

Even after he said that she had lain on this forest bed and sinned with him as pine needles pricked her naked backside. Sometimes she liked what they did, liked his touch and the sounds he made while they were doing it. He was always on top, the lookout, and she wondered how he would be able to see anybody coming when his eyes were always closed. Nobody had ever caught them, but now she wished somebody had. Then maybe she wouldn't be walking around with a swollen belly.

Alone in the forest, Mildred shifted her weight from leg to leg, tried to ignore the ache in her back that was circling her body, growing, and spreading. As pain forced her to give up standing, she slid to the damp ground. Above and below the surface of her pain was her anger.

"Don't say nothin' 'bout me 'til I get a job," Jonathan had told her. "Them fields ain't no place for me. But soon as I can, I'm gon' get a job and marry you, then won't be nothin' nobody can say. Promise me you won't say nothin'."

She had promised, and Jonathan had rubbed her belly, whispered love in her ear. Lying on the ground—not on top of her, but beside her—he shared with her his dreams. "One day I'm gon' have us a house bigger than Miss Dora's. It's gon' be made outta bricks, and I'm gon' have my own sto'. You ain't gon' have to want for nothin'."

She had worn her yellow dress because she wanted to look clean and pretty just for him. The dress was too tight and it added to her discomfort. She wanted to rip it off, only she couldn't walk around naked. A few months ago she had been a skinny little girl—well, not actually skinny, but smaller than she was now—with not much to speak of in the way of breasts. That had changed along with everything else. She had been able to run halfway to Cranston without getting tired. Since Mr. Blevins had closed his store, Mildred had begun to walk to Mays Spur with her mama to pick up things at Dupree's store. They would go once a month, and always on their way back through Cranston her mama would say, "Go see Li'l Brill for a spell." And Mildred would obediently head on off to the Everses' house, although little Brill was no more than three years old.

She knew that her mama used those monthly trips to visit with Miss Girlie.

Mildred wasn't supposed to know that, but she had followed her a few times. Her mama's name was Van Ida, but her mother's name was Katie. Mildred didn't know Katie so she settled for the mama who was always there. At home in the evenings Van Ida was like a shadow moving about silently. Mildred would see her sometimes touching her face where scales appeared every now and then. She wasn't pretty, and because of her skin people sometimes called her a swamp woman, a swamp hag, or a gator woman. The only women her mama would visit were Miss Girlie and Nadine Evers, and that wasn't very often.

Mildred would sneak into Cranston sometimes, sit on the Everses' steps, and wait for Jonathan's whistle. One day he had asked her, "You ever been out to the creek?"

She shook her head. "Nah. I hear there's snakes out there."

"Ain't no snakes out there. Come on, let me show you."

She had followed him all the way through the forest and out to the creek without seeing a single snake. Maybe there weren't any, but if there were, she'd rather see them coming than have them sneak up on her. Ruben had trapped a corn snake in their yard one day. When their Daddy sent him back outside to get rid of it, the snake was already gone. Mildred hated snakes. She preferred things that she could see coming and going.

Jonathan was much too brave to worry about snakes. He wasn't scared of anything, except maybe her daddy. Laughter came easy to him, and she often wondered how he could be so much fun when his mother was such a prune face. If she knocked at Miss Opal's door and Jonathan wasn't home, what reason could she give for being there? He had already told her, "I can't have nobody knowin' that's my baby, 'specially my mama. Not yet, Mildred."

Darkness now cloaked the forest, but out in the clearing she could still see Mr. Tarlo's squat little shanty and Mr. Neville's great white house beyond that. She could hear laughter of men making their way to Sloan's Place. She pulled herself up from the ground, realized that she had chosen a bad day to come into Cranston. Because of the weather the Cranston workers had not gone to the fields, which meant Miss Opal was probably at home. Mildred felt her stomach turn with worry like she was going to be sick, and a terrible salty taste pooled in her throat. It wasn't fair that she should worry alone. Jonathan probably thought that she was tucked safely away at home, had no way of knowing she was here waiting for him.

It was Friday, and no matter what the weather was like her daddy would make his routine trip to Sloan's Place. Cross Road, where Sloan's Place was located, was the quickest path to Hangling Road from the pines. If she went that way, though, she would run the risk of somebody seeing her and telling her daddy that she was in Cranston. If Jonathan married her, it wouldn't matter what anybody told her daddy. What if Jonathan still wasn't ready to get married? She would have to go back home and back to the fields.

From where she stood she could see the outline of the burial hill down on Willow Road. Mr. Tarlo's house was dark, but a dim light from a kerosene lamp was showing through a window at Mr. Neville's house. Mildred took the trail toward the county road. She had decided to bypass Sloan's Place and reach Hangling Road from Willow. Her courage momentarily faltered and she thought about turning for home, but quickly convinced herself that going to Jonathan was a risk she had to take. The baby moved, and she took it as a sign that she was doing the right thing, like the baby was urging her forward.

In the twilight, Spanish moss hung from trees like ghosts in waiting. Many times she had been on Willow Road, but never before had the place seemed so gloomy. She wished that she had thought to bring a lantern, but it hadn't been this dark when she'd left the house. Spitting the foul taste from her mouth, Mildred suddenly felt faint. A mile down Willow Road was the graveyard, straight ahead was the burial hill, and to her left was the county road with all the menacing trees. Darkness and distance lay ahead, and the baby was getting fidgety. It shifted again and seemed to fall heavy against the bottom of her belly. Mildred didn't know what it was doing, but it hurt something awful. She placed her hands against her abdomen, pressed firmly to still the baby. Nausea rose in her throat, and a pain that she couldn't describe rolled through her body.

What was happening to her? About snakes, people, animals, everything, except ghosts—her mama had always told her, "You stand a chance long as you can see it comin'." She hadn't seen this coming. She waddled over and leaned against the muddy burial hill. Too much walking and worrying, she told herself as she stifled a cry. So much pain, and yet she knew it wasn't time for the baby to be born. Her mama had said that it probably wouldn't come until sometime in July. She wasn't even sure now that she could make it back home. She wondered if this was how it felt to be a woman. It wouldn't be so bad if Jonathan was here with her. He would soothe her with his words and his touch. "Be still, baby," she said aloud as she rubbed her belly. "I gotta make things right. If you be still, I'm gon' get to yo' daddy so he'll marry me. He'll maybe want you to call him daddy 'cause that's the way he is. You gon' have yo'self a real smart daddy."

Resting against the hill had been a mistake. Mildred could feel the mud on her hands, knew it was covering her yellow dress. Jonathan would see the dress, and he would call her a nasty sharecropper girl. She moaned in pain and despair, rolled her head from side to side, could feel the dampness soak into her hair. The light moved away from Mr. Neville's window, and she suddenly felt more alone than she had ever felt in her life. As thought sensing her gloom, the baby began to settle down. It shifted again with one long scrape against her insides, then stilled. Mildred pushed herself away from the hill, took one unsteady step, then leaned forward in a dry heave before residual pain dropped her to her knees.

Get up and go home!

Mildred glanced up toward the sound of the voice. She saw no one, but she was relieved that somebody was with her. "I hurt," she whimpered. "I can't move."

You'll have to. For you and the baby.

"Do I know you?" Mildred asked as she curled her body on the ground.

Yes. You've known me all your life. I'm the woman folks speak about when they teach their daughters to be afraid.

"My mama told me not to be scared of nothin' but ghosts. Are you a ghost?"

I am, but I was once just like you. I was in love with a man and heavy with his child, heavier than you are right now. He didn't want me anymore than that boy wants you. They say I went crazy for the love of that man. I killed him, took an ax and chopped off his head while he slept in another woman's bed. I killed them both.

Mildred fought to keep her eyes open as the ghost blew a cool breath against her face. It chilled her entire body, made her shiver. "I ain't gon' kill Jonathan. He ain't done nothin' to me," she managed to say.

He's done everything that wasn't right, but you knew from the start that he was no good. He's not gonna marry you.

Mildred groaned at the horror of those words. She rolled over in the mud, wanted the ghost to be gone, but it wouldn't leave her alone.

Get up and go home while your baby still has a chance.

"Leave me alone," Mildred mumbled. "You makin my stomach hurt. You died crazy over in Mays Spur befo' I was born. Why you over here botherin' me?"

So you'll know from me what happened to me before you make the same mistake.

"But I ain't crazy just 'cause I love Jonathan."

No, not because you love him, but look at what you're doing. Crazy is just not having good sense, and crazy didn't come to a standstill all them years ago over in Mays Spur. You're about to lose that baby over some boy who doesn't even want you. Get up and go home!

A heavy weight on Mildred's chest pinned her to the ground. Without ever seeing a face, she felt a breath against her cheek, a death kiss on her lips. She struggled to breathe, could not hear her own moans of desperation. She had no sense of time, knew only that she could not rise up from the ground. A light appeared and caught her tearing at the neckline of the constricting dress so air could get through to her lungs. A voice that she recognized spoke to her. "Gal, what's the matter wit' you? You havin' that baby? Get up from there."

It was Mr. Tarlo holding a lantern, but he wasn't alone. The feet of three other people neared Mildred's head, and then Helen People's face came into focus as she leaned down to stare.

"Move 'way from 'er!" ordered Mr. Tarlo. "She bein' rode by a witch."

A hand reached down to lift Helen up, to pull her to safety. Mildred's shriek was pitiably unnatural when she witnessed Jonathan wrap protective arms around Helen. Mr. Tarlo was yelling above the screams that somebody should go get Mary Grady to come see if Mildred was having her baby. Through her tears Mildred searched Jonathan's face for some sign of recognition, love, pity, disgust that she was stretched in mud, anything. He showed nothing as he turned and walk off with Helen. It was Paul Brown who went to get Mary Grady. Mildred's screams echoed through the trees, then tapered into moans. For the first time she felt herself the fool her daddy had warned her not to be. It hurt awfully bad.

CHAPTER 4

Alabama had watched a new kind of ugliness etch Van Ida's face as she fretted about a child who didn't even belong to her. Not that he had to tell her anything, but Alabama told her anyway that he was going to Sloan's Place, that if he happened to see the girl he would send her home. The boys could walk with him and search for their sister.

Maybe he shouldn't have forced the girl to work today in a soggy field, but they needed to work now in order to have work later. No doubt it would rain again soon, maybe harder, maybe longer. Thoughts were stumbling over each other in his head as he walked along beside his boys.

Alabama was a man of few and simple words, and mostly those words tangled up in his head and came out flat. A few years back, when Mildred had shown that she could manage the household chores, he had tried to put Van Ida out of his house. There had been no fussing. In his simple words he had tried to tell her that he was tired of looking at her, that she was no longer needed or wanted in his house. Mildred's melancholy at the thought of losing Van Ida had transferred to the boys, and their work suffered as a result. Rather than taking a strap to all his children, Alabama had decided to let the woman stay.

By the time they reached Cranston all Alabama could think about was getting himself a drink. He deserved it after working so hard and being so disappointed with his life. "Y'all go knock on some doors, see if anybody done seen your sister," he told his sons. "I'll be waitin' on y'all over at Sloan's Place."

"You sho' you don't wanna look wit' us, Daddy?" Ruben asked.

He knew the boy was trying to dissuade him from going to the hall, but he said, "Nah. Y'all better at findin' her than me. If y'all don't find her soon, come get me and we'll all look together. Start at Theron's house. She mighta gone over there."

He gave the lantern to James, watched his sons walk off toward the pines, then he turned for Cross Road and Sloan's Place. From the outside he could hear Donald Grady strumming his guitar. It was a welcoming sound spilling out into the dark, damp night. In his pocket was a dollar in coins, and he was thinking how a drink should be given to him at no charge since he had helped remodel the old barn into a gathering hall. Neville always charged him, though, and Alabama always fumed until the corn whiskey burned into his gut and soothed his mind.

NOVELS

As he opened the door, he was stunned to see a slender young woman in a bright green dress dancing alone at the center of the floor. With her hands raised and swaying gracefully above her head, her hips rotated, and she right away caught and held his attention. Donald Grady strummed his guitar to the rhythm of her movements, or to encourage them. Alabama stood long enough at the edge of the floor to catch her attention. He thought she winked at him, but maybe she didn't. Maybe the glow of a lamp had shown on her lashes. She was pretty, and everything about her warned him that she was trouble, but what did trouble matter to him? He had an ugly woman, a pregnant daughter, one dollar worth of coins in his pocket, and a field to hoe come morning. Mumbling to himself, he made his way across the floor to Neville sitting at his table of brews.

"Who's that woman, Neville?" he asked.

Neville glanced up. "Hey, Alabama. That's my cousin Wondrene from Atlanta. What can I get you? Wine or whiskey? You look like you need some of my best."

Alabama looked down at the jugs and bottles surrounding Neville's chair and lined across the table, then he glanced back to the greedy, overweight man. "You know I don't drink wine and I don't want yo' best," he said, suddenly angry. "How you know what's the best anyway? All that whiskey come outta the same damn still, don't it?"

"Don't start no mess with me, Alabama."

Alabama shook his head. "Nah. I ain't startin' nothin', don't feel like startin' nothin'. Just give me a drink, Neville."

While Neville lifted a jug to pour, Alabama glanced back at the woman out on the floor. He didn't know how long she had been dancing, but she showed no signs of tiring. He accepted his drink, dropped coins in Neville's outstretched hand, then said, "You say that's your cousin out there?"

"Yeah, she's my cousin, but you stay away from her, Alabama, and I mean that."

Neville's protective, strong-man bravado was wasted on Alabama. The were both large men, but Alabama was taller and more muscular. Neville carried the flabbiness of a man who had never known a day of hard labor.

"I ain't gon' bother her," Alabama said as he turned back to face Neville, "but you oughta tell her to stop shakin' her behind like that or ever'body ain't gon' stay away."

"Yeah," Neville mumbled. "Like they didn't stay away from your girl?"

Alabama came close to smashing his glass against the man's head. "What'd you say, Neville?"

Neville wasn't a stupid man. He was fat and greedy, but he wasn't stupid. "I don't want no trouble, and I ain't gon' have no trouble," he said.

"You say anythin' else 'bout my girl, you gon' have a sho'nuff mess in here. I'll tear this place apart, wipe this flo' wit' yo' fat ass," Alabama retorted.

Neville glanced over at his cousin and his face unwillingly softened. "Wondrene is a young girl," he said. "It's my place to look out for her while she's staying with me. That's all I'm saying, Alabama."

Cleophus Bender, the chicken man, was curious to know what the two men were saying to each other. He was a grubby, ragtag man of fifty-eight who found it troublesome to pump enough water from a well to bathe or wash clothes. Around his neck he wore a pouch filled with the remnants of his trade—crushed chicken bones and eggshells along with seven assorted split roots that he had obtained from Wash Gibson. The odor from his body mingling with the scent from the pouch kept most people at a distance, although it was meant to deter evil.

Cleo always looked for and found something to talk about. He reached the back of the hall and stood a few feet away from the table in the darkest area of the room. His odor drifted over to Neville, who didn't even have to glance up to know that Cleo was nearby.

"Cleo, I ain't putting you out," Neville said, "but you gon' have to find somewhere else to stand."

Alabama finished his drink and searched the room for another spot. There was no table open that would allow him a clear view of the dancer, and he didn't feel much like sitting anyway. He looked down at his empty glass, then dropped the last of his coins on the table. As Neville refilled the glass, Alabama asked. "How long your cousin stayin'?"

"She's leaving tomorrow. Why you wanna know?"

"Just wonderin' how long she can keep dancin' like that. Don't worry 'bout me, Neville. I got enough troubles."

Cleo found his opening and stepped over to the table. "What kinda troubles you got, Alabama?"

Alabama's face and sigh conveyed his disgust at the odor Cleo brought with him. The man was harmless enough, but he had to be fed from a long-handle spoon, preferably a ladle. "Cleo, why don't you move on back where you came from?" Alabama asked. "Ain't it time for Wash to change them roots?"

"He gon' change 'em tomorrow. What kinda troubles you got?"

"Just troubles, Cleo, like you and ever'body else."

As if to justify that statement, a visibly shaken James entered the barn and, after glancing around, came straight toward Alabama. "Daddy, we found her," he said in a near panic. "She layin' out there in the mud by the burial hill. Mr. Tarlo and some mo' folks was already there and they sayin' a witch ridin' 'er. Me and Ruben tried to stop 'em from pourin' salt on 'er."

"Witch?" Cleo questioned.

Alabama was trying to make sense of his son's words. It had been a long time since he'd heard anybody talk about witches. He took another swallow from his glass before shoving what remained toward Cleo. He didn't want the man following him, but as he and James reached the door, Alabama could hear Cleo shouting above voices and guitar music, "Alabama's girl being rode by a witch."

"I swear, Daddy, she so covered in mud it look like somebody drug her up the road," James said as they hurried for the burial hill.

Nothing comes darker than a starless Cranston night, and the lantern that James carried was so unsteady that the light cut waves through the darkness. Alabama told himself that the whiskey hadn't had time to touch him, that he was as sober as a man could be. He thought it was the wavering of the light that made the ground shift beneath his feet. He reached over once to still his son's trembling hand.

They reached the burial hill to see a small group of people and a few lantern lights. What Alabama focused on was his daughter lying flat on her back with Ruben's shirt spread over her. As he leaned down to touch her, he felt the salt that had been sprinkled around and on top of her, even in her hair. He could hear the people around him speculating, whispering about witches, bad omens, and the baby his daughter carried.

"I heard a strange noise comin' from back here, Alabama," Tarlo explained. "When I seen who it was, I thought maybe she was havin' her baby, so I sent a boy to run get Mary Grady. But it ain't no baby, nah sur. It's a witch." Tarlo nodded his head as he always did when his opinion was not to be questioned. "She was grabbin' at her throat, couldn't hardly breathe, tearin' her own clothes off. That's sho'nuff the ridin' of a witch. It's got 'er good 'cause she ain't said nothin' since she stop screamin'."

"Daddy, here come some of them folks from Sloan's Place," James said.

They were coming alright—the curious who would stare from a distance and later wag their tongues with assumptions. Alabama could hear their approach, but he never glanced back. Without a single word or grunt he lifted Mildred from the ground. In the light of the lanterns the people watching could not see the small holes in his shirt. They could not see that his overalls would be thread-bare by summer's end. They could not see much, but they sensed the strength of his broad back as he effortlessly lifted and carried his daughter. He held her close to his chest—salt, mud, and all. "Mildred, baby, I'm gon' take you home," he said in a voice that threatened to break with sobs.

Alabama was an angry and confused man. Salt from his daughter's hair fell onto his arms as he weaved his way through the crowd. He loved Mildred, but he had shown her nothing but anger over the past few months. He regretted that, and as he walked he mumbled, "I'm sorry, baby."

All the way through Cranston, over to Marshall Road, to where Marshall narrowed into Blevins Stretch, Alabama carried his daughter. Mildred wouldn't open her eyes or speak, but he could feel her breaths against his neck. When he tried to stand her on her feet she went limp, and he had to lift her again. His boys walked silently behind him. Although they had both offered to carry their sister, Alabama wouldn't turn her over to them.

They were less than half a mile from the house when he stopped. "James, you and Ruben take her on home." he said. "Carry her between you and leave the lamp on the stoop so I can find my way."

He watched the light bob and fade, then he dropped down to the road and wept. When the tears dried and he was done with the self-damning, he pulled himself up. He stumbled through the night until he saw the light waiting on the stoop, and still he wasn't sure that he had found his way.

. . . .

Her dress was ripped. Mud with lines of salt made patches along her skin. More than anything in the world Van Ida loved this child. Mildred, with her easy laughter and constant chatter, brought joy to Blevins Stretch; she always had. Van Ida imagined that the girl had burst from her mother's womb in search of freedom only to find herself chained to a farm. For the most part she gave work more importance than play, but carrying a baby had slowed her down.

"Mildred, baby, talk to me," Van Ida coaxed as she bathed the girl. "Open yo' mouth and say somethin'."

The girl had been silent save a few low moans, but with so much patient coaxing she finally opened her mouth. "I hurt all over, Mama," she murmured. "I wanna see you, but my eyes is burnin'. I hear 'em say a witch got me."

"It's awright. You home now where can't nothin' hurt you."

"I thought it was a ghost, but they say I was rode by a witch."

Van Ida was torn between relief that the girl was speaking and fear at the mention of ghosts. She had never been afraid of witches, though. Witches could be handled with salt to shrink the cast off skin. After easing the girl's head down to the pillow, she stepped away from the bed, pulled the salt down from a kitchen shelf and began to sprinkle it across the floor.

"Put that damn salt down!" Alabama barked. "She got enough in her hair already to cover this whole flo'. I didn't bring her home just so you can start actin' a fool like them folks in Cranston."

"I ain't puttin' it on her," Van Ida explained. "She say somethin' got her, Alabama. I'm just puttin' a li'l on the flo'."

"Put it down," he repeated. "I got enough on my mind already."

Light as a feather Van Ida moved across the floor to replace the salt. Alabama wondered how a woman so tall could walk without putting an enormous strain on the floorboards. That one thought shifted to gators lying silent in the swamp, resting like logs, waiting to spring some brand new terror on a man. She had bathed Mildred and dumped the water. Now as she neared him, he wanted her to just be quiet, be still, be gone from his life.

"I reckon she gon' be alright," she said. "I done washed that mud off, now I think it's best we gon' and let her sleep."

Sitting at the kitchen table with his sons, Alabama involuntarily shifted as Van Ida pulled out a chair and sat down next to him.

"She gon' be alright, Mama?" Ruben asked.

"I reckon so. We'll know mo' by mornin'," Van Ida told him.

Alabama looked at his sons and felt the burden of everything that had ever gone wrong in their lives as well as his own. He tried to remember how and when they had begun to call Van Ida "Mama." He shook his head and it felt as though something inside had broken loose. "This ain't right," he said.

"What ain't right, Alabama?" Van Ida asked.

Because Alabama could not settle on any one particular thing, he said, "None of it. None of it ain't right."

Mildred was too young to have a baby. She should have waited until she had a husband who could take care of her—a better man than he was, he hoped. If she would just tell him who the boy was, he could maybe break a few bones, make the boy marry her and take care of her. Through the cloud of anger in his head, he visualized the hazy faces of the young men in Butcher County. One by one, and for one reason or another, he discounted them all. His own choices in women had cursed his daughter, he believed. He had chosen his children's mother out of physical desire, and given a chance, he knew he would do it all over again. Those had been the happiest years of his life. He had chosen this last woman out of desperation, and it left a sick feeling in the pit of his stomach. He wasn't doing well at all. He wanted to be numb, didn't want to feel angry, tired, defenseless. *When there's nothing you can do, then there's nothing you can do*, he thought. "Let's get to bed. It'll be mornin' befo' we know it."

Van Ida rose from her chair and started for the back room, but he put up a hand to stop her. "Where you goin'?"

"Goin' to bed."

"Nah, not you," he said, and tilted his head toward the curtain. "You stay wit' Mildred. Make sho' she don't need nothin' durin' the night. Make sho' she be awright."

Van Ida turned and slowly dropped back down onto the kitchen chair. When she knew that Alabama was out of the room, she got up and drew the curtain back to give herself a clear view of the girl. She knew that Alabama was troubled. Deny it and it'll all be better by morning. *This is bad*, she thought. *They all layin' they heads down 'cause they think I know what to do. I don't know what to do 'bout nothin'.* She watched the girl, listened as the boys gradually began to snore.

Mildred tossed and turned, moaned when she took a notion, screamed when she could do nothing else. Van Ida tried to calm her with words, cleaned her

NOVELS

up when she wet the bed. James woke up once to ask if everything was alright, Ruben slept on, and Alabama never made an appearance in the room.

In a moment of nighttime chill, when the dampness from the ground rose up into the house, Mildred lifted her head. "What's wrong wit' me, Mama?" she asked. "Do it hurt this bad to be rode by a witch?"

CHAPTER 5

They could have let it pass, but they did not. Tarlo Medfield armed himself with a dozen of the most boisterous, garrulous men and women in Cranston. Adorned in crudely carved and beaded charms to ward off evil spirits, they walked out to Blevins Stretch and demanded an audience with Alabama. It was early morning, the hour before the workday would begin, when they stood in the yard and called out until Alabama appeared at his door holding a lantern.

Tarlo was a thin, dark man with a patch of white hair that stood straight up on his head. As spokesman for the group, he braved the anger of the man in the doorway, and asked, "What you gon' do 'bout that gal of yours, Alabama? Ain't natural the way she was actin'. I know a witch got a hol' of 'er last night. She was scratchin' at 'er own throat and carryin' on. You know we don't allow nothin' like that in Cranston."

"This here ain't Cranston, Tarlo," Alabama said.

"Yeah," Tarlo agreed, "but she brought her witch to Cranston."

Warning his sons to stay inside, Alabama stepped out onto his stoop, stared at his neighbors. Most of them were people he saw everyday, worked beside in the fields. "She be alright in a day or two," he told them, and hoped he was speaking the truth. "Just havin' a little trouble. Y'all done seen folks get sick befo'."

"That girl been conjured!" Opal shouted. "Was bound to happen wit' the way she strut 'round like she some angel wit' wings. Some man's wife done worked a spell on that girl. Ain't nobody to blame but you, Alabama. You oughta had a woman bring her up 'steada some swamp hag."

"I don't believe in no cunjuh, no witches, none of that stuff," Alabama insisted, "but you seem to know what you talkin' 'bout, Opal. You done had somethin' done to my girl."

"Not me," Opal answered indignantly, "but I ain't ever' man's wife. I ain't no man's wife. I'm just sayin' you oughta been keepin' a better watch."

"Well, I 'preciate y'all's concern," Alabama told them, "but I think I'm able to take care of my own child. Y'all can gon' now, get on off my land."

"Memory serves, I believe this here Mr. Blevins's land," Tarlo asserted. "We don't want the Mays Spur law comin' over in here troublin' us, and they bound to hear 'bout yo' gal sooner or later. She was bein' attacked at the throat, Alabama, to where she couldn't even breathe or speak. She was scratchin' at her own throat and that's sho' nuff the ridin' of a witch."

"That's right," Wilbur Johnson agreed. "Lay the broom, Alabama. Lay it 'cross yo' do'step. Sprinkle some salt all the way from yo' window to the girl's bed. That'll keep the witch out."

"That woman I got done already tried that," Alabama admitted. "I knew she was wastin' her time when she done it. I don't believe in none of that stuff. Now, I'm gon' ask y'all again, right politely, to get on off my land."

"The broom and the salt—they never fail," Sally Blackmon said with conviction. "We ain't seen it, and maybe it ain't no witch. But if it ain't, it's likely somebody done laid a root on you. Somebody out to do you harm. You ain't had nothin' but bad luck since you come to Cranston."

"You know you right, Sally," Opal remarked. "First, Katie took off and left him stuck wit' them three chilluns. He don't know whose seed his daughter carryin', and she won't tell nobody. And he got that swamp hag livin' under his roof. Could be she done fixed 'im and ever'body else in that house. Looks that way. Sho' looks that way."

For years Alabama had listened to their nonsense, had watched their ridiculous rituals as they tried to ward off witches, ghosts, conjures, and other evils. He would sit with his friend Theron Evers at the rear of the Philpot store and watch people make the sign of the cross when they stepped out of their houses, tremble in fear at the sight of a black cat crossing their path, spin in circles, hang trinkets on their doors, sprinkle salt, spit over their shoulders. He and Theron would laugh about it, but Alabama sometimes wondered how many of their beliefs had rubbed off on him.

"There's other ways of keepin' the evil 'way from yo' do'," Cleo said. "You need to go over and see ol' man Wash or Miss Girlie. Bet it won't cost you no mo' 'an two bits to get that spell took off. You gotta do somethin', Alabama, or the law gon' handle it they way."

Alabama stood two inches under six feet. He was a heavy, hairy man with facial features that were pleasant enough when he wasn't scowling. "You must be some kinda fool, Cleo," he said. "The law ain't got no need to bother us. I'll keep my girl 'way from y'all, and y'all need to stay 'way from us."

"Now you wait just one minute," Opal said. She was a stout, ginger-colored woman, late thirties, and missing most of her teeth. She took a step forward, and the others followed. "I packed my boy up this mornin', sent 'im on away from here. He couldn't sleep last night 'cause yo' girl had 'im spooked on witches. Nothin' I said would settle 'im down. He wanted to go, and I sent 'im. Now I ain't got nobody. You all time talkin' 'bout what you don't believe, laughin' 'bout things you don't understan'. Let's see how much you laugh if somebody tell the law what's goin' on out here. I just might tell 'em myself so they can take that girl away and I can get my boy back home."

The door opened behind Alabama, and Van Ida stepped out beside him. Tarlo, Opal, and the rest took a communal step back, away from the eyes with elongated lids, away from the cold-blooded creature they were sure Van Ida was.

"I knows for sho' all y'all didn't come out here jus' 'cause that po' chil' got sick," she said in her deep, daunting voice. "Opal, I hear you say somethin' 'bout Katie leavin' Alabama stuck wit' three chilluns. They some good chilluns, and he doin' awright by 'em."

Alabama suddenly felt powerful standing beside Van Ida, and he was sure he stood a little taller. "Look at these folks, Ida," he said, holding his lantern even higher. "I want you to remember ever' last one of 'em. If it look like somebody tryin' to bring harm to this house, I want you to remember these faces."

Just as abruptly as the power had come, it began to drain from his body when he heard Mildred's whimpers from inside the house. Alabama could see that Van Ida was torn between going to see about the girl and staying to help him fight. He knew, though, that there would be no fight. Most of the folks in his yard were afraid of their own shadows. They would resort to voodoo before they ever swung a fist. Their earlier aggression turned to fear as Mildred's moans amplified and spilled out into the yard. They began to slowly disperse, some turning for the fields, others turning for Cranston. The only one to glance back was Wilbur Johnson, the slow-walking cripple who was convinced that his ailment stemmed from a conjure that had put lizards in his legs. "Go see Wash Gibson," he called out in a concerned voice. "Let 'im help the girl."

"We don't need his help," Alabama said. "How come he didn't help you?"

"Ol' man Wash—he say the woman had this done to me done passed on," Wilbur explained. "Ain't nowhere to send these lizards now."

"Couldn't be rheumatism, now could it, Wilbur?"

"Ain't no rheumatism. Sometimes I feel 'em crawlin' through my legs. If I look hard enough, sometimes I can see 'em, too. Ain't nothin' to be done for me,

Alabama. Nothin' at all. But maybe it ain't too late for you and that girl of yours. You better hope the news of this don't reach Mays Spur."

Alabama's eyes shifted from left to right as he watched to departure of his neighbors. He thought them the most ignorant people he had ever encountered, and he could not resist yelling out, "If I happen to see that witch that y'all talkin' 'bout, me and Ida gon' catch it, maybe send it to one of y'all houses."

"You ought'na said that," Van Ida scolded after the group was out of hearing distance. "S'pose they go get ol' Wash to lay a cunjuh on us?"

CHAPTER 6

The Wheatons' home was an unpainted, board-thick, two-room dwelling with three windows and a single door. A rope had been strung across the main room where a curtain was hung to separate the girl's space from the boys'. A kitchen table stood less than a foot away from the edge of the curtain and it was the first thing they saw whenever they entered the house. The curtain had been drawn back by Van Ida, and Alabama could see his daughter lying in a heap on her mattress. Last night he had listened to her scream, had heard the squeak of the coiled bedsprings as her body trembled and jerked on the mattress.

As much as he tried to denounce the existence of witches and the ability to conjure, Alabama had to consider the idea that somebody had done something to his daughter. After the way she had been found lying in mud by the burial hill, he knew that something was terribly wrong. She was too much like her mother, Katie. No amount of talking had ever mattered when Mildred set her mind to something. It had always been easy keeping his boys in line, but he had never known what to do with his girl. He walked over to her bed, leaned down, touched her face. "Why you go to Cranston actin' like that?" he asked. "Folks sayin' a witch done got a hold of you."

The girl moaned but did not answer him. He turned to his sons, who were fifteen and sixteen years of age. "I don't want y'all goin' nowhere near Cranston 'til Mildred is better," he said.

"What's makin' her act like that, Daddy?" James asked. "Look like she real bad sick."

"I know," Alabama agreed. "She havin' a little trouble, but that don't mean she bein' rode by no witch. Folks 'round here tend to get the wrong idea."

"I seen what she was doin', Daddy, befo' you got there," Ruben said. "The way she was scratchin' at her throat can't be nothin' but a witch or somethin' evil. Mama say it's gotta be somethin' mo' than that baby she carryin'."

Alabama glanced at Van Ida, who was standing beside the door. She was staring out as though waiting for the Cranston people to return. She had begged him to take the girl to Miss Girlie, but he didn't trust the old woman. He had heard of spells worked by Miss Girlie that had messed people up for life, and of how, if you crossed her in any way, she could lay a disease on you that would have you buried within a year. Although he did not want to, he believed the tales about Miss Girlie, and he stayed away from her. Van Ida swore by her, but he had made it clear early on that there would be no roots, magic, or foolishness in his house or around his children.

He supposed Van Ida couldn't help thinking like most of the others since she had been born in Butcher County. It did not matter that she was one of them; they ridiculed her because of her looks, the fact that her face sometimes broke out in a scaly rash. They said she had not been born of a woman but had hatched from a gator's egg. Alabama had laughed at that until he realized he was the only one laughing. He had been born and raised in North Georgia, where people had their beliefs, but nothing as farfetched as the ones in Cranston.

An ailing uncle had landed him in Butcher County, where he met Katie during his first week—like it was meant to be. He courted her for all of four months before asking for her hand in marriage. All that time, he realized later, her interest had not been in him. She had wanted to know what was out there in the world, what he had seen, and would he take her some place exciting. He nodded that he would; he would have promised her anything. Katie married him and bore him three children, then ran off one day before the oldest one turned three. The youngest, Mildred, had been only a few weeks old.

Alabama's nearest neighbor had been Van Ida, a woman-child of about fourteen or fifteen, he guessed, who had recently moved from the Jepson plantation and into the worst shack on Mr. Blevins's property. Alabama was as guilty as the rest when it came to Van Ida. He had heard the rumors and had not approached her until he had needed her help. On their first encounter, his first close look at her, he had found himself studying her face for the scales that were said to grow there. She hadn't had them at that time. She had dark, patchy skin from where he assumed the rash had faded. She had nice white teeth, but she was every bit as unattractive as he had heard—something about her hooded eyes and so much height for a girl. She had been nearly as tall as he was already, and still had some growing to do.

"I'm Alabama Wheaton from up the way," he said in introduction as he neared her stoop.

"I knows what you done heard," she responded, "and I didn't come out no gator's egg. My name is Van Ida, and I was born to Thomas and Matilda Raynor right up yonder a ways on the Jepson plantation. I done seen you sneakin' by here tryin' to get a good look at the swamp woman. What you want, Alabama Wheaton?"

Alabama had been relieved that she did not believe herself hatched from an egg. Still, he was hesitant about getting to the point, and he was not sure that he wanted her around his children, but there was no one else close by. He couldn't very well wake three children, get them dressed, then haul them into Cranston every morning. He'd have to double back to get to the fields, then make the same trip again in the evening.

He looked at Van Ida and cleared his throat. "Well," he began, "I'm havin' a bit of trouble over at my place."

"I knows all about yo' troubles," she said. "You shoulda come lookin' for help befo' you married Katie. Anybody 'round here coulda tol' you she wadn't no good. Now you done went and found out the hard way."

"I have," Alabama admitted, while trying not to shudder under her stare. "You see, the thing is, Miss Van Ida, I don't rightly know how to take care of no baby, 'specially no little girl baby. I was hopin' you could help me out. If I don't get on back out there to them fields, we gon' starve to death. I wanted to ask you if you'll watch my children."

"Well, say." She took a step down from her stoop. "Don't you see me ever'day goin' to them fields myself? You think I live for free? Yeah, I see. You think I'm some swamp woman, don't gotta eat food like ever'body else."

He didn't know what he had been thinking. Of course she had to work the same as he did. She was new to Mr. Blevins's fields, though, and he had never paid her much attention or worked beside her. All he knew was that he needed a woman's help, and she was supposed to be a woman.

"I beg yo' pardon, ma'am," he said as politely as he knew how. "I guess I'm just a li'l desperate. Wadn't thinkin' like no rational man." He tipped his old felt hat. "Sorry for troublin' you."

Alabama went home to where he had left his three babies asleep on a single bed. He thought about packing them up and taking them to Kingston where his mother lived. He had no money for that, and the uncle that he had come to care for had died a penniless man. By the time his uncle died Alabama was already married to Katie, and they had one son and another child on the way. He thought about Katie's family. They were sharecroppers on the Dean property, a few miles outside of Butcher County. Even as he thought about it, he knew he could not leave his children there. Everybody in Katie's family worked, and there would be nobody to look after a baby during the day.

He never knew what changed the swamp woman's mind. A few days after he had spoken with her, Van Ida arrived at his door with a bundle of clothes on her arms. She moved out of her tiny shack and into his larger one, brought her handful of chickens along to mingle with his. It was not what he had had in mind, but he accepted what he could get. Nothing had ever slowed her down. From day one, she had taken all of his children to the fields with her, made the oldest one watch over the younger ones. Her rest periods had been spent tending his children. And that's the way things had been for the past thirteen years. Never did it occur to Alabama that he could have done the same thing. He could not have.

As he prepared to leave for the fields, Alabama thought about the number thirteen. It was the age of his daughter, the number of years he had been with Van Ida, and the number of people who had entered his yard—four women, nine men. He tried hard not to be a superstitious man. He had weathered the worst of times, natural bad luck things like everybody else—floods, droughts, boll weevils, bad crops, being down to his last penny—and he had survived. Maybe he *was* due another turn of bad luck.

CHAPTER 7

Van Ida emerged from the swamp, stomped mud from her boots, and laughed aloud. Only when she was alone did she allow laughter to bubble up from deep inside and spill out into the world. There was no reason for it other than the solitude of the place that allowed her the freedom to be herself. This time, though, it might have come from not knowing what else to do. Across her shoulder she carried a short canvas sack, and in her heart she carried love for Alabama and his children.

Glancing back toward the swamp, she heard as well as felt her laughter trickle into silence. Alabama had told her to remember the faces of the Cranston folks. Even if he hadn't said that she knew that she'd never forget. They were some of the same ones who said that she had been born in this swamp, hatched from an egg. The way she was able to move freely among the swamp creatures sometimes made her think that maybe she had been born here. Fading memories of a mother and father always put that thought to rest.

She paused to extinguish the light of her lantern, then glanced briefly at the sky before heading for the path that led up to the road. It was a cool morning for late May, and clouds were lingering. She needed to get back to Mildred before another downpour hindered her path. The girl had the dropsy that had swollen her legs and feet to twice their normal size. Yesterday evening she had clamped her teeth together and began to twitch violently on the bed. Froth filled her mouth and bubbled around clenched teeth, and her eyes rolled up like she was trying to see inside of her own head. She'd had a fit like folks who were said to swallow their own tongues. When the fit ended, she had fallen into a deep sleep. Van Ida had slipped quietly into the Sunday twilight, made her way into Cranston to ask Miss Girlie for help.

"You can't brang the girl to me, and I sho' can't walk way out there," Miss Girlie had said. "What that man you got gon' say 'bout you askin' me for roots?"

"He don't know nothin' 'bout this, Miss Girlie, but the girl is real bad sick, and nothin' I got ain't workin.'"

Miss Girlie had patiently listened as Van Ida described Mildred's ailments, then she'd said, "I ain't got sto'd up in my house the thin' that can help 'er. You gon' have to go get it yo'self, and do just like I say. Out in the swamp is a root that can ease pain, calm the restless, and get ridda the swellin'. It's a night bloom. You go get it, Van Ida, and do just like I say."

NOVELS

When Miss Girlie was done explaining, Van Ida had nodded her understanding. Now in her canvas sack was the long-stem reward of her all-night search—a single zyma root. It was a long walk from the swamp to Blevins Stretch. The route took her around and across smaller farms, through acres and acres of Mr. Blevins's fields, and past the old shack that she had abandoned so many years ago. As she passed her old place, she stopped to peer inside the sack again. She needed to be certain that she had not wanted the zyma root so badly that she had only imagined it. The root was still right where she had placed it. The coarse black stem seemed to pulsate with life as the large oval-shaped petals dripped their purple blood onto the canvas.

Her feet, laced in waterlogged boots, made a slushy sound as she trampled through the cattails near Blevins Stretch. She was tall—nearly as tall as Alabama. Her head was covered with rust-colored hair that had never grown long enough to pin or braid. The peach-sized mounds on her chest and the slight curve of her hips were the only things that outwardly distinguished her from the male gender. She was the kind of dark that came from working too many years under a blazing Georgia sun—the kind of black that baked into the pores. Although she was only twenty-seven, she felt that she had always been old. She wanted to be something that she probably never would be—a mother. Alabama's three children loved her and called her "Mama," but it wasn't the same as actually being their mother.

Since the Cranston folks had come out to the house before daybreak on Saturday morning, Van Ida had been unable to stop worrying. Maybe Opal had been telling the truth when she'd said that somebody had laid a root on the girl. If so, it was a powerful one, one that Van Ida had never seen before.

She reached the house, pushed open the door. Alabama would be angry with her for missing a morning in the field, but some things couldn't be helped. Mildred was just a child, and no matter what she had done there had to be an end to the suffering.

"Mama? Is that you, Mama?" Mildred questioned in a barely audible voice as Van Ida stepped inside.

Placing her lantern on the table, Van Ida turned and answered the girl. "It's me, chile. I done went and got somethin' that gon' take yo' pain away." She removed the sack from her shoulder, pulled off her boots, then stepped deeper into the room to where the girl lay on her bed.

The house was hot and smelled of everything that had ever graced its walls. It was crammed with all of their earthly possessions. Van Ida shared the small back room with Alabama. The boys slept out front by the window, and the girl slept against the west wall of the same room. A stove, the beds, one dresser, a table, and five chairs filled the house to capacity. The table, chairs, and two wall shelves had all been crafted by Alabama and his sons. Van Ida felt blessed to be a part of this family, and she intended to show her love and gratitude by helping the girl. She touched Mildred's head, satisfied herself that there was no fever. The girl's eyes were troubled, though, appeared sunken in her head.

"I don't feel so good, Mama," Mildred said in a shaky voice. "I ain't never felt this bad befo'."

"It's gon' be alright, chile," Van Ida assured her.

Mildred did not think that things were going to be alright. Although it was still morning, she already dreaded the coming of the night. Her daddy would come home and the house would grow even quieter than it was now. Everything in her life hurt: her body, the sadness in her daddy's eyes when he looked at her, and knowing that Jonathan had made a fool of her. Last night in her dreams Jonathan had been holding her in his arms beside their tree, but it had faded into Jonathan running away, and she hadn't been able to get him back. She had screamed for him not to leave her, but it had done her no good. She had awakened with Jonathan on her mind and a cramp in her belly that still hadn't shown any signs of easing.

"Jonathan gone, Mama," she said as sadly as though it were a death. "This his baby in my belly. He say he was gon' marry me."

For a moment Van Ida could not respond. For sure Mildred had been with somebody, but Van Ida never would have thought it was Opal's boy.

"Don't tell Daddy," Mildred pleaded.

"I ain't got nothin' to tell nobody," Van Ida said reassuringly.

"I heard Miss Opal out in the yard when she say Jonathan gone. You reckon he gon' ever come back?"

"Maybe. I don't know, chile."

Mildred's body shuddered against the mattress, her face contorted with pain, then she clutched the sheet and drew it up to her chest. Her swollen legs were stretched and her feet extended from beneath the sheet. For a while she puffed air around moans that sounded like wind through cracks in the house on a cold winter night.

This is bad, Van Ida thought as she reached down to rub Mildred's feet. She couldn't bear to look at what pain did to the girl's face.

"Help me, Mama," Mildred whimpered.

Van Ida glanced over to where she had left her sack. She went over to the stove, lifted the warm kettle that was still nearly half filled with water. She poured water into a wide, wooden bowl, then took a knife from the wall shelf and removed the root from her sack. She studied it, tried to remember everything Miss Girlie had told her.

Starting at the top of the plant, she plucked three petals and sliced them into fourths. She dropped the purple portions into the warm water, watched as the petals disintegrated into scores of tiny sickle-shaped particles. Still holding the knife, she cut a slit along the length of the stem. The juice that bubbled from within was odorless and as black as the stem itself. Finally, she mixed the black and purple juices of the zyma root together in a cup.

"You needs to take this," she said as she moved the cup toward Mildred's lips.

Mildred did not question the woman who had been her mama for as long as she could remember. She parted her lips and slowly swallowed down the liquid.

"I'm gon' rub yo' body down," Van Ida said. "This be between me and you. Yo' daddy ain't never gotta know."

Van Ida bathed Mildred, then took the bottom part of the drained stem and began to rub it onto the girl's skin. There was no protest from the girl even as the wetness of the swamp rolled across her body. Her daddy would object to the use of the root, but she seemed not to care what happened to her as long as it eased the pain.

"Help me, Mama."

There was nothing more Van Ida could think to do. She sat on the bed beside the girl and waited for the root to work. She turned from the girl, pressed her hands together, and prayed the way the way she had learned to do as a child.

The rumble of thunder in the distance drew Van Ida away from Mildred's bed. Hurriedly, she scraped together all that remained of the root and tossed it out the door. It was going to rain again, and the rain would wash it away. She stood just inside the doorway staring out, and that was where she was when the rain finally came. Behind her, Mildred was silent. In front of her, heavy rain made sludge of the soil and washed away all evidence of her deceit.

Van Ida stood in the doorway feeling as though a heavy, dark blanket had been draped over her head. Worry didn't visit her often, but it was here now. She wondered what Alabama would do if he found out about the root. He would probably put her out of his house or kill her. Dying wasn't so bad, she guessed. Anything would be better than returning to the isolation of her old abandoned shack.

After a while—a long while—Van Ida saw her men moving toward the house in the pouring rain. She stepped away from the door and began to gather dry clothes. Mildred had dozed off, and Van Ida could tell by the constant creak of the bed springs that it was not a peaceful sleep. Alabama and the boys entered the house and began to change. They hung their wet clothes over the ropes to dry, then they sat at the table, and Alabama asked the expected question, "Where was you last night, Ida? Where was you all mornin'?"

"The girl chile," Van Ida whispered. "She don't seem to be gettin' no better."

CHAPTER 8

• •

Mildred had been asleep when he first came in, but now her moans was grat-
ing on his nerves, crawling under his skin. Alabama wanted to pull her up,
maybe hug her against his body to absorb her pain, maybe shake her into
silence. Enough was enough. Hadn't he told her so many times not to go out
and be a damn fool? He watched Van Ida as she gave the girl sips of water
from a jar.

Alabama stayed close to the door with the thought of escape heavy on his
mind. "I don't reckon Mr. Blevins gon' have no work for us come mornin'," he
said regretfully. "Fields gon' be too wet."

"Sound like it's stoppin'," offered James.

"Nah." Alabama shook his head. "It's comin' in spurts. Might rain all night."

"That's good that it's rainin', Daddy," Ruben said. "Better than the way it was
last year."

"Ain't no good for me," Alabama remarked. He wanted to be out of the house,
away from his daughter's suffering. He needed a shot of whiskey.

Mildred lay curled on her bed hugging the pain in her belly and moaning.
Between screams and moans she told them that something was stabbing her in-
side her body, and she wanted her daddy to get it out. His poor Mildred thought
he could protect her from everything, but he knew he couldn't.

"Daddy, it's crawlin' through my face," she screamed.

Because he had to get away from it, Alabama stepped out onto the stoop.
There was a moment of silence before Mildred's cries came out to keep him
company. *What do men do at a time like this?* he wondered. They don't high-tail
it through the rain, although that was what he wanted to do. He was even con-
sidering Miss Girlie's voodoo roots, anything to quiet his daughter.

"It's in my chest, Daddy," the girl yelled, and Alabama felt pain in his chest
as well.

James eased his way to the door. "Daddy, you reckon we oughta take her to
the doctor? I can go get Mr. Edward to bring his wagon 'round here."

Alabama had no money to pay the doctor, but he knew the boy was right. For
the sanity of everybody in the house, he knew they had to do something. "Yeah.
You and Ruben gon' over and get Edward," he answered.

He turned to go back inside. From the door he could see Van Ida standing over the girl's bed, staring down at her. "Her skin's breathin', Alabama. It's really breathin'. Look like settlin' porridge," Van Ida told him.

More foolishness, he thought as he made his way over to his daughter's bed. The boys were pulling on their boots, getting ready to leave out. Mildred was thrashing about, thrusting her hips so forcefully that the sheet had slid away to reveal a swollen belly that quivered like ripples in a creek.

From a wall shelf, Van Ida grabbed a knife, then returned to the bed. She eased the knife beneath the girl's pillow to cut the pain. "It be alright, chile," she soothed. "It be alright."

"Hurry up and do somethin', Ida!" Alabama insisted.

"I think that baby must be comin'," Van Ida told him, although she had no way of knowing. "It probably won't be alive if it come, Alabama. It's too soon."

Alabama pulled the curtain halfway across the ropes, then halted his son's departure. As much as he needed to be away from it, he also needed to know what was happening. "Is that what it is, Ida? Is she havin' the baby?" He called through the opening of the curtain.

Van Ida did not answer him. She tried desperately to calm Mildred, rubbed her back, placed a damp cloth against her head, talked to her. The moaning was unending now, breaking only for little gasps of breath.

"If it's time for the baby, this'll all be over soon," Alabama said to his sons. "I can't see movin' her in no open wagon in this rain if she havin' the baby."

Time passed slowly as heat swelled within the closed confines of the house and rain pitter-pattered against the roof. Van Ida had never delivered a baby before, and the gloom of the space made it hard for her to tell what she should do next. She pulled the curtain all the way across the rope, mainly to keep Alabama from talking over her shoulder while she tried to figure out what to do. She wished she had another woman with her to hold a lantern and guide her along. Alabama and the boys would never come into the girl's space at a time like this. She needed the lantern, but there was no place in the girl's area to set it so that it would be high enough for her to see by. The only light she had to work with was the bit that filtered in through the sheet, and it wasn't enough. Van Ida pressed a hand against Mildred's belly, then she checked to see if the baby's head was coming. She prayed, "God, let it be a head and not feet."

"What's goin' on in there, Ida?" Alabama asked.

Van Ida still didn't answer. Her strength went into straining to see while pleading with Mildred to push. "One a y'all hold that lantern in here so I can see what I'm doin," she called out, and an arm reached through at the corner of the makeshift curtain.

Other than the one holding the lantern, Van Ida couldn't even imagine what the men were doing. Maybe they were staring at each other, mumbling, pacing. She thought she heard the thump, thump, thump of heavy footsteps on the other side of the sheet, but it just as well might have been her own heartbeat. She was wet with perspiration and she felt like she had been working for days when she finally felt the baby's head. "One mo' good push, Mildred. Just one mo.'"

At some hour of the night when the light in the lantern was dimming and the arm extending it was drooping, Van Ida was able to separate a tiny girl-child from the mother. She stared down at the quiet, blue baby, placed her on her mother's belly, then cut the umbilical cord. She was not at all surprised that the baby was dead.

When she glanced down at Mildred's face, she thought they would be burying the two together. Mildred's breathing was shallow, no more moaning, and the only movement she made was the slight twitching of one finger. Her skin appeared ashen in the gloom, and no matter that Van Ida prayed from the very core of her heart, the girl's eyes never opened. A soft, single sigh escaped Mildred's lips, and the blue baby stirred. Although she could not see it, Van Ida felt it. Mildred had blown her last breath into the baby, and souls were shifting within the cubicle.

Van Ida stumbled back against the curtain, nearly tore it down, and the arm extending the lantern disappeared. Her hands, though unclean from the birth, clutched at the collar of her dress. "The zyma root," she gasped, because it could be nothing else. "The zyma root."

The baby began to cry, and Alabama pushed back the curtain to see.

Girlie　Folks want absolution. There was a preacher man used to come through here years ago, travelin' wit' his horse and buggy. That preacher man had so much religion that he could be anythin' folks needed him to be—Baptist, Methodist, Presbyterian, Catholic—just about anythin'. I suspected that sooner or later he might claim to be Jesus. One day he come though here talkin' 'bout savin' souls and how we needed absolution. None of us knew what the heck he was talkin' 'bout. He say he was talkin' 'bout savin' souls, givin' folks a pardon for they sins. That's what he say.

I went wit' ever'body else over to Willow Road. It was nighttime after harvest when we put our pennies and nickels in that preacher man's hat and turned our sins over to him just like he say we oughta. I give two pennies and one nickel 'cause I knew I had done a lotta wrong in my life. But the next day I didn't feel not one drop different. I guess I just didn't have no faith in the man. He never did come back through here after that night, and I reckon all them sins we loaded on him, right along with our pennies, musta weighed on him so heavy 'til he couldn't come back. Tarlo say he was gon' kill 'im anyway if he ever come back through here.

I'm thinkin' 'bout that absolution 'cause yesterday Van Ida come to me wantin' to know what I could do 'bout her sins. She had that li'l baby wit' her all bundled up in a cut-down blanket. She say she had done killed Alabama's daughter. After she had done told me all of it, I knew she hadn't killed that chile.

"You didn't kill Mildred," I say, "but you gon' kill that baby— bringin' 'er out when the whole world still damp. We havin' a rainy season, Van Ida, and you ought not be brangin' 'er out. What she? 'Bout two months ol'?"

You don't set fire to somethin' that's already burnin' outta control, so I ease up on her and say, "Mildred was in a rush to get nowhere. All rushin' do is put you in a early grave. Pray for this baby she done left in this here world, then pray for yo' self, Van Ida. Pray over the sins you know befo' you get to them you don't."

"I done prayed myself stupid," she say. "I done prayed so much 'til even Alabama tired of it. I can't tell 'im 'bout that root."

"You sho' it was a zyma root?" I ask. "Sounds like the girl died from the childbirth fever. And I don't see a thin' wrong wit' this baby. She could'na been no blue baby. But, Van Ida, you musta done somethin' wrong."

"I know," she agreed, noddin' her head and lookin' like sin was heavy on her brow. "Mildred ain't had no fever, Miss Girlie. And I know this here baby was dead when she come out."

'Cause she kept on me to do somethin', I wave my han's in front her face a few times like that preacher done, then I say a prayer from the bottom of my heart and tol' her it was absolution. I think she left here feelin' the way I felt when that preacher man was gone—like it was all a bunch of poppycock and her sins was still wit' her. I watched her leave my porch, holdin' that baby 'gainst her chest, and I felt bad for 'em both. I start to call Van Ida back, give her a cup of my berry wine. My berry wine make most folks forget they troubles, but I think Van Ida needed her grief mo' than anythin' I had to offer.

I been knowin' her all her life. She musta been 'bout six or seven the last time I set foot on the Jepson plantation. She was tall, and folks worked her by her height 'stead of her age. Her folks had done left here searchin' for a better way a life, say they'd send for her when they found the right place. They never did. Now she livin' out there on Blevins Stretch wit' some man that come from who knows where, who don't know nothin' 'bout our ways. I feel bad for Van Ida, but I ain't the one to give no absolution.

Part II

CHAPTER 9

Sleep allowed him to forget, but morning brought with it an ache in a heart that was no longer there. He had heard it said that time heals all wounds, but time had done nothing to close the gaping hole that grief had left in his chest. Mildred had been buried at the very end of Willow Road in the Cranston cemetery. It seemed so far away, and she was so young to be out there with people she had never known. Prohibition had ended a few years back, but Alabama's financial situation held him to moonshine, and often he couldn't even afford that. Sometimes he would find himself in a single or widowed woman's bed, but he never found relief.

Every evening he went home from a field with an ugly woman and a strange child. James and Ruben had stayed long enough to work and help pay for Mildred's burial, then they had stolen away in the middle of the night without a word to him. He hadn't raised his sons to desert anything, and above all family. What bothered him most was not confronting them when he first knew that they wouldn't stay, couldn't stay. They were fearful of a child that never should have been born. The raising of another girl-child was a little more than Alabama could tolerate, and he had more or less turned the responsibility over to Van Ida.

"You may as well go on and do it, Alabama. She ain't much to look at, but she done stuck by you all these many years. And I ain't never seen no woman work so hard. It'll be the best thing for you if you just gon' and do it. If you don't, you may have mo' losses than you can take."

Those had been Theron Evers's words to him six years ago, at a time when Alabama had been grieving the loss of his daughter and wondering if he'd have to bury her baby, too. Right away people had wanted to know if the baby had been born with teeth or a veil. He couldn't have answered their questions even if he had wanted to. During those first months, during that first year, he hadn't even been able to look at the child. Too much had happened too fast.

Although it had to be done, Alabama couldn't seem to wrap his mind around picking cotton today. His thoughts were on his sons and the way they had abandoned him. When they'd left, it had made him wonder about Van Ida. Would she stay and raise another child that was not her own? He hadn't known. Since he trusted Theron more than any other man alive, Alabama had considered his advice.

"I'm still married to Katie," he had said.

"She been gone so long I doubt if anybody remember who she is," Theron reminded him. "Tell folks she died."

"But what if she come back?"

"Then you'll have to kill her."

"Don't even joke like that, Theron. And how I'm gon' stand in front of Reverend Smith, tell him I wanna marry somebody else when he the one married me to Katie?"

Theron thought about it for a minute, scraped at his round chin with a thumb, then said, "Tell you what. I'll borrow Neville's truck, drive you to another county where don't nobody know nothin' 'bout you and Katie. But I tell you, Alabama, Reverend Smith too old by now to even remember y'all."

Alabama knew his friend meant well, but it was something he'd had to think on long and hard. Finally, he began to tell people that Katie was dead, realized too late that nobody would have asked if he hadn't brought it up. He had been forced to keep lying. He had tried to answer questions, tried to keep his lies straight. *When did she die? How did she die? Where is she buried?* He prayed his lies would not reach Katie's family out at the Dean place. He kept expecting Katie to show up and ask why he had killed her off before her time. When she did not, he married Van Ida.

He didn't love her, and it really didn't matter. He had needed her at first to take care of his children, and he had never felt obligated to marry her. Things had changed, though. Van Ida seemed restless, and he had feared she would leave the way Katie had done, not hang around to raise yet another child. He supposed he could have gone searching for a better-looking woman, but Van Ida worked the fields better than most men. She kept his house neat, cooked his meals, and he had gotten used to her. She wasn't a beauty, but how many men looked for beauty in a cotton field? How many women would feel as duty-bound to please him as Van Ida?

Alabama glanced up the row to his right and could see Zyma trailing behind Van Ida. Van Ida wore an old straw hat and a dark green dress with full sleeves—the same dowdy dress she had worn on their wedding day. Zyma, full of questions, paused in her chatter long enough to pluck a mousy amount of cotton from a boll and drop it into Van Ida's sack. Van Ida was patient with the child, actually smiled with her. Alabama wondered what they found amusing because there wasn't very much to smile about. It was a damn hot September day. He was sweating from every pore in his body, couldn't seem to take in enough water.

In the row to his left, Theron was stooped and picking. Alabama took the time to glance out at the heads and backs of the other pickers. Sometimes he wondered if one of the men was Zyma's daddy. Was he one of the farm tenants or one of the workers from town? Van Ida said it didn't matter, but it did matter to him. If he found out, though, what could he do about it? Kill the man? Make the man take responsibility for Zyma? Probably, he would never know, and he also knew that he wasn't going to kill anybody.

"You need water over there?" he called out to Theron.

Theron shook his head, never glanced up. The man wasn't a field worker, but he would come out when work was slow elsewhere. Most often he worked for Miss Dora Cranston, did repairs on her aging but eloquent home and kept her yard and shrubbery spruced up. Whenever there was a rumor of decent work with decent wages, Theron would find a way to get there, too. Often he invited Alabama to join him on some of the jobs in neighboring towns, but Alabama always refused. Transportation was scarce in Cranston. There were a few trucks, fewer automobiles, and men like Neville Sloan and Robert Union charged for a ride whether you found work or not. There were three Negro farmers in the area who owned mules and wagons. They didn't mind providing a ride sometimes, but it wasn't something Alabama was prepared to depend on.

"You good wit' yo' hands," Theron had told him once. "You need to come on, show folks what you can do."

"I'm gon' use these good hands to keep workin' Mr. Blevins' fields," Alabama had said. "Folks ain't plantin' crops like they used to. I ain't gon' cross Mr. Blevins. This is for sho' work in his fields, and I can't be tryin' to hitch no ride to all them places you go. Nah. I'm gon' stay here and do what I know."

Alabama wiped his brow and threw himself back into the tedious job of picking. He decided to work a while longer before sending his granddaughter to the shade for his water jar. There was a water boy he could call out for. The boy would come with a bucket and dipper, but Alabama had seen some of the mouths he had been drinking behind and had decided to bring his own water. He didn't want his teeth to start dropping out like Opal's.

Had the girl not slowed Van Ida down, Alabama was sure he never would have caught up to them. They were now nearly abreast of each other. He stood and watched Van Ida, tried to work the word "wife" across his tongue. He couldn't do it. Each time she straightened her tall frame, he could see the dark skin of her neck glistening with perspiration. She wore her cotton sack as though it were another garment, with her head through the hole made by the strap, and the strap pressed into her left shoulder.

It stood to reason that he would get tired long before she did. He figured that he was about eight or nine years older than she was. As he watched her nimble fingers sweep through the bolls, it occurred to him the work that Van Ida did each day before and after the fields. He had to admit that she had been a godsend.

Alabama abandoned his thoughts of Van Ida and glanced at Theron, who was already ahead of him. "Theron, I reckon this row gon' end somewhere in Tennessee," he said. "What you think?"

"I think you headed in the wrong direction."

"If it was up to me, I wouldn't plant cotton like this. I'd make the rows shorter so a man can feel like he gettin' somewhere."

"If you'd stop talkin' and tryin' to slow me down, you'd get to the end of that damn row," Theron said. "Ain't nothin' stoppin' Van Ida. How you gon' feel tonight when she weigh in at two hundred to yo' fifty? Do you even have fifty pounds yet, Alabama?"

Alabama tugged at the wrists of his threadbare gloves, then stooped and began to snatch cotton from the bolls. He did not answer Theron. He figured they had been in the field for about three or four hours already. Every man, woman, and child should have more than fifty pounds by now. Theron was right, though. It always bothered him when Van Ida weighted in with more than he had managed, especially when he had given the day and the field all that he was worth.

He saw his granddaughter coming toward him, heading back down the row. He assumed Van Ida had sent the girl for water. He would catch her on her way back, nab the water jar, and take him a long, cool drink. He waited.

Van Ida was ahead of him again, but only by a couple of feet. He experienced a smidgen of satisfaction when she removed the strap from her shoulder and pressed her hands against the small of her back. She was just as hot and tired as he was, but too stubborn to admit it. Her hands moved up to her shoulders and briefly massaged the muscles there. She was working the kinks out. What caught Alabama's attention was the sway of her hips in that worn-thin dress each time she shifted her body. Briefly, her backside reminded him of a girl he had seen dancing at Sloan's Place one night. She had been a young, beautiful creature by the name of Wondrene. Alabama would never forget that name, nor would he ever forget her gorgeous hips, like the ones Van Ida was now flaunting in his face.

He wiped his brow for about the hundredth time. It had to be the heat. The heat was getting to him because those hips were starting to look quite tempting. Over the years he had seldom touched Van Ida, had never desired her. He told himself that he had no desire for her now; however, if he could brush up against those hips, fill his hands with those hips instead of fiber, maybe that would take him the rest of the way down the long, long row of cotton.

"Daddy! Daddy!"

Alabama turned to see his granddaughter advancing between the rows. Her head was swathed in yellow cloth, but he could see her face clearly. He couldn't say exactly what it was that she was wearing, just something or the other that Van Ida had thrown together. It looked like an old dress sewn lengthwise through the skirt. She was holding the water jar against her chest with both hands. As she approached, Alabama stayed where he was—not wanting to remove his cotton sack, not wanting to drag it—waited for the water to come to him.

"Daddy, Mr. Wilbur keep breathin' in my ear," the girl said. "Make him stop it!"

Alabama was not sure he understood the child. He leaned down. "What'd you say, Zyma?"

"Mr. Wilbur. He keep breathin' in my ear."

Zyma was a small six-year-old. She had his pecan-brown complexion, and her mother's gleeful, brown eyes. Somebody on her father's side must have had a thin, upturned nose, because she had that, too. He studied her eyes for some sign of fear. There was no fear, no conception of danger.

"What's Wilbur been sayin' to you?" he asked.

"Nothin', Daddy. He just breathes in my ear." The girl said it as though it were some game she had been playing and had suddenly grown weary of.

Alabama dropped his sack, sat down on it, and waited for anger to take control of him. He wasn't angry, though, because Wilbur Johnson did not strike him as the kind of man who would bother a child. Wilbur was close to sixty, limped when he walked, and was as slow as a turtle. As small as she was, Zyma could outrun him if she needed to. He pulled his granddaughter closer to him, eased the water jar from her hands, then took a drink that nearly emptied the container. Finally, he called Van Ida and Theron over and shared with them Zyma's revelation.

"You gon' stomp him?" Theron asked.

Alabama shook his head. "Nah. I'm gon' talk to him first. But if he look the least little bit guilty, I'm gon' march his ass out to the swamp. Whatever happens to him happens. Won't be no blood on my hands."

Van Ida had been looking out over the field. There were about forty rounded backs moving along the rows. She could not tell which one was Wilbur's. "Where Wilbur at?" she asked.

"You can't see him from here, Mama," Zyma answered. "He down on the ground."

"Did he try to make you get on the ground wit' him?" Alabama asked. And the thought of it brought on the anger. It surged through him, yanked him up from the sack. He thrust the water jar at Van Ida as rage propelled him blindly forward. "Yeah, I'm gon' stomp him," he said.

"Anybody seen Wilbur Johnson?" Theron's booming voice called out across the field. Backs straightened, and heads turned in the direction of the voice.

Zyma rushed to catch up to her grandfather. "I know where he at, Daddy. I know."

Alabama took his granddaughter's hand and allowed her to lead him. Others had abandoned their work and were now following, sensing that there was going to be trouble. Out on the road at the weigh-in, they found Wilbur Johnson stretched on the ground. It looked as though he had been trying to crawl to the shade and hadn't quite made it. He was covered in sweat, so much that it poured from his hair and face and wet the ground beneath his head. One hand was clutched into a fist and rested against his chest. There was a severe scowl on his face when the group surrounded him, but he never said a word.

"You think it's heat stroke?" Alabama asked Theron.

"I don't know what it is, but he sho' looks bad."

Van Ida knelt beside the man and attempted to give him water from her jar. The water dribbled from one corner of his lips, and he gave a short, dry cough. She could hear him struggling to breathe. "Some of y'all needs to move on back," she said to the crowd. "Give him a little air."

They did as she asked, but only a step or two. Curiosity held them there to gawk at their fallen neighbor. He looked as though he was about to draw his last breath, and nobody wanted to miss it.

Zyma stepped away from her grandfather and dropped down next to the man. She touched the fist that rested on his chest. "I don't like it when you breathe in my ear, Mr. Wilbur," she said. "Why you do that?"

Wilbur Johnson was trying to open his eyes, his lips were moving, and the scowl eased from his face. He took in a heap of breath that expanded his lungs and allowed him to exhale slowly. He seemed to be coming around.

Van Ida, on the ground across from Zyma, could see the pained expression that came over the child's face. Her small hand clutched Wilbur's heavy fist, and she shuddered. She shuddered again, and then her body began to shiver violently, as though she were freezing. Through it all, she never released Wilbur's fist.

"What's wrong wit' her?" somebody asked.

Van Ida lifted the girl's hand, pulled her away from Wilbur. She wrapped Zyma in her arms, rocked her, tried to rub the shivers out of the girl's small arms. When the trembling finally subsided, Zyma squirmed to free herself. She glanced up at Van Ida. "I helped him, Mama."

"She done killed him!" Opal Lester shouted. "That's what she done done. She done killed him."

Wilbur Johnson was as still as death for sure and his face was now a picture of serenity. The people waited for him to breathe, to move, but he didn't. When Theron Evers knelt and pressed his ear against Wilbur's chest, he heard no heartbeat.

Maude Baker took a step closer. "Is he really dead?" she asked.

"Sho' he dead," Opal answered. "Alabama's girl done killed him just as sho' as I'm standin' here. They come over here to kill 'im. Y'all heard that girl say somethin' 'bout him breathin' in her ear. Y'all know Wilbur ain't done nothin' like that."

"Maybe it was the heat, or his heart," Lawrence Anderson suggested. He was currently courting Opal, and he wanted her to be quiet.

"Nah," Opal disputed. "Y'all seen, just like me, how that girl had a fit on top of Wilbur's chest. It's the work of a witch."

"Who ever heard of a witch at the noon-day hour?" Maude asked.

"Ahhh," Opal exclaimed. "They might come out at night, but they can leave they evil out all day long. This here's the work of a witch."

Van Ida rose to her full height, and eased Zyma behind her to shield the girl from the scornful eyes of Opal Lester. She had promised herself that she would be stronger for Zyma than she had ever been for Mildred. "You say that one mo' time, Opal, I'm gon' have to knock all seven of yo' teeth out." She stated it flatly, firmly. "Wilbur is dead for sho', but ain't nobody killed him."

They parted for the field boss who had finally made his way to their circle. Rather than asking questions about the man on the ground, he gave orders. "Two of you men stay here to get him loaded on the truck. The rest of y'all get on back to work. Theron, I'm gon' need you to ride with me to the doctor."

Alabama and Theron lifted the body onto the back of the truck. The others slowly began to head back to their rows. They glanced up at the sun, worried about the heat, worried about the time they had lost away from their work. Nobody worried much about Wilbur.

. . . .

It would be late when Alabama came home, if he came at all. He had left the field headed for Sloan's Place. Sloan's Place was where the men in Cranston went to swap stories and drink their troubles away. Sometimes a few of the women would join them. Tonight they would discuss what had happened to Wilbur Johnson. Women would speak only good of the dead, but the men would speak the truth, and nobody was going to believe that Wilbur had bothered Zyma.

Van Ida knew that it was up to her to speak to the child about what had happened in the field. Zyma was her cross to bear. At the birth of the child, Van Ida had audibly cursed the zyma root, and had unintentionally named the child. Alabama and the boys thought she had said Zyma Ruth, and that was the name that had stuck. She had seen no way or reason to correct the mistake and had let it stand as a reminder of her sin. She did not think that anybody other than Miss Girlie would associate the name with a swamp root, since most folks had no knowledge of the root.

She waited until the girl was done eating and was tucked away for the night, then she sat on the edge of the bed, which had belonged to the child's mother. Van Ida touched the girl's hair. It was long, thick, and tangled. She had no hand for hair and didn't like to fool with Zyma's anyway. It was easier to tie the girl's hair up during the day and let it loose at night.

"Zyma, chile, we need to talk 'bout what happened out there in the field today," Van Ida began. "You need to tell me how it come to be that Wilbur was breathin' in yo' ear."

"He wanted me to come to him, Mama," Zyma answered. "He was loud in my ear, and I wanted him to stop it."

Van Ida stared at the child. Zyma had been with her all day, except for the few minutes it had taken to go for the water jar. "Did he do that when you went for the water?"

"All day, Mama. He did it all day."

"But you was wit' me all day, baby. He wadn't nowhere near us."

"I know. But I could hear him."

"Did he talk to you, say anythin' to you?"

Zyma shook her head. "Just breathe."

"Well, how you know it was Wilbur? How come it could'na been somebody else?"

The girl shrugged. "It was him, Mama. I know it was him."

Out in the field, Zyma had followed Van Ida back to their row. The only thing she had said was, "Mr. Wilbur gone now, Mama. I don't hear him no mo."

Van Ida thought that there had to be confusion jumping around inside the girl's head. "What you know 'bout dyin', chile?" she asked.

Zyma lay on her back, stared up at the ceiling. "It's when you go away and don't never come back. Like Miss Shirley did, and like y'all say my Mama Mildred did when I was born. It make you and Daddy sad when y'all say her name, so I be sad, too. But it ain't nothin' to be sad. Mr. Wilbur wadn't sad—not after I help 'im change somethin'." The girl lowered her voice to a whisper. "It was a bad thing."

The girl had it partially right, but Van Ida knew that the dead sometimes came back. She stood, paced the floor of the small house, wrung her hands. At the door she peered out into the night, wondered if she should wait for Alabama before she asked the child about the bad thing. Always she had tried to keep a close watch over Zyma, did not want to repeat the mistakes she had made with Mildred. She needed to know who had done this bad thing, though. The child, or Wilbur, or both?

When Van Ida turned from the door she saw that Zyma was watching her, staring, patiently waiting to tell her about the bad thing. She took a kitchen chair and placed it beside the child's bed. As she sat on the chair and leaned forward, she could feel dread creeping along her spine.

"Who done this bad thin' that you talkin' 'bout, chile? Was it you or Wilbur?"

Zyma sat up in the center of the bed. She giggled, then momentarily covered her mouth. "Mr. Wilbur, Mama," she answered. "He took off his clothes."

"Go 'head," Van Ida said with a nod. "Tell me 'bout it."

"I seen Mr. Wilbur. He wadn't so old, and he could walk good—like Daddy. He opened the door." Zyma almost sang the words. "And then he look at a woman who was on a bed. She didn't see him. I think she was asleep. Then Mr. Wilbur, he pulled down his pants and he tried to make that woman naked, too."

Van Ida nodded. "Go 'head."

"Mr. Wilbur fell on that woman, and they was bouncin', and the woman start screamin' 'cause I don't think she like to be bounced. Then Mr. Wilbur, he told her to shut up, but she didn't do it." Zyma slapped a hand over her mouth, then removed it. "He covered the woman's mouth just like that, Mama, but she was still tryin' to scream. Mr. Wilbur, he say, 'Shut up, Evelyn! Don't make me hurt you.' He put both his hands on that woman's neck. And her head was bouncin' just like the bed. Then she wadn't screamin'. And when Mr. Wilbur got up off that woman, she never did move no mo'."

Van Ida sat silent for a long while, staring at the wall behind the bed. "Then what did Wilbur do?" she finally asked.

"He touch her neck and her face. And he touch his own face 'cause he was bleedin' where she scratch him. I think he was scared; he look like it. Then he pull his pants back up, and he ran outta that room. You wanna know how I help 'im, Mama?"

Van Ida could not answer right away. She was remembering. It had been sixteen years ago when Robert Winston's daughter, Evelyn, was raped and murdered right in her own house. The law had come over from Mays Spur to investigate, but nobody ever found out who committed the crime.

Van Ida could feel her heart pounding in her chest. She straightened her back, used one hand to rub at the dull ache that was starting behind her forehead. "Go 'head, chile. How you help 'im?" she asked.

"It was makin' Mr. Wilbur sad, so I made it so it never did happen. It was awright for Mr. Wilbur to die, Mama, 'cause now he never did bounce that woman. But I know he did."

"Oh, chile! Chile," Van Ida groaned. "You be my burden to bear, my reason to breathe. This gotta stay 'tween me and you. Don't you say nothin' to nobody else."

"Why?" Zyma wanted to know.

"Cause it ain't right what you sayin'."

"But, Mama, I saw it."

"Don't matter what you saw, just don't say nothin' to nobody."

Van Ida kissed Zyma's cheek, then watched as the child stretched on the bed and closed her eyes. She was certain that Zyma had just described a rape and murder. She would be alright, Van Ida guessed, since the worst thing to her had been the sight of a naked man—the bad thing.

After replacing the chair at the table, Van Ida went to stand outside on the stoop. Had it not been so dark, she would have worked in her garden, or maybe pulled water from the well to take a bath. She suddenly felt dirty on the outside and empty on the inside. The night sang out its strident notes, the sky was filled

NOVELS

with stars, and yet Van Ida felt hollow—like she was in the world alone. Alabama was somewhere out there. She closed her eyes and willed him to come to her, to hold her in his arms—just hold her for a spell. She had seen Theron do that for his wife, Nadine. But Nadine wasn't straight-up tall and ugly. She didn't work in a field; she worked in one of the big houses in Mays Spur, and her hands probably weren't rough and calloused. Theron would kiss the palms of Nadine's hands sometimes like she was special. Alabama had never done that for her, probably never would, and still she willed him to come.

CHAPTER 11

Theron Evers lived in two rooms of a row house on a dirt road that had no name. When he thought of Cranston it put him in the mind of a big, flat, deformed foot with one gigantic bunion and too many toes spiraling in too many directions. Willow Road ran about as straight as anything could get in Cranston. It was a mile-long road that ran south into the county road and terminated north at the cemetery. Three shanties, one house, and the old Philpot store stood on Willow. Across from those were overgrown weeds and open space.

Theron had no gripes with Cranston. The outlying fields stretched forever, and a man could usually find work. A number of farms in Butcher County had been repossessed, and Miss Dora's landownership had shrunk over the years, due mostly to her husband's negligence before he died. Theron had seen a peach orchard grow on land that had once belonged to Miss Dora, and he had thought how it should have been him growing peaches. Miss Dora had two nephews who would come in from Albany and sell off parcels of her land when ever they took a notion and could convince her that they were doing it for her sake.

Miss Dora's house was showing its age and still managed to be one of the most stately homes in Mays Spur. Her nephew, Stanley, had come from Albany with another man on Wednesday while Theron was laying sod in the yard. Miss Dora's maid, Inez, had come out to the bring him water that he hadn't asked for. She lingered as though she had something to say, and Theron waited.

"Mr. Stanley up in there fussin' wit' Miss Dora," she finally said. "He say she gettin' ol', but ain't we all?"

"Yeah," Theron agreed.

"He goin' over there to look at some mo' of her land in Cranston 'cause he say these ain't no times for things to go to waste. That's a lawyer man wit' 'im, and they keep talkin' 'bout how Miss Dora gotta recover her losses. I think he tryin' to take that land from her. Ain't no tellin' what he gon' do wit' it, but I thought I oughta let you know since you live over there. He keep tellin' Miss Dora how she never oughta married Mr. George. He right, you know, but I don't think nobody oughta throw that in her face."

A couple of days had passed, and now Theron climbed the steps and crossed the porch of his own residence. There was a hallway that separated his two rooms from the two rooms of his neighbor. Every room in the house had a door

NOVELS

that opened off the hallway. He stood in the dim space and could hear voices coming from both dwellings. Ulysses Sampson was preaching to his wife, Lynnette, telling her how the Good Book proved something she had done was a sin before God. They were a young couple. Ulysses worked at a lumber mill during the week and preached in an open space on Willow Road on Sundays.

From his own place, Theron could hear the mumblings of a conversation taking place between his wife, Nadine, and his son, Brill. He wanted to pace while he contemplated how to best do what he needed to do. He didn't move, though, because pacing footsteps on the weak floorboards of the hall would have drawn attention. He did not want somebody opening a door and asking him what he was doing marching through the hallway.

What he was doing was trying to find the right words to tell his wife that he wanted to buy a house, and to ask his nine-year-old son to teach him how to read and write. Mr. Stanley had convinced Miss Dora that she needed to unload this house—the house that Theron had lived in for the past twelve years—and the two neighboring houses as a package deal.

"Aunt Dora has come to terms with selling off some of her property," Mr. Stanley had said, "but she wants to offer it to you first. If you can't buy it, she'll understand and we'll look for another buyer."

Theron had a choice. He could either buy the houses himself, or he could sit back and let someone else get them. What if somebody else who had scraped and saved the way he had got wind of the offer and bought them first? He figured men like Wash Gibson and Neville Sloan could probably come up with the money, but Neville already owned more property than he needed. What if some man from Mays Spur bought the three houses and tore them down to build something else? Money was scarce, but people were looking for ways to survive, and what better way than owning land?

Theron tried to think of something that the land would be perfect for, but all he could think of was himself, his family, his home. He did not want to pack up his family and move. Where would they go? For sure, he did not want to live in some shack like a majority of the people in Cranston were doing. He liked sitting on his front porch, even though his view was a dirt road and a forest of pine trees.

This house had been a step up for him. When he first moved to Cranston from the Esterfield Plantation, he had lived in a one-room house on Marshall

Road. Marshall Road was where Mr. Blevins's field boss came with the truck in the early mornings to pick up the workers who wanted to ride out to the Blevinses' fields. Theron would ride sometimes, but mostly he liked to walk. He had been out on Tuesday, and he had watched an old friend die. He had seen Alabama's little granddaughter give more comfort with the touch of a hand than anybody could have done with words.

On Thursday Mr. Stanley had wanted to visit the Cranston property and had asked Theron to show him where people usually saw snakes out on the land. His lawyer friend had come along, too. They didn't see any snakes, and they didn't seem interested in anything on the land, except maybe the trees.

Theron had been approached again by Mr. Stanley. The man asked him if he had made a decision about the three houses on the two acres of land where Theron lived. Theron had always worked and had saved every penny he could for all these many years. He was thirty-seven, and ready to have something to show for all of his hard work.

Standing in the hallway wasn't getting him closer to anything. He sighed, then pushed open the door to his front room. His wife and son were startled by his early arrival. They fell silent and glanced over at him.

"You home early today," Nadine observed.

"Yeah," Theron nodded, "that's 'cause I got something I need to talk to y'all about."

He could tell that Nadine was trying to read the expression on his face. He purposely kept it neutral. He was nearly busting at the seams at the prospect of owning property, but there were drawbacks. The major drawback was that they purposely had no material goods, had been saving for a reason, and now he was about to propose that they spend their life savings on three houses that were barely standing. The room he had entered held two beds, a backless wooden bench, and two hardback chairs. Nadine and Brill occupied the bench, so he pulled up a chair and sat facing them. The smell of supper was drifting in from the kitchen. It was a combination of green beans, potatoes, and onions.

"Girl, you sho' got this house smellin' good," Theron commented as he leaned forward to kiss his wife.

Nadine was a healthy woman, thick all over, from her hair to her legs. Long before he had ever tasted her cooking, she had won his heart with a smile. No matter how sad or worried he was, if Nadine smiled, he'd have to smile, too. That's just the way it was, had always been, but she wasn't smiling now.

"What's troublin' you, Theron?" she asked.

"What make you think I'm troubled?"

"Them lines in yo' face that's runnin' ear to ear and chin to hair. Now, you gon' tell me what's wrong, or you gon' make me sit here and worry, too?"

"Mr. Stanley is talkin' 'bout sellin' this house for Miss Dora," he said. "This one and them other two out there."

"Oh, my God!" Nadine exclaimed. "I know you ain't tryin' to tell me we gotta start lookin' for some place to live."

"Let me finish, Nadine. He ain't told nobody yet, 'cept me. He givin' us a chance to buy 'em if we want to. I know for sho' that he tryin' to get rid of just about all Miss Dora's property. So I gotta know what you think. I gotta know what Brill think, too."

"We gotta have somewhere to live, Daddy," Brill said. "I done seen folks ain't got no place to live. I don't want that to be us."

"We ain't gon' be wit'out a place to live," Theron explained. "Could be somebody we know might buy 'em, and we can keep right on livin' here. But I was hopin' y'all might see things my way. We can buy 'em."

Nadine was silent and staring. Her fingers were interlocked, and she was twiddling her thumbs. "Did he say how much?" she finally asked. "I don't wanna waste all our money on these houses. We can't trust Mr. Stanley, and ever'body know Miss Dora been soft in the head for some time now. Look how they sold that land to Walter Baker, waited 'til he built him a house, then took the land back. How you know they ain't gon' do the same thing to you? S'pose we buy 'em, and ever'body move out. Times is hard right now, and we'd be stuck wit' three empty houses. I gotta sleep on this, Theron. And I thought we was savin' that money so Brill could go to school and be a doctor or somethin'."

"We'll save the money up again, Nadine," Theron assured her.

"I ain't gotta sleep on it, Daddy," Brill said. "Buy 'em! And I ain't sho' I wanna be no doctor no way. We got enough doctors 'round these parts. We got Mr. Wash and Miss Girlie, that doctor in Mays Spur, and two animal doctors. How many doctors we gotta have?"

"Stop it!" Nadine snapped. "I mean you stop it right now, Brill. I done saved since the day you was born so you could grow up and be somethin'. We ain't never made you go out to them fields or down to the fishin' boats. You don't even know what hard work is. Don't you see them other boys yo' age goin' out to them fields and boats ever'day? Don't you see how my feet swell up when I come home from cross town, and how yo' daddy come draggin' in her ever' night? All we ever ask you to do is study hard and get some learnin'. And that's what you gon' do."

"Yes, ma'am." Brill dropped his head, but not before Theron saw the tears brimming in the boy's eyes.

They were silent, and so were the couple across the hall. Theron hoped the Sampsons had not heard his plea, Brill's whining, or Nadine's outburst. He got up, went out to the kitchen to fix himself a plate of food. He figured Nadine was too angry to be bothered. After a while, he heard his wife apologizing to their son.

"I'm sorry, Brill," she said. "I don't mean to be cross wit' you, but sometimes you gotta think about things befo' you jump into 'em. And you ain't never gon' have to worry 'bout where to live. You got a daddy that's gon' always make sho' you got a roof over yo' head."

Theron sat down and ate. He ate everything on his plate, but for the first time since he had married Nadine, the food didn't taste so good in his mouth. He knew it was wrong to count chickens before they'd hatched. That was what he had done. All the way home he had made plans of how he would buy the houses, fix them up, and collect his own rent for a change. Nadine was right, though; they had to think about their son.

Without meaning to, he had roused hard feelings between his wife and son. An apology had been given and accepted. Theron had heard it, but when he reentered the front room he was met by two gloomy faces. Brill was on the floor trying to hide his face behind a writing tablet. Nadine was sitting on the bed concentrating on sewing the ripped sleeve of a shirt. Theron went over to his son, dropped down on the floor beside the boy.

"Show me how to write my name." He said it quickly, before he could change his mind. "I guess I gon' need to know how if we gon' be buyin' us a house. Don't wanna be makin no X's on somethin' that's gon' be yo's one day."

"I thought we wadn't gettin' no house," Brill said sullenly.

"Yo mama said she was gon' sleep on it. So I guess we just have to wait and see." They both turned to glance at Nadine, but her gaze was fixed on her sewing.

Brill gave his father a pencil, then placed the writing tablet on the floor. "How many letters of the alphabet can you write?" he asked.

"I can make the X and the I."

Brill took the pencil back and wrote some letters on the paper. He began to sound the letters out for his father.

Learning to read and write was going to be harder than Theron had thought, and he was ready to change his mind until he saw how enthused the boy was about teaching him. They remained on the floor for hours, wasting page after page of valuable paper. Nadine had finished her sewing and had fallen asleep. Brill finally went off to bed, but Theron stayed where he was, kept trying to get his letters to look like Brill's.

He dozed and was awakened by Nadine shaking his shoulder. The pencil was still in his hand, and the only thing that kept his face off the bare floor was the writing tablet. "Is it time to get up?" he asked sleepily.

"Nah," she answered. "I come to talk to you 'bout these houses."

"You done slept on it?"

She stretched on the floor beside him, draped an arm across his chest. "I slept on somethin' that wadn't my man," she said, "and I didn't like the feelin'. You gon' and tell Mr. Stanley that we gon' buy these houses. It ain't gon' be easy, Theron. Times is hard, like I said. Even the white folk losin' they land, they farms and tractors."

"I know," he said, "but we'll make it, Nadine."

"I let doubt come creepin' in," she said. "I done always trusted you, and I ain't 'bout to stop now."

Theron wanted to pull her into his arms, pick her up, spin her around. He was happy, but he thought that to move from his spot would disturb the moment, turn it back on him somehow. He kissed her lightly, then woke his son with laughter.

Girlie Odell Grady died some months back, and now Wilbur Johnson. Must be gettin' close to my time 'cause ever'body know folks go in threes. I don't reckon I'd be thinkin' like this if Miss Dora didn't get her driver to bring her out to my house. She knew Odell, but she say she can't recall no Wilbur, wanna know if he was a decent, God-fearin' man. I say, "I reckon ever'body on this land fear God in one way or another." After that, she ain't had nothin' else to say 'bout Wilbur. Miss Dora done got so ol' 'til I hadda creep down my steps to help her up in here. I guess her driver don't go inside colored folk's houses. Usually, she don't, neither.

"Girlie, you don't come to visit me like you used to," she say. "All of my friends are gone, except you. And I get so lonely in that big house all by myself."

I ain't never been to visit Miss Dora in my life. Been there to see after her sickness, but never no friendly visit, and we sho' ain't never been friends. "Miss Dora, don't you still live in that big house on Lowell Street?" I ask. "Look like to me you ought never get lonely. You can watch ever'thin' in that town right from yo' window."

"It's not the same," she say and fumble in her pocketbook for a handkerchief, one of them fancy kind wit' flowers sewed on ever' corner. "I remember a time when people were falling all over each other to visit with me," she say. "That doesn't happen anymore. And do you know they keep changing sheriffs? I tell you, Girlie, I didn't like that last one, and I don't like this one, either."

White folk business is white folk business. I wadn't 'bout to let her hear me say nothin' 'bout that white sheriff. I don't know 'im no way.

"This one took my keys," she say.

I knew what keys she meant, and it was 'bout time somebody took 'em.

"Did you ever use them keys, Miss Dora?" I ask.

She dabbed at her face wit' her fancy handkerchief, rubbed down the puffs under her eyes, but them puffs sprung right back. "No. I never used them myself," she say. "One day, some years ago, they locked up one of my Negras. I sent a man around there in the middle

No Ordinary Rain   277

of the night to set that boy free. I have the right to decide what happens to my own Negras."

"You don't own no Negroes," I say. "Maybe yo' folks did a long time ago, but slavery times is over, Miss Dora. Don't nobody own us no mo'."

She laugh and I heard a bit of the young Miss Dora in that laugh. "This is Cranston land," she say. "I own all the Negras on my land. There's no other way it can be. I'd like to give you your freedom, Girlie, and I probably will in a few more years."

My fingers start movin', countin' up my numbers. Now, I'm seventy-one; she gotta be close to seventy-five. Her hair is all the way gray and her back done curved over. She ain't got no "few more years." I got up from my chair, feelin' dizzy in my head, and made my way to the do'. I wiggled my fingers at the driver to come up to my steps and get Miss Dora. I helped her to her feet and led her out to the porch. "It's gettin' late, Miss Dora," I say. "You don't wanna be over in here when the snakes start comin' in out the sun."

"You're right," she say. "I could always count on you to look out for me, Girlie. You come on over and visit with me real soon. I'll give you a chair that's more comfortable than that old thing I was sitting in."

The driver took Miss Dora's han' and led her down the steps. When she reach the ground, she turn and look up at me. "Electrification is coming to Cranston," she say. "That means that all the houses over here will have electric lights."

"I don't want no electric, Miss Dora."

"You have no say in the matter," she tell me. "That's what I've been trying to tell you. This is my land. My daddy left it to me. My brother and nephews are trying to take it from me, but they'll never get their hands on it. Everything that grows around here comes from my soil. I've allowed you to live here, Girlie, and I've never troubled you, but all the Negras here belong to me."

"I'm free, Miss Dora. Yo' daddy give me this house when he move me here."

"Do you have a deed?" she ask.

I stood there knowin' I didn't, don't even know what a deed look like. I felt like cryin', somethin' I ain't done in over forty years. "No, ma'am," I answer, "I ain't got no deed, but I'm free, Miss Dora. I'm free to leave yo' land, go anywhere I wanna go."

"No, Girlie, you're not," she say. "If you try to leave, I'll have you thrown in jail. Stanley's lawyer estimates that you owe me hundreds of dollars, dating all the way back to the day my daddy died."

"You send the law after me, I'm gon' send the snakes after you," I threaten. I was madder than Hell.

All of a sudden she was in a rush to leave. She need to be usin' a walkin' stick, but I reckon she got too much pride to use one. I watched her backside in that white dress as she was helped into the automobile. Funny how the backside of ol' fat women start droppin' wit' time, and I don't reckon they make no harness to hol' that up. I put my han's behind me and touch my own narrow backside. It's done dropped, too, but I didn't know it 'til I seen Miss Dora's. Her visit done made me tired. I'm gon' go in there to my back room and rest for a spell. Tired as Miss Dora done made me, I just might lay there 'til I pass on over to Glory.

The Lord works in mysterious ways. That was what Alabama thought on that Saturday afternoon as he sat in Sloan's Place across the table from Wondrene Louise Barry. He had her full name now, and she had his undivided attention. Because she was sitting on the hips that had first attracted him, he concentrated on her other assets. Stylish in dress—she had long, slender legs, a flawless ginger complexion, and naturally wavy hair. The depression hadn't touched her in any way. She was without a doubt the most beautiful woman he had ever seen.

She said she was in town for Wilbur's funeral. Wilbur had been a cousin, just like Neville was, just like a lot of people were. She said she couldn't believe it when Neville sent the telegram to her in Atlanta telling her that Wilbur was dead. She'd had to come see for herself. Wilbur's children were scattered, and she hadn't known she'd have to wait around for them to come in from Maryland and New Jersey. As soon as the funeral was over she would be off again. She wasn't sure where she'd go, but maybe back to Atlanta.

"I'm like a homin' pigeon, honey," she said. "Atlanta is home, but I gotta flap my wings. You know what I'm talkin' 'bout? I ain't gon' just sit down and stay put in one place. Maybe I'll go to New Jersey wit' one of the cousins."

He had known right off that she was trouble because she was so much like his Katie. Still Alabama leaned in closer to her. "If you a bird, you must be a hummingbird," he said. "I hear music when you talk."

She picked up a Chesterfield from the table. He reached for her matches to light it for her, but she shook her head, did it herself. She blew smoke in his direction. When it cleared, she winked an eye at him. "I think you tryin' to sweet-talk me, you cute little country boy," she said. "Be careful! Wondrene Barry will break yo' heart."

Alabama had downed two shots of Jim Beam, compliments of Wondrene, but it wasn't touching him the way she was. She had a voice as smooth as silk, and a throaty laugh that seemed to wrap him in a cozy warmth. "Break my heart," he whispered. "Break both my arms, one of my legs. Do what ever you wanna do to me."

He had worked all day and was still wearing his overalls. He had not gone home, not for a bath or even a bite to eat. For the past three days, Van Ida and Zyma had walked around the house being quiet, acting as though they were keeping something from him. It made him angry. When he asked what was wrong, all Van Ida said was that she was not going to Wilbur's funeral. Everybody who could get time away from work would be there. They would look around and see that Van Ida was not with him, and they would take it as a sign of disrespect.

"Yeah, you goin', Ida," he had told her quite firmly. "We all goin'."

"I ain't, Alabama. I ain't goin'."

He hadn't spoken to her since. Forget about Ida. Wondrene Barry had her soft hands on his face. She parted his lips with her tongue, drew him into a kiss that nearly took his breath away. When she released him, his breath came out like broken wave, and his body prickled from head to toe.

She stared at him, a devious smile on her lips. "How long it's been since you had good lovin', honey?" she asked. "I gon' take you wit' me. But I want you to come out the gate nice and easy. Don't you go jumpin' the gun on me."

Alabama was about to do wrong. Like a child looking to see who saw him, he surreptitiously surveyed the room. The crowd would be coming in soon, but for now there were only three other men in the place—Bud Williams, Neville, and Lawrence. They were playing dominos at a back table, and no one seemed to be paying attention to him or Wondrene. *Imagine that*, he thought to himself, *three grown men, and not one of them staring at this beautiful woman beside me.* For all of two seconds, he felt a tinge of guilt. But then he convinced himself that Katie had deserted him and he really wasn't lawfully married to Van Ida. And Van Ida was a woman is some respects, but not for what he needed now.

Alabama reached for another drink, but she lightly patted his hand. "It's my bottle and we taking it wit' us," she said. He followed her out of Sloan's Place and up the road a distance to Sloan's house. Neville Sloan had a real house, and he was particular about who he invited inside. It was Alabama's first chance to take a look around, but he wasn't interested in what Neville had. He was more interested in what Wondrene intended to do with him.

She led him up some stairs and into a nicely furnished bedroom. On an ordinary day he would have stopped to admire the oak finish of the dresser and chiffonier, would have run his fingers along the polished surface, gauged the grain. Not today. Moving quickly, he sat on the bed to remove his shoes and socks and was up again in a matter of seconds. He unfastened the suspenders on the bib of his overalls, removed them, then turned to see how she was coming along. She was standing beside the dresser, fully dressed, smoking a cigarette and watching him.

"How old are you, honey?" she asked.

He felt something like a kick to the stomach, just knew she was about to tell him that he was too old for her. He was. "Forty-two."

She smiled, counted on her fingers, then said, "You nearly twice my age. I bet you wouldn't look so ol' if you'd get some of that hair off yo' face. You got what look like a strong body, I guess."

Alabama sat on the bed again, made up his mind right then and there that he would get a shave and haircut as soon as he left Neville's house.

"Don't look so sad, little country boy," Wondrene said, as she crushed her cigarette in an overflowing ashtray that stood on the dresser. "Come on over here and help me get this dress off."

He did as he was told.

"You one beautiful woman," he whispered, nearly choked on the words as he admired her naked body. Already his hands were caressing her breasts.

She gasped. "Rough hands, rough lover," she teased. "I'm gon' smooth you out a bit." She lightly kissed his lips, then pulled him with her as she dropped to the bed.

Alabama could feel an arousal surging through him. He remembered her words, *Nice and easy.* He stroked her flat belly, kissed a breast, took the nipple into his mouth. *Don't jump the gun.* Using one knee, he parted her thighs. There was no subtlety about it; he had to have her.

Wondrene—so young, so agile—slipped his grasp, shifted positions. She was beside him, and her throaty laugh, fused with the sound of his heartbeat, pounded in his ears. She kissed him again. He could smell the sweet scent of roses on her slender neck. She kissed his chest, nibbled, wrapped her cool tongue around one nipple, and then the other. It was so unusual, so unexpected, that it tickled at first, but then it sent a tingling sensation throughout his body.

He tried to take control, needed to get inside of her. Wondrene shifted again. She was somewhere near, but out of his reach. With his eyes closed and the hardness of his body ready for the softness of hers, he felt her stir like a cool breeze flowing over him. And then the most astonishing sensation. She held his rigid warmth in one hand, caressed it, took it into her mouth.

"Oh, Jesus! Jesus," Alabama moaned.

It had to be a dream. He opened his eyes and could see the flow of long, wavy, black hair. He sucked in his breath, stiffened his muscles, tried to hold on. *Nice and easy.* When she finally looked up at him, she puckered her lips and gave the air the tiniest hint of a kiss.

"How you doin' up there, honey?" she asked.

Alabama was glad she hadn't called him a little country boy again because he was sure he would have flowed like the Mississippi River. There was something about the way she said it, the twinkle in her eyes that translated into "you all man and I know it." He was being all man for her like he had never been for anyone else, even as she straddled him, even as she drew him inside. Her gorgeous hips rose and fell as her sweet wetness encircled him. And then it happened. *Don't you go jumping the gun on me.* He flowed like the Mississippi River, but it wasn't his fault.

She knows better than to beat a dead horse, Alabama thought as she dismounted and stretched beside him. He wanted to sleep, and it didn't matter to him that he was under Neville Sloan's roof. Wondrene nestled against him and began to talk.

"I like to go places," she said. "I went to New York once. You ever been anywhere?"

He shook his head, was not quite ready to speak.

"You can't meet nobody if you just stay in one place. You got some kinda ride?" she asked. "A car or a truck? A mule?"

He shook his head. "Nah. Got feet."

"Well, honey, you can't get too far on feet. If you had a car, I'd let you drive me to Atlanta. I betcha I could show you a good time. Had a friend of mine bring me here, but he said he wadn't stayin' 'round for no funeral. Guess I'll have to get Neville to drive me outta here in his ol' truck."

Alabama got up, started to get dressed. "Do you like me enough to see me again?" he asked.

"Sho' I do," she answered. "I wish you had a car so you could drive me outta here."

CHAPTER 13

All evening she had waited for him, had gone back and forth to the door, glanced up and down the road. Somehow he had eased home without her seeing his approach. He was in the yard talking to the child, only he did not look like himself. When Van Ida took a closer look, she thought he resembled that old, sick Wichita monkey Wash Gibson had owned some years back. All of the hair from his face was gone, and it seemed to make his lips thinner and his chin longer. He looked younger, but not quite as handsome.

"You don't look like my daddy, Daddy," Zyma told him.

"Just got myself a shave, Zyma," he said. "It'll grow back."

Van Ida noticed that he would not glance toward the door, although he had to know she was standing there. She stepped out onto the stoop. "You done that for Wilbur's burial?" she asked.

"Done it 'cause I wanted to."

"Humph," she grunted, then beckoned for the child. "Come on in the house, Zyma."

The girl stepped past her to enter the house, and Van Ida stood waiting for Alabama to follow. When he did not move, she asked, "You comin'?"

"I be there directly," he answered.

An hour or so later, he was still standing in the yard. Van Ida went back to the door. "Alabama, if you gon' stay out there all night, go stand some place downwin'," she said. "The smell of that woman is driftin' in this house, and it's makin' me sick."

"What woman?"

"The one you been wit'. The one whose smell is all over you, and you done brought it home in my face."

"Shit!" Alabama swore, then turned that anger where it did not belong. "You long, tall, woolly-head wench," he taunted. "Don't you keep comin' to that damn do' tryin' to sniff me. I ain't been wit' no woman."

Van Ida closed the door, shut him out of his own house.

Alabama paced. It was dark, except for the stars. Van Ida had extinguished the lamp in the house, meant for him to be in the dark. He knew he would have to go inside sooner or later, if for no other reason than to get his clothes. He had been with other women before, plenty of them. This was the first time she had confronted him about it, the first time he had known that he was going to leave her. Even before today, he had known his life was miserable, like he was trudging through an unending marsh of dung, where everything smelled and looked bad. He didn't know how to explain it exactly, but Wondrene was like waking on a spring morning lying in a field of daisies. She made him feel alive, and he wanted that feeling, needed it.

For a short time, Alabama had been able to put thoughts of hard work and sorrow out of his mind. Wondrene had done that for him, had said she would show him a good time. Now all he had to do was get in the house, pack some clothes, and get clean out of Cranston before Van Ida could get the old root woman to work a conjure on him. He was convinced she would do it. He had gotten Howard Reynolds to cut his hair and shave his face. He had gathered every bit of hair from the floor. He intended to burn it as soon as he got inside to the stove. He would leave Zyma with Van Ida, and when he cleaned out the money jar, he would leave enough for next month's rent.

He thought things through enough to clear his conscience as he stood in the yard. Finally, he stumbled his over to the stoop, leaned his head near the door, and listened for sounds from inside. It was quiet.

"Ida," he called out. She didn't answer. "Ida, I ain't been wit' no woman. But even if I had, you ought not be mad. It ain't like you my real wife no how."

A sound reached him from beyond the door—maybe a sneeze. Maybe she was crying. He stood, walked over to where he could make out the contour of the well. She had no right to make him feel guilty when he had done so much for her. He had taken her out of a shack that wasn't much bigger than an outhouse. He had married her and stayed with her despite what people had said about her. The thought of Van Ida standing in the house crying angered him even more.

"Ida, I shoulda listened when folks told me a gator hatched you. You crazy!" he shouted. "It take a crazy woman to think she married to a married man. You ain't got no say over what I do."

As soon as the words were out, he knew he shouldn't have said them. He stood with his hands pressed against the foundation of the well as the stars overhead twinkled into oblivion and the world got a little darker. A chill ran through him, reached deep down to his bones. His teeth chattered, he shivered, felt as though he were falling down a pit of jagged ice. He thought it had to be some sort of voodoo—something he had never believed in. He tried to reach for the hair in his pocket, make sure it was still there, but his limbs were immobile, frozen, seemed to crack from the effort.

Something horrible lurked somewhere close by, somewhere in the darkness behind him. He sensed it as a huge animal, dangerous, moving stealthily toward his back. He tried to turn his head but could not manage. He breathed in, breathed out, never heard the approach. Heavy paws clamped down on his shoulders, a fiery breath burned against his ear. He drew in a shuddering breath and screamed. Jim Beam soaked the crotch of his overalls, rolled down his left leg, wet his sock and shoe.

"You foolish man," Van Ida whispered against his ear. "Katie done passed on some eight years ago. I'm the only wife you got."

Trembling, he slowly turned to face her, stepped away from her touch. "How you get out here?" he asked nervously. "You done had some kinda fix put on me, Ida?"

"I ain't," she answered. "You got hell in you, Alabama."

"Stay 'way from me!" he shouted as he inched away, putting the well between himself and her. "Stay 'way from me, Ida. And I don't believe Katie is dead."

Van Ida moved off toward the house. He could clearly see her tall figure as she stepped up onto the stoop. He glanced up, saw the reemergence of stars twinkling in the sky, saw that light had returned to earth.

"A feelin' come over me some years back when Katie drew her last breath. It was a feelin' like I didn't have to worry wit' her no mo'. I ain't gon' worry wit' you, neither. So you believe what you wanna believe, Alabama," Van Ida said. "And draw yo'self some water befo' you come up in this house. You smell bad."

Alabama bathed because he needed to. He put two chairs together, sat on one and propped his feet on the other, slept in a very uncomfortable position. He wasn't dissatisfied, though, because he knew that as soon as Wilbur's funeral was over he would be leaving Butcher County with Wondrene Louise Barry.

CHAPTER 14

At first, life had been easy in Cranston, maybe too easy. Tarlo had been young and the sole male on the land. All Mr. Henry asked of him was that he clear away the few and infrequent squatters and make sure that Girlie and the animals were taken care of. Over the years Tarlo had learned the hard way to take the good with bad. As soon as Mr. Henry died and the animals were gone, the tenants came. They were Mr. George Philpot's doing. With the influx of tenants, Mr. George appointed Tarlo the eyes and ears of the land, the keeper of peace. Tarlo had never wanted the job, but he had come to expect the monthly pay that Miss Dora sent over to him.

It had made him feel important when folks began to move in with the understanding that he was to be respected. He could have them arrested by the Butcher County law, or he could have them evicted from the land. One unsolved murder, two convicted thieves, several domestic disputes, and the riddance of many wild animals were his contributions to the town over the years. He was the one Miss Dora sent for whenever there were rumors of trouble on her land. It was for that reason that the largest and smallest of infractions were brought to his door.

He was getting dressed for Wilbur's funeral, feeling the fatigue of age as noticeable as the old black suit he had worn to each and every funeral for decades. There was a knock at his door, but he took the time to tuck in his shirt and glance at his reflection in the cracked mirror that rested on his single table. He opened his door to see Opal Lester preparing to knock again. Rather than inviting her in he stepped out into his yard. "What can I do for you, Opal?"

On her head was a bright yellow hat with a frayed brim. She wore a shapeless, multicolored dress, and the morning sun brought out the bright red stripes of the garment. Her face, though, was dark with the appropriate sadness for mourning.

"Tarlo, I think you need to do somethin' 'bout them Wheatons," she said. "That swamp woman and that li'l girl killed Wilbur, and ani't nobody doin' nothin' 'bout it."

"I don't quite reckon that's what happened, Opal. Wilbur was gettin' ol', too ol' to work them fields. It was heat and hard work got to 'im."

"You got to admit that somethin' strange is goin' on out at that Wheaton house, Tarlo," she said. "Somethin' wrong wit' that li'l girl."

No Ordinary Rain   287

NOVELS

Tarlo sighed impatiently. "Opal, it seems to me that you wanna blame ever' bad thin' in this county on Alabama's family. Tell me what it is you got against 'em, and what you want me to do 'bout it."

She was quiet for a minute, dropped her head. "Nothin', Tarlo. I ain't got nothin' 'gainst 'em. I just think you oughta have the sheriff go out there and talk to 'em. I was in the field and seen that girl all over Wilbur's chest. How you know she didn't smother 'im or crush his heart or somethin'?"

"Mr. Milton already looked at the body and said Wilbur died from natural cause," Tarlo explained. "The sheriff done spoke to everybody that was in the field that day. Didn't he talk to you?"

"He don't listen to nothin' I say."

Tarlo wasn't in much of a mood to listen, either. He changed the subject by asking, "Opal, when the last time you heard from yo' boy?"

She immediately perked up. "Last month. I hear from 'im ever' month. Sometimes there be letters stacked up at the post office 'cause he have so much to tell me. I write to 'im and tell 'im to come on home, but he say he doin' just fine in Pittsburgh. He keep tryin' to get me to come."

Tarlo knew she was fibbing. There had never been letters stacked at the post office. The only two letters that she'd received from the boy had been shown all over Cranston for weeks, and the last one had come more than three years ago.

"Well," he said, "that's really somethin' that he want you to come to where he at. He oughta be a good-size boy by now."

"He's a man now, Tarlo. He's twenty-two, and he got a job. Sometime I think I wanna go where he at, but what would I do in Pittsburgh?" She fanned a hand as though to wave off the idea as absurd.

Opal was lonely and afraid to venture too far from home. Lawrence Anderson kept her company, but she was never even a shade close to happy. Lawrence would tell her how she ought to stop thinking about her boy all the time and pay more attention to him. He would bring up all the devilish things that Jonathan had done as a child. "Remember when he hit blind Odell upside the head wit' a rock?" he had asked her one day. "I tell you, Opal, you better off wit'out 'im."

When he said things like that, they would fight, part ways, and it would be days or weeks before they got back together. It was always Lawrence who made the effort to reconcile. He was weak. Opal wanted herself a strong man like Alabama Wheaton, had wanted him ever since her Booker died. She'd almost had him once, and she found it hard to accept that she had lost out to a swamp woman. Back when she'd had all of her teeth, she had flashed a smile just for Alabama, but he had rejected her so soon after Booker's death. Nothing ever seemed to work out for her. The more Alabama had avoided her, the more she pursued him. Then one day out at the fields, she had bumped into the swamp woman at the weigh-in scale, and the woman had stared right through her. Opal had felt pain in her mouth, and a tooth had fallen from her gum. They had been dropping from her mouth ever since.

Opal had stopped chasing Alabama and had taken up with Lawrence, but that hadn't saved her teeth. She didn't believe in coincidences, and she hadn't believed Miss Girlie or the doctor when they'd said she was suffering a bad case of gum disease because none of their remedies helped. Opal thought that if she showed fear, the swamp woman would be able to finish her off. Every morning she would tell herself, "I ain't scared of nothin' and nobody." She mumbled the words now, then glanced up to see if Tarlo had heard her.

Tarlo was looking out toward the road. "That walks like Alabama comin' there," he said. "Maybe you oughta talk to 'im 'bout his girl."

"Don't wanna talk to him," Opal mumbled as she glanced over her shoulder at the man coming up the road. She sucked at her remaining teeth, then eased away.

Tarlo watched her go, then he turned his attention back to the approaching figure. The man coming up the road walked in long, rapid strides. He had a clean-shaven face, wore a white shirt, dark pants, and a cloth hat. Tucked beneath one arm was a bundle of burlap.

"What you done had done to yo'self, Alabama?" Tarlo called out. "And where you goin' in such a rush?"

Alabama nodded a greeting and continued on. He had a plan, a change of clothes, and nothing to say to anybody except Wondrene. He had seen Opal standing in Tarlo's yard. Anything Tarlo had to say would mean trouble, and it was too early in the morning for that.

Having decided that he would hide his bundle behind Sloan's Place until after the funeral, Alabama made his way toward Cross Road. As expected, the hall was closed and there was no one around. He hid his roll of burlap in the grass that grew close to a side wall of the barn, then he leaned against the building and stared out toward Neville's house. Neville's house, with the yard and apple trees, stood between Willow and Cross Road. From the rear of the house Alabama watched a kitchen window hoping to get a glimpse of Wondrene.

People began to move along Cross Road making their way to the church. Alabama noticed that he was drawing the attention of a few. He kept his eyes averted, discouraged greetings and conversation. He thought he should go ahead and knock at Neville's door. What could it hurt?

If Wondrene took her exit through the front door, he would miss her. He took a few steps away from the building and glanced around, then cursed himself for hesitating long enough to allow Neville to spot him. The man's pudgy face appeared at the kitchen window, and he stared straight out at Alabama. A minute or so later, he brought his huge bulk out the backdoor, past the apple trees, and across the road.

"You know I won't open this place until after the funeral," he said. "What's troublin' you that you need a drink this early in the mornin', Alabama? Wilbur's death?"

"I don't need no drink."

"People don't come here for no other reason than to drink or dance, and I know you ain't wantin' to dance this early in the day. So if it ain't a drink you want, what do you want?"

Alabama didn't care much for Neville, never had. The man was too full of himself. What bothered him was how hard Neville worked at being tough. He was sure he could have knocked the fat slob over with one punch, but then where would he go when he needed a drink? He had seen Neville ban men from his place, and there was nowhere else to get booze for miles around.

"Just standin' here waitin', Neville, that's all," Alabama said.

"Well, I hope you ain't waitin' on Wondrene. I bet that's it. I bet you thinkin' my cousin wants you. She done made some kinda fool outta you, ain't she? I bet that's why you done shaved up, cleaned up, and come standin' by my place at this time of mornin'."

"I'm just standin' here, Neville, waitin' on the church to open. Ain't nothin' wrong wit' that, is it?"

"Yeah. I think it is since the church is 'round the corner and up the road a piece. I bet you waitin' on my cousin, but I hope you ain't. She gone. Left here 'round two o'clock this mornin'. Fellow who dropped her off come back through here, picked her up, and off they went."

Alabama tried to pull himself together. There was no way a woman could love him the way Wondrene had done and then leave town with another man. He glanced back at the barn, knew that he could not retrieve his bundle with Neville staring at him. He would get it later. Right now he needed to get away, find Wondrene, prove that Neville was lying.

"Guess I could open up and let you have one drink," Neville offered.

Alabama shook his head. "Nah. I'm gon' get on over to the church."

He could feel Neville staring at his back as he moved along Cross Road. He was glad when he reached Hangling Road and Neville could no longer see him. A mangy dog loped down the center of Hangling, trailed by six of Cleo Bender's tarnished chickens. Cleo had dug holes in his yard to search for a conjure bag that he believed had put a curse on his chickens. Tarlo had made him coop the chickens so that they did not mingle with other people's. They always found a way out, though, and in the evenings, Cleo could be seen rounding them up. Eggs kept hatching, the chickens multiplied, and they lived a good life as far as Alabama could tell.

Alabama made his way to the church and took a seat on a rear bench where he could watch the people as they entered. Wondrene would have to come through that door sooner or later. She had said that she was in Cranston for Wilbur's funeral, and a person did not up and leave without saying farewell to a cousin.

When Alabama took a moment to study his surroundings, he saw that Wilbur's casket was already up front. The casket made him think of his Mildred. It made him sad, and it set him to reminiscing. He thought of Katie. He watched the entrance for Wondrene.

Opal Lester entered wearing a hideous yellow hat. Behind her were Theron and his family. Theron's wife helped the root woman to a bench, and the old woman turned her head back to glance at him. It was a brief glance, but Alabama didn't like it.

Theron spotted him and came over. "You alright?" he asked.

Alabama nodded.

"You got folks talkin'," Theron said. "I try to make it a habit not to listen to gossip, but sometimes the words is out befo' you can stop 'em. I can see by yo' face that some of what they sayin' is true. We can talk about it later if you want to."

Alabama did not respond. He was too ashamed to speak, and finally Theron left him alone. Neville came through the door followed by two of the oldest men in the community—Tarlo Medfield and Wash Gibson. Wash wore a shabby black suit that had probably once fit perfectly. It now hung loose on his frail frame. His head was bald, he wore glasses, and he used a cane to guide his steps. Alabama was not fooled by his feeble appearance. He knew Wash was a devil. He watched other devils enter the church with their solemn expressions of grief. The worst devil, Wondrene Barry, was not among them. And true to her word, Van Ida did not show up.

By the time people began to leave the church for the cemetery, Alabama thought of the few dollars in his pocket, and decided he would pay Robert Union to drive him out to the Deans' property. If Katie's folks were still living there, he would find out if she was dead or alive. It didn't matter to him either way, but he had to know.

CHAPTER 15

Theron was wearing a pair of britches and no shirt or shoes. He had been asleep when Alabama knocked at his door. Alabama was still dressed in the clothes he had worn to the funeral. It was late and Cranston was quiet as they sat together on Theron's front steps. Theron was younger, a couple of inches shorter, and definitely broader through the chest, but they were both muscular men.

Alabama was gripping the roll of burlap he had retrieved from Sloan's Place. He laid it across his lap, stared out toward the trees across the road. They both had things they needed to talk about, but Alabama's seemed more pressing. Theron waited for him to speak.

"Katie's dead," Alabama finally said. "She been dead since nineteen thirty-one. Eight years, Theron. I went out to see her family today, and her sister, Ruby, told me about it. She say they thought I knew. Ain't that one hell of a thing? Say they thought I had done washed my hands of Katie what wit' the way she left me and all. Say they thought that's the reason I didn't come to the funeral. I woulda gone if I knew about it."

"Sorry, man," Theron said. "You alright?"

"I'm alright. Somebody coulda let me know, but I'm alright. Say she drop dead in they kitchen tryin' to fix herself a cup of tea. They think it was pneumonia. But I'm alright, Theron. Never knew Katie that well to start wit'. Bothers me that she was this close and never stopped by to see her own children. I tried to tell myself that maybe she was too sick to come, but she coulda sent word. Maybe Mildred would'na died if Katie had come to see her."

Theron thought they knew each other too well for him to allow his friend to get away with such nonsense. "I can't even imagine what you must be feelin', Alabama," he said, "but I know you don't believe that."

"The thing of it is, Theron, I'm mo' mad than sad. I ain't never had no luck wit' holdin' on to no woman. If I was doin' somethin' Katie didn't like, that was me, and she shoulda told me. She didn't have to take it out on our children, but she did. Sometimes I think I shoulda stayed in Kingston. I coulda worked the fields there just like I'm doing here."

Alabama was getting deep into his sorrows. Always when he had troubles, he would talk about Kingston, remember the good times, the years before he met Katie. But the truth of the matter was that he had Van Ida and Zyma now. He needed to go home and try to smooth thing over.

"I'd sho' miss you if you moved away," Theron said. "I'd miss little Zyma and Van Ida, too. You would be takin' Van Ida wit' you, wouldn't you?"

Alabama sighed wearily, a culmination of the day's events and what he still had to face. "Sometime I just don't want her, Theron," he said. "There be nights when I be tempted to come over here and put my foot up yo' ass. It's yo' fault I'm stuck wit' that woman. You should'na never told me to marry her. Shoulda told me to marry somebody look a lot better."

Theron chuckled. "You married her because you needed her. She the only decent woman you ever had, and I think that scares you. You got folks talkin' 'bout you and Neville's cousin. Talked about that mo' than they talked about Wilbur today. If you wadn't so down tonight, I'd tell you somethin' 'bout yo'self, Alabama. You all the time chasin' after women, and Van Ida just sit out there and takes it. You think she don't know 'bout it? If I did what you do, Nadine woulda had me laid out in the graveyard by now."

They sat in silence for a while, absorbing the coolness of a late September night. Alabama shifted on the step, ran a hand across the burlap on his lap, thought about going home to face Van Ida. "Why don't you put me up for tonight? I can sleep in the hallway," he said.

"Go home, Alabama!" Theron said sternly. "I ain't gon' help you wrong Van Ida. She probably worried 'bout you."

"She knew 'bout Katie. Never bothered to tell me 'til the other day," Alabama said. "She say some feelin' come over her when Katie drew her last breath. Why you reckon she wait so long to tell me?"

Theron thought about it, could not bring himself to put any blame on Van Ida. "That woman been wit' you nearly twenty years—married and unmarried. She done looked out for you and yo's. She had to look out for herself, too. I reckon she probably sat in that house nervous, waitin' on Katie to come back, not knowin' what you might do. I woulda done the same thing, just kept quiet. You would'na believed her no way. And why she gon' tell you anythin' 'bout Katie when she the one tryin' to be yo' wife, livin' under yo' roof? You need to go home, Alabama, talk to Van Ida."

Alabama knew his friend was right, but he couldn't move. He thought that he might stay and sleep on the porch. He glanced over at the house next door. If he fell asleep on Theron's porch, one of the neighbors might get up early and see him there. That would give people something else to talk about. Worse yet, he could wake up with Ulysses Sampson staring down at him, praying over him.

"Guess I'll get on home," he said, but made no effort to move.

After a long moment of quietness, stillness, Theron said, "I done bought these houses—almost. Gon' put my name on the paper right proper come Wednesday. Got the money right out, and some left over. Nadine say I oughta go on and buy me a truck wit' what we got left over. We gon' have to start savin' all over for Brill."

"Yeah?" Alabama questioned. Envy tugged at him for a second, until he thought of the sacrifices Theron had made, all that going from town to town, doing whatever was necessary to make a dollar, going without things to save. "I'm happy for you," he said, and meant it.

"Gonna take a lotta work to get 'em where I want 'em to be," Theron said. "I was hopin' you might help me out. I'd be willin' to pay you whatever I can. Maybe you can take a day away from the fields ever now and then."

"How many of these houses you buy?"

"All three."

"All three," Alabama echoed. "I guess I can help you out. Don't know 'bout takin' time from the field, but I can come on some Saturday afternoons and maybe some Sundays."

"That's good. That's good," Theron said contemplatively. "Now, I gotta get on in and get to bed. I been gettin' up early, practicin' how to write my name. Buyin' a house is somethin' I always wanted to do, and I aim to do it right."

He lingered long enough to allow Alabama to stand first, did not want to give the impression that he was rushing him. Alabama rose slowly, alternated kicking his legs out and shaking his feet. He moved down the steps, tucked the burlap beneath one arm, then glanced along the row of darkened houses.

"You bought all three?" he asked again.

"All three," Theron answered.

Alabama sighed wearily. "I'm gon' leave her, Theron," he said. "I'm leavin' Ida. I'm gon' save up some money, and as soon as Zyma get ol' enough to see after herself, I'm leavin'. I just can't do this no mo'."

"This got anythin' to do wit' Neville's cousin?"

"Nah. Maybe. I don't know. I was raised up believin' that when you marry somebody you was s'pose to stay wit' 'em. Katie done proved that wrong. I wadn't really tryin' to marry Ida. You know that, Theron. I was just tryin' to get her to stay."

"So she stayed," Theron said, "and she still stayin'."

Alabama nodded, then started up the road. He did not know how he could expect someone to understand something he did not understand himself. Dogs barked at the sound of his footsteps as he weaved his way toward Blevins Stretch. The few and scattered lights from windows fell behind him, darkness stretched before him. He kept walking.

He reached his yard, stood beside the well, and drew up a bucket of water. He took a drink, then finally headed for the door. The house was quiet when he let himself in, but he knew Van Ida was awake, probably watching him in the dark with her gator eyes. He had made up his mind that he would not feel guilty when he faced her.

"I thought you wadn't comin' back." she said. Her deep voice reached him from the bed as soon as he stepped into the room.

He sat on the side of the bed. "This where I live."

"I know you do," she said. Her hand reached out, touched his back.

Alabama sprang up quickly under the pretense of getting undressed. As he removed his clothes, he thought about the changes he would make. Tomorrow he would go to the field and do the work of two men. He would save the way Theron had. Maybe one day he would have enough money to buy a car, and if Wondrene ever came back, he would be able to drive her anywhere she wanted to go.

Had they kept the boys' bed, Alabama would have slept there, but they had moved it out to make more room in the house. He stretched on the edge of his own bed, as far from Van Ida as he could manage. That didn't stop her from touching his shoulder.

"Don't wanna know her name, don't wanna know nothin' 'bout her," she said, "just want you to hol' me the way you hel' her."

Alabama squeezed his eyes shut. He heard the squeak of the bed springs as she moved away. When he was able, he turned toward her, touched her, heard her sigh. He thought of what his friend had told him, and he knew Theron was right. Van Ida had always been there for him, had looked out for him and his. He tried to push thoughts of Wondrene from his mind and searched within himself for a longing to love Van Ida the way she deserved to be loved.

He kissed her face, brushed his lips against hers. "I'm sorry," he mumbled in her ear, but the words sounded more like Theron's than his own.

"You be my reason to breathe," she whispered.

Alabama wanted to love her, only the emptiness inside of him would not allow it. He tried, and tried, but it would not come.

Girlie : The electrifyin' folks done finally been through here, put electric in ever' house that could hold it. They cut limbs off Mr. Henry's trees and made a bunch of racket. Neville Sloan got electric first, then them row houses, then these other two houses on the north road. I didn't want it. Don't nobody got money to buy nothin' run on electric.

They had a big shindig over at Neville's place to celebrate, and folks start seein' things that wadn't there. Opal swo' she seen her boy's face in one of them electric light bulbs. Nobody else seen 'im. She got drunk and start fightin' wit' Lawrence over somethin' or the other, scratched 'im 'cross his face like a cat. Well, whatever it was about, he told her he was done wit' 'er. Mary Grady help me walk 'round there, but I wish I hadn't gone 'cause what I seen hurt me to the bones.

Van Ida's man got drunk and start reachin' for some woman dancin' on a tabletop. Nobody else seen that, neither, but he could tell 'em right down to the last stitch of clothes what she was wearin'. Po' Van Ida was just standin' there lookin' and she could see it all in that electric. Don't nobody pay no mind to what Opal say, and I say Van Ida done married herself a fool.

She come by the other day. She say Alabama don't want her nowhere near me, but she hadda come. I invited her in and offered her a seat. It was night outside, and nearly dark inside 'cause my lamp don't give out much light and I don't use that electric.

"I don't think Alabama care nothin' 'bout me," she say. "He care 'bout the girl-child and them boys that's done run off, but nothin' 'bout me."

"Why you say that, chile?"

"A man s'pose to touch his wife, Miss Girlie. They ain't s'pose to share no bed wit' they backs to each other. Not all the time. I always heard that if I work my han's for a man, I'd feel the spirit of his love comin' through my palms. If I work my feet, I'd feel it comin' through my soles. I keep waitin' on some feelin' to come 'cause I been workin' everythin' I got."

"Ooh, child," I managed to say as I struggled up outta my chair.

"I'm gon' fix us some tea, and we gon' talk for a spell. I gotta straighten you out."

I knew if I start to move, she'd get up to help. That's just what she done. I fell back in my chair, told her to use the water off my soaked leaves to make the tea, then I watch her out the corner of my eye. Now, I ain't one to call nobody ugly, don't judge nobody on what they can't help, but that chile is just plain pitiful. She had on some ol' dress look older than me, and a raggedy blue rag tied 'round her head. She don't hardly never smile. But maybe what I see is just comin' from my lack of light.

"What that man do wit' you out there on Blevins Stretch?" I ask.

She brought my tea over, then sat down in the chair by the do' wit' her teacup. "He don't do nothin' wit' me."

"Humph," I grunted as I swallowed what I believed to be the truth. Takin' my time, sippin' from my cup, I tried to decide how much I wanna tell Van Ida. If I tell her too much, I'd just leave her all mixed up in the head, but the chile needed to know somethin' 'bout life.

She placed her cup on my money table, then she start fidgetin', movin' her hands about on her lap. "I can't stay out here too long, Miss Girlie," she say. "I gotta get on back."

"Humph." I nodded to let her know I understood. "What is it you want from me?"

She had been waitin' for that. She lean forward on her seat— whoosh—like a shadow in the night. "I want you to look inside me, tell me what Alabama see. Tell me if he ever gon' care anythin' for me."

"I can't tell that through you. I can't tell that at all."

"You know you can, Miss Girlie. You can put them han's on me and know everthin' there is to know."

It was a thoughtful chuckle that I give to Van Ida's words. I needed her to know that I ain't laughin' at her, although what she said was kinda funny. I waved a hand toward the table that held her cup. "Drink yo' tea, chile," I say, then I start pullin' my thoughts together.

After she wadn't fidgetin so much, and I knew the tea was doin' its job of calmin' her, I ask, "Do you believe in God?"

"I do," she say.

"Why you believe?"

"I don't know, Miss Girlie. I guess it's 'cause He been here all my life."

"But do you feel Him to know He real?"

Over in the dark by the do', I couldn't tell if she was noddin' or shakin' her head. I know she didn't answer me.

"If you don't feel Him, then you believe in God 'cause folks told you He was real. You ain't never seen Him," I said. "I believe, too. But sometimes I feel Him in this room wit' me, and it makes me wanna shout 'cause I be so happy."

"Miss Girlie, you gon' help me?" she ask, tryin' to rush me.

"I am helpin' you. Listen to me," I say. "Life is 'bout what you believe, Van Ida, and them beliefs is measured. Look at it like a dandelion. At the tip top, the part that blow in the win', is the thangs you hear and can just wave yo' han's at. They don't matter. Then you get to the center, and them the things that start to shape who you gon' be. That's where you wanna prove it either is or it ain't. At the bottom, down at the root, is who you is. Them the beliefs you can't get rid of, the ones you take to the grave. You ever tried to get the root of a dandelion up outta yo' yard. Them thangs just keep growin' back. You can't get rid of 'em."

I thought I had her thinkin', but she put her cup down and rose up from the chair. "I gotta go, Miss Girlie," she say, "but where is Alabama on my dandelion?"

She wanted to leave and I wanted her to stay for a spell, so I made her wait. I tilted my head and stared up at her. "Ain't nothin wrong wit' them chickens," I say.

She stared down at me wit' worry on her face. "You alright, Miss Girlie?"

"I'm alright. Them chickens alright, too," I say. "I was singin' one mornin' when Cleo come by this house. I seen him starin' over here all wide-eyed. He went on and told folks I was chantin' up the evil spirits, had Tarlo comin' 'round here. Nobody else ask me 'bout it, not even you, and I know you done heared it."

"I heard it. Alabama told me, but I don't question what you do."

"I wadn't chantin' up nothin', Van Ida. I was singin' to my Lord. When word reached me what Cleo was sayin', the devil got in me. I took my cane and walked 'round to Hangling Road. I told Cleo I had done laid a cunjuh on his yard, and if he eat one of them chickens he gon' drop dead."

It was funny even now when I thought about it. I laughed, but Van Ida didn't join me. "He believe me," I say. "I bet he ain't et no chicken since. That's one of them center weed beliefs, Van Ida. Prove I did or prove I didn't. It's easier to just gon' and believe. That's where Alabama is on yo' dandelion—smack dab in the center. Now, I say all that to say I don't know nothin' 'bout that man or how he feel 'bout you. The important thang is what you think."

"He scared of you, Miss Girlie."

"I know that. He didn't get scared of me 'til you move in wit' him to take care of his young'uns. You and me—we don't share no blood, but we kin. The Jepson plantation make us kin. He think I'm gon' give you somethin' to put in his food to fix 'im, but I ain't. That's why he don't want you 'round me. Why I wanna fix 'im, less he raisin' his han's 'gainst you? Is he doin' that, chile?"

"No, ma'am. I can't rightly say that I know what his han's feel like."

She went back to the chair by the do', sat down, and let out a weary sigh. "Miss Girlie, can you fix up somethin' to make him love me?" she ask.

"I can," I say, "but I ain't gon' do it. You don't want that kinda love."

"I want any kind I can get," she say, then she rose up and drifted on outta my do' like she had never been here.

CHAPTER 16

The letter was addressed:

> Alabama Wheaton
> #7 Blevins Stretch
> Mays Spur, Georgia

It had been delivered by Cleo, courtesy of the Mays Spur post office. Alabama held the envelope between his palms, then ran his fingers across the letters of his name. Wondrene, he thought. She's ready to come back, or maybe she wants me to come to her. Whatever she wanted, he was willing to do. He had known almost from the start that he loved her. He had convinced himself that it had nothing to do with their lovemaking or her beauty. It was all about light, freedom, being able to breathe without discomfort. He put no blame on her that she played tricks with his mind. Folks didn't believe him when he told them he had seen her right here in Sloan's Place dancing on a tabletop. He had seen her walking the dirt roads in her bare feet, winking at him, then glancing up toward the sky. He had heard her laughter.

Alabama held the letter in his hand and shook his head. No, my Wondrene would never come back here to live, he thought, so she must be asking me to come to her. This place is too dreary, shaded by too many trees, populated by too many dull people.

Alabama rose from his seat, moved away from the table where Theron and Lawrence sat. He settled himself in one of the stalls that Neville had turned into booths. He needed privacy. Love swelled in his heart and he took in a deep breath before ripping the envelope open.

"Wondrene," he whispered as he removed a single sheet of paper, unfolded it, and began to read.

> Dear Daddy,
> How are you? Fine I hope. I am married now. My wife's name is Christine and she is writing this letter with me. We have a son, and I named him after you. He make me think of Mildred. I hope her little girl is alright. I been living in Washington, D.C., and I don't know where James is. We was together until we got to Toledo, then he said he was going to California. I didn't want to go, so I came to Washington. Daddy, I hope you still live in Mays Spur and that you get this letter. I hope you and

Mama are happy like me and Christine. I don't think I'm ever coming back to Cranston, but you can come live with us if you want to. I told Christine all about you, and she wants to meet you. Christine is a good woman. She said I ought to write my Daddy, so that's what we doing.

Your son,
Ruben

Disappointment settled in. Alabama had been expecting to read Wondrene's words of love, her plans for him, but all he got was the ramblings of a long-lost son. The boy had deserted him, now here comes a letter saying that he has a wife, that he's happy. Alabama was not happy, nowhere close. He was stuck in the same old place. The cotton crops were dwindling, and he thought, *When it's all gone, there'll be no more of me.* He crumpled the letter, walked out of Sloan's Place and over to Hangling Road. Wondrene was heavy on his mind. He sniffed the night air for the sweet scent of roses, a fragrance of her. He couldn't have her tonight, but he could sink himself into something soft, and pretend.

He knocked at Opal's door and was greeted by a sunken smile. Lawrence had said he had no more interest in Opal, and that was good because she wasn't worth fighting over. Alabama had no interest in her, either, but she would have to do for tonight.

Van Ida was feeling uneasy. "You gon' move us close to that graveyard," she accused. "We alright out here, Alabama. Out here we ain't gotta worry 'bout no ghosts movin' 'round in the middle of the night. I know a lotta folks that's buried out there. I don't think I done none of 'em no wrong, but you don't never know what a ghost be thinkin'."

Alabama continued to pack. Already he had placed his clothes in boxes, and he had both of the beds stacked against the wall beside the door. All he was waiting for was Theron to arrive with the truck. It wasn't as though Van Ida hadn't known about the move before today. Alabama had patiently waited for somebody to move out of one side of one of Theron's houses. It took Alexander Chavers leaving for the army to clear a spot for Alabama, and he intended to be in it before nightfall.

"You can stay out here in a empty house if that's what you wanna do, Ida. Me and Zyma—we movin'. Theron ain't gon' charge us no mo' for rent than we payin' out here in this place."

Van Ida stared at him. He kept his face clean-shaven now, and she had gotten used to it. What she could not get used to were his eyes that had dulled over the years, the slump of his shoulders, and the way his arms hung stiff and weighted. She knew he was bored with the solitude of Blevins Stretch, was eager for something more. As it was, he spent most of his free time in Cranston. She thought he would probably leave her out here and never glance back. He didn't really need her anymore. The girl-child was eight, almost old enough to see after herself. Reluctantly, Van Ida began to place dishes in a box, and still she tried to dissuade him.

"There's a lotta folks in Cranston," she said. "Ain't we been doin' just fine out here?"

"I wanna feel like I'm gettin' somewhere," Alabama said. "I'm talkin' 'bout movin' a few miles up the road; that's all. I tol' you, you can come wit' me, but I ain't gon' tell you no mo'."

Van Ida moved slowly, knowing that nothing she said or did was going to deter him. She had gotten too comfortable having a family to even think about being without them. At her command, Zyma came over to help pack the dishes. Van Ida wrapped a plate, placed it in a box, picked up another one. The girl did the same.

Van Ida ignored the sound of Theron's truck as it pulled into the yard. She knew she should have been grateful for a better place to live, but she was not. Alabama had tried to make it all sound wonderful. He talked about Zyma being close to the school in Mays Spur, and of how Van Ida would not have to walk so far to get to Dupree's store. Since Theron had bought the truck, Alabama made plans that did not include her or the child. One day he rode off with Theron. When he came home, all he could talk about was how good he was with his hands, of what all he could be building if he lived someplace else.

Theron and his son stepped inside. They spoke, took a minute to look around, then began to help Alabama carry the beds out to the truck. Ordinarily Zyma would have been following behind Brill, talking the boy's ears off, but not today. She followed her mother's lead, moved slowly, worked gently.

"You don't wanna move outta this house?" Van Ida asked as she glimpsed the worried expression on Zyma's face.

"I ain't never lived no place else," Zyma answered, "but I don't care if we move. Daddy say things gon' be better."

"Maybe they will. Don't you worry 'bout it, chile."

They worked across the table from each other, filling one box and replacing it with another while the house was emptied out around them, until the sounds of paper and dishes seemed to echo through the space, until the men stood waiting for something else to load onto the truck.

"We can get everything on that truck, Ida," Alabama said. "Why don't you move a little faster wit' them dishes?"

Van Ida heard Alabama, but she was watching the child, saw tears slide from Zyma's eyes.

"Mama, I gotta tell you something," the girl said.

"Well, say it, chile," Van Ida responded tenderly. "Just say it. It be alright."

Zyma glanced over at Alabama, Theron, and Brill, then she leaned forward. "I can't, Mama," she whispered. "This be between me and you."

Alabama heard her and responded angrily. "You done set the chile to turnin' 'gainst me, too, Ida?"

"I ain't," Van Ida said as she continued to watch the girl.

"What you gotta say, Zyma, that I can't hear?" Alabama asked harshly. "You spit it out!"

"I can't, Daddy," Zyma said nervously.

"You will, or I'll wear yo' little behind out."

"Tell him, chile," Van Ida encouraged.

Zyma turned hesitantly, spoke softly. "It's Miss Sally, Daddy. She want me to come to her, but I can't come. It's too far."

"What you talkin' 'bout, Zyma?" Alabama demanded. "That woman ain't thinkin' 'bout you."

"I hear her, Daddy. She keep breathin' in my ear."

Alabama stepped around the table. His scowl was more pronounced now that he didn't have the facial hair to camouflage the deep lines. "Zyma, you get them dishes packed and stop talkin' yo' foolishness!" he barked.

"The chile tellin' you the truth, Alabama," Van Ida said. "What reason she got to lie? You done forgot 'bout Wilbur? I believe this chile, and I believe Sally Blackmon is someplace takin' her last breath."

Alabama rubbed his hands together, stared down at his granddaughter. He didn't want to believe her, yet he knew she wasn't lying. "How Sally sound in yo' ear?" he asked.

"She sound like she all by herself. She breathe, then she hum, then she whisper my name." Zyma tilted her head, listened. "I don't know if it's my name she whisperin', Daddy. I think it's my name, though."

"Sally Blackmon is somethin' like two miles from here, all the way over in Cranston," Alabama said. "You tryin' to tell me you can hear somebody that far away?"

Zyma nodded, used the hem of her dress to wipe away the tears that were spilling from her eyes.

Theron glanced from Zyma to Alabama. "You wanna go over there?" he asked.

Alabama paced, chewed on his bottom lip. "Nah," he finally said. "If that woman ain't dyin', well, that's good. If she is, I don't want it to be me walk up on her."

Zyma eased around the table to stand beside Van Ida. "She ain't gon' die, Daddy," she said. "Miss Sally ain't gon' die if somebody go help her, and I can't help her like I helped Mr. Wilbur."

"Helped Wilbur?" Alabama asked dubiously. "How the hell you help Wilbur?"

"Zyma, you and Brill, y'all go on outside for a spell," Van Ida commanded. "You ain't gotta tell it no mo'. It be my burden to bear."

Van Ida waited until the children were out in the yard, then she returned to the table and continued to pack the dishes. This time she worked rapidly, kept her hands busy while she told about Evelyn Winston and Wilbur Johnson, about how Zyma believed she had snatched the memory from Wilbur and replaced it with a more pleasant belief. "Course, Evelyn just as dead as she always been, but Zyma say Wilbur don't know that when he died."

Alabama and Theron were now sitting at the table staring up at her. They asked many of the same questions that Van Ida had asked Zyma. They put their heads together and tried to come up with a feasible explanation.

"Maybe somebody told her 'bout Evelyn's murder," Theron suggested.

"You know somebody in Cranston would sit on a murder, wait all these years to tell it to a chile?" Van Ida asked.

"Coulda been what Wilbur was whisperin' in her ear," Alabama said. "How else would Zyma know?"

"She claim that while she was touchin' Wilbur, she could see it all," Van Ida explained. "Now, I know a lotta peculiar things is known to happen, but I ain't never heard of such as that."

"Why you wait all this time befo' you tell me 'bout it, Ida?" Alabama asked.

"Humph. I gave yo' head some rest, somethin' you didn't have to think on. I'm tellin' you now, Alabama, so what you gon' do 'bout it?"

The men left Brill behind as they drove off with the loaded truck. They found Sally Blackmon in her bedroom, crumpled on the floor just inside the door. The left side of her face was sagging, and drool had settled at one corner of her lips. It seemed to Alabama that she was watching them and trying to speak, but nothing lucid came from her mouth. Rather than taking the time to search for her husband, the men took her out to the truck and drove her all the way through Mays Spur and over to the hospital in Frankton.

Alabama was wondering if the hospital would charge for bringing Sally Blackmon in. He thought they should have taken the time to locate her husband. Theron was wondering how Zyma had known.

Girlie Folks been knockin' at my do' since the sun come up, passin' each other on my front porch. Opal brought me another one of them dolls she make. It's the tallest one yet, and it's made outta dark blue cloth, but it ain't got no eyes, or nose, or nothin'. She oughta be savin' that cloth to make somethin' useful, 'stead of all this foolishness. She say it's a pin cushion. We in the middle of a war, savin' ever'thin' we can save, and she makin' a damn pin cushion.

"Opal," I say, "if I live to be a hundred, I ain't never gon' have that many pins."

"Ain't you a hundred already, Miss Girlie?" She ask.

My cockeyed look done got kinda weak over the years, but I give her one all the same. "You know, Opal," I say, "I can change a few stitches here and there, add a bit a stuffin', and cut out a bare mouth in this here doll. Then I might have some fun stickin' it up wit' pins."

I could see her tryin' not to be scared, but she was scared alright. "You take it on back now. Maybe you can use it. Maybe one day you'll have a li'l girl you can give it to, or you can use it as a scarecrow in yo' garden."

"Miss Girlie, you know I'm too ol' to have anymo' chilluns," she say, bare-mouth smilin' and tryin' to be all innocent. "Jonathan the only baby I got, and my garden is comin' along just fine."

She didn't wanna take that doll back, but I didn't give her no choice. I ain't no fool. I knew that doll was intended to be Van Ida, and Opal wanted me to stick it up wit' pins 'cause she think I know voodoo. Humph. Shame on her. Ever'body jumpy just 'cause Sally Blackmon had a stroke. She over there in the colored ward at the hospital in Frankton. Folks lookin' for someplace to point a finger, and it seems to me they pointin' it at Van Ida and her chile.

Billy Wiggins come by here to get somethin' for the ache in his back. I give him sassafras root tea—some to drink and some to bathe in. He put his money on my table, then he sat down to drink his tea and talk about what the Wheatons done to the Blackmons.

"Ya know, Steve Blackmon is talkin' to Tarlo 'bout havin' 'em run outta town," Billy say. "I'm of a mind to agree wit' him. Po' Miss Sally all laid up like that. And I hear she can't even talk, don't even know who Steve is."

"Billy, ain't you done ever seen folks have a stroke befo'?" I ask. "Remember Martha Jennings? That chile wadn't even born yet when Martha had her stroke."

"Yeah, but that was different," he say. "Miss Martha was ol', and we all knew she was gon' die sooner or later."

He was workin' on my last damn nerve. "We all gon' die sooner or later," I say. "The graveyard is fulla sooner or later folks. You gon' and finish up yo' tea, Billy. I got things I gotta do."

He finished up like I ask him to, and he didn't say nothin' else to me 'bout that chile. Billy can't be no mo' than thirty, but I guess that's enough years to give him a lot to talk about 'cause that man know he can gossip. He oughta been off fightin' the war, but even the army didn't want 'im. I was glad when he finally left here.

Nadine Evers dropped by to talk about the war, and to tell me that the Wheatons had moved into one of the houses she and Theron bought. I already knew that.

"Why you worried 'bout them movin' in next to you?" I ask.

"People talkin', Miss Girlie," Nadine say. "They think that li'l girl got a way of fixin' folk. They say she can make it so you live or die."

"That's what they say 'bout me, but that's just foolishness, Nadine," I say. "Don't you go to church ever' Sunday? Ain't you done heard Reverend Smith talk about how no man knows the day or the hour? Now what you gon' believe—what folks 'round here sayin' or what the Bible tell you?"

She wadn't gone five minutes befo' Tarlo knocked at my do' meddlin' all in my business. "Girlie, you gon' have to do somethin' 'bout Cleo's chickens," he say. "Ain't a day go by that somebody don't come to me 'bout them damn chickens."

"Lawd have mercy!" I say. "Tarlo, all them chickens oughta be dead by now."

"That's just it," he say. "They ain't all dead. Eggs keep hatchin' and mo' keep comin'. Folks worryin' the curse you put on 'em done reached they hen houses. Minnie Bell brought me a speckled egg the other day. We cracked the thang, and sho' nuff blood was hangin' from the yoke. She say yo' curse done made it ovah into her chickens."

He scratched his ol' gray head, looked down, then back over at me. "Girlie, you and me come to this place together. I sho' don't wanna have to ask you to leave," he say, "but folks sayin' you gotta go."

"Go where? Go where, Tarlo?" I tried to shout at 'im, but my voice tricked me. It came out all hoarse and tangled like I'd done forgot how to talk. I moved over to my stove and got me a jar of soaked-leaf water that I use to make certain teas. I drank me a swallow, then I turn back to Tarlo. He'd done got my blood boilin' hot.

"Tarlo, do you own that li'l run-down hut you live in?" I ask in that same piece of voice.

He didn't even have to think about it. "You know I do, Girlie."

"You got a deed?"

"Naw, I ain't never needed nothin' like that. Mr. Henry give me that house befo' he died."

"That's what I thought, too, but Miss Dora come by here some years back, she say we don't own these houses. She say she own us, and we can't leave here or she'll have us locked up in the jail. So you see? Can't nobody run me 'way from here."

My words troubled him for a minute. Sunlight comin' through my window, shinin' on his ol' face, made 'im look like a burnin' ball of coal. His fiery eyes stared at me like I was the one who had done wronged 'im. "I don't think you right, Girlie," he say. "I think we free, but even if we ain't, I still get to live in my house. Miss Dora been kinda decent all these years. I can't see her runnin' me off this land or puttin' me in jail."

"Humph. Tarlo, what she pay you to be the law over in here?" I ask. "Miss Dora done used you for so long that you done forgot how to think. Mr. George used you, too. He had you countin' heads over here so he could get his rent. You done let them white folks make you so big in the head that you start runnin' folks outta town. Now Miss Dora say you owe her money for ever' day since her daddy died."

That sobered him up a bit. "How much you reckon that come to?" he ask.

I almost cussed, but I held my tongue. "Don't matter what it come to, you can't pay it."

He dropped his head, looked down at the flo'. "Well, if she say I owe her, then I reckon I do. Maybe I'll get work down at the lumber mill 'til I can get her paid."

"That lumber mill closed five years ago," I say. "They would'na hire you no way. You done got too ol'."

"What I'm gon' do, Girlie?"

I told him to gon' home and rest his bones, stop meddlin' in other folks' business. "Let Miss Dora run her own land," I say. "I reckon she do own you, Tarlo, but she don't own me."

I'd done a good job of messin' up his day, and I felt kinda bad. When he left here, I stood on my porch and looked up at the sun, wondered if God could hear me pray through that big ball of fire in the sky. I reckoned He could, so I stood there and prayed for ever'body on Miss Dora's land. I went back inside, got my hat, and headed out for Hangling Road wit' two of my walkin' sticks.

Two roads over was like fifty miles of wilderness as the sun dried up my brain through the holes in my hat. Folks had start to follow me, and I reckon that's 'cause they don't see me out that often. They musta figured I was up to somethin'. Lawd, have mercy! My steps done got so slow. I 'member a time I could run from one end of this land to the other and never get tired.

"Miss Girlie, what you doin' out here in all this sun?" Opal had done come up behind me. "You gettin' ready to work yo' voodoo on somebody else? You need to stop all that mess 'cause you pickin' on the wrong folks."

"Whoooo, whoo," was the sounds comin' outta me. I was 'bout to parch, and my snail steps was getting slower. "Opal, get me a drink of water," I say.

"I ain't gettin' you nothin'," she say. "For all I know, you may be over here tryin' to work yo' voodoo on me. You wouldn't take my doll, and ever'body know you up to somethin'."

NOVELS

Mary Grady brought me out a jar of water. I drank, and when I thought my throat was wet enough to talk, I say to Opal, "Why you standin' out here troublin' me? You'd best mind yo' own business, Opal. You keep foolin' 'round wit' Van Ida's man, you gon' lose mo' than yo' teeth."

She didn't have but 'bout three left, and I declare, when I said that, one of 'em fell out in the dirt by my foot. She made this loud gaspin' sound and covered her mouth, then she drew that hand back and whacked me 'cross my face.

"Oh-oh, you done done it now," somebody said to Opal, but I walk on 'way from her, on up the way to Cleo's house. I was thinkin' how now would be a good time to know some voodoo for real 'cause I sho' woulda worked it on Opal. I wade my way through chickens, hens, roosters, crows, whatever all that mess was in Cleo's yard, then I had one of them folks followin' me to call Cleo outside. My face was stingin', and I didn't have the voice to yell.

When Cleo come outside, I took both my walkin' sticks, stuck 'em deep inside one of them holes in his yard, and shook 'em there for a second or two. "There," I say, "now you can have chicken for supper."

He come on down the steps, stanking like sunk turd, kiss my stingin' face. "Thank you, Miss Girlie. Thank you," he say. Tears come up in his eyes, and I felt bad that I had done made him suffer for so many years, but I had to leave 'im wit' a warnin'.

"Don't tell no mo' lies on me," I say.

CHAPTER 18

Zyma walked to and from school with Brill Evers. Their school stood on a paved street in the Negro section of Mays Spur. The best part of her school day was listening to Brill talk. Brill was in sixth grade, and his parents were already talking about sending him to Macon after he completed the eighth grade. They wanted him to stay with Miss Nadine's aunt so that he could go all the way through twelfth grade. One day after school, Brill encouraged Zyma to climb the burial hill with him, and he gave her her first lesson in geography. It was two days after a heavy rain. They slipped and slid along the side of the hill until they made it to the top.

"What you see down there?" Brill asked.

At first Zyma was too busy rubbing the mud from her hands and looking down at the mess the hill had made of her dress. When she finally looked, she could see nearly everything. Down on Willow Road, she saw the old Philpot store and the open space where Mr. Ulysses held his Sunday meetings. There was a parked car in front of a house, and two men standing beside it smoking cigarettes. When she looked farther out, she could see the Baptist church and the graveyard, rooftops of houses, and even more trees and mud. On the Marshall Road side of the hill, she saw houses, chickens, trees, and more mud. She could see Mr. Neville's house on Cross Road.

"Houses and mud," she answered with little interest, still concerned about the mud on her clothes and what her mama was going to say.

"Take a good look at the roads," Brill said.

There were about a dozen or so roads in Cranston, but she couldn't see them all. The north road, Pepper, and Hangling could not be seen from the top of the hill, but she could see some of the roads that did not have a name. The road she lived on, Marshall, and Willow were the only ones that ran in a straight line. All the rest seemed to have been made by rolling a wagon around everything in its path.

"Ain't nothin' down there but mud," she said.

That's right. That's 'cause Cranston ain't nothin but a crater. You gotta go up a hill to get anywhere you wanna go. God did this on purpose so Negroes could have someplace to live. I think He musta threw somethin' down here and made this big hole for us to live in. This ain't nothin' but a little hill, but I bet somewhere there're great big mountains wit' all the Negroes livin' at the bottom."

NOVELS

"That's crazy talk, Brill. White folks live here, too. Out on the county road and on Blevins Stretch," Zyma said.

"Yeah, they do," he agreed, "the poor ones, but not folks like Miss Dora and the Jamisons." He took her hand and guided her back down the hill and onto the road. "We gotta find some grass and try to get this mud off our shoes."

They reached their road and wiped their shoes off in the grass at the corner of Zyma's yard, then they went up to sit on the steps. As they sat, Zyma kept thinking about her visit with Miss Girlie. She wanted to tell Brill about it, but she knew she couldn't. Whenever her mama said, "This be between me and you," she knew it was meant to be a secret, but still she asked, "Brill, do you think it's something wrong wit' me?"

His stare was a bit too long before he shook his head. "Nah, ain't nothing wrong with you. Why you ask that?"

She shrugged, couldn't tell him how Miss Girlie had dipped her fingers in root water and pressed the tips against her scalp. Miss Girlie hadn't tried to whisper when she said, "Van Ida, when I die, don't brang this chile 'round me 'til I'm all the way dead. I done a lotta wrong in my life that ain't nobody got no need knowin', 'cept me an' the Lord."

There was one house between Brill's and Zyma's. Darlene Kincaid lived on one side of the house between theirs, and the Green family with their five children lived on the other side. Darlene was in seventh grade, had a sister who was too young for school, and a brother, Tommy, who had already finished the eighth grade. The Harper family lived across the hall from Zyma. They were just a husband and wife with no children.

"You ever been fishin'?" Brill asked and moved out of her reach so that her hand fell from his hair.

Zyma shook her head.

"If you cut through them trees out there and keep walkin' for a spell, you'll come up on a fishin' hole. I go out there sometimes wit' Tommy. You can come wit' us if you want."

"I don't want to. I don't like worms."

"There's a man be out through there. Sometimes you can see him sneak out. He got tin and stuff nailed to a tree, and that's where he live. I'll take you out there one day and show you."

"Will he bother us?" Zyma asked.

"I don't reckon he will unless we got somethin' to eat. He might try to take that away from us, but he ain't never bothered nobody that I know of."

Zyma stared out through the trees trying to get a glimpse of the man. Brill saw her and said, "You can't see him from here. He's way back out through there."

"I bet my mama don't know nothin' 'bout him. She don't like it here. Sometimes she can't sleep 'cause she think ghosts in the graveyard gon' come after her. Maybe that man out there is one of them ghosts."

"Nah. He ain't no ghost. Ghosts don't walk around in the daytime, and they don't eat food," Brill said.

They kept sitting and staring at the trees. Zyma was waiting for her mama to come home from the fields. It was too quiet in the house when she was inside by herself. Van Ida had planted herself a garden behind the house, and now Zyma worried that the man from the trees would come and steal stuff.

Miss Nadine came up the road, and Brill got up to go meet her. She was always the first of the adults to get home. She stopped at the bottom of the steps and spoke. Zyma stared down at her feet to see how much mud was on her shoes, and to see how big her ankles were today.

"Zyma, you wanna come on and wait in our house?" she asked.

Zyma knew she could if she wanted to. Some days she did, but not today. "No, ma'am," she answered. "I'll just wait right here."

Instead of moving on up the row toward her house, Miss Nadine came up and sat on the step next to Zyma. Brill stayed in the yard.

"Zyma, I know you don't know the people I work for," Miss Nadine said. "They be the Jamisons over in Mays Spur. It's the mama and the daddy, and they got two little girls ain't too much older than you. The one little girl, Clair Anne—sweet little thing—been sickly since she come in this world. She be real pale, white as a cloud."

Miss Nadine glanced up at the sky. Zyma did, too. She had seen white folks before, but never anybody as white as a cloud. She thought the little girl had to be awful sick.

"Theron say you got a way of knowin' when folks gon' die," Miss Nadine said, then she got quiet, and Zyma knew she was waiting for her to say something. Zyma remained silent.

"Them Jamisons, they keep prayin' for Clair Anne. Ever' mornin' and ever' night they pray. They don't wanna know if she gon' die; they just wanna know if she gon' live, if she gon' be alright. I told 'em a little 'bout you, and they'd like for you to come over to they house. You think you can go over there wit' me one day and take a look at that little girl?"

"Mr. Scott got a telegram said his son Earl had done died in some place called Kentucky," Zyma said. "I didn't know nothin' 'bout it 'til I heard Daddy tell Mama. I think people die all the time, Miss Nadine, and I don't know nothin' 'bout it. Daddy say it ain't right that I should know stuff 'bout folks, that I should mind my own business."

Miss Nadine rested a hand on the girl's knee. Zyma could feel her staring. She could feel Brill staring, too.

"Could be that God gave you that gift 'cause He want you to use it," Miss Nadine said.

"Could be," Zyma agreed, "but I can't be goin' over to no white folk house in Mays Spur. Mama and Daddy wouldn't like it."

Nadine stood and walked down to the yard. "I'll ask Alabama, see what he say. If it's alright wit' him, then I'll take you over there."

Brill stayed with Zyma, and they watched his mother walk past Darlene's house and climb the steps at her own. All three of the houses looked the same. When the Wheatons first moved in, they had a front room that was nearly as big as the house they had moved out of. Van Ida had told Alabama and Theron to put a wall up and turn that one room into two. Now they had three rooms, and so did the Evers. Zyma had a room of her own with a window, and a door that opened out into her Mama's and Daddy's room.

"Mr. Alabama ain't gon' let you go over there, is he?" Brill asked.

"I don't know," Zyma said, "but I don't know no Clair Anne. I don't wanna see nobody that's white as a cloud. But I don't want Miss Nadine to be mad at me."

"She won't be mad. She'll just pray for that little girl, then she'll get over it. I saw her once—Clair Anne. She can't walk. They say she ain't been able to walk since she was three years old. I think she's about ten or eleven now."

"Did she look like a cloud?"

"Not when I seen her. I guess she must be gettin' worse," Brill said. "You wanna go in yo' house and study yo' lessons?"

"Nah. I don't like schoolwork."

Brill sat down on the step below her. He stared past the yard to where there was a vacant lot. "I gon' build me a house out there one day," he said. "It's gon' be bigger than Mr. Neville's."

They were looking out toward the lot when Tommy Kincaid turned on to the road. Tommy didn't walk tired like the others when he came home from the fields. He was always ahead of everybody else. Brill got up to go talk to him, and Zyma waited on the step for her Mama and Daddy to turn the corner.

After supper that night, Brill knocked at their door and asked if Zyma wanted to help him and Tommy put up a sign. "We gon' make a sign and nail it to a pole, then we gon' put it up right out there at the corner," he said, pointing toward the end of the road. "I think we oughta be a road or a street. I'm gon' call it Evers."

"Evers Street, Brill," Zyma said excitedly. "Make it Evers Street. I ain't never lived on no street befo'. If you make it a street, maybe they'll pave it like the streets in Mays Spur. Then we won't have to walk in so much mud."

"You wanna help us?" Brill asked.

"Yeah."

They put up the sign, and everybody from all three houses came out to take a look. The sign had only one word on it—Evers. Mr. Sampson said it was an uppity thing to do, and that Brill was an uppity boy. Theron said that if anybody didn't wanna live on Evers then they were free to move. So they lived on Evers, and they knew it wasn't a street because nobody ever came along to pave it.

Girlie Miss Dora done died. A few days befo' she done it, she sent a man out here to give me and Tarlo our freedom. It wadn't nothin' but the deeds to these ol' houses, and I laugh when that man tell me what it is. Course I didn't know Miss Dora was 'bout to die or I would'na been laughin 'bout nothin'. Folks say she had done got too old to live, but I say it was her brother's greed that killed her. Mr. Stanley's boy come to Mays Spur last year wit' his wife and two of his sons, moved into Miss Dora's house. That oughta been enough to kill her right there, but she hung on long enough to get a few of us workin' in that mill. Now they tell me that place make stuff for the gov'ment. I ain't been over to Mays Spur, but they tell me they got colored and white women workin' in that mill.

That gov'ment is somethin' else. It's tellin' folks what they can grow on they own land, and it sho' ain't cotton no mo'. They growin' food crops to feed the men that's off fightin' the war. Last week a airplane flew by here. Folks was runnin' 'round yellin', "The Japs is comin. They gon' bomb us like they did Pearl Harbor."

Wadn't no Japs up there. Wadn't nothing' but Mr. Stanley flyin' over our heads in that airplane. I shoulda knew trouble was comin', but it didn't hit me til Mr. Stanley sent them men over here to get rid of the snakes. Why he wanna kill the snakes now? They ain't never bothered nobody, matter of fact, they keep the place peaceful. They don't sho' up at yo' do' meddlin' in yo' business. If one of 'em come up in yo' house, you just throw it on back out the do'. One of them mean kind might get under yo' porch sometime, but we all got hoes and we all know how to use 'em.

It's two men that's huntin' for them snakes. They made it over to the north road, ask me if I'd seen any snakes 'round my place.

"That how y'all look for snakes?" I ask. "Y'all just walk up and ask somebody if they done seen 'em?"

"No, ma'am," one of 'em said, "but this is a large area to cover. We need to know where to start our search."

"Not here," I tell 'im, "ain't no snakes troublin' me."

They laugh—both of 'em—the little round one that look like he'd done swallowed a cottonmouth whole, and the other one that look like he might be good at catchin' snakes. He was tall, thin, and willowy. Look like to me if he stretched out on the ground he'd slither like a snake.

"What Mr. Stanley up to?" I ask. "I done been on this land for mo' than fifty years, and ain't nobody been over here lookin' for snakes 'til now. What he up to?"

"We don't know," say the round one. "He's paying us to find the den and get rid of the snakes."

"How you gon' do that?" I ask.

"Burn 'em out," said the thin one.

I laugh, let 'em see me laugh befo' I waved my hand at them chilluns and told 'em to stop followin' them snake hunters. Closed my do'.

CHAPTER 19

On a clear night, under a starlit sky, Van Ida moved silently across the road. She feared no attack from man or beast, but if confronted by a ghost she was not sure how she would handle it. She thought that as long as she stayed awake she could ward it off. She never wanted one to come up on her while she slept, though. For years she had waited for Mildred's ghost to appear before her and demand restitution. She owed the child a life, and there was only one way to pay that back.

She stepped into the forest of trees and traveled a path that her feet alone had made. The trail kept her away from the roads and the houses of her neighbors, and it took her home to a place where she felt comfortable. The little shack was barely standing now. It leaned and was nearly hidden by ivy and overgrown weeds. It was the house where she had lived before she ever met Alabama Wheaton.

She had learned to give a warning before opening the door. The first time she had barged in on him, Calvin Brown had landed a forceful chop that might have decapitated her had she been just a few inches shorter. As it was, it caught her chest and knocked the wind out of her. She had come around to find him sitting on the floor watching her. He had lit the lamp, and it stood on the floor between them. She thought she saw a mixture of fear and concern in his eyes.

"My God!" he'd said. "I thought I had killed you." Ignoring the pain in her chest, she managed to say, "I'm alright, Calvin. I done been hit befo'. Can't say it was ever that hard, but I done been hit."

Now when she came to the house she would stand off a distance, then whistle before heading for the door. A facade of foliage veiled the day-to-night routine at the all but forgotten shack. Van Ida had brought Calvin here after having known him for just a short time, had offered him the things she had left behind—a bed full of mold and mildew, a table and stool both barely standing, a stove that had not been used in over two decades, solitude.

She first met him in her own backyard on one of those rare occasions when she had been too sick to go to work. It had been a morning spent with blackberry root and rest. As she began to feel better, she got up with thoughts of walking the miles out to the Blevinses' farm, working the remainder of the day.

Through her kitchen window she had spotted a man in her garden kneeling beside the turnip patch. At first she had thought he was one of the snake hunters. He was reaching for something on the ground, and she wondered if he had followed the trail of a snake into her yard. When he stood, though, his hands held nothing but grass and dirt. From the shadows of the kitchen, she watched as he moved over to her tomato vines. She stepped into the hallway, opened the back door. The man heard her, and they stood for a moment staring at each other. He spoke first.

"Wasn't stealing, ma'am," he said. "Was trying to help you out. That's all. Garden needed weeding."

He had a pleasant voice that seemed strange coming from a mouth that was hidden beneath a scruffy beard and mustache. His shirt and overalls were tattered and filthy. His hair was matted on his head. He was a tall, thin man whose age Van Ida could not readily determine. She thought an old man.

"Where you come from that you end up in my yard?" she asked.

He stood with his head low and began to roll the soil between his palms. When it seemed that he was not going to answer, Van Ida said, "Don't wanna see you in my yard no mo'. We got men folks 'round here. If I see you again, I'm gon' tell 'em."

Those words loosened his tongue. "I won't come back," he said, as he eased around toward the Harpers' side of the house.

Van Ida rushed up the hallway, then stood at the front door and watched as he crossed the dirt road and disappeared into the woods. Of the six families who lived on Evers, only Lynnette Sampson, little Brenda Kincade, and three of the Greens' children were home during the day. Lynnette was expecting her first child. Van Ida thought for a minute that she should go check on Lynnette, make sure she was alright. She quickly dismissed the notion, reasoning that her presence at the door would probably frighten the woman more than a stranger roaming the yards.

Feeling guilty for having missed a day of work, Van Ida decided to make up for it by working in her garden. Except for the weekends, she had little time to tend her vegetables. It was always dark when she left home, nearly dark when she returned. She spent a few hours in the garden, then went inside and gave the house a good cleaning. She kept thinking about the man in the yard, found it unsettling that someone had slipped behind the house without her knowledge. She had seen people like him before—men, women, and children—hungry and homeless.

The runoff from the river and the shelter of the trees made the forest a haven for drifters. Sometimes they would jump from a train as it slowed on its approach into Mays Spur, then they would walk the mile or so north toward the trees. Others would come in from the highway to take a rest. It seemed as though an invitation had gone out along the roads and rails that one could find peace in Cranston. And maybe that was so, as long as a person did not steal or cause any problems.

During the afternoon, after her supper was cooked, Van Ida prepared a plate of food, then left the house and entered the woods. She had no idea where to begin looking for the stranger, or if he had remained. As she walked, she called out to him, "Mister man. Where you at, mister man?"

She was no more that a quarter mile into the woods when she felt his presence, felt him watching her. She stopped, slowly turned in a complete circle, peered around the tree trunks.

"I'm over here," he called out.

He was sitting on a sheet of cardboard with his back against a tree. Squalor best described the area of his retreat. Cans littered the ground around him, some too rusted out for use. On one side of the tree, scraps of tin formed the worst hovel she had ever seen. In front of that were four large rocks, two on each side, holding another piece of tin with numerous holes punched through the center.

"You one of them snake hunters?" Van Ida asked.

He jerked away from the tree, glanced around the area, then looked at her. "What snakes?" he asked.

"This place is full of snakes," she said, and saw fear flicker in his eyes.

"I ain't seen no snakes," he said.

"Not yet. But if you stay out here, it's likely you will."

"From the looks of this place, I ain't the first one to stay out here," he said. "Look like a lotta people done been out here at one time or another."

"You see any of 'em out here now?"

"Look, lady," he responded angrily, "I ain't bothering you. Don't want you bothering me. If I see a snake, I guess I'll have to kill it."

"Didn't come to bother you. I come to thank you for tendin' my garden, and I brought you a plate of food."

He reached up for the plate. "Alright. You done said your thank you, and you welcome. You can go on now. And ain't no need to tell nobody nothing about me."

Van Ida had noticed that he did not stare at her the way most people did. Maybe because he was guilty of something, maybe because he was polite, or maybe because he was too busy gobbling down the food while glancing around for snakes. Whatever the reason, she appreciated it. "I ain't gon' tell nobody," she'd assured him. "You can keep tendin' my garden if you want. Take yo'self a few things when they ready. We ain't gon' miss 'em."

He'd nodded. "Thank you. I already took one cucumber, two tomatoes, nothing else."

Van Ida turned to leave. "You oughta clean up some of this mess if this where you gon' be," she said. "How long you plannin on stayin?"

"Ain't gave it much thought."

From that day on she had begun to go out to the woods every night after work. She would take him cooked meals sometimes, talk to him while he ate. She found out that he had been watching everybody who lived in the houses across the road. He knew of their comings and goings, knew when it was safe to come out of hiding. One day, after having eaten her food for a full two weeks, he told her his name was Calvin Brown.

"You down on yo' luck, or you hidin from somebody?" she asked.

"I guess a little bit of both."

Before she told him about her old house on Mr. Blevins's property, she had gone out one Saturday afternoon, cleaned it up as best she could. It wasn't hers to offer, but she offered it anyway, and hoped he would accept. Carrying a lantern to light their path, she had taken him out one night to show him the place. She warned him that a family lived about a half mile up the road in Alabama's old house.

"Funny thing is," she said, "don't nobody remember this ol' place is even here. But they'll remember if they see somebody 'round here. They'll go up there and tell Mr. Blevins, and he'll come down here snoopin 'round. Be careful, Calvin."

He was thankful for shelter in this isolated place. He heeded her words of caution because he had to be more vigilant than she could ever have imagined.

Calvin opened the door of the little shack, and Van Ida came out of hiding and went inside. Although he was friendly, and she enjoyed his company, she remained as secretive about herself as he was. Sometimes she would come out to the shack and expect to find him gone. Always, though, he was there to greet her. He sat on the bed. Van Ida sat on the old stool that wobbled beneath her weight. Calvin had said he was thirty-nine. Now that he kept himself clean and he regularly shaved—thanks to her supplying him with soap and a razor—she could see that he was not as old as she had originally thought. He was a few inches taller than Alabama, but just a little too thin.

He reached out and took her hands in his. "I been knowing you for several months now," he said. "I know I can trust you. You ain't never brought nobody to that door, and ain't nobody been out here looking for me. Not to know me or nothing about me, you been real decent."

Van Ida allowed her hands to linger on his, but she looked away. She knew what loneliness could do to a person, how it could make you melt under kind words and attention. Calvin, she thought, had to be the loneliest person in the world.

"It ain't right what I'm thinking, what I'm feeling," he said. "I know you got a husband and that little girl. I done seen them both. It's just that sometimes I don't want you to leave."

Van Ida quickly withdrew her hands, rose from the stool. "I ain't gon' be bothered wit' no man that's scared of his own shadow," she said. "You need to do somethin', Calvin. Go on over to Edward Small's farm. He ain't gon' ask you too many questions. If he need help, he'll give you work."

"That's one of the colored farmers?" he asked. "Which way do I go to find his place?"

She nodded. "It ain't that far from here. He ain't gon' be able to pay you much. But somethin' is better than nothin', and you needs to be 'round people other than me. All this time, and you ain't told me what you scared of."

Calvin went over to his table, used a dipper to scoop water from a bucket, then took a drink. He had gotten comfortable with hiding. He didn't have to talk or explain anything to anybody. He didn't want to scare Van Ida away, but he knew it was past time he told her the truth.

"Come on back and sit down," he said, and tilted his head toward the stool.

She hesitated at the door, stared at him, then finally returned to the stool. She thought about when she had lived in this very house, how lonely she had been, how there had never been anybody to talk to. It had been a relief when Alabama had come along needing her help. She'd at least had the fields to occupy her days. Calvin had nothing but a small garden out back. He had even asked her to bring him seeds for a garden and a book for company.

"I left a man for dead in Decatur County," he said, and watched her face to see if she was shocked by his words. She didn't move, just sat with her hands resting on her lap.

"It's a long story," he continued, "but I want you to understand that I didn't have no choice. Man was trying to show off for the woman on his arm, I guess. I had walked in the store about a second or two before them. He said I was disrespecting the woman, that I had nearly knocked her over when she came through the door. I knew I hadn't touched her, but I apologized anyway. That wasn't good enough for him. He came stepping up to me like I was a child and he was gon' spank my ass. Things just kinda got outta hand from there. I hit him. After I realized I had hit a white man, it didn't make no sense to stop, so I kept hitting him."

"You know for sho' that man died?" Van Ida asked.

"Nah. But I put my hands on a white man, Van Ida. I kicked him, stomped him, tried to beat his face in. Don't get me wrong, I ain't never been no violent man, but when the grocer man came from behind his counter and tried to grab me, I hit him. That woman was screaming, and I started to knock her ass down, too, make all the trouble seem worthwhile."

"You think what you done was so bad that somebody gon' run from town to town chasing after you?"

"Maybe not. But since that man was already down, and I knew I was gon' have to run, I just reached on off in his pocket and took every dollar he had. Could be the law want me for robbery, too."

He saw a puzzled expression come over her face. She sat a while longer, stared at him, then rose from the stool. When she started for the door, he did not try to stop her.

"I ain't gon' be the one say if you right or wrong," she said, "but you can't keep hidin' out here away from the world. It ain't what a man s'pose to do."

"I ain't hiding from you. You all the company I need. And didn't you tell me I need to stay hid so Mr. Blevins don't know I'm here?"

The sincerity and worry in his voice caused Van Ida to pause for a moment. "I said you need to be careful," she told him. "I didn't say you need to stay hid the rest of yo' life."

When Alabama had needed help, she had been the only biting fish in a very small pond. She had begun to depend on him and cling to him. She decided that she would help Calvin Brown as far as she could, and then he would have to turn her loose.

CHAPTER 20

On summer Saturdays, most of the young people would come home from the fields or groves and find fun things to do, like swimming, fishing, and playing in the field on Evers. On one such Saturday, Zyma went out to the fishing hole with Brill and Tommy, and she made herself touch the worms. Darlene went, too. It angered Zyma that Darlene kept giggling and asking Brill stupid questions. Tommy told his sister to be quiet because she was scaring the fish off. Nobody caught anything.

Zyma wanted to see the man hidden in the trees, but Brill shrugged his shoulders and said, "I guess he's gone."

It was late when they returned home, and everybody went inside to eat supper. Zyma stayed in long enough to eat, then she went over to the Everses' house, hoping that Brill would come out and join her. She could hear Miss Lynnette's baby crying from inside the Sampsons' part of the house. Alabama and Van Ida had been home from the fields, but they had both left out again. Zyma thought her Daddy might be over at Sloan's Place. She had no idea where her mama was—just out through the woods somewhere.

When she knocked at the Everses' door, Miss Nadine said that she should stop trying to take up so much of Brill's time, that there were things he needed to do around the house. Unless Brill told her that himself, she was going to take up as much of his time as she could. He would be leaving soon, going to Macon to attend school there. He had told her that he was almost a man now. He said that he had to be because so many of the other men had gone off to fight the war. He had heard about it on the radio, and everybody was talking about it.

Miss Nadine always worried that the war would last until Brill was all the way grown, and drafted, and killed. She worried that Mr. Theron was going to be drafted, although he had told her that he was past the age. Miss Nadine still saw him as a young man, but he wasn't young. Zyma knew for a fact that Miss Nadine had paid Miss Girlie to make the war end. Zyma had gone with her to the north road, and she had put a penny on Miss Girlie's money table because that was all she had. She wanted the war to end, too.

It was taking Brill a long time to come outside. Little dark lines were stretched out across the sky, moving slow like they couldn't decide if they wanted to make it completely dark yet. The sun was all the way gone, but it was still hot. Drifting pass Zyma's nose was the smell of something like a butchered cow that nobody had bothered to wash. Using her fingers, she pinched her nose closed and could still smell it.

Brill came out, sat on the step beside her, and asked why she was holding her nose.

"Can't you smell it?" she asked. "I think somebody done butchered a cow, and they trying to cook it wit'out washin off the blood."

"I don't smell nothin," Brill said.

"I think I'm gon' be sick, Brill."

"Well, don't be sick right here. Go 'round to the back, or over in yo' own yard."

She moved to get up, but then Lawrence Anderson started breathing in her ears, and she sat back down again. Brill was talking to her, but it seemed like his voice was a long way off. What she heard the most was Mr. Lawrence's breathing. He was making all kinds of sounds in her ears—two loud whooshing breaths, and then something like when you flush the toilet on the back porch and everything won't go down the hole.

"Mr. Lawrence want me to come to him, Brill," she said.

"Where he at?"

"In some bushes by his house."

"How you know that?"

She shrugged. She couldn't see Mr. Lawrence, but she knew where he was. "He dyin', Brill," she said. "We better hurry up."

Brill stared at her for a minute, then he said, "I'm gon' get my mama."

The three of them struck out toward Lawrence Anderson's house over on Pepper Road. They cut through people's yards where there weren't any fences to stop them. The closer they got to the house, the more afraid Zyma became. In her ears, the breathing kept changing until she thought there wasn't going to be any breathing at all by the time they got there.

Mr. Lawrence lived in a small one-room house. Through his side window, they could see a lamp burning, and they could hear his dog barking in the back-yard. Miss Nadine started for the front door, but Zyma stopped her. "Back here, Miss Nadine," she said as she moved toward the backyard.

If the light had not been on in his house, they probably would not have seen Lawrence as quick as they did. They saw his legs first. They were sticking out from beneath a bush. Miss Nadine and Brill pushed back the branches of the bush while Zyma dropped down beside the man. She could not see his face clearly because of the way he was laying. She was so afraid that her hands began to tremble, but she knew she had to touch him. She brought her hand down to settle in a warm, sticky wetness on his chest.

Touching Mr. Lawrence was making Zyma weak. His pain was in her, but she could not move her hand. His blood was like glue holding her to his body. It became difficult for her to breathe. She could feel the two of them floating back to where he needed to be. Miss Nadine's voice kept drifting in and out. "Zyma! Zyma!"

Zyma could not answer Miss Nadine because she had drifted into the space where Mr. Lawrence thought he had a chance to make things right.

"Zyma! Get up from there, child. Look how you shaking," Miss Nadine said as she tugged and pulled the girl to her feet. "You come on and stand over here by me. Brill gon' be back soon wit' Tarlo and the others."

Zyma's abrupt departure from her connection to Mr. Lawrence left her weak and dizzy. She blinked her eyes, then glanced around for Brill, who was no longer in the yard. "Mr. Lawrence come out here to feed his dog," she said. "Can't nobody help 'im now, Miss Nadine," she said. "He dead."

"You don't know that for sho."

"Yes, ma'am, I do," Zyma said, and tried to stop myself from trembling.

Alabama was with the others when they came into the yard. Some of them were carrying flashlights, and all of the beams were aimed at Mr. Lawrence's legs. Zyma didn't know how much blood was on her clothes and hands until Mr. Silas came over and turned his flashlight on her. "You alright, Zyma?" he asked.

Alabama reached for her hand, but she put both hands behind her back. She did not want to get blood all over her daddy. "You shouldn't be out here," he said. "Who brought you over here?"

"I didn't bring her, Alabama," Miss Nadine explained. "She was gon' come, anyway, so I come wit' her. She already knew Lawrence was dyin'."

"Hush up!" Alabama snapped.

Miss Nadine fell silent, but it was too late. The others had heard her. They began asking Zyma how she had known that something had happened to Lawrence Anderson. Mr. Tarlo wanted to know what she'd had to do with it and why was blood all over her.

Alabama gripped her hand, paid no mind to the blood on it. He led her out of the yard. More and more people were making their way toward Mr. Lawrence's house and around to his backyard. Zyma did not see Brill, but she did see Miss Opal. She knew the woman had something to do with Mr. Lawrence being dead. Zyma's knees went weak as Miss Opal passed her. She was dropping to the ground when Alabama hoisted her back up.

"You gon' have to walk, Zyma," he said roughly. "I done got too ol' to carry you. You ain't had no business 'round here no way."

Van Ida was on the porch when they reached the house. Lanterns lit the yard, held by a circle of people, as though the sun had fallen on Evers. People who did not usually speak to Van Ida were standing in the Wheatons' yard. The Sampsons, the Harpers, the Greens, Darlene Kincaid and her entire family had all come out, just like they did when Brill put up his street sign. They were staring at the blood on Zyma, asking if Mr. Lawrence was really dead.

Alabama rushed Zyma inside and kept telling her not to open her mouth. Van Ida went in behind them. She didn't say anything right away. She helped Zyma pull off her dress, then she fixed her a bath in the tin tub in the kitchen. The water was warm, but Zyma was cold and could not stop shaking. Van Ida bathed her—something she had not done in a long time.

Alabama left the house while Zyma was having her bath. When he came home again, he was angrier than they had ever seen him. They were sitting on the large bed, and Van Ida had not begun to question Zyma. She had been waiting for Alabama.

"Zyma, we needs you to tell us what happened," she said, keeping her gaze on the child and away from Alabama's angry scowl.

The look on Alabama's face was scaring Zyma. She wished her mama had talked to her before her daddy came back. She tried not to look at him.

"I could hear Mr. Lawrence breathin' in my ear," she said, "and I could smell somethin', Mama, smelled like blood, I guess. I told Brill to go 'round there wit' me, and he went and got Miss Nadine."

"Go 'head," Van Ida said, and Zyma knew she was going to have to tell it all.

"I saw the man that killed Mr. Lawrence," Zyma said. "And when I went back wit' Mr. Lawrence, he killed that man. He goin' to Hell, Mama. That ain't no good way to help nobody, is it?"

"Zyma, baby," Van Ida said, and shook her head the way people do when they are sad or just don't know what else to do.

Alabama did not shake his head; he shook Zyma. He rushed over to the bed, grabbed her by her shoulders, and began shaking her like he had lost his mind. "You can't tell nobody no nonsense like that," he shouted. "I'm sicka hearin' 'bout this breathin' in yo' ears mess. You gon' get us all run outta town. You oughta hear what folks is sayin'."

After he thought he had shaken some sense into her, he let her go, and stepped away from her. She fell to the floor and thought how it would be good if nobody asked her anything else.

"Ida, you shoulda been home wit' Zyma," Alabama said, turning his scary face toward Van Ida. "Where was you, anyway, that you couldn't be here to stop her from goin' over to Lawrence's?"

Van Ida got up from the bed and walked toward him. "Where was you?" she asked.

Zyma did not like the way her mama's voice sounded, how it had gotten deeper than it usually was. They were talking about her, but it seemed they had forgotten all about her, as they stood facing each other in the center of their bedroom floor.

"If you'da been here, Nadine would'na had to go 'round there openin' her mouth. You'da been here, you coulda stopped Zyma from goin' 'round there," Alabama accused. "Now Tarlo done sent for the Mays Spur law. Folks is upset, talkin' how it's Zyma's fault Lawrence is dead."

"You ain't gon' put the blame for this on me," Van Ida shot back. "I can't be wit' that chile day and night."

"How come you can't? If you can't look after her, ain't no reason for you to stay here. I goin' to see what mo' I can hear. I want you gone by the time I get back."

Alabama started for the door. Van Ida followed the trail of perfume that emanated from his clothes. She grabbed a hold of his shoulders to spin him around. Alabama pushed her off, but she sprang right back. She caught his head in the crook of her arm, and for a minute all Zyma could see were her daddy's legs following her mama's back across the floor. They struggled, made grunting sounds. Her daddy's head was stuck like swollen feet in brand new shoes. She did not think her mama was trying to break his neck, but if she had twisted a little more, a little harder, she probably would have.

When he got his head free, Alabama came out all puffed up and hunched over like somebody who wasn't meant to be bothered. Van Ida was falling.

It took her a long time to hit the floor because she fell in parts—knees, hips, shoulders, head. They were both breathing pretty hard, but Alabama was the first to speak. He looked down at Van Ida and said, "I want you outta here. Out there, folks callin' Zyma a witch all over again. That's 'cause you fill her head wit' foolishness, got her thinkin' she can hear folks dyin'. And she ain't got sense enough to keep it to herself."

Van Ida lifted her head, and then the rest of her body. She didn't get too close to Alabama. "You needs to stop talkin' so loud," she said. "You shoutin' our business for all the neighbors to hear."

Alabama made a fist as though he was going to hit her, then he turned and walked out. Zyma was glad to see him go. She watched her mama take a shirt from a drawer, unbutton it, and spread it on her bed. She took some of her clothes, laid them on the shirt, then tied the shirt sleeves around them to make a bundle. While she packed, she kept asking Zyma questions about Mr. Lawrence. Zyma told her everything.

"Well, when the law come," Van Ida said, "and they gon' come, this is what I want you to say. . ."

The lie she told Zyma to tell was the biggest lie Zyma had ever heard. Van Ida told her to say that she had seen everything with her eyes instead of inside her head. She made Zyma repeat it twice, then she said, "That's good. Whoever that man is, he gotta pay for what they done."

When Van Ida started toward the door with her clothes tied in the shirt, Zyma followed behind her. She was scared, and she didn't want to be left alone.

"Don't go, Mama," she begged. "Where you goin'? I wanna go wit' you. I don't wanna be by myself in this house. What if that man come for me wit' his knife? He a ghost now."

"He ain't no ghost," Van Ida said. "Did that man see you?"

"No, ma'am, but I seen him. It was Mr. Cleo, Mama."

"You sho', Zyma?

The girl nodded. "He stab Mr. Lawrence in the back, then when Mr. Lawrence turn around like he was gon' fall, Mr. Cleo stabbed him in his chest over and over again." Zyma's hand made a stabbing motion as she talked, then she stopped. "How come you gotta leave, Mama? How come Daddy can't go if he the one mad at you? He ain't never here no way."

Van Ida dropped her bundle to the floor. She squatted and pulled Zyma into her arms. "You be my burden to bear," she said. "Zyma, child, you be my reason to breathe."

When she said that, Zyma knew that she was not going anywhere. She had never spent a day or night without Van Ida in her entire life, and she did not want to. She picked up the bundle from the floor, untied the sleeves, and began putting her mother's clothes back in the drawer.

CHAPTER 21

Van Ida stayed awake all night waiting for Alabama, had left the dangling bare bulb burning for him. The light hurt her eyes. It seemed that was all she did anymore—wait for Alabama. She stared at the clock on the bedside table, watched the hands move, waited. She had never bothered to put on nightclothes, and that was alright because soon she would have to get up and get busy whether Alabama came home or not. He was not the reason she had been unable to sleep. The Mays Spur law had come to her door with Tarlo, and their faces and voices remained in her head long after they were gone. They had barged into her house, questioned her child, and wanted to know how Zyma just happened to be on Pepper Road when Lawrence Anderson was murdered.

"I was looking for Daddy to come home for supper," Zyma told them.

Van Ida was pleased with how quickly and convincingly Zyma had lied, but she knew that was not the end of it. The law had left her house and had gone straight to Cleo's. They hadn't found him. Even in the middle of the night, she had heard the angry voices of her neighbors coming through her walls, saying that Zyma had sent them to Cleo. It was nearly morning now, quiet, a new day.

When the small hand was on the five and the big hand reached the ten, the front door opened and Alabama stepped inside.

"There's gonna be trouble if you try to go to the fields today," he said when he saw that she was awake. "I don't know that Tarlo put the word out on you, but I'm hearin that folks don't want you or Zyma nowhere near 'em."

Already fully dressed, Van Ida rose from the bed. She did not mean to sniff him, but the smell of a woman was overpowering. Her perfume, her sex, her total presence clung to his skin and clothes. It bothered her that Alabama looked well rested because it meant he had been able to sleep. Somewhere he had been able to rest his head beside some woman where he felt safe and comfortable.

He moved off toward the kitchen. She stepped into her shoes and followed. She wanted to ask him where he had been all night, but she didn't.

"They ain't sayin nothin' 'bout me," he continued, "but the way I see it, if they talkin' 'bout you and Zyma, then they talkin' 'bout all of us. We a family."

His talking family, keeping a distance between them, and not being able to look her in the eyes were all signs of guilt, Van Ida thought.

He took a seat at the table and Van Ida did what came naturally. She began preparing breakfast for him. As she cracked an egg on the edge of a bowl, she felt like she had cracked the same egg yesterday and the day before. She had been cracking the same egg on the same bowl for a hundred years.

Every Saturday since the beginning of summer, Van Ida had been going over to Miss Girlie's house. She would take a dime and leave it on the money table, and Miss Girlie would always say, "Won't be too much longer now." She never gave Van Ida powder, or charms, or any rituals to follow. Maybe, Van Ida thought, what she had asked for was something that Miss Girlie had never been able to conjure up before. Van Ida was trying to buy a little happiness. She hadn't said that to Miss Girlie. What she had said was, "I want you to get this dark cloud off me. It's hangin' down in my face, makin' me blind, suffocatin' me." When Miss Girlie took the first dime, Van Ida had assumed the old woman could move the cloud, but she was still waiting.

"I don't think we no family, Alabama," she said. "I think we just folks passin' each other in the same house ever' day. I remember when you asked me if I loved you. I did, but I don't no mo'. I never did asked you that question 'cause I done always knew you didn't love me. You stayed wit' me then for the same reason I stay wit' you now. That child in there."

"I didn't really mean for you to leave last night," he said, by way of an apology.

"I know, but I wish I'da left, then I would'na had to smell that floozy all over you this mornin'."

"Nothin worse than a ugly woman gettin uglier," Alabama mumbled to himself.

Van Ida heard and let it pass.

Alabama watched her as she worked at the table. He had started not to come home, and now he wished that he hadn't. His Wondrene was back, and he had spent the night with her, feeling younger and happier than he had in a long time. His gaze traveled the length of Van Ida's body, settled on her eyes. He placed his thumbs together, pressed them against his lower lip. He thought that if he could take all of the good from inside of her and put it into the body of Wondrene Barry, he would die a happy man.

"You want me to love you?" he asked, and silently prayed that she would so no, because he did not have the strength or desire. "Want me to take you in there to that bed and love you, Ida?"

"Nah." She shook her head. "I don't care if you don't never touch me no mo'. I done forgot what it felt like, and it's good I done forgot."

He sighed audibly and witnessed the knowing look that she gave him. Right then and there he decided he would never again eat anything she prepared.

They could hear Zyma stirring, the sound of her bedroom door opening. Van Ida called out to the child, did not want her to think she was in the house alone. When Zyma entered the kitchen, Van Ida said, "When you get done eatin', I want you to hurry and get dressed. You goin' wit' me today."

"That ain't a good idea, Ida," Alabama said. "Theron's goin' up to Rootsville. I'm gon' ride up wit' him, and we ain't comin back 'til sometime tomorrow. I ain't gon' be here if trouble get started, so I think it's best if you and Zyma stay at the house."

"Do what you gotta do, Alabama. I'm goin' to work like I do ever' day. Ain't nobody gon' try to stop me."

"Ida, they done took Mr. Cleo to jail. Folks sayin' what happened was by Zyma's hands. They sayin' she done lied on Mr. Cleo."

Zyma was not hungry. She knew that wasting food was not allowed, but she thought she might be able to get away with it since her daddy wasn't eating his food, either. All night, in and out of dreams, she had seen Lawrence Anderson's face. Over and over again, she had watched Mr. Lawrence take the knife and kill Mr. Cleo. He hadn't really killed him, though, so what if none of what she had seen was real? Maybe Mr. Cleo didn't kill Mr. Lawrence. Maybe it was somebody else. She pushed her plate away and stared down at the table.

"Daddy, can't we move outta Cranston?" she asked. "I don't like it here. Things was better befo' we moved."

Alabama stood, looked down at her, then said, "I ain't got no way to take you outta here, Zyma. If I had a truck, I'd move us all to Kingston. What I want you to do is stay in this house today."

"By myself?" Zyma whined.

"Don't worry 'bout it, child," Van Ida said. "If he don't take you wit' him, I'm gon' take you wit' me. You ain't gon' be by yo'self."

"I'm tellin' you, Ida, it ain't a good idea," Alabama said sternly, although he knew he was wasting his breath.

He headed for the door. He did not want to see in Van Ida's eyes what he knew to be the truth. He was not going to Rootsville with Theron. He was going back to be with Wondrene because he could not stand the thought of her leaving Cranston again without him. Instead of running off to be with a woman, he should have been going to the field. If he thought there was going to be trouble, he should stay and face it with Van Ida. He stepped out into the hallway without giving her a chance to say it. He would have had to say something back, defend himself. That was a hard thing to do when he knew he was wrong.

Without a word, Van Ida watched him go. While Zyma got dressed, she washed the breakfast dishes and sang a song from her past, words she had learned from the great mothers. *Ol' blue sky, I need yo' clouds today. Let yo' rain wash my troubles away.*

The field truck was already waiting when Van Ida and Zyma reached Stanley Road. The darkness was beginning to separate into little spaces here and there, not yet enough to bring light to the earth. Seven dark figures stood on the bed of the truck, and three others stood on the road talking. Their early morning murmuring ceased when they spotted Van Ida. She could feel their coldness, could have reached out and touched it if she had wanted to. She ignored them.

Van Ida helped Zyma onto the bed of the truck, handed the girl the canvas bag containing their lunch and water, then climbed up herself. Almost immediately the seven on board eased away from her and climbed down. They joined the others on the road, and there was total silence, except for the idling of the truck.

From the center of the group, Maude Baker finally spoke. She did not look up at Van Ida, who stood as tall as a tree, tall enough to fall over and squash them all.

"They done took Cleo to jail," Maude said. "I was there when they found Lawrence's blood all over Cleo's clothes." She hesitated as though waiting for someone else to pick up the story. No one spoke, so she continued. "We keep wantin' to know how that blood got on Cleo's clothes. What make Mr. Cleo wanna kill Lawrence? He ain't had no reason to, 'cept bein' touched by the wicked."

"Folks thinkin' it had somethin' to do wit' yo' girl," Silas said. "They say there was a owl on Lawrence's roof when Cleo got to him. We know that's how the witches come sometimes, and they can make folks do some strange things."

"What you sayin', Silas?" Van Ida asked.

The big man hooked his thumbs through the straps of his overalls as a gesture of bravery. He glanced over at Maude, then up at Van Ida. "I'm sayin' it's likely yo' girl had somethin' to do wit' it. We think it'll be better if y'all stay away from ever'body 'til we get this straightened out."

Mr. Blevins's driver stuck his head out the window of the truck and warned that he would be pulling off in one minute. Gabriel Hawkins and Henry Winston stepped over to the driver's door. They sheepishly glanced up at Van Ida while they whispered to the driver, and Van Ida knew that trouble was brewing.

In Cranston, when the people wanted to run somebody out, they shunned them and robbed them of their livelihood and shelter. They made life unbearable. They had all seen it happen, usually with thieves and those who posed a threat of attracting the attention of the Mays Spur law, but never with a child.

Van Ida felt Zyma holding onto her dress. She reached a hand down and touched the top of the girl's head. "Tarlo know y'all out here troublin' me?" she asked the group. "Tarlo send y'all?"

"We think yo' girl done laid somethin' on Tarlo," said Thelma Green, a woman who lived next door to Van Ida. "He can't see what ever'body else can see. He can't see that there's somethin' wrong wit' that child."

Van Ida laughed, a low humorless laugh. "What's my girl s'pose to be?" she asked wearily. "Is she a witch, or a root worker, or a demon?"

The driver had gotten out of the truck. He was a thin, bowlegged white man with hairy arms. He came around to where Van Ida stood, looked up at her, and said, "You gon' have to come on down from there. These folks saying that they ain't riding wit' you. I ain't got nothing against you, but I can't drive out there and tell Mr. Blevins that I brought a woman and a little girl to work his fields and left all the others behind."

Beside Van Ida, Zyma dropped the canvas bag and began to hum. She locked her fingers together and moved her arms in a swinging motion. The humming grew louder as she stepped toward the edge of the truck's bed. Everybody stared up at her.

"That girl is evil and wicked," Silas said. "When the law find out she lyin' on Cleo, I hope they lock her away in that little dark hole under the jail."

Zyma unlocked her fingers, reached both hands toward the sky, then stared at Silas Rodman. "Mr. Silas," she said sweetly, tenderly, as thought he meant the world to her. "I done caught me a mess of bees. Come nightfall they gon' be swarmin' and stingin' inside yo' head."

For a moment Silas could not find his voice, could not believe what he had heard. He tried a laugh that came out loud and awkward, then he glanced around at the others who would not meet his gaze. When he turned back to the truck, he saw that Van Ida and the child were gone. He turned again, saw them walking up the road. His voice finally surfaced full of fear and disbelief. "Did y'all hear what that chile said?"

Not one of his neighbors answered him or looked at him. To them he was a cursed man, and they did not want it to rub off on them. They climbed onto the truck and left him standing alone on the road. Silas didn't know what to do. If he tried to go home, he would have to go in the same direction as the woman and girl. He watched the truck pull off without him, then he hurried along the road toward Wash Gibson's house.

Zyma It was sunrise when the truck finally pulled off. Mama took me over
to sit on the steps at the back of the Philpot store. We were facing
Stanley Road. We saw Mr. Silas rushing off in the other direction.
The early morning sun was crowning his knotty head, and I thought
he could have stood several month's worth of haircuts.

"You ought'na said that to that man," Mama said after we had been
sitting for a while, but there was no anger in her voice.

"Daddy said if they gon' call me a witch that I oughta act like one."

"When he tell you that?"

"When I first started to school."

"Well," Mama said, "I'd hate to be you when he finds out what you
done."

"I know," I agreed and leaned my head against my mother's arm.

Mama chuckled. "I ain't never heard of no witch puttin' no bees in
nobody's head. Zyma, chile, where'd you get that from?"

Mama laughed her way into tears, and it was a strange sound
coming from her throat. She wiped at her eyes and kept right on
laughing. When she was all laughed out, she lightly slapped me
across my thigh. "Don't you never do nothin' like that no mo'," she
said.

Although Mama laughed, I knew she was going to punish me.
When we got up from the steps, she made me carry the canvas sack
with our lunch and the heavy water jar inside. We walked back down
Stanley Road to where the truck had stood. I thought we were going
home, but we turned and started up another road. We passed Mr.
Lawrence's house on Pepper. It looked cold, dark, and empty, like
nobody had ever lived there, and there was no sign of the dog. I kept
thinking that I was going to see Mr. Lawrence's body again, and it
scared me, but I didn't say anything to Mama.

We traveled on that road until it curved into another one, and that
one curved into another one, and the roads kept curving and we kept
walking until I was sure that we were headed for the end of the earth.

"Mama, don't you know no shortcuts?" I asked. "Where we going,
anyway?"

We passed a forest as thick as the one across the road from our

NOVELS

house. We passed houses and cows and fields. We came up on a snake that was lying on the road. Mama said she thought a tractor had probably run over it, but I didn't see no tractor tire tracks, and I wasn't sure the snake was dead. Mama walked on by it, and I didn't have no choice but to follow.

Mama told me how snakes shed their skin. She said if Daddy had done talked me into being a witch that I was gonna have to learn how to shed my skin, too.

She left the road and cut through a cornfield. I rushed to keep up. I was right on her heels when she stepped out of the field behind a stable. We came around to the front of the stable, crossed a lane where wagon wheels had made furrows in the dirt, passed a small house and a large vegetable garden.

We were at Mr. Edward Small's place. I knew that the minute I saw Lucinda Small and her grown-up sister, Imogene. They both had baskets and were busy picking vegetables from the garden. Lucinda used to go to the Mays Spur School, and Mr. Edward would come with his mule and wagon to pick her up sometimes. She didn't go to school anymore. Both of the girls were wearing britches. I had always wanted to wear some, but Mama wouldn't let me. She said britches made girls look like boys.

I waved to Lucinda, and she waved back. Mama walked up to the edge of the garden and spoke to Imogene.

"I'm looking for Calvin Brown," Mama said. "You know where I can find him?"

"He's 'bout half a mile down the road wit' Daddy," she said. "They clearing land to build a house for Robert and his wife. Robert's getting married next month."

Mama started out toward the road. I hung back, staring down at the baskets of tomatoes that Lucinda and Imogene were sliding along the row. I was still carrying the canvas sack, and I wondered what Mama had packed in there for us to eat.

"You want one?" Lucinda asked.

I nodded. She pulled a small tomato from a vine and gave it to me. I wiped it against my dress, then popped the whole thing in my mouth. I was wishing that I had eaten my breakfast.

"You going to the Jubilee this year?" Lucinda asked.

I nodded, although I was probably lying. We never went. I think Daddy would go sometimes, but Mama never did, and I was always left at home with Mama. The Jubilee was held at the end of August down on Cross Street. There would be plenty of food, music, and dancing. Folks would come in from all of the farms, and some from as far away as Mays Spur. Folks always had a good time, and they would talk about it well into the picking season.

The girls were working, and it seemed I should have been doing something, too, other than walking along beside them carrying a heavy canvas sack. I swallowed the last of my tomato, then asked, "Who Robert gon' marry?"

"Margaret Jordan," they answered together.

I didn't know her, and I figured she must be from one of the farms.

"Mama's sewing me a dress to wear to the Jubilee," Lucinda said. "I'm gon' dance 'til it's time to come home. Maybe I won't even eat that much. I'll just dance."

She was pulling tomatoes and smiling like she could already see herself dancing. I was ready to catch up to Mama, but I wasn't sure which way to go. I glanced around.

"Which way to where yo' Daddy clearing land?" I asked.

Lucinda said she would show me, and I walked beside her up the lane the way Mama had gone. When we got to the end of the lane, Lucinda pointed to her right. "You just keep walking that a way 'til you see 'em. They'll be on this side of the road."

As I started down the road, Lucinda walked with me like she was in no hurry to get back to the garden. She was about the same age as Brill. I had always liked her because she had never made fun of me at school.

"It's gon' be good having Robert and Margaret living just down the road," she said. "It'll give me someplace to visit. I can't wait 'til they have a big family." She pointed to a pole that had a strip of red paint around it. "That's where Imogene's house gon' be if she marry a man that ain't got no land. Mine gon' be up the road the other way. But I think I'm gon' marry somebody that's gon' move me into Mays Spur. I'll probably marry somebody like Brill Evers or Edward Rice."

"Why you wanna marry them?"

She gave that giggle that older girls sometimes give when they're about to explain something to a child. "Brill is gonna be a doctor or something else important," she said, "and Edward can sing. He's gonna be on the radio one day."

"Oh," I said, like she had made it all clear and now I understood. I liked her, but I didn't want anybody to marry Brill.

"Imogene's got her eyes on Calvin Brown. Mama don't like that. She say Imogene gotta find somebody closer to her own age, but she can't meet nobody out here on the farm, 'cept men that Daddy hire to work the land. Mama want her to look for a husband at the Jubilee. But I think all the best young men done gone off to the war. We'll see."

"Mr. Lawrence died yesterday," I said. "I saw his body. Mr. Cleo killed him." Before she could say anything else, I ran off to catch up with Mama. I didn't know why I had told her about Mr. Lawrence. I think it was because I needed something to say.

When I caught up to Mama, she had already stepped off the road onto a plot of downed trees. Five men and two mules were working to clear the land. Mama walked over to where Mr. Edward and another man were standing beside one of the mules. I heard her ask about work. Mr. Edward said something about how he wouldn't need any more help until picking time, which was still a few weeks away.

"Glad you sent yo' cousin to me when you did, though," he said. "Calvin was here to help us mop for the weevils, and it looks like we got a good crop this year. He's been a big help."

The other man stepped around in front of the mule. He stood beside Mama. "You a sight for sore eyes, Van Ida," he said, and Mama looked embarrassed for a minute.

"It's good to see you, too, Calvin," she said.

"Mama, do you need a drink of water?" I asked, hoping she would remember that I was still carrying the sack.

Mama's cousin Calvin squatted down beside me. "How you doing, little Zyma?" he asked. "I could stand a drink of water."

I stepped away from him and gave the sack to Mama. I didn't know anything about no cousin, and Daddy had told me to be careful about who I drink and eat behind.

Mama reached into the sack and gave her cousin the water jar. Mr. Edward moved on off across the yard with the mule. I just stood there beside Mama.

"When you gon' get on into Mays Spur, buy yo'self some clothes?" Mama asked her cousin.

"I don't know that I'm up for that yet," he said.

"Them you got on 'bout to fall off. You can't be no cousin of mine and dress like that," Mama said.

Calvin was holding the water jar, but before he took a drink, he threw his head back and roared with laughter. It had a happy sound, like nothing I had ever heard come from any of the men in Cranston. It seemed his whole body had to be smiling at that laugh. I decided right then and there that I liked Mama's cousin. I was wearing a dress that Mama had sewed me from two of Daddy's old shirts. Mama's dress was mismatched like mine because she'd had to sew on a different kind of cloth to make hers long enough. I guess we didn't look too much better than Calvin, just cleaner.

"What happened that you ain't working at Mr. Blevins's place no more?" Calvin asked. "This ain't the kind of work for you out here at Edward's. He ain't got nobody 'cept me and two other fellows and his son, Robert." Calvin stared out to where Robert was sawing on a tree trunk. "He got his wife and two daughters, but I ain't seen no other women out here. This a lot of land and a lot of hard work. This ain't the kind of work for no woman. Not out here."

"If Eleanor and her girls can do it, me and Zyma can do it, too," Mama said.

Calvin screwed the top back on the water jar. He took the sack from Mama, put the jar inside, then stood there holding the sack in his one hand and Mama's hand in his other. I had never seen Mama hold hands with anybody besides me.

"You gon' tell me what happened?" Calvin asked.

Mama slid her hand from his and touched the blue bandanna that was tied around her head. "Tell you 'bout it when you get home from work," she said. "I'll be waiting at yo' place."

Calvin was leaning over close to Mama like he wanted to whisper something to her when Mr. Small called out for him to come help do something. Calvin lifted Mama's hand and put his lips to it. Mama snatched her hand away like his mouth had burned her. She glanced down at me with a look on her face that made me think he had scared her.

Calvin grinned. "You sho' you gon' be waiting?" he asked.

Mama took her sack from him. "Maybe not," she snapped, and I knew she was mad about something.

On our walk back home, we stayed on the road and passed the cornfield that we had cut through earlier. Mama was walking fast, but at least this time she was carrying the sack. All I had to do was keep up with her.

"Why you mad at yo' cousin?" I asked, hoping that talking would slow her down.

"'Cause he ain't no cousin of mine, and he ain't got no sense," she said, and I swear she started walking even faster.

"I like him," I said. "How many mo' cousins we got, Mama?"

I was just about running along beside her when we came up on that dead snake again. I stepped right on over it like nothing. After we walked around the curve of the road, I just stopped. I had to do something to let Mama know she was 'bout to walk me to death. Talking wasn't slowing her down. I started to cry, and finally she stopped.

I had been wanting to cry all day, ever since we passed Mr. Lawrence's house this morning. I had held it in so I wouldn't have to explain anything to anybody. I was scared because I wasn't sure Mr. Cleo had killed Mr. Lawrence, and I had told the law that he did. Mr. Silas had said that the law might lock me away in a little dark hole under the jail.

Mama came back to where I was. She squatted down on the road beside me. "It's gon' be alright, Zyma," she said. "Whatever it is, I feel it inside me that it's gon' be alright."

Mama sometimes told what she called needed lies, but I didn't think she had ever lied to me. On that road with her holding me against her body, I tried to believe that everything was going to be alright.

Zyma Lawrence Anderson's funeral was the only one I had ever been to. Daddy said we had to go, pay our respect, show folks that we weren't guilty of anything. We even went out to the graveyard. Miss Opal was real pitiful. She didn't have nobody to hold her up, but Mr. Tarlo and Miss Annie stood beside her. Miss Opal could be mean sometimes, and still I felt sorry for her. I felt sorry for a lot of things, like how most folks didn't wanna get too close to me and Mama, or how they would stare at us until we caught them doing it, then they'd turn their heads.

When folks started leaving the graveyard, I wanted to walk with Brill, but I knew I couldn't. Mama and Miss Nadine didn't talk to each other, and it wouldn't be right for me to leave with Brill's family instead of my own. I stayed where I was, took Mama's hand, and asked her if she would show me where my Mama Mildred was buried.

She looked over at Daddy. "I can't be walking 'round out here in this graveyard looking for nobody."

"She's right over yonder," Daddy said. "Right over yonder by that tree."

There was anger in Mama's eyes when she saw Daddy pointing at the tree. Real quick like, she slapped his hand down. "You know better than to point in a graveyard, Alabama," she said.

"What's gon' happen 'cause Daddy pointed?" I asked.

"Finger might rot off," Mama said before she walked away from us. With both hands, she was holding the front of her dress right over her stomach. She was walking fast, passing all of the other folks who were leaving the graveyard.

"Ain't nothing gon' happen, Zyma," Daddy explained. "Ida always been scared of the graveyard. She got ideas in her head that ain't never gon' change."

Daddy walked me over and showed me where Mama Mildred was buried. There was no headstone, just some rock gravel and a piece of tin. I couldn't even tell what had been scratched into the tin. I glanced around the graveyard at the spots where headstones stood, making sure not to point. It didn't matter what Daddy said, if Mama thought it was a bad thing to point, then I wasn't going to point.

NOVELS

"How come she ain't got no headstone like everybody else?" I asked.

"Everybody ain't got no headstone. Some folks ain't even got gravel to mark they spot. Folks do the best they can when somebody die, do what they can afford. I always thought I'd get one for her. Just never got around to it."

Daddy said that most of the folks were taking food over to Mr. Lawrence's mother's house down on the north road. He said some would go to Miss Opal's house. "I ain't feeling too hungry," he said, "but I'll take you to the north road if you wanna eat."

I shook my head. "I wanna go home and eat what Mama cook."

We walked home. Daddy was sweating, and I was feeling hot all over. Everybody had scattered one way or the other, and we didn't see nobody on the roads. It seemed like even the dogs, cats, and chickens were being quiet out of respect for Mr. Lawrence.

"It was sort of like this when we buried Mildred," Daddy said. "It was in May, but almost as hot as it is today. Folks brought food over to the church 'cause we lived so far out. I couldn't eat that day, either. She was pretty just like her mama. I shoulda packed her up and moved her away from here. That's what I shoulda done."

"You think I'm pretty, Daddy?"

"Not like Mildred," he answered without looking down at me. "I don't want you to be pretty like that. It's like a curse, and folks don't stop bothering you 'til that make you ugly or hurt you some kinda way."

Our yard was empty, and so was the house. I looked out back for Mama, but I couldn't find her. There was nothing cooking in the kitchen. I wanted to change my mind and go down on the north road, but one look at Daddy made me know that I didn't even need to ask about it. He really wasn't hungry. I was. Daddy got a glass of water and went to sit in his old chair on the front porch. It was cooler outside than inside, so I sat with him. The sun was baking down across the steps, but the porch roof gave us a bit of shade.

"Reckon Ida went down to the north road to get her some food?" Daddy asked.

I didn't bother to answer him. We both knew that Mama hadn't gone anywhere near any of the women in the community. She would go over to Miss Girlie's, but that was usually when she needed something for sickness, and she hadn't been sick, not that I could tell.

"Maybe she went to see her cousin," I said. "I didn't see him at the funeral."

"What cousin?" Daddy asked.

All bunched together and walking as a group, the Everses, the Kincaids, and the Greens turned onto the road and caught my attention. They walked toward the houses. They were all quiet, even the little ones. I think they were being what Mama called mournful, like they were still in the church and Mr. Lawrence's body was still in the casket up front.

"What cousin?" Daddy repeated.

"Calvin," I said, then I jumped up and ran down the steps and toward the road to meet Brill.

CHAPTER 22

Calvin heard the familiar whistle. He opened the door and watched as Van Ida stepped out of the weeds. She was wearing a black dress and had a plain black hat pulled down on her head. In the sunlight he could see that the dress was old, patched in places, shorter than she usually wore them. He guessed she'd had no matching material to make it long enough. For a moment she looked startled, like she was seeing him for the first time, like she didn't know who he was. He hesitated before calling out to her. Maybe she was troubled about the funeral, he thought. He was glad he hadn't known the dead man. He didn't want to be sad, but he would be if she needed him to.

"Come on in," he invited. "You alright?"

She nodded, stepped through the doorway. He offered her a seat, but she stood glancing around the room. It pleased him that she seemed to be observing the changes he had made, the work he had done. The old stool was now sturdy, there was a clean blue spread on his bed, he had two drinking cups, and a new dipper for the bucket. There were now two chairs placed at his table. They didn't match, one had a higher back than the other and they were different shades of oak.

"What you do?" she asked.

"I went into Mays Spur with Edward." Calvin smiled, allowed some of his pleasure to show in his voice. "Got myself some clothes so I can be your cousin. Got myself a couple of books, too. They keep me company out here."

Van Ida took a good look at him. He was wearing a white shirt and brown pants. He had a broad grin on his face. "You a handsome man, Calvin," she said, "but you ain't no cousin of mine. I don't need no cousin."

He laughed. She had a way of making him do that. Her words were plain, direct. "What do you need, Van Ida?" he asked.

"Need to get off my feet. Need something cold to drink."

She reached for a chair. He stopped her and led her over to the bed. "Sit over here where it's soft," he suggested. "Kick off your shoes. I want you to be comfortable."

She sat on the bed, but she did not remove her shoes. Calvin pulled the stool over to the bed, lifted her feet, and removed her well-worn black oxfords. He rested her feet on his lap, ran his thumbs along her soles. It felt good to her, so good that she pulled away from him, placed her feet flat on the floor.

Calvin smiled, then bounced up from the stool with the agility of a young boy. He went over to the door, glanced back at her, winked an eye. She watched him disappear outside. After a while he came back in carrying a jug. He filled the two cups from the jug, then came back, gave one of the cups to her, and reclaimed his spot on the stool.

"Wine," he said. "I got it from Edward. I have to keep it under the house so it'll stay cool. Go ahead, taste it. It ain't bad."

Van Ida stared down at the dark red liquid in the cup. She had never tasted wine before, but she needed something cool to soothe her throat. She could have asked for water, but she didn't. She tilted the cup, took in a small amount, just a taste. It wasn't bad. She took another swallow, glanced over at Calvin, and smiled.

"Girl," he said playfully, "that's 'bout the nicest smile I ever seen in my life. I didn't think I was ever gon' see one, but there it is."

They sat in comfortable silence. The world outside was just as quiet as inside—no birds chirping or dogs barking—not even the sound of a breeze rustling through the weeds. Calvin rose from his stool and sat on the bed beside Van Ida. He didn't touch her, gave her enough space to relax. He finished off his wine, then placed the cup on the stool.

Van Ida took another sip of wine, and finally spoke. "This the first time I ever really saw you. I don't mean I couldn't see you, but you been just a shadow. Everything been just a shadow."

"You been having trouble with your eyes?" Calvin asked.

"Nah." Van Ida shook her head. "I had a cloud over my face, but I think Miss Girlie done took care of that."

"I done heard that name before out at Edward's place. Ain't she a root worker?" Calvin asked. He was moving again, reaching inside a wooden box that stood at the head of the bed. He pulled out a folded red and white bandanna. "I bought this for you." He held it out to her.

Van Ida did not take it, would not even glance at it. "Why you spending yo' money on me?"

"What I'm gon' spend it on?" Calvin asked. He placed the bandanna on the bed between them, then he took Van Ida's cup and set it on the stool beside his own. "How come you act like you don't want nothing, don't want nobody to do nothing for you?"

She did not answer him.

Calvin leaned forward and turned his head so that he was looking directly into her face. It was a frozen face, a face that worked well at hiding all emotions. "Van Ida, you care about me," he said. "You done walked all the way out here in the heat, dressed in all that black stuff. You didn't come so you could be by yourself. You came to see me. How come I can't rub the tiredness out your feet? How come I can't give you this little scarf that I done bought for you?"

"You ain't got no business touching my feet," she said, and she turned her head and looked him straight in the eyes. She picked up the bandanna, then rose from the bed. "I got a husband. His name is Alabama Wheaton."

"I know his name," Calvin said angrily. "I done seen him—a old sorry something. If the man was treating you right, Van Ida, you wouldn't be walking 'round looking so sad all the time."

She walked over and placed the bandanna on the table, ran her fingers along the cover of a book he had been reading before she arrived, then pulled out a chair and sat down. "There's a swamp 'bout a mile or so from here," she said.

Calvin nodded. "I know. I done walked all over this place."

"Folks say I was born outta that swamp," Van Ida continued. "Say a gator spit me out. Just might as well say I'm the tallest and the ugliest woman they done ever seen. But I ain't never tried to stoop my shoulders to get no shorter. Long time ago I got used to being pointed at. Even the great mothers out at the plantation didn't know what to make of me. There was three of 'em, had done been there since before the freedom come. They had done seen a lot, but never nothing like me."

Calvin made a fist, brought it to his mouth, and blew through it. He was trying to imagine a child being ostracized because she was taller than the rest. Van Ida was not an ugly woman, but he could understand how years of scorn could make her believe she was. He wondered if anybody had ever told her how smooth her skin was, or how her smile brightened her entire face.

"I can't remember my own mama or daddy," she said. "I think they left the plantation to get away from the awful thing they had done made. The great mothers took care of me 'til they started dying off one by one. By then I was old enough to take care of myself."

The happiness Calvin had been feeling when Van Ida first arrived was now gone. He had thought he would be sad if she needed him to be, but he had not expected this. He listened intently, hung on to every word, and wondered what good was listening if he could not make things right. He wanted to touch her.

"I ain't such a good woman like you think," she said. "And Alabama ain't so bad like you think. I killed his daughter, Zyma's mama. He don't know it, but ever' day I wake up and remember how I poisoned that child wit' a swamp root. I didn't mean to, Calvin. I was trying to help her, trying to save her. She was so sick. I went and got a root. I done wished a hundred times that I hadn't done that. Today the first day I been out to that graveyard since we put that child in the ground."

Van Ida began to cry. She turned her face from him and used her hands to wipe away her tears. She was the personification of sadness, dressed in black—black on black—her shoulders hunched and shuddering. There was no hesitation on Calvin's part now. He got up from the bed, went straight to her, and rested her head against his body. Her tears soaked the front of his shirt.

"How you know that child wasn't gon' die anyway?" he asked. "If nobody else could help her, how you know she wasn't gon' die?"

Van Ida cried herself dry. It took her a long time to get there, but after she was all cried out, she straightened her back and looked up at him. "I killed her, Calvin," she said. "I owe that child a life. I can't give it to her, so I have to give it to Alabama."

"That ain't no way to live," he said, shaking his head disapprovingly.

"I know," she agreed solemnly. "I ain't been living. Not living can make you tired when you still gotta breathe. Zyma be my reason to breathe—and now you."

"Me?" Calvin questioned.

"You, Calvin," she answered. "'Cause I think you the only somebody want me just like I be. The great mothers tried to tell me what loving a man was gon' be like. Wadn't no good thing, just something had to be done. I moved in Alabama's house to take care of his children. That's the only reason I was there, but I kept hoping for that feeling they said was gon' come—the pain and the pleasure of knowing I had done satisfied my man. I don't guess he was ever my man. It took five years near 'bout fo' he ever touched me. Come home one night smelling of whiskey, needing a woman, and I guess I was the closest thing to a woman he could get that night. Wadn't no pain, no pleasure. Wadn't nothing."

"Humph." Calvin grunted. He didn't know what to say.

Van Ida raised her hands, spread the fingers apart on one, and held up two fingers on the other. "All these years," she said, "and he done touched me these many times. Sometimes I think I need him to, but I don't know. I done forgot how it felt. How 'bout you, Calvin?"

He didn't know whether he should go for inhibited or boastful. He pulled the other chair closer to hers, sat down, and decided to go for honesty. "Some things you don't never forget, Van Ida."

It was her turn to grunt. "Humph." She rose from the table like darkness and blocked the sunlight that streamed in through the opened door. Calvin had known her to walk out in the middle of a sentence, and once in the middle of a word. If she walked out in the middle of a conversation, there was nothing he could do about it except swallow his frustration, make sure she got her shoes, and wait until she showed up again. He cared about her, and he was glad she knew it.

She turned from the door, removed her hat, and placed it on a chair. Stands of rust-colored hair stood up on her head. There was only one mirror in the house, just a piece of glass he had found and placed in a corner against the back wall. She could not see it from where she stood, but somehow she knew the hair was sticking up. She used a hand to smooth it down. When she brought her hand away, the strands popped back up.

"Ain't no breeze coming in here," she said. "Nothing coming through that door 'cept flies and bees, and all that sun that followed me out here."

"You want me to close it?"

She nodded.

She was closer to the door than he was, but he got up and moved toward it. "You ain't gon' be able to see much," he told her. "Those two little windows don't let in that much light." He smiled to himself when he remembered that she had lived here before him. She knew how dark the little shack could get. He closed the door, then turned back to face her.

She stood beside the bed, in front of the window, where a narrow stream of light shown through. Her back was to him, and he thought she was staring into the wilderness outside. She glanced back at him.

"Turn 'round," she said. "Don't want you staring at me."

He did as she asked.

Her black dress was a slipover. She reached down to the hemline and pulled it over her head. She unfastened her undergarments and removed them. When she was done undressing, she picked up her dress, held it in front of her body to hide her nakedness. She turned to see that Calvin was still standing by the door with his back to her.

"You think you can love me?" she asked.

"I'm pretty sure I can," he answered, turning to face her. "I want to. Why don't you let that dress go? Ain't nobody here except you and me."

Van Ida clutched the dress tighter. She glanced back and down at the garments she had removed. Calvin could see her hesitation, sensed her indecisiveness, her inhibitions. Finally, she let the dress drop. It fell to the floor beside her shoes.

She stood in the stream of sunlight like perfectly cast glossy black porcelain, something too delicate to touch, to even think about touching. Her small breasts were firm, high-perched with darker nipples that seemed to point straight at him. His gaze traveled the length of her body, took in the curves of her hips, the flatness of her belly, the long, strong legs that stood like a pedestal holding up a portrait.

Desire rolled through him, nearly took his breath away. "Shit," he whispered. "Did he ever see you like this?"

"I ain't never been naked in front of nobody," she answered. "I feel foolish standing here, but I feel free. You coming?"

It was a stupid thing even as a thought, but Calvin said it aloud. "I'm scared you gon' break."

"I ain't gon' break, but you better come on over here 'fo I change my mind."

Zyma   "Don't nobody 'round here know nothing 'bout you having no
cousin, Ida," Daddy said. "I been asking folks all evening, and don't
nobody know nothing 'bout it."

"Don't you be throwin' yo' questions at me, Alabama." Mama said.

She was sitting on her bed beside me, and Daddy was standing in
the doorway that led to the kitchen.

"Folks don't care whether I got no kin at all," Mama told him.
"They think I come out a gator's egg. Why you wait all these years
befo' you start wantin' to know who my kin is? Who yo' kin?"

"You know I ain't got no kin 'round these parts, 'cept Zyma. If I
did, folks would know 'bout it."

"Well, say," Mama said, as she reached over and touched my head.
She untied my scarf, took a look at my hair, and acted like Daddy
wasn't even standing there. "Zyma, get the comb out the drawer. I
gotta wash yo' hair."

Daddy was getting a little bit mad. I could tell by the way he was
staring at Mama. "I don't care what you got, Ida," he said, "but kin
ain't somethin' you spring on somebody after they been knowin' you
for years."

"You don't know me, ain't never wanted to know me. And I ain't
sprung nothin' on you. If it mean that much to you, I can tell you
'bout the great mothers that raised me up."

Daddy stepped away from the door. He came closer to the bed. "I
already know 'bout them ol' dead voodoo witches," he said.

"Be careful what you say, Alabama. They can hear you."
Daddy said a few ugly words, then he stepped out into the hall. We
could hear his footsteps as he left the house. I guessed he was going
back over to listen to the radio with Mr. Theron. That's what he had
been doing before Mama came home.

"Mama, I'm hungry," I said.

She chuckled. "Zyma, you nine years old. You better go on out to that
kitchen and fix you somethin' to eat. Ain't I done showed you how?"

I nodded. "But it don't taste like yours," I said.

"Don't matter. If you hungry, you gotta know how to get somethin'
to eat. Yo' daddy gon' probably put me outta this house befo' long, and
this time I'm goin'. I done got you up old enough to see 'bout yo'self."

I could either get the comb so she could wash my hair or go out the kitchen to find something to eat. She had told me to do both. I decided eating was more important. I remembered the leftover cornbread in a covered bowl on the table, and I went out to get it. If I had known Mama wasn't going to cook, I would have stayed out in the yard. Before she came home, I had been running around and across the yards.

....

A dying breath carries the scent of the person alive and doing well. I didn't know that until the day that Miss Emerson died. Her smell was light and delicious like the taste of cucumber or watermelon. It was the fragrance that clung to her clothes and drifted in the air inside her house. I sniffed that fragrance minutes before her breathing reached my ears.

I woke up struggling to catch my own breath. At first, I thought that a witch had gotten into our house. I stepped out of my room and looked for Mama and Daddy. Neither one was home. I got the broom and the salt from the kitchen, laid the broom across my bedroom door, then sprinkled salt from the front door to my bed the way I had seen Mama do. I got back in bed, made a fist, and puffed air through it.

The breathing grew louder—soft, broken breaths. A heartbeat in my ears seemed to flutter, stop, then start back up again. It worried me that it was my own heart trying to quit, even though I knew deep down inside that it was Miss Emerson's.

Brill was away in Atlanta. He was staying with his aunt and going to school there. He could have gone closer to home, over in Mays County, but Mr. Theron said he wouldn't be able to take him over there every day because gasoline was being rationed. If Brill had been home, I would have gotten him and taken him with me to Miss Emerson's house.

It was dark outside. I wasn't afraid of ghosts the way Mama was. Ghosts were just dead people who wanted to be remembered. Witches, though, were something else. They would ride a person, suck the breath right on out the body. Witches came like cats creeping through the night, leaping through the air, landing on folks' chest, and doing all kinds of foolishness.

In my ears and my head, Miss Emerson was getting desperate. She reached me like gusty wind on a starless night, made her noises, drifted away, then came back again.

I got dressed and went over to the Everses' house to get Miss Nadine. She believed me right away when I told her about Miss Emerson, and so did Mr. Theron. It was just a short distance, but Mr. Theron drove us there in his truck.

Miss Emerson's door was open, as though she had left it that way for me. Miss Nadine knocked, but I went on inside because I knew nobody was coming to that door. The light was on in the front room, and Miss Emerson was sitting on a chair with a folded newspaper on her lap. On the table beside her chair stood a lamp and a teacup on a saucer. The teacup was full. She could have been dead already, except for the quiet breath that came nearly a full minute after we had entered her house. It was low, but it sounded in the room and echoed in my ears.

Mr. Theron picked her up and placed her on her bed. I got down on my knees beside the bed, touched her, and waited for some horror to take me back in time the way it had happened with Mr. Wilbur and Mr. Lawrence. I had always liked Miss Emerson, and if there was something I could change for her, I wanted to be able to do it.

When I held her hand, all I felt was the coolness of her fingers. But then a mood came down on me like I, or maybe Miss Emerson, was eager for something. It was the feeling I got when I knew Brill was coming home for the summer. I would get up early, sit on the steps, and wait for Mr. Theron to drive up with Brill. Brill would step down from the truck, smile at me, and I would go running across the yards to wrap my arms around him. So I held on to Miss Emerson because it was pleasant.

....

Daddy and Mr. Theron were good friends, Brill was my best friend, and I could not understand why Mama and Miss Nadine hardly spoke. At first, I had thought they were angry with each other because Mama had not let me go to see Clair Anne. But that had been nearly four years ago, and Clair Anne was still living; she just couldn't walk. The war—where people were fighting all over the world—well, it had come and gone, and still Mama didn't want anything to do with Miss Nadine. Even Darlene and I had made up.

Occasionally people would come out to our house wanting me to conjure somebody. I had never worked a conjure, couldn't even imagine how to begin. That didn't stop people from saying that I had used a spell to kill Wilbur Johnson and Lawrence Anderson. They said that I had put bees in Silas Rodman's head.

"You see?" Daddy had said to Mama one day. "You see how rumors get started, Ida? That's the same way they got started 'bout Miss Girlie, Wash Gibson, and the rest. Can't none of 'em do nothing, but people keep taking money to 'em."

For Daddy's sake, Mama tried to rid herself of beliefs she had had all of her life, things she had taught to me. Like the time we were walking on Stanley Road and the black cat crossed our path. Mama had been terrified and so had I. We turned around and started back home, but then Mama said she was not going to let a black cat stop her from going where she needed to go—which was over to Miss Girlie's. She had tried not to be scared, but we had both been nervous for the rest of the day.

Mama tried so hard for Daddy. Sometimes she would say that he be her reason to breathe. She would tell me the same thing. I knew it was her way of saying she loved us. I loved her, too. In Cranston, Mama was always going to be a gator woman, and I was always going to be some sort of witch, or root worker, or whatever people decided I should be. When folks got a hold of something different about you, they stuck to it like sap to a tree bark.

Daddy said I should act like I know something about roots, and just go on and take the money of the fools who come trying to give it to me. Mama said conjuring was real, and it was nothing to be played with. Then one day when Opal Lester came to our yard asking if my conjures were stronger than Wash Gibson's, Mama did something really strange. She puffed up and turned what Daddy called blue-black.

"Wash Gibson can't cunjuh nobody," she said. "He just a ol' fool living wit' his dreams. He sit over there in his house mixing up his powder and stuff that ain't never done nobody no good. He just take folks' money, then he grin 'cause he know he done caught hisself another fool."

Miss Nadine up on her porch, me, Darlene, and her little sister, Betsy—we all watched Mama as she stood in the yard, raised her hand over her head, and made a fist, "I done caught me a mess a bees," she said. "Come nightfall they gon' be swarming and stinging inside yo' head. 'Cause I'm 'bout tired a you, Opal Lester. Now, you go see if Wash Gibson can't get this fix off you."

Opal Lester stammered and stuttered, then she touched the string on her neck that had a cross attached to it. She held the cross out toward Mama. "You wait and see what I bring down on yo' head, Van Ida," she said. "You, Alabama, and that bastard child, all y'all gon' be sorry you ever laid eyes on me." Then she took off back up the road.

Mama made a chuckling sound that grew loud and strong. It seemed she was too tickled to make it back up the steps. She sat down and laughed until tears formed in her eyes. I thought at first that she was crying because I had never seen her laugh so hard. Finally, we were all laughing, including Miss Nadine.

I didn't want to say anything in front of the others, but once we were inside, I asked Mama if she could really put bees inside Miss Opal's head.

"I can't do nothing like that," she said. "I just wanted to scare Opal. She probably left here and went straight to Wash Gibson to get that curse took off her. I'd sho' like to see her face come morning. Don't you mention this to yo' daddy."

"Miss Nadine heard you," I said. "What if she tells him?"

"She ain't gon' tell him," Mama said. "I done fixed her wit' the evil eye so she ain't never gon' tell another thing I do in this world."

"Mama, you told me conjuring wadn't nothing to be playing wit', but you was just playing wit' Miss Opal if you can't really do it."

"I wadn't playing, Zyma. I was hoping I could do it. I think God'll forgive me for that."

I did not care what happened to Miss Opal, but I did not want

Miss Nadine to be fixed. I liked her, and, anyway, there were too many fixed people walking around in Cranston. I thought that if I never mentioned the evil eye to anybody, Miss Nadine could go right on laughing, being happy, and making my hair look pretty.

People had all sorts of beliefs. Brill said I should believe half of them because they were true. He said I should just junk the rest, but he never told me which was which.

In all the years we had lived on Evers, not one ghost had ever come to our house looking for Mama. Maybe it was because we had bones hanging over our door. All three houses had them. Maybe the bones were the reason the man in the woods had gone away. I asked Brill about it.

"He was probably down on his luck," Brill said. "People all over the country been having a rough time. It's likely that man found himself a job and moved on. I told you he wasn't a ghost, Zyma."

When Brill was away in Atlanta and I started to miss him really bad, I would walk down to his street sign and rub my hands against the pole. Once I got a splinter right in the middle of my hand, and Mama said it was a sign of Brill being in my blood. Now when Brill came home, he spent more time with the Kincaids than he did with me. Sometimes he would drive off in Mr. Theron's truck, and he would take Tommy Kincaid with him.

Tommy wasn't clean like Brill. He didn't have a daddy to teach him anything, but he had always worked hard to help out his mama and his two sisters. I think he looked forward to Brill coming home almost as much as I did so that he could ride off in the truck.

One summer day when Brill was sitting alone on his front steps, I went across the yards and joined him. Mama had said what a handsome man he had turned out to be, so I guessed he was a man. He was tall enough to be, and he had big, healthy bones like Mr. Theron. His skin color was the same brown as mine, somewhere between Miss Nadine's light and Mr. Theron's dark. He had a thin line of hair over his upper lip, and it made me sad to see it there because I knew soon he would be old like Daddy and Mr. Theron.

"When you coming home for good?" I asked.

He smiled. "And do what, Zyma? What would I do in Cranston?"

Treading Paths through Forests of Words

Delores Phillips's Creative Choices

Trudier Harris

"*A people*," Alice Walker once commented, "*do not throw their geniuses away. If they do, it is our duty as witnesses for the future to collect them again for the sake of our children. If necessary, bone by bone.*"[1] Walker modeled her own words in playing a pivotal role in recentering Zora Neale Hurston into American and especially African American literary studies. In editing this volume of works by Delores Phillips, Delia Steverson is following in Alice Walker's path and is, as James Baldwin said of Lorraine Hansberry in her truthful depiction of characters in *A Raisin in the Sun*, assuredly a witness. While Phillips may not have been relegated to the outermost dustbins of African American literary history, she is nonetheless generally unknown. Her only published novel, *The Darkest Child* (2004, 2018), received scant attention from most scholars until the last few years. Some graduate students began to focus on it in their seminars and dissertations, and, upon graduation, continue their interest in Phillips. Then, in 2018, Soho Press reissued *The Darkest Child* with an introduction by novelist Tayari Jones, whose reputation must surely have given Phillips's a boost. While that attention has not yet reaped a plethora of scholarly endeavors, it has succeeded in bringing more attention to Phillips.

With *Stumbling Blocks and other Unfinished Work*, Steverson provides general reading audiences, professors, students, and scholars with opportunities to engage with a talent that was bred in Cartersville, Georgia, and honed in the snowy regions of Cleveland, Ohio. From poetry to short fiction to unfinished novels, Phillips creates worlds that invite engagement. While her fiction is informed by social, political, communal, historical, and folkloristic subjects that place Phillips in conversation with many other African American writers, her poetry is quiet, mostly personal, and generally eclectic. There are few shouts or amens informing her poetic creations. Some read as observations, such as "Riding with a Friend," in which the persona comments on her problems with LSD. Positioning the drug as a "friend" misleads readers into thinking that the poem's subject might be different from what it actually is

(Phillips uses a similar technique in her short story "Grand Slam"). This "relationship" is perhaps just as disappointing as the one Phillips portrays in "Ashes," which is about a human-to-human relationship. "Riding with a Friend" is certainly more emotionally inflected than "Ashes," which might suggest that drugs evoke more of a response from the creator/poet/persona than human relationships do.

In the few instances in which Phillips broaches difficult topics, such as racial violence, the presentation is rather subdued, given the subject. Consider, for example, "Cousin Nathan." A Black man has obviously been dispatched violently. Yet Phillips begins the poem as if she were a Black Arts poet decrying the use of creativity on the frivolous. Then she turns to the real subject: Nathan has been run down and decapitated by a group of men in a truck when he mistakenly thought he could outrun them and live (echoes of James Baldwin's "Sonny's Blues"). Despite the tense and horrific subject matter, the poem comes off almost as reportage. The tone is so contained that readers must surmise the speaker's anger. Equally contained is "Sister, You Wear It Well," which focuses on child abuse. A younger sister is unaware that a slightly older one is being abused by their stepfather (or at least the man in their mother's life) until later in their lives. Lack of awareness of matters of sex and sexuality could be the only reason that the young girl, who lives in such close proximity to her sister, is unaware of what has occurred. The horror is compounded when the abused child finally shares her pain with an aunt and is simply told to go home and take a bath. That rejection is perhaps matched, again, by Phillips's sleight of hand. The image of wearing something well is usually applied to clothing and superficial matters; to apply it to how a younger sister responds to her older sister's being abused perhaps unintentionally deflects the traumatic impact of abuse.

Throughout this poetic sampling, it is clear that Phillips is not committed to any particular subject or to any particular form. Her poetic creations range from short, eight-line sentiments ("Ashes") to couplets ("Jesters") to lengthy meditations ("Queen of Rub-a-Dub"). Occasionally, Phillips echoes other writers. When I read "Forgive Me, Child," for example, I think immediately of Gwendolyn Brooks and her poem, "the mother," in which a woman who has had at least three abortions begs for forgiveness from the unborn children she has killed. What happens between mothers and children is a private matter that positions readers in the voyeuristic position of being relegated to looking over the shoulders of the mothers as they speak to their children. Both Phillips and Brooks contain readers just as they contain the events in the poems they create. Noticeably, the overall tone of most of Phillips's poetry compares well with Brooks in the absence, as Richard Barksdale and Keneth Kinnamon assert of Brooks, of "hallelujahs" and "amens"; instead, "clinical brevity" dominates.[2]

Most of Phillips's poems are somber, if not downright sober. A rare exception is "Uncle Sam Needs You," in which the speaker plays upon the literal meaning of "uncle" to negate the nationalistic, patriotic, emotional hold on Americans that Uncle Sam is designed to elicit. This brief nod to politics substitutes biological family for patriotic family and suggests humorously that the country has no legitimate claim on the speaker. The speaker can thus comfortably elide any call to citizen responsibility. Readers must surmise, however, the historical and racial background that informs the speaker's position and rejection of "family." By contrast, "I Never Thought" reclaims the original meaning of family through biology, when an uncle generously assumes responsibility for the speaker after her mother's death. He provides food, shelter, and emotional support that is far beyond any the speaker could have expected. Despite her initial negative response to being taken in, she comes to realize that her uncle has performed an invaluable service, one for which she is intensely grateful.

Phillips seems to have a surer hand with most of her stories. That, I would suggest, is because the majority of them are as much reportage as they are creation. Consider Langston Hughes's poems that take the shape of blues lyrics. With the form already established, Hughes had only to slot words into it. A valid question, then, is, How much is the form shaping Hughes, or how much is he giving to the form? In the stories that focus on Renwood Circle, the nursing home in which several of the stories are set, Phillips comes off as much as a reporter or documentarian as she does short fiction writer. Anyone who has spent time in a nursing home, or anyone with a general interest in the delivery of health care, will recognize the character types Phillips presents—the overbearing, overreaching nurse, the exhausted and complaining administrator, the harried dispenser of medication, the nurse desperate to save the life of a rapidly declining patient, the hourly workers who try to be invisible, the hourly workers who cheat by taking too much time from their duties, the residents who violate the spaces of other residents, the residents who are violent, the residents whose families have deposited them and disappeared, and the residents who, for whatever reason, would rather spit out or toss their food than eat it. "Gardenia Sue" and "Renwood Circle" are especially indicative of these patterns. "Choices" is poignant in its capturing of the issues surrounding many elderly people, that is, deciding which one of the incompetent offspring is best suited to provide a permanent home. "The Good Side of a Man" is perhaps most memorable in its ability to capture what most observers cannot begin to imagine. Comparable to William Faulkner in his effort to render Benjy visible to readers in *The Sound and the Fury*, Phillips captures what an elderly man thinks and feels after he endures a stroke that leaves him a shell of what he was before. Ultimately, love rules, even when it cannot be spoken.

"Grand Slam" had me curious for a bit as to whether Poppy was human or another animal—disappearing and dashing across the road in front of cars are dog-like actions.

When it becomes clear that Poppy is the young man's grandfather, I had to salute Phillips for her ability to maintain the suspense for as long as she did (as with the "friend" in "Riding with a Friend"). Indeed, it seems as if she were executing an experiment in the manner of Toni Morrison in "Recitatif," that is, trying to keep from readers the knowledge they believe they have about certain characters and actions. Morrison experiments in keeping away from her readers that one of the two characters in her story is white and the other one is Black. The two meet as young girls in an orphanage and encounter each other periodically over the years. Unlike Phillips—or so she believes anyway—Morrison never reveals the Blackness or whiteness of her characters, though stereotypical evidence throughout the story offers clues that readers constantly try to decipher.

Like many migrants from the South, Phillips may have left physically, but she could never leave psychologically or emotionally. She echoes Ernest J. Gaines, who moved permanently to San Francisco yet continued to write about Louisiana and the quarters and plantations on which he grew up. Similarly, Phillips returns to the soil of the South for inspiration again and again. The rural and small-town South that defined the fictional world she creates in *The Darkest Child* shapes the narrative in the previously unpublished novel *Stumbling Blocks*, as well as in the previously unpublished *No Ordinary Rain*. Indeed, Phillips limns the landscape and her characters with such minute detail that readers can conclude easily that she had traversed the territory and knew intimately people who served as models for her characters. For example, Rozelle "Rosie" Quinn, who first appears in and dominates just about everything that goes on in *The Darkest Child*, so captures Phillips's imagination that she looms over *Stumbling Blocks* and Tangy Mae and Laura's pseudo escape from Pakersfield, Georgia, to Knoxville, Tennessee. There must have been some real-world woman, I conclude, who so shocked Phillips with her sense of motherhood and charmed existence that Phillips could not be content to allow that woman to have space in only one novel. Rosie Quinn might be physically absent for the majority of *Stumbling Blocks*, but she hovers over and motivates characters nonetheless. Tangy Mae's sense of perverted loyalty to Rosie—or perhaps her embarrassment about possibly revealing ugly family secrets—prevents her from sharing with Miss Francine Yardley, her grandmother, what the real situation is in Georgia. Though Phillips writes Miss Francine as an injured (she has a broken leg) but impressive matriarch, her portrayal still pales in comparison to that of Rosie Quinn.

Arguably, Rosie's shadow is what causes Tangy Mae's stagnation in Knoxville. Unlike the character we see in *The Darkest Child*, who seems competent in many areas, the Tangy Mae of *Stumbling Blocks* is much more passive than readers familiar with *The Darkest Child* might expect. Or, perhaps Phillips is so accustomed to having Rosie as antagonist that it is difficult to write other familiar characters in a different setting where that central character is absent. So Tangy Mae wanders around in *Stumbling Blocks*, not exactly directionless but not exactly with purpose either. Her passive stay-at-homeness gives the novel a sense of mundanity that repetitive actions in *The Darkest Child* do not elicit. It is thus incumbent upon readers to try to see the two novels as separate entities, even as they remark the fact that *Stumbling Blocks* is the sequel to *The Darkest Child*. With Rosie only appearing in the last few pages, after Tangy Mae's father, Crow, forces Tangy Mae and Laura to return to Pakersfield, readers might reasonably ask, "Why allow Tangy Mae any form of escape if she is going to be forced to return to the mother and the circumstances from which she sought release?" Thus Rosie and the small-town South remain foremost for Phillips, which emphasizes even more the reality that must underlie the fiction.

An equal dose of reality informs *No Ordinary Rain*, at least in the folk content that stymies the lives of most of the characters. As an African American southerner, Phillips was obviously aware of folk traditions and specifically the conjuring traditions that she incorporates into *No Ordinary Rain*. They are so prevalent that readers might reasonably ask, "Why are these dirt-poor people, most of whom have neither a pot nor a window, so embracing of traditions that make them look more backward and ignorant than forward-looking and progressive?" Conjuration, as Hurston, Langston Hughes, and many others have documented historically and as Charles W. Chesnutt documents literarily, was often an alternative solution to medical as well as other issues for those without more financial or educational resources. The risk any author runs in portraying such characters is that it is almost impossible to make them look good. So, Opal, the woman whose son, Jonathan, has impregnated Alabama Wheaton's daughter, Mildred, comes off as a buffoon, a woman who is incapable of seeing beyond her own limitations to imagine a world where human beings are not always scheming to assault, denigrate, or kill other human beings by extra-natural methods.

The world of *No Ordinary Rain* is one in which Phillips is clearly attracted to a lot of characters, not the least among them Girlie, the woman who has remained on the plantation after others have moved away. And she obviously likes Van Ida and Zyma Ruth (a character named Zyma Root also appears in "Gardenia Sue"). On the other hand, Phillips could not seem to make up her mind about how to feel about Alabama Wheaton or some of the other characters. The novel thus showcases numerous characters whose storylines are perhaps curtailed because there are so darned many of them. Point of view becomes an issue as well, for, while Girlie relates her story in first person, others for whom third-person limited holds sway are still just out of the grasp of readers. Readers are understandably surprised when they find themselves inside Zyma's head, but they may still be hopeful for some information that will explain the heretofore inexplicable in terms of Zyma's extra-natural abilities. Such explanations, however, are not forthcoming. We have no clearer sense through Zyma's eyes as to why Zyma has the special knowledge that she has than through the omniscient narrator. And what's with the snakes? They have portended Zyma's mother Mildred's death, and they might have more significance in terms of the folk world that Phillips creates, but passing references to them as well as to snake catchers do not ultimately serve to glue the narrative together. Nonetheless, readers will remain engrossed in this fascinating world of country folk, folklore, and the extra-natural beliefs that undergird both.

From poems to short stories to novels, *Stumbling Blocks and Other Unfinished Work* offers readers opportunities to look into the imagination of a writer who worked tirelessly to perfect her craft and whose creative output for that effort definitely warrants much more attention. Phillips's creative choices will undoubtedly invite scholarly engagement for years to come. The collaboration between Delia Steverson and Phillips's family that enabled this project to come to fruition is one of the triumphs of recovery in an era when such work is more necessary than ever before. With this addition to the published corpus of her work, Delores Phillips can be situated rightly as a neglected genius put solidly on a path to full scholarly recovery.

NOTES

1. Walker, Alice. "Foreword: Zora Neale Hurston: A Cautionary Tale and a Partisan View." *Zora Neale Hurston: A Literary Biography*, Robert E. Hemenway, University of Illinois Press, 1977, p. xviii. Italics in original.

2. Barksdale, Richard, and Keneth Kinnamon. *Black Writers of America: A Comprehensive Anthology*. Macmillan, 1972, p. 714.